# "WHY ARE WE HERE?"

"We are going to convince the earl that our marriage is irrevocable," Damien told her.

"No!" Kathy cried. Her face flamed bright red.

Damien's patience frayed. "Do it, Kathy, or, so help me, I won't come to your rescue again." He yanked off his shirt and was startled as he heard Kathy's gown hit the floor.

She stood before him in her shift, her body trembling. Her hair fell over one shoulder, a wild, curling mass of brightness against creamy arms and shoulders. Oh God, he wanted her . . .

Voices outside the door grew louder and Damien reached out, grasped Kathy's hand and jerked her onto the bed. She lay beneath him, her breasts rising with each breath, pressing into his chest as her whole body began to tremble. Then, his passion overruling his sanity, he took her mouth in one swoop, his tongue thrusting between her lips, swallowing her gasp . . . He broke the kiss to string small hungry nips along her neck, her collarbone, and farther . . .

She cried out and slid her hands into a frenzied hold on his head, not to fight his caress, but to ask for more. She wanted him as fiercely as he wanted her.

# LOVE ME NOT

## EVE BYRON

AVON BOOKS  NEW YORK

LOVE ME NOT is an original publication of Avon Books. This work has never before appeared in book form. This work is a novel. Any similarity to actual persons or events is purely coincidental.

AVON BOOKS
A division of
The Hearst Corporation
1350 Avenue of the Americas
New York, New York 10019

Copyright © 1996 by Connie Rinehold and Francie Stark
Published by arrangement with the authors
Library of Congress Catalog Card Number: 96-96462
ISBN: 0-380-77625-1

First Avon Books Printing: December 1996

AVON TRADEMARK REG. U.S. PAT. OFF. AND IN OTHER COUNTRIES, MARCA REGISTRADA, HECHO EN U.S.A.

Printed in the U.S.A.

RA  10  9  8  7  6  5  4  3  2  1

To Ann McKay Thoroman and Carrie Feron
for guidance and inspiration

# Prologue

*Blackwood Manor*
*Spring 1807*

They were Bassett's bastards.

Papa had said so two days ago. He'd said that she and her brother Bruce weren't his children.

*Bassett's bastards.* Kathy heard it over and over again all day long. She heard Papa yelling and the sound of his fists hitting Bruce, nearly killing him. And at night when she closed her eyes, she saw the way Bruce's mouth bled because he bit his lips together, refusing to cry. He'd lain there on the ground, glaring up at Papa, hitting Papa with his eyes because he couldn't move his arms.

Kathy grabbed the first dress she found in her wardrobe and jerked it over her head. She had to hurry. She had to hide before Papa jumped out from a dark corner and tried to kill her, too.

It seemed like she'd been scared forever and it had been only two days since she and Mama had been outside in the garden when Smithy, Bruce's groom, had run up to them, his face as white as her petticoats.

"Lady Elizabeth," he panted. "His lordship's done kicked over the traces. He's beating master Bruce to death."

Mama dropped the basket of flowers in her hand and ran.

Kathy ran too, fear tearing at her insides. Papa hated Bruce as much as he hated her.

Across the back lawns she'd run, trying her best to keep up with Mama and Smithy, but she couldn't. They stopped at the edge of the woods. And then, Kathy saw why.

Papa was sitting on Bruce's chest, hitting him over and over with his fists. Bruce bucked his body and flopped his legs, trying to get away.

"Stop it! Stop it, Robert!" Mama screamed. "You're killing him."

But he wouldn't stop.

Suddenly, Mama jumped on Papa's back, screaming and clawing at him.

Kathy ran faster. Her heart felt as if it were going to explode and her side hurt and her legs felt as if they were on fire. By the time she got to them, all she'd been able to do was cry and scream for him to stop. If only she could have done what Smithy had done. He'd found a big stick and given it to Mama. She'd hit Papa over the head with it.

He'd fallen right over, and Kathy had been glad.

But, she hadn't been able to help. She was too small and weak and all she'd been able to do was scream and scream and scream.

She hated being only seven years old.

And now, she hated feeling like everyone had forgotten her. The servants were busy helping Mama take care of Bruce. And they were always looking straight ahead, over her. They didn't look down and they didn't look in corners and behind furniture where she'd scurry whenever she heard someone coming. She wasn't sure if anyone had even been in her bedroom for two days.

But Papa wouldn't forget her. He'd look for her and when he found her he'd—

Heavy footsteps sounded down the hall. A door opened and closed.

Fear swelled like a monster inside her, pushing at her chest and up into her throat.

*Papa.* He'd waited as he always had, until there

was no one to see him stick her with pins or pull out her hair or smother her with a pillow. Mama was out riding with her friend Bassett. The servants couldn't protect her. She was alone, except for him.

She ran to the door and opened it, ran into the hall, and looked left and right before turning toward the stairs. She ran down the long corridor, not caring that her hair wasn't brushed or that she hadn't had time to put on her shoes.

She reached the head of the stairs and whirled, glancing back to make sure he was not behind her. She hiked her dress up and hooked her leg over the shiny wood banister and climbed on. She didn't like walking down. This way if Papa came, she'd be able to see him. If he came, she'd be going too fast for him to grab her.

"One, two, three," she counted silently and pushed off. Hanging on tight, she held her eyes wide open and watched for him as she sailed backwards, praying that her hiding place was still there.

She flew off the end of the banister and landed with a hard thump on the Persian rug at the foot of the stairs. She scrambled to her feet and rubbed her aching bottom as she raced past the drawing room toward the open doors of the dining room.

She darted inside and circled around the big table to the china cabinet. Falling to her knees, she yanked open the lower doors. It was still empty. The dishes that had been taken out to be washed had not been put back.

"Thank you, God," she whispered as she climbed inside and pulled the doors shut behind her. She couldn't hear anything except the thump of her heart and her own short gasps for breath. Not even a sliver of light leaked inside. She couldn't see anything at all. She felt safe again.

She had learned that what you could see was much scarier than what you couldn't.

Pressure built in her chest as she wedged herself

into a corner. Tears ran freely down her face as she hugged her knees tightly against her chest and again tried to understand what had happened two days ago. Somehow she knew that it had something to do with why Papa seemed to enjoy hurting her when no one was looking.

Why he'd never cared about her or Bruce.

Like a nightmare, it came back to her again, making her feel cold and sick and scared all over again as she remembered the blood and the horrible sounds as something cracked and she'd thought Bruce's face was being broken.

She hugged her knees tighter to her chest and buried her face in her skirt, her dress muffling her sobs and soaking up her tears. She'd thought her brother was truly dead. He hadn't moved for the longest time. She'd never seen so much blood. It had run from his nose and from cuts on his cheeks and around his eyes like bright red ribbons.

"Bruce? Bruce?" Mama had said and dabbed at his face with the hem of her dress.

Suddenly, his eyes opened. "Is it true?"

"Yes," Mama said.

Bruce had looked away then and he'd started coughing, and Mama had wanted to get him home as fast as they could. They'd left Papa where he lay.

With a shudder, Kathy pushed the pictures from her mind and thought about what Papa had said. She didn't understand what a bastard was. She only knew it must be something bad. And if it was something bad, how could she and Bruce be Bassett's bastards?

Mama called Bassett her dearest friend. He was a duke. Kathy thought that must be something like a king, since that was how he acted, and he looked the way she thought a king might look. He had light hair and was much bigger than Papa, and he had eyes as blue as her own.

Once, Mama had told Kathy it was all right to call him Uncle Alex, but Kathy knew he really wasn't her uncle. So, she'd settled on calling him "Bassett" like Papa did.

Bassett didn't seem to like that very much, but Kathy didn't care. He didn't seem to like anything but Mama anyway.

As long as Kathy could remember, Bassett had come to Blackwood to visit Mama when Papa was away. Except that this time he'd come the day after Papa had hurt Bruce and there had been three strange men with him.

She'd been hiding in a tree in front of the house when he'd spoken to them on the portico. "Comb the woods. When you find Blackwood, take him to Westbrook. Under no circumstances are you to bring him here."

Mama had told her that the strange men were Bow Street Runners. Kathy had not asked who they were looking for. She had known it was Papa. She only hoped that Westbrook was far away.

But she didn't know if they'd found him. Blackwood was a big place with lots of places to hide, and Papa knew them all. She felt safe only in the china cabinet because it was too small for Papa and it was usually filled with dishes.

Fear crawled up her spine. Papa was out there somewhere and he'd come back. She just knew it. She was afraid to sleep in her bed.

For two nights, she'd crept downstairs and slept in the china cabinet so if Papa came back, he wouldn't be able to find her.

Today, Mama and Bassett had gone riding. Bassett had said she needed some fresh air, and Smithy would sit with Bruce. Kathy wanted to sit with Bruce, too, but Mama wouldn't let her. Just like the servants, Mama hadn't looked down at her, but stared at something else like she did when she was thinking or sad.

On a shuddering breath, Kathy lifted her head, scrubbed her nose with the back of her hand, and stared into the blackness of her safe place. She'd just wait here until Mama and Bassett came back. When Bassett was here, Papa wasn't.

Her mind returned once again to the things Papa had said. How could he say he wasn't their papa? That confused her more than anything and she hadn't yet been able to ask Bruce or Mama to explain it to her.

Still, if it was true, it explained why he did terrible things to her. Things she'd never told anyone about, because he'd told her if she did, he'd kill Mama and Bruce and her.

She'd never told, and it hadn't done any good. He'd tried to kill Bruce anyway.

She frowned into the darkness. Maybe Papa thought she'd told—

Her stomach clenched as she heard footsteps again, louder this time.

*Papa.*

Her breath froze in her chest and her heart pounded in her ears as they came closer and closer. Very slowly, she raised her hands and pressed her palms together. "Dear Lord," she silently prayed, "please let it be the butler or Bassett—"

A dull thud sounded on top of the cabinet. He was standing right in front of her.

A sob rose in her throat and she swallowed it down. She must not cry. She must not make a sound. She must not be found.

A moan slipped out. She wanted Mama.

The door to the cabinet opened. Light poured in, blinding her.

Kathy jerked upright; her head banged into the top of the cabinet. Her eyes began to focus and she saw black boots with tassels. Bassett's boots had no tassels.

Papa's did.

He had found her. He would kill her.

She closed her eyes and screamed.

"Good God, child! Cease your histrionics at once," he said sternly.

She barely heard him. She kept her eyes squeezed shut and pressed back as far as she could into the corner, her throat aching from the scream she couldn't seem to stop.

Suddenly, his hands reached in and lifted her out. "I said be silent," he commanded as he set her on her feet.

Her legs collapsed beneath her. She sat flat down on the floor with a bone-jarring thud. The scream died and on a gasp and hiccup; she realized he didn't sound like Papa.

With a quaking breath, she opened her eyes and stared up. A huge man glared down at her with his hands braced on his hips and his long legs planted wide apart. He was as big as Bassett and scarier than Papa, with a ferocious frown on his face. His cheeks looked sort of blue, like a shadow that ran into his shiny black hair and one long eyebrow that slashed above his mean, green eyes. He was an ogre. A giant ogre.

"You will explain to me the reason for your display this instant," he ordered in a voice like a boom of thunder. "What were you doing in the china cabinet?"

"I was hiding," she whispered, too afraid not to answer him, too afraid to even push to her feet.

"Hiding? Why?"

He sounded like Papa did when he told her to "come here" and she knew she had better obey. "I was hiding from my Papa," she blurted. "I was afraid he had come back to kill me."

The ogre's frown grew more fierce as the ends of the black slashing brow drew up at the corners. "Don't be ridiculous, child. He'll never be back."

Kathy cringed. His voice still sounded like thunder. Yet, he spoke as if he knew her papa, as if he knew something she didn't. "How do you know?"

"Are you being impertinent?"

"I don't think so," Kathy said, not sure what that word meant.

He took a step back, his mouth twisting as if he had a bad taste in it. "I see," he said.

He was going to leave. "Wait," she said. "Please tell me. I have to know. He promised me he would kill me and Bruce and Mama if I told. But I didn't tell, and he thinks I did."

"Told what?"

"The things he did to me."

"What did he do to you?" he said and his voice sounded like a growl.

She lowered her gaze. She couldn't stand to look at him; it made her heart beat too fast. His green eyes were glittering like those she saw sometimes when she looked out her window at night. Bruce had told her they were the stable cats, but she believed they were panthers watching her, waiting to eat her up. This man looked like the picture she'd seen of a panther—a big, black cat that could see everything, even in the dark.

"Answer me now," he said as he stepped toward her.

She jumped and scooted backward, afraid the ogre would step on her and squash her. Kathy tightened her lips and swallowed hard. Ogre or not, she couldn't tell. She stared down at her lap. "I don't want to talk anymore."

The ogre said nothing. She waited and waited, and as she waited, the funniest thing happened. She began to feel better because someone besides her knew she was afraid of Papa, even if it was only a mean old ogre, with panther eyes.

She peeked up at him. The ogre's arms were folded across his chest and he stared straight ahead. For the first time, she saw that he really had two eyebrows and the blue on his cheeks was really only whiskers.

He stared down at her. His eyes looked funny, like

something had hurt him. "Blackwood won't come back," he said gruffly.

"Papa always comes back," she said as she plucked at her dress, wanting to believe him and knowing she didn't dare.

From the corner of her eye, she saw the ogre's feet shift. "He is on a ship making its way toward America," he said and his voice seemed smoother, as if the thunder had moved away. "Soon, he will be an ocean away."

Her head snapped up. She remembered how Bassett had told the Bow Street Runners to take Papa to Westbrook when they found him. She'd hoped Westbrook was a long way away. Now, she knew it was in America and she couldn't imagine a place further away than America. Bruce had told her it took months to get there. Still she had to be sure. "How do you know?" she asked warily.

"I escorted him on board and watched the ship sail away."

Tears stung Kathy's eyes. "He's truly gone?"

The ogre nodded gravely.

Her breath shuddered with relief. Still, as happy as it made her, she didn't believe Papa would stay away. "What if he comes back?"

He sighed like Bruce did when she asked too many questions. "He won't."

Oh, how she wanted to believe him. But she couldn't. "Yes, he will."

The ogre frowned. "If he ever comes back, then I'll come back. I won't let him harm you."

"Promise?"

He rubbed the side of his face next to his eye like Mama did when her head hurt. "I promise."

"Cross your heart?"

His lips tightened and his eyebrows ran together again. She was making him angry. She knew she was, but she couldn't stop. A promise was good, but she needed more. "Please?" she asked.

He raked his hands through his hair. "I promise

that as I long as I live, I will protect you from the Earl of Blackwood."

She stared up at him, thinking hard. He looked so big and strong and fierce that he made her feel safe. He didn't try to hurt her like Papa did even though she made his head hurt. Deciding she could believe him, she nodded. "Do you think you'll live long?"

He blinked and his mouth dropped open. "If I should die," he declared, his voice rising a note as he looked up at the ceiling, "then my son will protect you."

"Is he like you?" she asked.

"Yes, he is very much like me," he growled and his feet shifted again, as if he wanted to get away from her.

Kathy smiled. His son was a panther, too. She'd be able to sleep in her own bed again. She could play in the garden. She could walk down the stairs. "All right," she said.

He nodded and turned and walked toward the door.

Kathy felt a wave of panic. When Papa came back, how could the ogre and his son protect her if she didn't know their names? "Wait," she called. "What's your name?"

"The Duke of Westbrook," he said.

Westbrook. It was a man instead of a place. "And your son's?"

"Damien," he said softly.

# Part 1

# Chapter 1

*London*
*Spring 1817*

*I promise that as long as I live, I will protect you from the Earl of Blackwood. If I should die, then my son will protect you.*

Kathy had clung to that promise for years. Even though she had never seen the Duke of Westbrook again, she had believed with all her heart that he would come back if she needed him. She had believed until she was old enough to understand that the Earl of Blackwood would never return.

Nor would the Duke of Westbrook. He had drowned over a week ago.

Sorrow swelled inside her for a brief moment. It seemed she should feel more than a fleeting moment of sadness for the man who had made such an extraordinary promise to her. Yet, she could barely remember what the Duke of Westbrook had looked like.

A book sailed across the drawing room and crashed into the wall beside the fireplace. Kathy flinched and met her mother's feverish gaze.

"What is keeping Bruce?" Mama demanded. "He promised to take me to the harbor."

The Duke of Bassett had drowned as well.

Bassett—the man who had fathered her and her brother, Bruce. The thought brought another glimmer of sorrow. She should feel more, but he had been a stranger to her, a man who walked past her

13

and Bruce on his way to their mother, as if they were mere decorations in the hallway.

The only genuine grief she felt was for her mother. Since they'd received word of Bassett's death, Mama had not eaten or slept. She had not wept, refusing to believe Bassett was dead. The only thing Mama had done was come to London to take up residence in Bruce's townhouse so she could go to the harbor every day and wait for Bassett's return.

Yesterday, Kathy and Bruce had decided not to allow her to return to the harbor. Her brother's absence today was deliberate.

Mama rose and brushed out her gown. "I cannot wait any longer. Alex has probably already arrived."

A terrible sense of desolation seemed to cloud the room. Kathy was beginning to fear for her mother's sanity. "No, Mama," she said, rising to her feet. "He's not there."

Mama pressed her hand to heart, her expression stricken. "How can you be sure?"

"Listen to me, Mama," Kathy said as she went to her, eased her into a chair, and knelt on the floor in front of her. "Bassett and Westbrook were racing their yacht in the middle of the ocean. There were two gentlemen sailing alongside them. Suddenly, they found themselves in the midst of a storm." She paused and took her mother's hands, holding them firmly. "Remember how that can happen in the ocean? One moment the water is calm and in the next moment it changes and the water is raging all around with towering waves?"

Mama nodded, her gaze fixed on empty air, as if she were seeing it.

It broke Kathy's heart to speak to Mama in such simple terms, as if she were a child. She wanted to stop, but she couldn't. She had to make Mama accept the truth. "The yacht capsized under a huge wave. They drowned, Mama. *Bassett* drowned. He is *dead. He isn't coming back. Ever.*"

Mama snatched her hands from Kathy's hold and

doubled over, burying her face in her lap. "Alex," she cried in an anguished wail that rose in the air and dissolved into a storm of weeping.

Hot tears streamed down Kathy's face. She leaned forward and wrapped her arms around her mother, absorbing the shudders of her body, wishing she could absorb some of her pain.

After a while the sobs subsided and Kathy straightened to look at her mother. Her beautiful auburn hair had lost its luster and her eyes no longer sparkled. Her porcelain skin now seemed to have a gray cast, as if the life had gone out of her. Kathy blinked. Had Mama looked this way a few moments ago?

"I'm very tired," Mama said, her voice weak. "I should like to go to bed now."

She leaned heavily on Kathy as they made their way up the stairs. After she was in bed, Kathy pulled the covers around her, remembering all the times her mother had tucked her in and soothed her after a nightmare.

"Perhaps I shall dream of him," Mama whispered.

"I'm sure you will," Kathy replied, the ache in her throat unbearable.

"He loved me," she said, her gaze anguished. "I know he loved me."

Kathy brushed back her hair with a tender hand. "Of course he did," she said.

"I loved him. I loved him so much . . ."

*Too much,* Kathy thought as she blew out the candle and settled in the chair beside the bed. Never would she allow herself to love a man as her mother had loved Bassett.

Her mother had loved Bassett for most of her adult life, devoting herself to raising his bastard children and living in virtual seclusion while the duke came and went on a whim, giving her random moments of his presence, assuming that Mama's love was his due.

Mama moaned in her sleep. Kathy reached out and stroked her hair, realizing now why it had disturbed her to present the details of Bassett's death in such a simple fashion. It was yet another tragedy he had left for someone else to explain away.

Just as he had left it to Mama to explain his role in their lives.

It had been years before Kathy learned the entire truth. It had taken her just moments to comprehend the full measure of power Bassett held over them all.

The Earl of Blackwood had married her mother knowing full well she loved another man and carried his child. He agreed the marriage would be in name only. He was to recognize her child as his own. In exchange, the Duke of Bassett had paid him a fortune, retrieved the Blackwood jewels and art collection and kept him out of debtors prison.

But the earl had become unhappy with the arrangement. He had not been able to take out his frustration and anger on her mother, so he had tortured her and Bruce. She had never discussed the dark days of her childhood with anyone save the Duke of Westbrook, and even then, she had just voiced her fear of the earl. Aside from the beating the earl had given Bruce, she was not sure to what extent he had tormented her brother. They had never talked about it.

There had seemed no need after Bassett and Westbrook had stripped the earl of his fortune and left him no better than a beggar in America where even his title was useless.

It amazed her that she had could have ever believed the earl was her father. Sometimes, she found it difficult to believe he was human. What kind of man would treat children as he had, no matter that they were not his own flesh and blood?

Yet, the Duke of Bassett had been just as wicked in his own way. He had been the coldest man on earth, like a statue in their lives, seen from time to time, yet as blind to them as a piece of stone. He even ignored his legitimate child.

Kathy shook her head in disbelief. She had a half-brother she'd never seen—Maxwell Hastings, heir to Bassett and ironically, Bruce's closest friend. And although Max was aware that Bruce was the son of his father's mistress, he had no inkling of the real truth.

As a child, Kathy had burned to meet Max, to know him, but now that she was seventeen the yearning had faded. She'd come to understand that to reveal that truth could destroy the carefully constructed web of lies they had lived their entire life. As it stood, Bruce was Viscount Channing, heir to the Earl of Blackwood, and she was Lady Kathleen Palmerston.

She was to have made her come-out this season. Now it would be delayed. Her mother would need her in the months to come.

A shaft of light spilled across the carpet as the door creaked open.

"Kathy?" Bruce called in a low tone.

She rose and went to her brother, closing the door softly behind her.

"She is finally sleeping?" he asked.

"Yes. She accepts that Bassett is dead. All that is left is for her to get through the memorial service and overcome her grief." Kathy sighed, knowing it wouldn't be that easy, that Mama might never recover from the loss of the man who had been her life.

They had sat in the back of the church, the last mourners to arrive, the first to leave when it was over.

The service had been interminable with the archbishop droning on and on about their virtues as if the dukes were listening from their watery graves and he sought their approval.

Mama held up well, a straight and silent figure in her mourning clothes and veiled hat.

Behind her, Kathy could hear the low murmur of voices as other mourners spilled from the church, casting slanted glances their way as they passed. Bruce had warned her that they would be objects of curiosity and whispered comments. All of England, it seemed, knew of the long affair between the Countess of Blackwood and the Duke of Bassett. Bruce had also assured her that all of England believed her and Bruce to be the earl's offspring. It made sense since Bruce looked nothing like Bassett and hopefully, no one would look further than her red hair, so different from the blond features common to the Dukes of Bassett.

Still, she had the urge to escape the probing stares that seemed to penetrate her own heavy veil. But Bruce was firmly in control between them, holding Mama steady and keeping Kathy to a sedate and dignified pace as they walked toward their coach.

Mama came to an abrupt halt, pulling Bruce up short.

"Mama, what is it?" Kathy asked.

"I want to speak with Max," she whispered.

Bruce shot Kathy a questioning look. She wanted to shake her head in negation. She had lived her entire life without meeting her half-brother and had no wish to meet him today of all days. "Mama, are you certain you're up to it?" she asked.

Mama gave a firm nod. "Yes, I want to see him."

Kathy sighed in defeat, grateful that she was veiled. Though Max and Bruce were friends and Max was aware of his father's liaison with her mother, he had no idea that the connection included blood ties. From Bruce's description of Max, she knew that her blue eyes were a striking match to those of her half-brother. If Max ever looked closely at her, she feared that he would see a resemblance to himself.

"All right," Bruce said, gripping her forearm. "But only for a few moments."

Tightening her grip on Bruce's arm, Kathy forced herself to put one foot in front of the other and walk the short distance to the carriage bearing the Bassett coat of arms, to meet the man who was now the Duke of Bassett.

Kathy's breath caught as Max gazed directly at them. He *was* Bassett—every cold and arrogant inch of him. He stood as tall as his late father, as hard and golden as his father, his shoulders and chest broad enough to bear the weight of power that was synonymous with his title. His mouth was straight and tight, his expression hard, remote.

But then, as they approached him, she saw a small spark in his eyes, heard a touch of warmth in his greeting. "Bruce, it is good to see you." His voice was sincere and smooth and he seemed to relax a bit. It intrigued her to see the subtle transformation, the small evidences of humanity his father had lacked.

"I thought you might appreciate a friendly face," Bruce said.

"Bruce," Kathy prompted, forgetting her initial reluctance to meet Max. Suddenly, she wanted to have some kind of contact—even verbal—with this man, her half-brother. Until she'd come face to face with his resemblances to his father, both in manner and countenance, she had not realized how heavy the burden of hers and Bruce's parentage weighed on her.

She barely heard Bruce's introduction for her fascination with this man whose eyes were so much like hers. Eyes that did not look at her mother with scorn or condemnation as he nodded toward her with an expression that had warmed even more.

"Lady Blackwood, Kathleen," Max said nodding toward each of them in turn, his voice gentle, as if he understood and sympathized with her mother's grief. "Bruce speaks of you often."

"It is good to finally meet you," Mama said.

"Hello," Kathy whispered, she could not think what to call him. He was a duke, yet, she had always thought of him simply as "Max."

Vaguely, she heard him introduce the small woman at his side as Lady Jillian Forbes. Westbrook's daughter. Bruce had spoken of her, too. She and her brother had grown up with Max and according to Bruce, Jillian and Damien were as close as she and Bruce. Apparently, Jillian and Max were close as well, for in his brief glance at Jillian, Kathy saw undisguised affection.

"I am very sorry about your fathers," Mama said, her voice beginning to quiver.

"Please excuse us," Bruce said. "As you can see, my mother is unwell."

"Then I am doubly grateful for your presence here, Countess," Max said, rigidly formal once again. "I'm sorry our first meeting is under such grim circumstances."

And grim Max looked as he withdrew, becoming once again a stone pillar of British nobility.

Mama leaned forward slightly, her hand fluttering up and down again as if she wanted to touch Max and thought better of it. "You are like your father," she said softly.

Max stiffened even more, his transformation complete. Kathy couldn't bear to look, to see him become "Bassett" rather than "Max." In the course of a few impersonal introductions, her feelings for her half-brother had become very personal. Now that she'd met him, he had inexplicably become hers as much as Bruce was hers. She wanted to shake him and shout at him to come back, to be the man who showed warmth and concern.

Yet, she knew she had no right.

She stared straight ahead toward the cathedral and the last of the mourners trickling out of the doors. . . .

Her gaze snagged and held on a man standing at the top of the stone steps. He was tall and sleek, with gleaming black hair and black slashing brows. And though she was too far away to see, she knew his eyes were green.

Her breath caught in profound recognition of the man who had been as much an invisible presence in her life as Max. The man whose name she'd heard before she'd ever known that Max existed. A name that comforted her with the promise of protection and gave her peace throughout her childhood.

She could not doubt that he was Damien Forbes.

Now, she remembered what the Duke of Westbrook had looked like, what he still looked like. For there, in the man standing so proud and magnificent above the crowd, she saw all that the late Duke of Westbrook had been and more.

So much more that she could not tear her gaze from him as her heartbeat became loud in her ears and the world faded into insignificance. Only he had detail and dimension as his gaze restlessly skimmed each cluster of mourners, passing over her . . . returning.

Her breath stalled and grew into a lump in her throat and a strange warmth flowered in the pit of her belly as his stare seemed to close the distance between them and penetrate her veil. She wanted to reach out to him then and smooth the hard line of his mouth into a softer expression, to trace his tense jaw and the patrician slant of his nose, to soothe the lines of weariness and strain from around his eyes. She shivered at the idea of touching him, of perhaps discovering that he was less than the hero she'd always thought him.

She lowered her gaze with a jerk, forcing herself to bring the world back into focus as Bruce took her arm and helped her into their coach. Still, she felt as if Damien Forbes was staring at her, imprinting sensations on her that she'd never before felt—of

anticipation and excitement, of awakening to find a
dream had come to life and stood waiting for her to
claim it.

She glanced out the window and watched him
descend the steps, every movement of his body
suggesting power barely contained, as if the restlessness she'd sensed in him were a part of him.

She felt it, too, and knew that she would never
forget him. And as he raised his head and again
seemed to stare at her through her veil, she knew
that in those few short moments, he had become far
more to her than a name and a promise she wielded
to chase away fear.

# Chapter 2

*Blackwood Manor*
*One year later*

*Bruce—*

*My deepest sympathies for the loss of your mother. Please convey my condolences to your sister. If I may be of any assistance, you have but to ask.*

*Damien*

**K**athy read the note over again, amazed that Damien Forbes would mention her in his missive. They had never met, though the memory of him had remained with her, as vivid and as startling as her first sight of him standing on the steps of the cathedral. Kathy had thought about him, the patrician elegance of his face and form intruding into her mind at the slightest mention of his name. At other times he popped into her thoughts for no reason at all.

In the past year, she'd wished that she could see him smile.

God knew there had been few enough smiles at Blackwood Manor since then.

The stunning memory she had of Damien Forbes could not overcome the memories she had of her mother suffering and dying by inches.

The past year had been a nightmare. After Bassett

died, Mama had taken to her bed and refused to
leave it. Day after day she'd lain there staring up at
the ceiling. At night, she wept endlessly. She ate if
Kathy coaxed her, but even then, only a few bites.

Kathy shook her head and laid Damien's note
aside as she stared at the portrait hanging above the
mantel to see the image of Mama as she had been,
smiling and happy and so full of life.

"Mother is at rest, Kathy," Bruce said from the
doorway. "Put your grief behind you."

She glanced up at him, startled that he should
know her thoughts without knowing the emotion
behind them. "I'm not grieving, Bruce. I'm angry.
Mama didn't even try to overcome her grief," she
said as he walked into the sitting room. "She allowed
it to kill her."

"Nonsense. Grief is not fatal."

Kathy met her brother's gaze levelly. "It was not a
mysterious wasting disease that sapped mother's
strength and stole her appetite," she insisted. "You
were not here at Blackwood to listen to her weep and
call his name night after night."

He paused at the sideboard and picked up a
decanter of wine. "I was here every fortnight. The
physician told us that her illness would make her
overly emotional."

"Grief was her illness." Kathy met his gaze as he
pressed a glass of sherry into her hands, saw the lines
of strain around his blue eyes, the furrows his fingers
had left in his auburn hair.

He cradled her face in his palms. "Mother would
not be pleased to see you dwell on this. She would
want you to get on with your life."

She sighed. She knew what was coming. They'd
had this discussion before and Bruce always began it
in the same way. "I don't want to go to London."

He straightened and added new furrows to his
hair as he raked his hands through the strands. "It's
time you got out in the world, Kathy. You've lived a

cloistered existence too long. I want to introduce
you to Max and Jillian." He grinned. "Now that
they're married, life in London should be quite
interesting."

Bruce was to have stood up with Max, but the
death of their mother a month ago had prevented
him from attending the wedding. She hadn't been
surprised at the news that Max and Jillian had
become betrothed. She'd seen the way Max looked at
Jillian after the memorial service for the late dukes
of Bassett and Westbrook.

She'd known that Max and Jillian were close
friends of her brother, but she hadn't quite been able
to shake the feeling that there was more to the
relationship that fed the rumors sprinkled throughout the London newspapers. Rumors Bruce had
blithely dismissed. Too blithely. She knew her
brother's penchant for mischief. There was something he wasn't telling her and it related to his
restless need to return to London.

"Think about what life has in store for you,"
Bruce said with a note of exasperation. "Next year,
you make your debut."

Kathy shook her head and wondered what other
enticements he would try to offer her. He didn't
understand that society held no interest for her.
"The Season will be over by the time our mourning
is at an end."

"There's always the Little Season," he argued. "If
you wait another year, you'll be twenty and almost
on the shelf."

Kathy was counting on it. The older she was when
she made her debut, the less she would be noticed by
aspiring bridegrooms. "You hate the Little Season,"
she reminded him.

He scowled. "You're right, of course. It's boring
and there are hardly enough people in London for a
proper debut. Another year won't make a difference." His eyes twinkled. "There is, however, noth-

ing to stop you from coming to London with me. You can enjoy the sights, get to know Max and Jillian."

"Why do you never speak of Damien?" The question just popped out before she could stop it. It had frustrated her over the last months that Bruce always had news of Max and Jillian, yet he rarely mentioned Damien. Of course she was interested in her half-brother and his wife, but she was fascinated by Damien.

"No particular reason. Perhaps because I spend more time with Max." Bruce glanced down at her with a speculative gleam in his eyes. "Why? Are you interested?"

"Of course not," Kathy said, annoyed that she'd almost told him that yes, she was interested. "I've never even met him."

"Come to London and I'll introduce you to him."

"I have no desire to meet him or anyone else at the moment," she said, relieved to have had the presence of mind to equate Damien with all the other "anyones" she did not know.

Bruce raised his hands and let them fall to his sides in a gesture of frustration. "You have to come with me, Kathy. We have an appointment to meet with Mother's solicitor."

"Why?" she asked, puzzled. "You already know what is in Mama's will."

"There are papers you must sign."

"Whatever for? Everything is in your hands."

"Not everything. You have a sizable inheritance of your own."

His announcement held no surprise for Kathy. Naturally, she would inherit her mother's jewels and perhaps an allowance. Why did Bruce insist on being so dramatic about it? Still, seeing him shuffle his feet as if he were impatient to go on, she supposed she should play along. "How sizable?"

Bruce sat down in the chair opposite hers and leaned forward. Rarely did she see him so serious.

"Your dowry is one hundred thousand pounds. There is an additional four hundred thousand pounds. You are to have all Mother's jewelry." Bruce grinned. "Those alone are valued at an additional three hundred thousand pounds."

She stared at Bruce, feeling out of breath and stunned beyond comprehension. She was rich.

Obscenely rich.

"What am I going to do with it all?"

"Anything you wish," Bruce said. "I believe that was Mother's intent. She knew that I would inherit the earldom and I've been in control of my own fortune for some years. She would not allow you to go wanting, nor to be dependent on me." Planting his hands on his knees, he rose from the chair. "The will is very specific. If you have not married by the time you reach your majority, your dowry and inheritance reverts to your control. You are one of the few truly independent women in all England "

She couldn't speak, couldn't absorb it all.

"Pack up, Kathy," Bruce said, taking advantage of her shock. "Tomorrow, we go to London . . . and by the way . . ."

She looked up at him, wondering what else he could possibly say.

He grinned widely. "Will you make me a loan of a few thousand pounds?"

Before she could answer, or better yet, throw a pillow at him for his quip, he strode from the room, leaving her to ponder her future. A future that was in her control.

Sighing, she leaned her head back and closed her eyes. It was expected that she would meet a man, fall in love, and marry. An image of an elegant man rose in her mind, standing tall and sleek and assured of his power. A man who had influenced her musings for over a year.

But, she would not allow herself to fall into the maiden's trap of assuming she would belong to someone like him—a man who would own all she possessed and then demand her heart as well. She wanted no part of such a fate, and she certainly wanted no part of love. She would not allow herself to belong to any man so completely that he held her very life in his hands even from the grave.

For just as surely as grief had been her mother's illness, love had been her disease.

# Chapter 3

**H**ow beautiful she was!

From the confines of his closed coach, Tony Edgewater watched Lady Kathleen Palmerston ride the narrow paths of the park beside her brother. Every day for the past week, he'd come here hoping to catch a glimpse of her.

Her beauty took his breath away.

The black mourning clothes she wore set off her brilliance as black silk set off the brilliance of jewels. He smiled at the thought. How beautifully it would fit into an ode, celebrating the mysterious depths of her sapphire eyes, the vibrancy of her red hair that caught the sunlight like the facets of a garnet, the elegant coolness of her demeanor that shimmered among more ordinary ladies like a diamond among paste beads.

He thought he might change his wardrobe to black, thus becoming an appropriate setting for her, and showing her how well they would suit.

She was meant for him; he just knew it.

Guilt tweaked him for his infidelity. Julia had been dead barely a year and he had cared for her; he really had. His wife, the only child of a successful merchant, had given him wealth and adoration. He'd been sincerely grieving since she'd slipped away, taking their unborn child with her.

But now, he wondered if it hadn't been providential. If Julia had lived, he would have been denied the one great love of his life.

Yes! That was it. He loved Lady Kathleen with all the passion he had not felt for his wife. He adored Kathleen. He worshipped her.

He burned with the desire to approach her . . . here . . . now. But he dared not. Not yet. She was in deep mourning for her mother. And Tony had to muster up some congeniality before he petitioned her brother, Lord Channing, a man he thoroughly disliked.

He had never forgiven Channing for humiliating him in a billiards room at Oxford so many years ago. He'd wagered his entire quarterly allowance on a game of billiards with Channing. He'd lost. Channing had given the money back to him after extracting Tony's word that he would bathe on a regular basis. As their classmates had looked on, he'd become horribly aware of the foul odor of his body. The hair matted to his scalp had felt heavy with grime and oil. His clothing had felt stiff and abrasive with the dirt and perspiration that stained it.

Tony shuddered at the memory of what he had been, of how his classmates had given him a wide berth, and how disgusted he'd been after Channing had forced him to see himself as others did. He'd hated it. He'd hated himself. He'd understood why they'd called him Anthony the Offal.

He'd worked hard to become someone else, to cleanse himself of Anthony the Offal and become Tony Edgewater, a man worthy of respect.

Ironically, Bruce Palmerston, Viscount Channing, had been the only one at Oxford who had called him by his rightful name.

He supposed he should be grateful to Channing. Because of him, Tony had become what he was today—a man devoted to all things beautiful: art, music, poetry. He had done well for himself in spite of being the second son of a baron. He had married wealth and inherited more when his father-in-law

and Julia had died within mere months of one
another.

Tony glanced down at his perfectly manicured
hands and straightened his immaculate coat. Yes!
He was certainly worthy of a gem like Lady Kathleen.

He searched the paths winding through the park
and caught a glimpse of her back as she and her
brother rode out the gate. His gaze clung to her as
she sat so straight and perfect on her horse, her hair
a flame that beckoned him and then disappeared
from view before he could catch his breath. And still
he stared at the last place she had been, imagining
that she waited for him to come to her.

Of course! He had to go to her. He could not—he
dared not—wait. She was too beautiful, too inviting.
There would be others who wanted her. He must
claim what he knew was rightfully his. He had to
speak with her brother immediately.

*Kathleen.* Even her name was a melody.

He couldn't get her out of his mind as he left the
park and returned to his townhouse to bathe and
change. It took hours to create just the right image.

He stepped back from the mirror and studied
his reflection.

Perfect! The black frock coat fitted his frame to
perfection. He turned sideways. Slim but not unat-
tractively thin. Tall but not awkwardly so. He raised
his hand and carefully smoothed his hair to make
sure he'd used just the right amount of pomade. He
had rather nice hair that laid sleekly over his head
like a shiny chestnut pelt. He bared his teeth and ran
his tongue over them. Yes, smooth and white and
perfectly straight. And he thought his eyes were an
interesting shade of gray . . . enigmatic perhaps. Or
arresting. That was it! His eyes were arresting.
Kathleen would be pleased with his appearance, he
was sure.

With a well-practiced glide to his step, he left his
chambers, ready to claim his destiny.

She seemed so close he thought he could feel her warmth as he climbed the steps of her brother's townhouse and lifted the knocker. The door opened and he met the butler's inquiring gaze and presented his card, only to be informed that Channing was at his club.

He returned to his coach, haunted by visions of Kathleen lying in her bed, dreaming of a man such as himself. Twenty minutes later, he entered the club and found Viscount Channing.

"Edgewater," Bruce said. "It's been a long time."

"Two years," Tony said. "I've been out of circulation, mourning actually."

"That seems to be going around," Bruce murmured, then frowned. "I apologize. I did hear that you lost your wife. You have my condolences."

Tony nodded graciously in spite of his impatience to be done with social pleasantries. "I was distraught to hear of your loss as well."

"Thank you," Bruce said. "Will you join me for a drink?"

Tony flushed with pride at the invitation. Perhaps he had been wrong to nurture a grievance against Channing, Tony thought as he took a chair at Bruce's table. After all, he *had* done him a favor and accorded him more respect than any of the others in school. Besides, it wouldn't do to have ill feelings about his future brother-in-law.

Brother-in-law. Yes! It sounded right.

Tony caught himself just in time to keep from placing his hands on the table. An unsightly ring marred the top, still glistening with spilled liquor. He was tempted to call a footman to clean it up, but held his tongue. He would just have to be careful to keep his hands on the arms of his chair.

He waited while Channing ordered their drinks and turned back to him, studying his air of command. The man was as sure of himself as his cronies Bassett and Westbrook. Tony decided that he must be equally confident. Channing was not a man to appreciate shilly-shallying about a subject.

"I should like to formally request the hand of your sister, Lady Kathleen, in marriage," Tony said bluntly.

Channing's brows shot upward. "I wasn't aware that you'd met my sister."

"I haven't. I've seen her riding in the park with you these mornings past."

Channing narrowed his eyes as he sat back in his chair and propped his chin on his hand. "I think an introduction after she is out of mourning would be more appropriate," he said softly. "Perhaps at her debut?"

"I don't require an introduction," Tony said firmly. "I have already concluded that we would suit. Of course, I understand that the marriage cannot take place until next year."

"You're serious," Channing stated with a note of bemusement.

Tony nodded, pleased with himself. "There is no need for you to go to the expense of a season. I wish us to be married as soon as propriety allows and will be honored to present her to society as my wife."

Channing's lips twitched. "I'm afraid I must decline on my sister's behalf."

Tony's stomach lurched. "She'll never want for anything. I'm a very rich man."

"Nevertheless," Channing said. "My sister's wishes must be considered. Once she has made her debut, I'll see that you have an introduction."

"No," Tony said desperately. "I don't want an introduction; I want to marry her. I insist you give your permission."

Channing set down his glass down on the table. "The subject is closed."

"But—"

"Edgewater, one more word and I'll forbid even an introduction." Glancing around the room, Channing pushed back his chair and rose. "If you will excuse me."

Stunned, Tony watched Channing weave his way through the tables, pausing here and there to exchange a word with Lord this and Sir that. All the old bitterness rose like bile in his throat. He should have known Channing would still be as arrogantly superior as he'd been in school. A man who would publicly humiliate another would be too callous to care what was best for his sister.

Channing stopped at a table occupied by Maxwell Hastings, the Duke of Bassett.

Tony watched their easy camaraderie and recalled the gossip that had circulated on campus about Channing's mother and her years-long affair with Bassett's father.

Channing's father, the Earl of Blackwood, had eventually fled England to escape the gossip. He wondered if the earl knew that his wife had died, or that the old Duke had drowned. He wondered if the earl knew that his daughter's future was being dictated by Channing without regard to her happiness.

Pressing his palms on the table, Tony pushed to his feet. He snatched his hand away, revolted by the sticky residue that clung to his hand. He glared at Channing's back, blaming him for that, too.

Tony breathed deeply and summoned his control. It wouldn't do to allow anger to cloud his judgment. Nothing had changed. Lady Kathleen would be his.

Channing was not the final word on his sister's future. She had a father who rightfully was the final authority over his daughter's life.

Surely the earl would see what a perfect match they were. After all, the earl had suffered a broken heart. He knew what it was like to love a woman and not have her. What other explanation could there be for the earl's departure to America over a decade ago? It gave Tony hope that the earl would understand his own predicament.

And Tony had ample resources to use in locating

the Earl of Blackwood. Yes! He must locate the earl.
He must begin immediately.

But first, he had to wash the filth from his hands.

# Chapter 4

**B**ruce was not himself today.

Kathy sat on the sofa in his study, ignoring the needlepoint in her lap as she watched her brother. Even though he was behind his desk with quill in hand, he was not working. He had not written a sentence for the past half hour, but merely stared at the sheet of parchment before him as if the answer to whatever he pondered would miraculously appear.

Perhaps he was bored. Lord knew she was. She wished he had left her at Blackwood. At least there, she could roam the estate freely, ride from dawn to dusk or visit the cottagers. She was restricted in London as she had never been at Blackwood.

They had been in the city for a week, and with the exception of last night when she had demanded that Bruce go to his club, she hadn't had a moment to herself.

He was with her every waking hour, making sure she did not brood over their mother. But she was slowly learning to live with the gaping hole Mama's death had left in her life.

Still, no matter how hard she tried to convince her brother that she was all right, he remained steadfastly at her side. He would not allow her to take a walk unless he was with her, using the need to protect her reputation as an excuse. Even their early morning rides in the park did nothing to alleviate her boredom. Bruce insisted they ride at a sedate pace, while she longed to gallop.

And every time she and Bruce went out for a walk or a ride, she found herself hoping they would accidentally cross paths with Damien Forbes. Contrary to what she had told Bruce, she very much wanted to meet him, for what purpose she was not sure. Perhaps she simply wanted to see if his eyes were really green.

She always returned home, restless and filled with a sense of disappointment.

"You are very thoughtful today," Bruce said.

Kathy traced the needlepoint design with her finger. "I was just thinking the same thing about you," she said, knowing it wasn't exactly true. She'd been thinking about Bruce until musings about Damien had intruded. It had been happening all too frequently since she'd first seen him a year ago. It was worse now that she was in the city and the inevitability of actually meeting him hovered in the back of her mind.

"I had an interesting evening at the club." Bruce leaned back in his chair and propped his feet on his desk. "Someone offered for your hand."

"What?" Kathy said, unsure she'd heard him right.

Bruce chuckled. "A widower. Seems he saw you in the park and decided you could end his loneliness. I declined of course."

"I should hope so," she said, dismissing the subject. She didn't want to know who would do such an absurd thing.

His expression changed, becoming serious, troubled. "I also spoke to Max last night."

"What is he doing in town? He and Jillian have been wed only a few weeks."

"Business matters," Bruce said.

"Oh," Kathy replied, battling back the urge to inquire if he had spoken to Damien as well. The thought annoyed her. Bruce was the last person she should ask, given his fondness for teasing. For that matter, there was no reason for her absurd fascination with a man she'd seen once, and from a distance at that. If she didn't know better she would think she'd developed a schoolgirl crush on him. But, she was no schoolgirl, and crushes were for those who believed love and marriage were worth dreaming about.

"I almost told Max about us," Bruce said quietly.

Her gaze snapped to his, every other thought chased away by Bruce's astonishing admission. It had always been understood that their secret would remain just that—a secret that didn't need to be told. "Why would you want to tell him?" she asked.

Bruce shrugged. "A momentary lapse into sentimentality."

Kathy searched his expression. Flippancy was second nature to Bruce, yet just then it seemed to be forced. It occurred to her that her earlier annoyance with his constant presence might have been selfish, that perhaps the weight of losing Mama added to the strain of keeping silent. Their parentage was unfinished business. Bruce hated loose ends. He had a special bond with Max, a bond that would either be broken or strengthened if their secret were told. Perhaps Bruce needed to know one way or the other before he, too, could come to terms with their diminished family. "Why didn't you tell him, then?"

Bruce sighed, another disturbing sign that something weighed heavily on his mind. "You know the relationship between the duke and our mother has always been a closed subject to Max."

"Do you ever intend to tell him?"

"Someday, perhaps." He grinned, but it seemed forced. "Max has just reluctantly acquired a wife. That's enough for any man to contend with," he said, as if that explained it all.

It explained nothing and raised a great deal of curiosity. According to the papers, the marriage

between Max and Jillian was the love match of the
century. Kathy had never doubted it was so. "Reluctant? What do you mean—"

"Bruce!" roared a deep, male voice from the
foyer. An angry voice.

Bruce ran his hand over his face and rose from his
chair. "I believe," he said as he strode toward the
door, "you might be about to find out."

Alarmed, she lurched to her feet.

He glanced at her over his shoulder and shook his
head. "Stay here," he ordered and stepped into the
hallway, pulling the door shut behind him, closing
her in.

She stared at the door, stunned by Bruce's actions.
He'd never commanded her to do anything before
except in a good-natured, teasing way. Bruce was
rarely grave, except in the most dire circumstances—

She jumped at the sound of a crash coming from
the next room. She ran for the door and wrenched it
open. She rushed down the hall as she heard another
crash, glass breaking, more loud thumps, like bodies
falling to the floor.

"Goddamn you, Bruce," the furious voice echoed
from the drawing room, followed by a loud thud.
"You can't deny it, can you?"

She stopped dead in the threshold, seeing the
toppled lamp, the chair that had been shoved across
the floor . . . her brother pinned helplessly to the
floor by a madman who pummeled him without
mercy.

The sound of a fist slamming against flesh and
bone resurrected all the fear and helplessness of her
childhood. A sound she had not heard in more than
a decade.

It still filled her with terror.

It was happening again—Bruce lying flat on his
back, his arms pinned to his sides by someone sitting
astride his chest, striking him over and over again.

She shook her head to clear it. She was no longer seven . . . no longer too small and too weak. She could help.

Dimly aware that someone else was pounding on the front doors, she rushed into the drawing room and pounced on her brother's attacker. "Stop it!" she cried as her fingers twisted in the maniac's hair.

"Get back, Kathy," Bruce rasped and rolled from side to side, trying to avoid his attacker.

"No!" She yanked on the beast's hair and pounded furiously at his shoulders with all her strength, ignoring the stinging numbness in her hand as her fist connected with hard bone and tight muscle.

Suddenly, hands gripped her waist and pulled her away.

"No, don't. He's killing Bruce," she cried, flailing her arms and kicking out at whoever held her.

"Be still and stay out of the way," a deep voice commanded.

She struggled more violently, tears stinging her eyes. "He's killing him."

Other, gentler hands gripped her shoulders. "Max won't allow it," a soft voice said. A woman's voice, full of reason rather than madness. "He'll stop them, but you must not interfere."

Kathy forced herself to take a deep breath, to focus on more than the men grappling on the floor. She sagged against the woman at her side as her attention fastened on the muscular blond man who strode toward the combatants on the floor.

Max. The Duke of Bassett. Her half-brother. A man she had seen only once before.

She blinked and glanced at the woman beside her. A woman she had seen only once as well, but Kathy knew her as Jillian, the Duchess of Bassett.

What were they doing here? Why now?

"Stop it," Max growled as he yanked the madman from her brother, whirled him about, and neatly pinned his arms behind his back.

For the first time, Kathy saw the face of the attacker. Her heart stumbled in her chest as she stared at a tall man, his black brows an angry slash above eyes filled with unbridled fury.

Green eyes.

Damien Forbes, Duke of Westbrook.

She reeled with the shock of recognition. The man who had occupied her childhood thoughts as her knight in shining armor, her kind and gentle protector. She'd imagined him to be all that his father had been and more. She'd remembered him as something beautiful and magnificent after she'd seen him on the steps of the cathedral.

She'd been wrong. He was nothing like his father. He wasn't—could never be—a protector.

He was a destroyer.

She heard Bruce groan as he raised to a sitting position and rested his back against the sofa. With a strangled sob, she ran to her brother and dabbed at the blood streaming down his face with the hem of her skirt.

"Let me go," Damien shouted. "He ruined Jillian."

"What?" Max said.

*Ruined? How could that be?* Kathy struggled to order her thoughts, to bring her fear and anger under control and understand what was happening. If Bruce ruined Jillian, why was she married to Max?

"It was Bruce," Damien spat out. "He tricked Nunnley into spreading gossip about you and Jillian."

Kathy's gaze narrowed on her brother's face, but Bruce was not looking at her. For a moment, he glanced at Jillian then leaned his head back on the cushions and closed his eyes.

"I think," Max said evenly, then broke off for the space of a heartbeat, "I think that one of you had better explain, now."

"Max," Jillian said, a note of panic in her voice, "can't you see that Bruce is in no condition—"

"Damien, I trust you're willing to enlighten me," Max interrupted.

Kathy's hand fell to her lap as Damien launched into a story that made no sense. He spoke of Bruce observing a seemingly scandalous encounter between Max and Jillian on a balcony at some ball. Jillian's gown was torn and she'd been seen sitting on Max's lap. Damien identified other witnesses as well, and it was obvious from the grim way he spoke the names of Viscount Nunnley, Arabella Seymour and her daughter, Melissa, that he had little liking or respect for them. From what Kathy could ascertain, Bruce had torn Melissa's gown, then threatened to initiate gossip about her and Nunnley if any of them breathed a word of the incident.

It sounded to Kathy as if Bruce had saved Jillian's reputation. Damien Forbes was insane, and without the capacity to recognize an act of kindness. She glared up at him, hating his arrogant stance, the demonic slash of his brows, the grating sound of his voice.

He folded his arms across his chest. "Apparently, Bruce had a change of heart the following morning. He tricked Nunnley into believing that Arabella had already begun to spread malicious tales about Jillian and Max. Nunnley naturally felt free to gossip about what he thought was a known scandal."

Kathy stiffened in outrage. How dare he accuse Bruce of deliberately manipulating Max and Jillian? She shifted her gaze to Bruce, waiting for him to name Damien a liar.

Bruce gave her the barest nod, confirming the tale.

*Why?* she wanted to ask, yet said nothing, afraid to disrupt the charged silence that had suddenly swept through the room. No one moved, but stood stunned and unmoving, like pillars of salt.

Shaking her head, she once again gathered the hem of her skirt and tried to staunch the flow of blood from the open cut above Bruce's eye. Whatever the reason for his actions, she refused to believe

Bruce meant harm. Never would he hurt these people. He cared too much about them. Surely Max would give him a chance to explain, as Damien, damn him, had not.

"Why?" Max asked.

Kathy's gaze jerked up. Max's expression was as cold and forbidding as his voice. Beside him, Jillian's face was white and pinched. Nearby, Damien stood with clenched fists and watchful eyes. Unable to stomach the sight of him, Kathy again focused on her brother.

Bruce met Max's gaze, shrugged, and glanced away.

Out of nowhere hands appeared and twisted in Bruce's collar. "*Why,* you bastard?" Max demanded and jerked him to his feet.

Kathy sprang up and latched onto one of Max's arms. "No! Don't touch him."

"Max!" Jillian grasped his other arm.

Max toppled forward. Bruce's hands shot out and splayed against Max's chest as he sat down flat on the sofa. Kathy felt herself being dragged forward and then abruptly jerked backward as Damien grasped Max's shoulders and held him upright.

"Turn loose of his bloody coat," Damien snarled from behind her.

The sofa toppled over and landed with a thud, taking Bruce with it. Kathy cringed as she heard the thump of Bruce's head bang against the floor. She could see nothing but his feet sticking straight up toward the ceiling.

"Get up, damn you," Max said as he tried to shake her and Jillian off of him. But Kathy held on, terrified of what he would do were she to let go.

"Enough, Max," Damien said. "This has gone too far."

Kathy glared at him, suspicious of his sudden change of heart.

"It will never be enough," Max said harshly. "The bastard ruined my life."

For Kathy, it was more than enough. She was sick to death of hearing the word "bastard." Hearing Max say it sent her beyond the edge of reason.

"He is a bastard," she blurted, then sobbed with the enormity of what she'd said, feeling as if she were coming apart inside. "So am I."

"Kathy, no!" Bruce said.

"Max, listen to me," Jillian said from his right. "Bruce ruined me because I asked him to. I could not allow Damien to put you out of my life."

Dimly, Kathy heard Jillian's confession, but it meant nothing to her. She had her own confession to make and no reason to keep silent. Bruce had already come close to admitting the truth himself. She wanted to be free of this dark secret. She wanted Max, to understand that whatever Bruce had done, he had done it for Max. He would do anything for Max.

"Bruce is your brother," she gasped, knowing it was too late to turn back and she had to say it all. "And I am your sister."

# Part 2

# Chapter 5

*London*
*June, 1820*

She was not impressed with the glamour of the Season.

Kathy stood at the edge of the ballroom floor, watching elaborately dressed aristocrats hop about in a country dance. Perspiration rolled down the gentlemen's foreheads and the ladies delicately dabbed at their upper lips and necks with handkerchiefs. In the last few weeks the temperature had soared, and the ballroom was stifling. Baskets of flowers adorned every available nook and cranny, adding a heavy scent to the humid air. Thousands of candles smoked profusely in the chandeliers.

Kathy felt as if her body was coated with a fine layer of black soot.

"Never again will I allow you to persuade me to host the last ball of the Season," Max grumbled.

"Let her be, Max," Kathy said, smiling at her half-brother. She was free to do that now, free to visit him and exchange banter with him . . . and to love him. Even though the true connection between herself, Max, and Bruce would never be publicly acknowledged, in the privacy of their homes and minds, she, Max and Bruce were as much a family as Damien and Jillian.

"Yes, let me be, Max," Jillian said. "I'm rather enjoying the sight of Lord Gardner's hair pomade melting down his face."

Kathy chuckled, then smiled fondly at Jillian, her first and only female friend as well as her unacknowledged sister-in-law.

The confessions that had been made nearly two years ago would be excellent material for one of the novels that were so fashionable these days, complete with a happy ending for them all. Bruce had indeed manipulated events that led up to the marriage between Max and Jillian, but as she'd surmised, he'd done it with the best of intentions. It had been a shock to discover that the initial plot had been Jillian's.

She'd loved Max and wanted to marry him, and had gone to extraordinary lengths to accomplish it. Things had not gone well for them after Bruce's and Jillian's confessions, yet Jillian had not given up in the face of her husband's rejection. It had taken Max a while to accept that he loved her, too. In spite of how it had begun, their marriage was everything to Max and Jillian.

Kathy admired Jillian's strength and courage. Most women would not be so tenacious, nor so creative, in pursuing a future of their own choice. Kathy was determined to follow Jillian's example, though love and marriage had no part in her plans.

In six months, she would reach her majority and gain control of her fortune. She would buy a house and live as she chose, answering to no one but herself. Life would be her own—no more Seasons or chaperones or coming to London if she didn't wish it. She was looking forward to being on the shelf, ignored and eventually forgotten by ambitious suitors, and she would no doubt be labeled as one of those "scandalous eccentrics" the ton whispered about. Only women committed to art or studies usually confined to men dared to flaunt the rules of society without concern. She had no such ambitions. To live alone in a home of her own and enjoy her family without living in their pockets was enough for her.

The orchestra struck a waltz. Jillian smiled up at Max.

"Go ahead and dance," Kathy said. "I will be fine."

"Are you certain?" Jillian asked. "Perhaps Max should fetch Bruce from the card room."

"You needn't drag Bruce away from his game," Kathy said. She didn't know why Jillian was so concerned about leaving her alone in the chaperone's corner. It wasn't as if any suitors would dare approach her. It had taken most of the Season, but she had managed to discourage the eager contingent of bachelors by being a thoroughly boring lump.

"Oh, there's Damien," Jillian said as she beckoned her brother with a wave of her hand. "I'm sure he will be happy to keep you company."

Kathy was sure he wouldn't be happy to keep her company just as she wasn't thrilled to be in the same room with him. She had been well and truly purged of her fascination for him when he had burst into her home like a wild animal and mauled her brother. In the beginning of their odd relationship, he had made several friendly overtures, but as she made her aversion of him more obvious, he became more annoyed with her.

Her mouth flattened in irritaton as she watched him stride toward them, arrogantly oblivious to the admiring female stares that collected in his wake. She had to admit that he did look spectacular in his black formal attire that seemed a mere accessory to his own inborn elegance. Sometimes, she wished that he would have just one hair out of place . . . or a nick on his chin from his razor. She found it distasteful to admire anything about him.

Still, she supposed that if she must have a chaperone, Damien was better than Bruce, who naturally assumed her goal was to find a husband and would advise her to smile so someone would ask her to dance.

Damien's imposing brows descended in a frown

as he drew near and his gaze briefly met hers before skipping to Jillian. "What is it?"

"Max and I would like to dance," Jillian said.

"You don't mind holding our places, do you?" Max said as he took Jillian's arm and guided her into the waltz before Damien could reply.

Kathy turned her head to hide her smirk. Max and Jillian were well aware that she and Damien went to great lengths to avoid one another. They simply chose to ignore it.

As she and Damien ignored each other now. Oddly enough, the silence between them was so familiar that it was almost comforting. She didn't like Damien, and he had the grace to accept her antipathy without comment. Standing with him was the same as standing alone—not a bad thing at all under the circumstances.

The hair on the back of Kathy's neck prickled. She felt as if someone were watching her every movement. She ground her teeth together as a man appeared out of the crush, his gaze fixed on her like the mouth of a leech.

She should have known. Tony Edgewater had not given her a moment's peace for six long weeks. Everywhere she went, he was there, watching her. She had learned that he was the widower who had offered for her right after Mama died. He'd offered again a fortnight after her come-out. At her request, Bruce had again turned him down, yet it made no difference. He continued to pursue her, besieging her with dozens of roses and assaulting her sensibilities with volumes of ponderously verbose handwritten poems. His presence was as oppressive as the heat in the room, as suffocating as the smell of roses and candle wax and perspiring bodies.

She didn't know why his attentions offended her so. More so even than Damien's presence. Tony was tall and more attractive than some of the men who had sought her attention. As tall as Damien, she thought as she darted a sideways glance at him. Yet,

Tony was a whittled stick while Damien was a polished carving.

In truth, Tony's company unnerved her. She had the feeling that he would do anything to gain what he wanted. That sort of desperation frightened her.

"Westbrook," he said as he stopped before her and nodded to Damien.

"Edgewater," Damien acknowledged.

Tony turned to her with a sickeningly adoring smile on his face and bowed over her hand. "My Lady Kathleen, it is the last waltz of the Season. Please say you will grant it to me."

"You know I do not waltz," Kathy said, employing the monotone that had been so off-putting to the rest of the ton.

"Surely you will make an exception for me," Tony entreated. "It will be a memory that will sustain me until I am privileged to look upon your countenance once more."

Damien cleared his throat and raised his hand as if to cover a cough . . . and probably a smirk.

"No," she said coldly, not caring how churlish she sounded. Tony's fawning was bad enough, but Damien finding amusement in her discomfort was more than she could tolerate.

Tony glanced at Damien, then back at her. "It's quite all right," he said as he straightened his waistcoat. "I really must be going anyway. I have an early business appointment." With a stiff bow, he turned and walked away.

"Was that necessary?" Damien gritted.

"Was what necessary?" she asked absently as she watched Tony disappear through the ballroom door.

"Your behavior with Edgewater."

"I do not like him," she said flatly.

"That is no excuse for you to be so bloody stiff-rumped."

"It is the only one I have," she said, inordinately pleased that she'd been so convincing.

"You could have been nicer to him."

"Why? I want him to leave me alone." Annoyed that she was explaining herself to Damien of all people, she stepped back. "Please tell Jillian that I will be in the ladies' retiring room." She turned away from him and wound her way toward the door, as glad to be away from Damien as she was relieved that Tony was gone. Now, she could move about without constantly looking over her shoulder.

Thank God that her first Season would also be her last. Her birthday was six months away, and she was going to spend it purchasing and furnishing her own home. She'd found the house she wanted—a modest twenty-room cottage a few hours' ride from Bassett House. Unfortunately, it was an hour's ride from Westbrook Court, one of Damien's residences and the one he inhabited most of the year. If only he would spend more time at Westbrook Castle. It was, after all, the seat of his dukedom and where he belonged. It was also at the far end of England.

At least he planned to go to the castle at the end of the season. She could hardly wait, for then she would have the opportunity to speak to Bruce and Max without Damien's presence to rattle her. She could just imagine his reaction to her desire to live so close to Westbrook Court.

Still, why should he care? It wasn't as if the houses were within sight of one another. It would be her house and her land. Of course, she had yet to broach the subject with her brothers and did not look forward to doing so. Bruce and Max would be none too pleased with her plans to live alone and would no doubt object strenuously.

Again, it didn't matter. Their power to control her would end when she reached the age of twenty-one.

Never again would she conform to any rules but her own.

Damien strode out of the ballroom and up to the second-floor library. He was suffocating in that bloody ballroom. And watching Kathy Palmerston treat someone as harmless as Tony Edgewater with rudeness rather than her usual cool indifference made his hands itch to shake her.

When she'd first made her debut, Kathy had made a spectacular splash. Women envied her and men clamored for her favor. Of course he could see why. She was beautiful. She was an heiress. Polite society had immediately proclaimed her *the* diamond of the first water.

It hadn't taken her long to prove just how hard diamonds were.

The men found her too formidable. It was not what Lady Kathleen did, but what she didn't do. She did not have a malleable nature. She did not laugh at jests and rarely smiled. She limited herself to cotillions and country dances, which required a minimum of contact. Damien made it a point to never ask her to dance at all. In fact, he made it a point to keep away from her altogether. Even he was not immune to her sapphire eyes and perfect porcelain skin, her willowy height and feminine grace. But what fascinated Damien most was her wild mane of bright auburn hair. Even tonight, with it caught in a loose bun on top of her head, he visualized it hanging to her waist in a mass of fiery curls that seemed to have a life of their own. No matter how she arranged it, her hair always looked as if a lover had recently run his fingers through the locks.

Her breasts were nice, too. Damien suspected they would fit perfectly in the palms of his hands. As for the rest of her body, he hadn't a clue. The current fashion of high-waisted gowns made it impossible to tell if a woman had a waist, or whether her legs were long and slender or short and chubby. Nothing aroused him like a pair of endless, shapely legs—

Impatiently, he strode to the sideboard and poured a snifter of brandy. What was he doing in allowing his mind to wander down lascivious pathways? After suffering the events leading up to Jillian's marriage to Max, he of all people knew that it was the height of stupidity to become even remotely involved with the sister of one's friend.

At least Kathy made it easy for him to avoid her. With him, she was frigid rather than remote. A diamond indeed, he reflected—unremittingly cold in her beauty and brilliance.

She'd never forgiven him for the thrashing he'd given Bruce two years ago. In light of how well everything had turned out, he supposed he should have tried to make peace with her. But her stubborn refusal to meet him halfway rankled. While he admired her loyalty to her brother, he had no patience for her stubborn refusal to comprehend that his own actions had been out of loyalty to his sister.

They'd reached an impasse that neither of them cared to change.

Damien loosened his neckcloth and stretched out on the long leather sofa, balancing the snifter on his chest. He couldn't imagine what had possessed him to interfere between Kathy and Edgewater, other than he'd felt sorry for the man. He felt sorry for any man who was so moon-eyed over a woman that he allowed her to hack at his pride on a regular basis. Particularly since Bruce had told him that Edgewater had offered for her hand and been rejected, not once but twice. Still, it was none of his concern, and he should have kept his mouth shut.

He should have visited his mistress tonight instead of subjecting himself to this. At least voluptuous Vicki was entertaining.

The door opened and closed with a soft click. Footsteps whispered across the carpet—definitely feminine. Damien stifled a groan. Had some marriage-minded miss followed him? He flicked his gaze around the room, searching for a quick means of escape. There was none. The best thing he could do was to lie still and hope he wasn't discovered. He stared longingly at the brandy as his fingers curled around the snifter on his chest, holding it steady. All he'd wanted was a moment of solitude and a drink.

A figure dashed past the end of the sofa in a flurry of yellow skirts, tendrils of auburn hair flying from their restraint. She halted and glanced over her shoulder, her gaze skipping over him, her body seeming to vibrate with urgency.

Good lord, it was Kathy.

He forced himself to be silent as she ran to Max's massive oak desk, pushed away the chair, and disappeared into the knee hole.

The door opened again and more footsteps sounded, heavy this time. "Lady Kathleen," Edgewater called. "I know you're here. Please come out."

What the hell? Damien thought. Hadn't Edgewater left?

"I didn't mean to frighten you in the hallway," Edgewater said. "I wanted a moment alone with you, my darling."

Damien frowned. No wonder Kathy had looked so desperate. Edgewater had no right to follow an unmarried lady into a private room, much less address her with an endearment.

He supposed he should put Edgewater in his place, but it really wasn't *his* place to interfere. Maybe Edgewater would go away when Kathy didn't answer.

"Why are you so cruel to me?" Edgewater whined as he came abreast of the sofa, his gaze searching the corners of the library.

"Perhaps because you are so bloody annoying," Damien said, unable to keep silent any longer.

Edgewater jerked and pivoted toward Damien, his face blanching. "Westbrook!" he gasped, then recovered himself and squared his shoulders, meeting Damien's gaze head on. "What are you doing here?"

"A better question is: what are you doing here in my brother-in-law's private library?" Damien said, raising up to finally take a long draught of brandy. "Didn't you say you were leaving?"

"Yes, I did," Edgewater said smoothly, expressionlessly.

Very carefully, Damien set the snifter on a side table, giving himself time to control his anger. He was beginning to understand why Kathy had such an aversion to Edgewater. There was definitely something reptilian about the man. Come to think of it, there always had been. During their first year of university, he had avoided Edgewater because of his slovenly ways. Over the next year, Edgewater had cleaned up nicely, but he'd become standoffish, keeping apart from the rest of the students, choosing to watch them rather than participate in their activities.

The thought gave Damien pause. Edgewater seemed to go from one extreme to the other, lurking in corners one moment and being improperly forward in the next, especially when Kathy was around.

Quelling his urge to toss Edgewater out the nearest window, Damien kept his seat and glanced up at him. "I'm going to assume that you have lost your way to the front door."

Edgewater nodded and turned on his heel to stride out of the library.

"And by the way," Damien called after him. "Lady Kathleen is not here. In the future, if you wish to speak with her privately, I suggest you ask her brother, Viscount Channing, for permission." He turned his head, seeing Edgewater pause stiffly in the threshold.

Damien arched a brow. "But then you've already done so, have you not? And if I'm not mistaken, your suit was rejected. You might remember that the next time your ardor overcomes your dignity."

Without commenting or looking back, Edgewater stepped into the hall and closed the door behind him.

Damien reached for his brandy and drained the glass, unrepentant at having been so brutally insulting. Apparently brutality was the only thing Edgewater understood.

Apparently, Kathy had known that.

Damien rose and strolled across the room to the door. He wanted no intrusions. As he turned the key in the lock, he stared at the desk, waiting for Kathy to emerge.

He counted to ten, yet still she remained tucked away.

"You can come out now," he said.

The rustle of silk preceded the bob of her head over the top of the desk. She glanced around the room, wincing as she gained her feet and held on to the back of the chair for support. Her gaze darted everywhere but at him. Lowering her head, she fussed with the fall of her skirt. "If you will excuse me," she mumbled.

"Not yet," he said, amused at her refusal to voice gratitude. In the two years he'd known her, she had never thanked him, even when he'd been forced to help her into a coach or hold a chair for her. He could carry her across a lake of mud and she would find a way to avoid expressing appreciation.

"Really, I must go," she said as she skirted around the desk and sidled along the edge of the library toward the door. There was something soft and vulnerable about her just then with strands of hair spiraling about her face and the ribbon beneath her breasts hanging free from its bow as she moved among the shadows. Something appealing.

Something alarming.

Damien narrowed his eyes on the dangling ribbon as he recalled what Edgewater had said. "What was Edgewater apologizing about? Did he accost you in the hallway?"

Her gaze jerked downward, to the ribbon, then back up at him. "Of course not. He never laid a hand on me," she said quickly as she retied the bow.

Suspicion rose full blown in Damien's mind.

Again, he eyed her dishevelment, studying the hap-hazard bow beneath her breasts and the high color in her cheeks. "Not even one?"

"I stepped on the ribbon," she said defensively. "It was a harmless incident."

"It was bloody well not harmless," he snapped. "Edgewater could have irreparably damaged your reputation, had the situation gone differently. I have no doubt that Bruce and Max will agree."

"There is no reason to bother Bruce and Max with this," she said quickly. She edged closer to the door, her gaze on him wary as her fingers continued to worry the ribbon. "It's over and I am fine."

She didn't appear fine to Damien. That Kathy was distressed was obvious in the glimmer of panic in her eyes. He had the queer idea that she was actually afraid he would turn the encounter with Edgewater into something sordid.

It unsettled him to know she distrusted him that much.

Impatiently, he raked his hand through his hair. Why should he be concerned over what she thought? For that matter, there was no reason to tell Bruce and Max about this.

Though she didn't know it yet, in a few weeks Kathy would be on a ship bound for America with Max and Jillian while Bruce attended to business in the West Indies.

Damien was looking forward to Kathy's extended holiday.

# Chapter 6

*F*<sup>*ool!*</sup>

Tony cursed himself over and over as he leaned his head against the seat in his coach and closed his eyes, willing the humiliation and anger burning inside him to dissipate.

Westbrook was just like Channing. He had no doubt Bassett and his wife were the same, given the way they all ran in a pack. They were all overweening prigs. All except Lady Kathleen. She didn't belong with them. She belonged with him.

He should never have waylaid her in the hall. He'd frightened her. But her cruelty in the ballroom had made him realize that she thought he was like the others and cared only for her money. The need to tell her that her fortune was of no consequence to him had overwhelmed him.

If not for Westbrook, he could have convinced her that she loved him. Tony was certain that she had been in that room somewhere. Westbrook had lied. Yes! He wanted Kathleen for himself. Who would not want her?

His mouth flattened. Westbrook would not have her.

In a few weeks, he'd have the permission he required to marry her. It had taken him almost two years, but his investigator had finally located the Earl

59

of Blackwood, and had sent word the earl would be on the next ship out of some godforsaken place called New Orleans.

Tony was anxious to meet the man he admired so much. A man who had given up everything for love.

He smiled as he thought of the letter he'd written to the earl. He'd labored over it as carefully as the poems he'd written for Kathleen and every word was engraved in his memory.

*My Dear Sir:*

*If you are reading this missive, then my search is at an end. Regretfully, I have grievous news to impart. Your beloved countess passed on, and though I am reluctant to bring his name into this, I feel I must inform you that the Duke of Bassett drowned in a yachting accident. I tell you this in the highest of hopes that you will return to England immediately. Your daughter Kathleen's future depends upon it.*

*The situation is most dire as she is in the hands of her brother, Viscount Channing, and he cares not for her happiness.*

*I am desperately in love with her and your son has refused me permission to wed her. I assure you that no other man will suit her so well as I. My lineage is impeccable and I am possessed of an impressive fortune, which I am prepared to dedicate to making Lady Kathleen the happiest of women. Your son, Viscount Channing, has done both myself and Lady Kathleen a disservice by denying her the life she so richly deserves.*

*You sir, have the power to right this injustice and secure a glorious future for your daughter.*

Filled with pride at his eloquence, Tony sighed. The letter was more persuasive than he'd thought.

Soon, the earl would arrive.
Soon, Lady Kathleen would be his.
Soon, she would realize that she loved him.

# Chapter 7

*Bassett House*
*June, 1820*

**H**e was soft as a freshly baked roll and smelled sweeter than a sugar plum. Kathy wanted to bite him, so she did.

James Alexander Hastings giggled at her playful nip and tangled his hands in her hair. "Top Kaffy."

Kathy laughed. At a little over a year old, James hadn't yet mastered "S" or "th." She took another nibble from his warm belly. "Oh, but you taste so good."

He shrieked and crawled away, pausing for a moment to climb to his feet. The garden at Bassett House was a veritable fairyland for a child, Kathy thought, complete with child-sized mazes, swings, and a gazebo. She loved it here, loved knowing she and Bruce had a whole week to enjoy the company of their extended family. She loved knowing the Season was over and she would never have to go through another.

Most of all, she loved sharing afternoons with the baby, watching his wonder as he discovered new things to study and found new ways to get into trouble. Like now, as he waddled across the thick carpet of grass as fast as his unsteady legs would carry him toward a fountain and pool stocked with fish.

"No, James," LadyLou called out. "Come look at the butterflies."

Kathy smiled at Lady Louise Forbes, Damien's and Jillian's aunt. Not only had LadyLou accepted the truth about hers and Bruce's relationship to Max without batting an eyelash, she had welcomed them into the family with open arms.

Kathy admired this woman as much as she admired Jillian. There was no artifice about LadyLou, yet she was most attractive with fine strands of silver threaded through her black hair and a youthful twinkle in her light blue eyes. More importantly, LadyLou had lived her entire life as she'd wanted and was one of the most contented and confident people Kathy had ever known.

Kathy could think of no other woman who could advise her so well as LadyLou, yet the information she sought was of a personal nature and she groped for a way to broach the subject. Tilting her head, she considered whether it would be too forward to ask outright.

LadyLou met her gaze and raised her brows. "You look as if you've something on the tip of your tongue. Would you like to talk about it?"

Kathy smiled in relief. Forthrightness was yet another thing to be admired about LadyLou. She gathered her thoughts and decided to ask the most brazen question first. "You never married. May I ask why?"

LadyLou regarded her thoughtfully for a moment before turning one eye on the baby's progress across the lawn. "If I may ask why you're so determined to avoid marriage."

The observation startled Kathy. LadyLou had attended few functions throughout the Season, spending most of the time with her friends. She hadn't attended Jillian's and Max's ball at all and had chosen to return to Bassett House with James the week before. How on earth could she possibly know what Kathy had been up to?

"I suppose because I'm selfish," Kathy replied,

answering bluntness with honesty. "I don't want anyone telling me what to do and I hate the idea of living only through my husband. I want to know what it's like to make my own decisions and carry them out."

LadyLou nodded. "Then I suppose I am selfish as well. I am a bluestocking with too much education to be satisfied living according to a man's whims."

"That's exactly how I feel," Kathy said, excited to find someone who understood, and had successfully established herself as a person in her own right.

"But there are sacrifices for such independence," LadyLou said. "Do you not want love?"

"No," Kathy said, unwilling to elaborate. To do so would be to speak of her mother and the late Duke of Bassett. She did not want to discuss what love had done to her mother. And she thought that even LadyLou would be shocked if Kathy told her she believed that love destroyed.

"What of children, Kathy?" LadyLou asked. "It's obvious how much you love James."

Kathy stifled a regretful sigh. The only disadvantage of never marrying was the children she would never have. "I will always have Max's and Jillian's children, and Bruce will surely marry one day. There will be more than enough children to love."

"It's not the same, Kathy," LadyLou said. "But I suspect you know that as well as I." She narrowed her eyes as the baby tottered near a rosebush, then relaxed as he righted himself. "I wonder though, why you have such a dismal view of marriage and love after having observed Max and Jillian."

"Max and Jillian are exceptions to the rule," Kathy stated. "Have you seen any others like them?"

"Yes," LadyLou said with a soft smile. "Damien's and Jillian's parents were the same way." Her gaze on James sharpened; she began to rise. "No, James. It has thorns. You'll stick yourself."

Kathy's vision blurred and turned inward at LadyLou's revelation. She did not want to hear that

Damien's parents had been happily in love when she'd believed his childhood had been as empty of emotion as Max's. For some reason, it unsettled her to think he'd learned to take tenderness and sharing for granted from an early age when all she'd known of him was his temper and coldness. It contradicted everything she wanted to believe about him.

LadyLou returned and settled back on the lawn as the baby squatted to pull out clumps of grass with his chubby hands. "What a lot of mischief they get into at this age."

Relieved that LadyLou hadn't picked up on the previous subject, Kathy focused on her next concern. "Did you ever consider having your own house?"

"I did have my own house until Jillian was born."

"Really?" Kathy said. "You actually owned it?"

"Not precisely. I had the Dower House at Westbrook Castle. It was all my brother, Jillian's and Damien's father, would allow. He was a stickler for propriety."

That wasn't what Kathy wanted to hear. Yet, she knew that about Damien's father. He hadn't been too pleased to find her in a china cabinet. She told herself that times were different now. Max and Bruce were different. She *would* have her own house.

And she did not need doubts encroaching on her plans for the future.

A high-pitched wail filled the air. Kathy lurched to her feet and ran toward the baby while motioning for LadyLou to remain seated. James had managed to get to the rosebush after all and pricked his finger in the process. His cries grew louder and more persistent as he held up his hand for her inspection. "Ow, Kaffy, ow."

She scooped him up and kissed his fingers one by one. "Didn't LadyLou tell you it would stick you?"

The baby regarded her with a serious expression as his sobs turned into little gulps.

Carrying him to a safer section of the flower beds,

she set him down and picked a daisy from a patch near her elbow. "Here, sweetheart," she said, extending her hand. "This one won't hurt you."

He pushed out his bottom lip.

She knelt down in front of him. "Still want that rose, do you? This one is more fun." She plucked a petal. "He loves me?"

James leaned closer and sniffed the flower as he studied the gap left by the missing petal. He had such thick, golden hair. Max's hair. And his large, thickly lashed eyes were an arresting deep green. Jillian's eyes. . . .

Damien's eyes.

She plucked another petal so forcefully several others fell to the ground. "He loves me not!"

"He loves me," an amused male voice intruded. "He loves me not."

Damien's voice.

With a sinking heart, she glanced up at him as he crouched down to sift through the fallen petals. Why did the sun have to cast blue lights in his black hair and emphasize his widow's peak where the wind had blown the strands back?

James squealed in delight. "Un Dame! Un Dame! See fowler."

"Yes, I see the flower," Damien said gravely. He lifted James as he rose, and swung him high in the air.

The baby shrieked and drooled on his uncle's snowy white cravat.

Damien chuckled.

Why did he have to like children so much when most men seemed to merely tolerate them?

Frustration increased as Kathy watched Damien play with his nephew until she wanted to shriek, too. Feeling at a distinct disadvantage with Damien towering above her, she rose to her feet, her gaze colliding with his.

Why did his bronzed face have to be such an elegant setting for his emerald eyes?

For that matter, why was he here? He was supposed to be far, far away at Westbrook Castle. She didn't want him here. Not now, when she planned to finally broach the subject of purchasing her own house with Bruce and Max. Damien could spoil everything.

Her conscience pricked her as she watched him settle the baby on his hip and carry him toward LadyLou several feet away.

She supposed she should be more gracious in her attitude toward him, considering how Damien had kept his word not to relate the incident with Tony Edgewater to Max and Bruce. And, thanks to Damien's actions in so neatly dispatching Tony from Max's library, she was certain Tony would never trouble her again.

She frowned and tried to banish the memory she'd so scrupulously avoided since the night Damien had rescued her from Tony's blatant attempt to compromise her.

Damien's actually being there when she'd needed him disturbed her beyond measure. It had been as if the promise his father had made so many years ago was being fulfilled, as if events had gone beyond her control and she was somehow now tied to him.

She shook off such nonsense and told herself that it was one thing to be comforted by the idea of having a protector at age seven, and quite another to feel incapable of looking after herself at age twenty. She'd felt so humiliated at having to hide beneath the desk as if she were again a helpless child. Worse was having Damien witness her vulnerability. She didn't want him to think that she needed anyone for any reason. She didn't need him. She didn't like him. She certainly didn't want to be grateful to him. The promise had nothing to do with it and had only concerned the earl.

And she certainly didn't want to have to worry about him tattling on her. Just because he'd kept his silence about Tony until now didn't mean he would do so indefinitely. If her bid for independence came to a battle of wills between her and Bruce and Max, she knew which side Damien would choose.

Disgusted that Damien's mere presence could so easily create anxiety, she strolled over to join Lady-Lou and Damien, determined to meet whatever threat he presented with as much dignity as she possessed.

Damien lay flat on his back across from his aunt, James sprawled belly down on his chest, fast asleep.

Why was she so fascinated with his large hands as they so gently held James, the long fingers gently stroking the baby's back?

"Where is everyone?" he asked.

"Max and Bruce are in the library," LadyLou said. "Jillian is somewhere about."

"And your aunt and I are right here," Kathy said, unaccountably miffed. It was as if she and LadyLou counted for nothing.

"Thank you for pointing that out," he said with a lazy lift of his brow.

LadyLou glanced from Kathy to Damien. "I should take James to the nursery."

"I'd hoped he could stay with us a little longer," Kathy said. "It seems that I never get to spend enough time with him."

"Well, you will certainly have your fill of him over the next eight weeks," LadyLou said as she lifted the baby off Damien's chest. "It will take all of us to keep him out of mischief on the ship."

"Pardon me?" Kathy said.

"Oh dear, they haven't told you, have they?" LadyLou said.

"Told me what?"

LadyLou sighed and smiled apologetically. "That you're going to America on holiday with Max and Jillian, and James and me."

Kathy frowned as she looked from LadyLou to Damien. When had Max and Jillian decided to go to

America? And whyever would they think that she would accompany them?

They were like bookends, Damien thought as Max and Bruce each leaned a shoulder against opposite sides of the mantel in identical poses of controlled patience. To the trained eye, they indeed looked like brothers, both radiating the Bassett pride and arrogance in the bearing of their tall bodies. The most significant difference between them was one that could not be seen at all. Max had been born the legitimate son of the late Duke of Bassett while Bruce and Kathy were the bastard children. Yet it made no difference. They were a family in every way that mattered.

At the moment, they were a family in discord.

Kathy glared at them. "I am not going."

"Why are you being so blasted stubborn about this?" Bruce thundered.

Fighting to control his impatience, Damien tilted his head to one side and waited for Kathy to reply. It hadn't entered his mind that she would refuse to go to America with Max and Jillian.

It should have entered his mind, given the way she'd reacted earlier in the garden when LadyLou had spilled the soup. There had been a brief flash of confusion and shock, but Kathy had recovered quickly with a mutinous line to her mouth and a militant stiffness to her posture.

It had been damned entertaining to watch.

Now, she sat perfectly still in a tapestry chair, her hands folded neatly in her lap and her mouth still set in a mutinous line. "Why do you insist that I arrange my life for your convenience?"

Why did she have to make life so bloody difficult for everyone? Damien wondered. What her family was asking of her was for her own protection.

Bruce had to travel to the West Indies to inspect a sugar plantation he had recently acquired. Max and

Jillian wanted Kathy to accompany them to America so she would not be alone in England. It wasn't as if they were asking her to enter a convent.

"If you will excuse me." Damien lurched to his feet, pulled a cheroot from his pocket and strode toward the door. He'd had quite enough of this nonsense.

"There is no need for you to leave the room to smoke," Jillian said from the sofa.

He halted and glared at the door. He'd very nearly made it. Reluctantly, he turned away from the double doors of the white drawing room at Bassett House. And as he faced his sister, he knew he was well and truly trapped. Of all of them, he thought Jillian might be the most formidable.

She made no distinction between bonds formed by blood and those formed by marriage. To her, every person in the room was family and each had a responsibility to the other.

He should have gone on to Westbrook Castle as planned. Regardless of what Jillian believed to the contrary, this was not his concern, and being drawn into this dispute did not please him. Still, he couldn't bring himself to walk out, not with Jillian glaring daggers at him. In spite of her diminutive stature and the way she wore her black hair caught simply with a ribbon at the nape of her neck, she filled the role of family matriarch admirably.

Defeated, he dropped into the chair nearest the door, distancing himself as much as possible from the argument taking place at the other end of the room. "I'll sit here then." He lit his cheroot and expelled a cloud of smoke. "No need to offend anyone's sensibilities," he said, ignoring the exasperated look Jillian gave him at the ruse. It was not as if any of the rules of polite society were strictly observed when the Hastings and Forbes families gathered.

"You cannot remain at Blackwood alone," Max

said, resuming the debate as if Damien hadn't
interrupted.

"A companion can be engaged," Kathy said.

"I suppose so, but why would you want to stay
alone with a stranger for company?" Jillian leaned
forward. "We could have such a lovely time together
in New York."

Kathy stared down at her fingers clenching and
unclenching in her lap, her forehead pleated with a
thoughtful frown.

They were wearing her down, Damien noted with
satisfaction. He might get away from here yet.

Kathy rubbed her temples. "I want to remain
here," she said haltingly, "because I've made plans
to search for a house of my own and have it
furnished before my birthday."

Silence descended, enclosing each person in their
own attitude of shock. Jillian sagged back against
the cushions. Max and Bruce sat heavily in matching
chairs that flanked the fireplace. Damien hid his own
shock with his hand as he lifted the cheroot to his
mouth. She would reach her majority in a few
months. He had a bad feeling. . . .

"And what do you plan to do with this house?"
Bruce asked.

"Live in it," she said in a low voice.

"Alone?" Max asked.

She raised her head to squarely meet her brothers'
gazes, each in turn. "Yes."

"No," Bruce said flatly. "I won't allow it."

"You cannot stop me."

"Yes, I can," Bruce said.

"Only for six months," Kathy conceded. "Mama
left me a fortune and the freedom to use it as I see fit
when I reach my majority. I intend to do just that."

Again silence fell as Max and Jillian and Bruce
looked at one another with expressions of frustration.

Damien stretched out his legs and studied the toe

of his boot. Good God, she was hard enough to manage already. With a fortune and a house of her own, she would be beyond control.

"Jillian and I will postpone our trip," Max said.

Jillian nodded. "Of course. Actually next spring would be a much better season in which to travel."

*Excellent idea,* Damien thought. Someone needed to remain behind to look after Kathy, talk some sense into her. Nine months ought to be enough time.

"No," Kathy said, rising to her feet in a flounce of bright blue muslin. "Why is it so difficult for everyone to believe that I am capable of looking after myself?"

"It's not that I don't believe you're capable; it's just that there's no need," Bruce said. "Just as there is no reason to have your own house when we have Blackwood Manor as well as the London townhouse." He rose and strode forward and planted his fists on his hips. "Not to mention that you have free access to all of Max's houses."

Kathy lifted her chin. "You and Max and Jillian watch every move I make. As much as I love all of you, I feel suffocated and bound by your concern. I need my own home where I can come and go as I please." She met Bruce's gaze levelly, a plea in her eyes. "I need to be free, as you are free."

A chill rolled over Damien at the desperation in her voice, the reverence with which she spoke of freedom. He'd never seen her this way before.

He could almost sympathize with her.

Since he'd become confident that Jillian was happily wed, he'd felt a sense of freedom he'd never experienced before. Until recently his entire existence had been centered on the duties required by his name and title as well as making sure his younger sister grew up with a strong sense of love and family. It had seemed as if he had to give so much there was nothing left for himself. He didn't regret it but he was relieved to be free of the responsibility of playing dual roles of father and brother. He was even free of his responsibility to LadyLou, his aunt, who now resided with Jillian and Max and looked after their son.

Now, at the age of thirty, he devoted himself to pleasing only himself, to discovering what pleased him rather than what was needed to please another.

It hadn't occurred to him that a woman might feel the same.

From the way Max's and Bruce's gazes connected across the room, Damien knew a decision was being reached. It fascinated him to watch the two communicate without any outward sign. He and Max often used the same method, but they still relied on facial expressions or gestures. Not so with Max and Bruce. They seemed to read one another's minds.

"You are determined to do this?" Bruce asked.

"Yes," Kathy replied firmly.

"Well then," Max said. "I suppose we should find that companion you mentioned earlier."

"I relent on two conditions," Bruce said.

Kathy gazed at him warily. "What conditions?"

"That you allow my solicitor to locate suitable properties for your inspection. And that Smithy remain with you, particularly when you are out and about."

Damien rolled his eyes at the mention of Smithy, Bruce's man of many talents. While Smithy had enough brawn to scare off any who might accost Kathy, he'd never be able to save her from herself. Not when he indulged her like a doting uncle. And not when he was a law unto himself, skirting and even flouting the rules that separated servant and master. Bruce tolerated it but the rest of society would not.

"I'd planned on calling on Mr. Goodman anyway," Kathy said, "and I would be most happy to have Smithy with me."

"It's settled then," Max said.

Bruce nodded.

At the confirmation, Kathy flew from her chair and ran to Bruce and then Max, hugging each fiercely. A sunbeam slanted in through the window and flowed over her, the light playing over her hair like the hands of a lover sifting through the vibrant, curling strands. Excitement and anticipation sparkled in her eyes and her mouth curved upward at the corners—

Good lord, she had dimples. Damien never knew she had dimples. But then, he'd never before seen her smile with a happiness that radiated to every corner of the room.

The beauty of it took his breath away.

Abruptly, he averted his gaze, stubbed out his cheroot and lit another. He didn't know what annoyed him most—her smile or his sudden urge to trace it with his tongue. He shifted in the chair and dismissed his fascination for a simple facial expression. The real source of irritation was Bruce's and Max's approval of Kathy's intention to purchase a house and live alone, not to mention their willingness to leave her in England with just a companion and Smithy, of all people, to see to her welfare.

Was there no one in this room who knew that Kathy needed a keeper?

"I still don't feel comfortable with this," Jillian said as she rose and strolled across the room to lean against the side of Max's chair.

Finally, someone who was still capable of reason, Damien thought. But then the hair on the nape of his neck prickled as Jillian's gaze settled exclusively on him.

"You intend to leave for Westbrook Castle immediately after we sail, don't you?" she asked.

"I do," Damien said firmly, feeling as if he needed to reinforce his own independence.

"Blackwood isn't so very far from Westbrook Castle," she mused.

"As the crow flies," he replied. He didn't like the considering look in his sister's eye.

His gaze skipped from Jillian to Max to Bruce. Like Jillian, they all stared at him with the same expression of expectation. His gut clenched. It didn't require imagination to know what they expected from him. He drew on the cheroot and stared at the ceiling, refusing to allow them to involve him in Kathy's mad scheme. It was not his responsibility. Bruce, Max, and Jillian were Kathy's family. He was not.

"I'm certain Damien won't mind looking in on Kathy," Jillian said to no one in particular.

Kathy inhaled so sharply, it sounded like a gasp.

Damien continued to stare at the ceiling. Obviously, she was as thrilled with the idea as he was.

"It would certainly ease my mind," Bruce said.

"And mine as well," Max said. "There is no one I trust more."

"Damien?" Jillian said.

He made the mistake of meeting his sister's gaze. Goddammit! He never could say no to her. He couldn't say no to any of them, not when he knew they would do no less for him if he asked it. Whether he liked it or not, Jillian's perception of their obligations to one another was accurate. In one way or another they *were* family, bound by loyalty and trust.

"Of course, I'll look in on her," he said evenly as he ground his cigar in the crystal tray beside him.

Jillian smiled. "If you have need of anything, Kathy, all you have to do is send word to Damien."

"Of course," Kathy said, her grim expression reflecting his own mood. And in her eyes, he saw her silent determination to develop her talent for avoiding him to a fine art.

He gave her a smile that mocked himself as well as the absurdity of the situation. Yet, it was his own fault. If he had told Bruce and Max about her encounter with Tony Edgewater there would be no question about leaving Kathy alone in England. And now he couldn't tell them without admitting his own selfish reasons for keeping silent. He hadn't wanted to be involved.

He'd been a fool to believe she would go quietly to America. He'd been more than a fool to agree with Kathy that there was no need to worry Bruce and Max with such a "harmless" incident. Nothing about Kathy was harmless. She attracted trouble without even trying.

Kathy Palmerston needed a keeper, and now she had one . . . for better or worse.

In Kathy's case it could only be for worse.

# Chapter 8

**"P**erfect!"
     Tony stood on the dock and watched a ship slide into its berth. He could not believe his luck. No, not luck, he corrected, but a sign from God that he and Kathleen were destined to be together.

Kathleen was alone at Blackwood with only a hired companion to stand between himself and the culmination of his dreams.

The Duke of Westhrook had retired to his castle. Channing had taken a ship bound for the West Indies. The Duke and Duchess of Bassett had left yesterday on another ship bound for America. The Earl of Blackwood was on the ship that was even now lowering a gangplank. Tony was becoming rather fond of ships.

A delicious thought darted into his mind. An erotic thought of kidnapping his lady love and carrying her off on a ship of his very own. They would be alone together, sharing the close quarters of a cabin, bathing in sight of one another, feeding one another across a small table, lying together in a narrow bunk, their bodies swaying in rhythm with the ocean—

But no, such a thing was not proper for a lady like his Kathleen. She was too demure and chaste to even think of kissing without the sanctity of marriage. It would take time for her to become comfortable with intimacy, to be willing to indulge freely. Far better that he court her with gallantry and gifts. And far better that they have a large wedding ceremony.

Yes! Fairy tales! She deserved the magic of flowers and organ music and a honeymoon in the country—Bath perhaps. Or the seashore. He ought to look into a suitable cottage somewhere.

He searched the passengers disembarking and staggering slightly as their feet touched solid land. None appeared grand enough to be an earl, particularly the rough-looking fellow who stood head and shoulders above the rest. The man had longish hair that appeared plastered to his head with grease. His clothes were so dirty they were all the same color of grime. Tony shuddered and stepped back. He could almost smell the oaf and felt dirty just looking at him.

He focused on the ship again. Perhaps the earl was waiting in his cabin until the crowd thinned out.

He couldn't wait to meet the man he so admired, couldn't wait to sign the marriage contract he'd had prepared and seek out Kathleen. He had to tell her that she needn't worry about his intentions. That he didn't give a fig for her fortune. That she would be loved truly and always for herself. How happy it would make her to know that she needn't mistrust him any longer. Yes! And how pleased she would be that he'd brought her father home to her.

The dirty oaf was coming closer, filling Tony's vision, forcing him to step back even farther to avoid him. Again, he anxiously searched the ship for the earl.

"Anthony Edgewater?"

Tony started at the voice and glanced down. He'd been so preoccupied with avoiding the oaf, he'd missed seeing the slight sparrow of a man standing directly in front of him, impeccably dressed in brown from head to foot.

"Yes," Tony answered politely. "May I be of service?"

"I believe I am to be of service to you," the man said. "I am the Earl of Blackwood."

"Oh." Tony jerked on his waistcoat and straightened to his full height. "Ah . . . my lord, what a pleasure it is to finally meet you."

The earl waved a hand. "Let us dispense with civilities. You requested permission to marry my daughter. You have it."

Tony beamed. Yes! It *was* divine providence. "Why, thank you, my lord. I knew you would understand. Shall we go over the details in the comfort of my coach?" He could see it now—the earl's nobility and consequence as he nodded and walked ahead of Tony. Only a man sure of his power would not bother to wear more noticeable colors. Only a man of the world would have such an uncanny ability to see him for the first time and so wisely judge him fit to wed his daughter.

"My lord?" Tony called as he caught up with the earl. "Have you baggage?"

"My man will see to it." The earl glanced back at the oaf.

Tony barely kept himself from recoiling. His man? Was America so primitive that someone as noble as the earl must suffer the presence of Neanderthals? "I'll engage a wagon to follow us then," he offered. For no reason would he allow such filth in or upon his new conveyance.

The earl snapped orders to his man, and climbed into the coach. Thankfully the oaf hailed a passing wagon.

Tony scrambled in after the earl and pulled the door closed, anxious to put a more solid barrier between himself and the stench of the waterfront. Immediately, he produced a sheaf of papers from his pocket. "My lord, I took the liberty of having contracts drawn up. As you can see, I have been most generous to Kathleen." He paused, wanting to deliver his *pièce de résistance* with the drama it deserved. "You need not offer a dowry, nor do I want her inheritance. With all the fortune hunters in the ton, I wish to impress upon her that I would love her if she came to me in rags."

"I see you have anticipated my terms for signing the contracts," the earl said.

"My lord?" Tony's thoughts wrapped around the earl's words. Yes! Of course. The earl had been in the wilderness for years while his wife and son had control of his holdings. He was likely land rich, but had little money. "I have indeed anticipated, my lord. I wish to sign over all of her inheritance to you upon our marriage."

"Fine. We'll procure a special license and the marriage will take place immediately," the earl said as he removed his hat and set it on the seat. "We have but one obstacle to overcome. We'll have to abduct my daughter in order to avoid her brother's interference."

"No!" Tony clamped his mouth shut as a vision of carrying Lady Kathleen off tantalized him. It would be more romantic than a large affair. "Of course," he agreed. "Though you needn't worry about Channing. He is en route to the West Indies."

The earl's eyes narrowed. "She is alone?"

"Well, she has a paid companion," Tony replied dismissively. "There will be no one to object. No one at all."

"Perfect!" the earl murmured, then threw back his head and laughed.

# Chapter 9

*Blackwood Manor*
*July, 1820*

**"I** shall write your brother at once," Mrs. Hilton declared as she swept through the front door in a flurry of outrage and navy blue crepe, her perpetually red nose stuck in the air.

"And I shall write to him as well," Kathy flung at her back, knowing it was an empty threat. It would take months for a letter to reach Bruce in the West Indies. Besides, Kathy had no intention of informing Bruce that her companion had turned out to be a sot. "I'm sure he'll send you a bill for all the brandy you've consumed in the past fortnight," she added.

Mrs. Hilton halted and whirled around, looking like an oversized ball turning on its axis, and nearly colliding with Smithy, who followed with her bags. "How dare you! I informed your brother when he engaged my services that I occasionally take a glass of spirits for my headaches."

"Yes, you did," Kathy agreed evenly, knowing now that it had been a gross understatement.

Mrs. Hilton's face crumpled and tears streamed down her face. She tugged a handkerchief from her sleeve and dabbed at her eyes. "You should be ashamed of yourself for dismissing me. You know my circumstances."

"Yes, I know," Kathy said and thanked her lucky stars that she did. Otherwise her conscience would not allow her to toss the woman out on her ear. Mrs.

Hilton had a widow's portion and certainly could maintain a modest residence of her own, not to mention that she had a son who lived in London.

It was the reason Kathy had chosen Mrs. Hilton as her companion. The fear of being saddled with someone she didn't get on with had prompted Kathy to examine the applicants closely. She had not wanted a person whose existence depended on the position.

Life had taught her to be prepared for any eventuality, but nothing could have prepared her for Mrs. Hilton.

During the fortnight since Bruce had left, Mrs. Hilton had drank herself insensible every night and rarely rose before late afternoon, complaining of a headache. Instead of Mrs. Hilton looking after her, Kathy had been looking after Mrs. Hilton. Instead of finding freedom with her overprotective family out of the country, Kathy was once again trapped with someone who was determined to destroy herself.

She shoved the thought away, refusing to dwell on the topic as she descended the front steps. "I've instructed the coachman to take you to the inn where you will be able to catch a coach to London." She glanced over her shoulder to make sure Mrs. Hilton was following.

Mrs. Hilton stuck out her bottom lip in a pout. "I haven't a ticket."

"Smithy will accompany you and purchase one."

"But where will I go?"

"Your son's home," Kathy suggested gently.

"I don't want to live with him," she wailed. "He doesn't understand about my headaches. He doesn't keep any spirits in the house."

Kathy steeled herself against the display of emotion, reminding herself yet again that she was not sending the woman out to starve. She nodded to Smithy, reassured by his burly frame that he would have no trouble controlling the woman.

"There now, Mrs. Hilton," he said as he led the

sobbing woman across the cobbled drive to the coach. His weathered features softened in sympathy as he produced a flask from his pocket and pressed it into the woman's hands just before he lifted her into the coach.

Kathy knew she should take him to task for encouraging Mrs. Hilton, but then, what better way to pacify her?

With a sigh of relief, she watched the coach roll down the drive and turn onto the main road. Freedom! How wonderful it felt. Laughing, she twirled about and flung out her arms toward the sky. Everything seemed larger suddenly, more open. The future lay before her, free of responsibility to anyone but herself.

Bruce's solicitor was compiling a list of suitable properties. She had tried to tell Mr. Goodman he needn't bother; there was only one house she wanted—Willow Cottage. But he wasn't certain the property she wanted was available and insisted on finding others for her to consider.

She'd humored him, though she couldn't imagine that the owner wouldn't be happy to rid himself of a house that had stood empty for years. If all went well, she would be able to surprise her overprotective family with her choice of a home so close to Bassett House. If she was fortunate, she would be firmly ensconced in Willow Cottage long before Damien got wind of her plans.

In the meantime, there was no one around to say what she may or may not do, no one to consume her time and energies, and she had every intention of keeping it that way. If no one knew Mrs. Hilton was gone, she wouldn't have to find a replacement. She'd already told Smithy that he wasn't to tell a soul. She hadn't named names, but Smithy knew who she meant.

The last person in the world she wanted to deal with was Damien Forbes. Whatever had possessed him to agree to watch out for her? she wondered. It had been obvious the prospect annoyed him as much as it had annoyed her.

She smiled at the thought. There was an amusing twist of irony in the whole thing. Damien had been hoisted upon his own petard by not revealing her encounter with Tony Edgewater. Damien regretted it, she was sure. Had he told, she would never have been able to convince her brothers to go along with her plans.

Her smile widened. It hadn't taken her long to see the advantages in the situation. In spite of her personal feelings for Damien, he was indeed the ideal "protector." For the most part, he would be an invisible presence, available should she decide she needed him. For all intents and purposes that left her completely on her own.

At last.

"What the devil," Damien muttered as he watched a well-dressed, middle-aged, and very portly woman make her way to the mail coach parked in front of the inn with the aid of a rather burly and rough-looking man of indeterminate age. He leaned forward on the seat of his coach to study the scene more closely from the window.

The woman was definitely Mrs. Hilton, Kathy's paid companion, and the man was unmistakably Smithy, who was all but carrying her to the coach.

She stumbled. She reeled. Her bonnet had slipped to the back of her neck, remaining attached to her person by virtue of the ribbon caught between her lower lip and her chin.

The woman was foxed.

"What's Lady Kathleen going to do?" she slurred and swiped at the ribbons that had nearly worked their way into her mouth. "Can't stay there alone. It's not proper."

"Don't you worry yourself none about it, ma'am," Smithy said as he shoved her bonnet back up onto her head.

She gave a mournful sob. "Tell Lady Kathleen that I forgive her."

Smithy grasped the woman by her waist and hoisted her into the coach with a grunt. "That I will, Mrs. Hilton."

"No, no, don't tell her that," she said, suddenly agitated. "Tell her she's a heartless young woman for turning me out."

An ache began to build behind Damien's left eye. Max and Bruce had departed a fortnight ago and Kathy had already found a way to rid herself of her companion. Given the woman's inebriation, he had to concede that Kathy might be justified, but he didn't have to like it. Just as he didn't like having to admit that Kathy's instincts about people were generally right. Edgewater was a perfect example. Kathy had known that Tony wasn't as harmless as he appeared long before Damien had caught on.

Still, he was tempted to order his driver to return him to Westbrook Castle with all due haste. He didn't want to know that Kathy was unchaperoned. Why hadn't he come yesterday? Or tomorrow for that matter? Kathy was enterprising. She would have found a way to keep him from finding out. He hadn't even intended for her to know he'd been here, but had simply acted on impulse to make some gesture regarding his obligations. He had planned to stop at the inn overnight, ask a few questions and be on his way. Kathy would have been none the wiser. Now it was impossible to escape without involving himself. He had no choice but to face his responsibility to Kathy.

*Why him?*

The answer came immediately to mind. He could do no less for Bruce and Max than they would do for him.

He waited until the mail coach rumbled away before leaving his own coach. He stepped down, his gaze never leaving Smithy. The man's step was a little too jaunty and the tune he whistled a little too lively as he ambled toward the tap room of the inn. It was annoyingly clear that Smithy was living up to Damien's predictions and indulging Kathy without a thought for the consequences.

Damien had no doubt that Kathy was crowing with delight over Mrs. Hilton's departure.

He so hated to ruin her celebration. He smiled at the thought and leaned against his coach. "Smithy," he called.

The whistle died as the servant halted and slowly glanced over his shoulder. He slumped and gave a little shake of his head, then turned and ambled toward Damien.

"Want to tell me about it on the way to Blackwood?" Damien asked blandly.

"Lady Kathy said not to," Smithy said.

Damien nodded toward the open door of his coach. "Now, why doesn't that surprise me?"

Kathy stepped from the mausoleum and tried to shake off the chill that had seeped into her bones. Yet, she knew it was not the absence of sunlight or the coolness of the marble that made her shiver. It was the idea that a drawer in a crypt had simply been opened and her mother's coffin slipped inside as if she were a nothing more than a discarded handkerchief shoved into a bureau.

She had hoped that a visit to her mother's tomb would appease the guilt that had set in after her initial glee over Mrs. Hilton's departure. Even though she had tried to avoid drawing a comparison between her mother and her former companion, it had slipped in anyway. In a different way, Mrs. Hilton was as bent on destroying herself as her mother had been.

But, this time, Kathy did not have to stand by and watch. The sense of freedom she'd experienced earlier returned. She wouldn't feel guilty, she told herself firmly.

Stepping lightly, she returned to the house and

entered through the kitchens. She smiled and nodded at the cooks and assistants, then lowered her
head and hummed a little tune as she fairly skipped
down the long, white-plastered hallway that led to
the front of the house.

"You're off-key."

Her step faltered at the sound of Damien's voice
echoing down the length of the passageway behind
her. She whirled around and halted on a stumble as
her gaze widened on the tall frame of her nemesis.

He stood with his legs braced apart and his black-
gloved hands planted firmly on his hips, outlined by
tight black doeskin breeches and knee-high boots.
He seemed to fill the end of the narrow hall, an
imposing shadow with his wide chest and broad
shoulders defined by a fitted black coat. His gleaming black hair lay in a smooth, disciplined pelt
except for a forelock dipping over his brow. The
only part of him that was not covered in black was
the flesh on his face and his glittering green eyes. He
was the very picture of a powerfully sleek panther
poised to strike in the stark white corridor.

Darkness at the end of the tunnel.

Her sense of freedom fled in the face of his grimly
set jaw and the arrow-straight slash of his brows.

*He knew.*

She wanted to turn and run. Yet, before she had
time to move or say a word a commotion erupted in
the front of the house. She frowned as she spun back
around in the direction of the entrance hall.

"Place my trunks in the master suite," a male
voice ordered.

Kathy felt her body jerk as if she'd taken a lash
from a whip. Even through the walls separating her
from the foyer, she had no trouble identifying that
voice. A voice from the distant past. A voice that
terrified her.

"Summon Lady Kathleen at once," the voice
barked.

Her body numbed with a sudden chill. A silent

scream rebounded inside her, shattering her. He was back. She hadn't expected him to come back.

She *had* to run. She had to hide.

Again she whirled around only to be brought up short by Damien's fierce scowl. A roar filled her head. Her breath came in shorter and shorter gasps. She could feel nothing but the terror that consumed her.

She was trapped. A devil waited for her in the foyer. A panther blocked her path to safety.

She ran toward the lesser of the two evils.

# Chapter 10

**K**athy was a blur of movement, her loose braid flying out behind her and her arms reaching out for him as she closed the distance between them before he could hold out his arms to catch her.

"Lady Kathy ain't here."

She halted as Smithy's voice carried from the entry hall, too deliberately loud for normal conversation. Damien didn't need Smithy's implied warning to realize that whomever had arrived a moment ago was somehow a threat. Kathy's behavior spoke volumes, in her suddenly pale complexion and wide eyes that seemed to cover her entire face, in the way her hands desperately grasped his forearm.

"Where is she?" the voice snapped.

"She may be out takin' a walk, milord."

"Find her at once!" the man shouted. "And be quick about it, Smithy. I need little reason to dismiss you."

Damien heard anger in the man's tone, could feel it building inside himself as Kathy's grip tightened on his arm. Who the hell was this person tossing out orders as if he owned the place?

Why was Kathy so terrified?

He fought the impulse to wrap his arms around her, to shield her from whatever danger loomed in the foyer. She was too wary just then, with her eyes narrowed and watchful and her nostrils flared like a fox sniffing the air for danger. The fear was so strong on her he imagined he could smell it.

He would not tolerate it.

Placing his hand firmly over Kathy's, he pulled her closer, ready to toss her over his shoulder if she should try to run. "Smithy," he called. "Lady Kathy is here."

Kathy leaned into him like a child hiding behind her nanny's skirts.

Boot heels clicked rapidly on the marble floor and were joined by heavier, more lumbering footsteps, sounding as if a gnome was clearing the way for a giant.

A man stepped around the corner, then paused and took a step backward, his brow knitted in obvious confusion as he stared at Damien.

A shudder vibrated through Kathy's body.

Bemused, Damien stared back. The man was no Goliath at all but a slight, rather short figure with a stiffly erect posture and impeccable attire. Certainly, he could see nothing in the man to explain Kathy's terror.

Damien studied the man's prominent forehead and square jaw, his hair and eyes that were an ordinary shade of brown. He saw recognition in the man's expression yet he knew they had never met.

"Westbrook," the man said. "I'd assumed that you'd met the same fate as Bassett."

Unease crawled up Damien's spine as he wondered where this man had been to make such a mistake? "You speak of my father and confuse the living with the dead," he said evenly.

"So I did," the man said smoothly, showing no signs of embarrassment. "Forgive me. You have the look of your father." His gaze roamed over the hallway as if he were reacquainting himself with the textured plaster walls, arched thresholds, and the bas relief bordering the ceiling in a shell pattern.

"You have me at a disadvantage," Damien said coolly as suspicion uncoiled in his mind.

The man did not reply as his gaze settled on Kathy.

It disturbed Damien to see the man scrutinize her with such cold calculation, as if she were an object whose value had yet to be determined. More disturbing were Kathy's tremors and the chill of her hands seeping through his sleeve.

She knew this man.

It was all Damien could do to control his sharp intake of breath as suspicion became realization. No man of breeding would burst into a private home, order the servants around, and look at Kathy with such proprietary interest unless he had a right do so. Damien had a nasty feeling that this man had every right. "You have me at a disadvantage, sir," he repeated, only needing confirmation.

The man's gaze slid to Damien. "Robert Palmerston, fifth Earl of Blackwood, at your service." He smiled at Kathy. "Don't you recognize your father, Kathy? Don't you wish to welcome me?"

Her whimper was so small, Damien knew that only he could hear it as her nails dug into his arm. He would expect shock, but not this terror that made her shrink against him. But then what did he know of the earl beyond the bare facts of his arrangement with Kathy's mother?

What did it matter? He knew he didn't like the earl, and was outraged at his presence and the way he toyed with Kathy, feeding off her fear as if it were an old habit. He knew that the earl was not Kathy's father. As she knew it. As the earl knew it.

Fortunately, the earl couldn't know that Damien was aware of the situation. Perhaps it would give him a small advantage should the need arise. "Kathy's reticence is understandable," he said, filling the silence because Kathy couldn't seem to utter a sound. "If memory serves, she was all of six or seven the last time she saw you."

"Forgive me for being rude, Westbrook," the earl said impatiently, "but I should like to conduct a reunion with my daughter in private."

Under normal circumstances, it would be a reasonable request. But the circumstance was not normal. The earl was using familial references like knives, stabbing Kathy at every opportunity, hurting her in some way Damien didn't understand. At the moment, he didn't need to understand anything beyond his conviction that he couldn't leave her alone. "Lady Kathy has invited me to dinner and I'm quite famished," he said, chafing against the need for restraint.

"I'm sure that you can find an adequate meal at the inn," the earl said smoothly.

Damien clenched his jaw as he fought an overwhelming urge to usher the earl out of the house by the scruff of his neck. Unfortunately, it was the earl's house and Damien would succeed only in getting himself thrown out. He smiled blandly. "The cook there has a fondness for boiling shoe leather. I'd much prefer the roast duck Kathy has offered," he said, grateful that he'd entered through the kitchens and seen the cook spit the fowl.

The earl gave a feral smile and glanced over his shoulder. "Freddie, escort the Duke of Westbrook off my property."

A massive man suddenly loomed behind the earl. Damien had to tip his head back to see the piggish face attached to the giant body. Here was the Goliath he'd been expecting.

Damien's free hand curled into a fist. "I prefer to remain."

"Your preferences count for nothing, Westbrook," the earl snapped. "Get out." He gave Kathy a penetrating look that both warned and threatened at once.

Her body jerked and she snatched her hand from beneath Damien's as she stepped back. "Go home," she said in a strangled whisper. "Please."

The defeat he heard in her voice sounded like the last breath before death, holding him frozen and staring at her. The desperation in her eyes and the bleakness of her expression alarmed him. This was not the contrary Kathy he knew, but a child so brittle with fright that she would shatter if she had to bear much more.

He wanted to hold her, to press her face to his chest and reassure her that he would not leave her, that he would allow nothing to harm her.

As if she knew what he was thinking, she straightened her shoulders and hardened her expression, holding herself aloof from him, from all of them. She knew what he did not want to accept. The earl was master here. In the eyes of the law he was Kathy's father and she was under his control. He could lock her in a dungeon and beat her once a day and no one would stop him.

Damien had no choice but to go. Kathy had no choice but to stay.

Reluctantly, he stepped away from her and captured her gaze, making a silent promise that he would return. He brushed past the earl and strode down the passageway and into the entrance hall.

Smithy stood at attention by the front door, eyes forward, gaze blank, the epitome of an apathetic servant.

"Watch. Listen. Come to me," Damien murmured as he waited for Smithy to open the door.

"Take her out of here soon, Your Grace," Smithy muttered. "He'll hurt her bad if you don't."

Smithy's fear for Kathy burned into Damien like acid as he walked out the door and down the steps, as he climbed into his carriage and settled into the squabs and stared out the window, unable to see anything but his own fear. A fear he had never felt before, eating at him, consuming him with the urgency to act rather than think. But he had to think. This was not a battle that could be settled with fists. Though he knew next to nothing about the earl or his relationship with Kathy, every instinct he had told him that the earl was cunning as well as dangerous.

One wrong move from any quarter and Kathy would be the one to suffer.

She was alone with the devil.

Why had he come back? Why had she ever believed he wouldn't? Why had she allowed herself to push him from her mind?

She was at his mercy, and even the silent promise she'd seen in Damien's eyes had no power to comfort her. *If I should die, then my son will protect you.* She was old enough now to know that such promises could not be kept, that some things were absolute. Damien had no authority to usurp the earl's control. She'd be a fool to believe otherwise.

How she wished she had the skill and strength to use her fists as effectively as Damien had when he'd attacked Bruce. She would beat her way out of this house, then run as fast and as far as she could. But she had only her wits with which to defend herself against the earl.

She could not show the panic that weighed her down like a sodden blanket. Drawing in a slow measured breath, she met the earl's gaze.

He grinned at her, showing an expanse of large teeth in a face that had not changed at all. His hair had not even grayed with the passing years. She was not surprised. Time would leave a demon untouched.

"My, but you have grown up nicely," he said with an expectant tilt of his head.

She was supposed to respond. She had not forgotten the rules. "Thank you, Papa," she said, forcing the words past the lump of fear in her throat.

"We have a lot of catching up to do, don't you think?"

"Yes, sir."

"I grow weary of standing about in the hallway."

He turned on his heel and strode toward the front of the house.

She was supposed to follow. That was the way of it. Because the earl had never been allowed to order her and Bruce around when they were children, he devised a way of phrasing commands without actually ordering them to do what he wanted. There had been penalties for disobeying. She shook her head and blanked her mind. She couldn't think of that, couldn't concentrate on anything but getting through the next few minutes . . . and then the next.

She trailed him into the drawing room.

He glanced at a chair.

She promptly sat in it.

He smiled in satisfaction. "I was sorry to hear of your mother's death."

She could think of no answer to such a lie. The earl had hated Mama, just as he hated her and Bruce. She knew he expected a reply, yet she could not think past the question that reverberated in her head. "Why did you come back?" she blurted, then clamped her mouth shut. She had not meant to speak the thought aloud.

He gave a burst of laughter that faded abruptly. "This is my home. I've waited an eternity to return. How convenient that Bassett has died and your brother has left the country."

She couldn't breathe for a moment, couldn't respond. Had he had them spied upon? How else would he know that the old Duke of Bassett and her mother had died? How else would he know that Bruce was gone?

"What was Westbrook doing here?" he asked as if nothing else had gone before.

"Bruce asked him to look in on me," she said.

"That's all?"

"Yes."

A knock sounded on the door. At the earl's call to enter, Smithy stepped inside. "Mr. Anthony Edgewater to see you, milord."

*Tony?* Why did he want to see the earl? Kathy wondered. How did he know the earl was back in the country? The world seemed to tilt dangerously, threatening to tip her off the edge as the earl nodded and Tony brushed past Smithy, entering the room on a wave of eau de cologne.

"Really, Robert, I would have thought you'd have a better class of servants," Tony said as his adoring gaze settled on her.

Dread choked her. She'd believed that Tony was out of her life forever just as she'd believed the earl was out of her life forever. Yet, Tony knew the earl well enough to use his Christian name, to walk into Blackwood as if he belonged here. Her panic redoubled. This couldn't be happening. The two men she hated above all things had converged on her at once.

The earl's gaze narrowed on Smithy. "Where is the butler who admitted me earlier?"

"He took sick," Smithy said.

Ignoring Tony's gaze on her, Kathy focused instead on Smithy, aware that he had dispatched the butler in order to keep close to her.

"Pack your things and get out," the earl ordered. "I haven't forgotten where your loyalties lie."

"Please, milord," Smithy whined in a dramatic display of humility. "I been here for years."

"You have one hour to leave of your own accord or I'll have you forcibly removed."

Smithy shot an uncertain glance at Kathy.

*Run while you have the chance,* she wanted to shout at him. Smithy could not help her, and she could not bear it if harm came to him because of her. She smiled weakly at him. "Goodbye, Smithy."

Smithy blinked and backed out of the room.

Tony cleared his throat.

The earl nodded. "I believe you're acquainted with Mr. Edgewater."

Tony bowed over her hand. "Lady Kathleen," he said. "We have much to thank your father for."

She snatched her hand away and sat as far back in

the chair as she could. "And for what do we owe such gratitude to my father?" she asked.

"Why, because the earl has so graciously approved my suit and granted me your hand in marriage," Tony said.

"What?" Kathy whispered in horror.

"We can be married now," Tony said. "Your brother can no longer stand in our way."

"Her brother has nothing to do with it." The earl sat on the sofa and crossed one ankle over the opposite leg. "I am her father."

A sick dread threatened to choke her. She'd been right about Tony. He was ruthless and would do anything and use anyone to get what he wanted. . . .

The earl. Tony had summoned the earl. He couldn't have known that the earl hated her, that he would go to any lengths to hurt her.

She couldn't tell him, not now with the earl listening to every word. Her best chance was to reason with Tony. "I've told you twice that I do not wish to marry you."

Tony took the chair opposite her and leaned forward, and gazed at her as if she were a goddess he worshipped. "How could you know such a thing when you've never had the chance to really know me?"

"Enough of this," the earl snapped. "The contracts are already signed. Edgewater has waived his rights to your fortune, and wishes to turn it over to me upon your marriage. I have accepted. You will be married tomorrow."

*Tomorrow.* The word echoed inside her. Her fortune. Her dreams. Her freedom. She'd been so tragically close to having it all, to being untouchable.

Her fingers dug into the arms of the chair as she stared at the earl, hating his falsely benign smile. It would be tragic only if she allowed it, if she didn't fight for what was hers. She had to fight or else crawl back into the china cabinet.

Fury such as she had never experienced overcame

her panic. She ruthlessly battled back the rage, forcing herself to be calm, to think, to meet the earl at his own level of duplicity. "I am already promised," she said.

"You are betrothed?" Tony sputtered.

The earl raised his hand, silencing Tony, and smiled viciously at Kathy. "Naughty girl. You lied about Westbrook's reason for being here."

"Westbrook was here?" Tony asked in a frigid voice, apparently recovered from his shock over her pronouncement.

"Yes," the earl said, "but it changes nothing."

"It changes everything," Kathy said, her mind racing, trying to outdistance the earl as she lowered her gaze to her lap and kept it there. She never would have thought to name Damien as her betrothed. But it was an excellent idea. No matter what she thought of him, he was the Duke of Westbrook, representing power, and power was the one thing Tony and the earl responded to. "Damien and Bruce have already signed the contracts," she added and smoothed her skirt to hide the tremble of her hands.

"Bruce has no say in the matter, and neither do you," the earl shot back.

"Vows must be exchanged," she replied. "That gives me all the say, does it not?"

The earl's face smoothed of all expression. "Edgewater, will you excuse us?" he asked politely. "I require a private word with my daughter."

"Certainly," Tony said on a note of relief, and strolled from the room as if nothing was amiss.

Before she could react to being left alone with the earl, he grasped a handful of her hair and yanked her from her seat. "I have been away too long," he hissed. "You have forgotten that I can force you to say or do anything I choose."

Tears stung her eyes. "And you overlook that I am no longer a child to be terrorized," she choked on a wave of renewed fear.

She could hear tiny little pops as he slowly twisted

his fist in her hair, pulling strands from their roots. "Careful, *daughter,* I no longer have to be concerned with leaving marks on your body." He released her hair and drew back his fist.

"You should be concerned," she gasped in desperation. "How will you explain marking me to Damien?"

The earl lowered his hand.

At his hesitation, she scrambled backward. "He is like his father, you know. And like his father before him, he has the Duke of Bassett at his back." Though he did not move, his face paled and his jaw tightened just enough to tell her she had drawn blood with her statement. A weapon. She had found a weapon to use against him, to make him stop if only for a little while. She knew that sooner or later, he would overcome his initial fear. He always had, but in the meantime, she would use it to keep him away from her.

. She pressed the point home, careful to keep her voice low, careful not to show her desperation. "Can you fight them both?"

"You little bitch," he snarled and reached her in two long strides. He grabbed her arms and shook her so hard her teeth rattled. "You think I fear them?"

"Yes," she managed. "Just as you feared their fathers."

The earl shoved her away from him.

Stumbling, Kathy found her balance and walked slowly to the door, her shoulders squared and her back straight, refusing to run, refusing to surrender her dignity.

Smithy sprang aside as she opened the door and slipped through, closing it quickly behind her, praying the earl had not seen Smithy lurking at the keyhole. She leaned back against the carved wood and swallowed the gorge that had caught in her throat.

Tony was nowhere in sight.

An angry pulse throbbed at Smithy's temple.

"Where is Tony?" she asked.

Smithy jerked his head in the direction of the front door.

So, she couldn't leave that way. Even if she did she knew she wouldn't succeed. Tony and the earl would be upon her before she reached the stables, and it would be impossible for her to get far on foot. She would have to bide her time, bear whatever torment the earl chose to inflict until she could devise a plan to escape.

"Stay away from him, Smithy," she warned. Her scalp stung as if it were on fire and she reached up to massage the tender flesh. She lowered her hand and stared dumbly at the hair caught in her fingers. "Do as he says and leave while you can," she said wearily and shook her hand until the strands fell to the floor.

"We'll get you out, milady," Smithy said and leaned over to pick up the clump of hair, then ducked his head and loped toward the back hallway.

"No," she said in a frantic whisper, but it was too late. He'd already disappeared around a corner. She wanted to run after him, to tell him that she had to do it alone. Bruce and Max couldn't help her, neither could Damien. No one could.

Tears built up behind her eyes as she scurried up the stairs like a mouse fleeing to its hole. Her heart pounded so hard that she imagined she could hear it echoing through the air. Topping the stairs, she turned toward her chambers and abruptly halted.

It was not her heartbeat that produced the dull thumps. The pounding came from inside her bedroom. Her maid, Frances, hovered at the end of the corridor, meeting her gaze with an apologetic shake of her head, then darted down the rear staircase.

Cautiously, she inched along the wall to the open doorway. The brute the earl had referred to as Freddie was hammering a nail into the frame of her window.

"What are you doing?" she demanded. "You have no right to be in my chambers."

The brute said nothing as picked up another nail and drove it into the wood with a single blow.

"Get out this instant," she ordered.

Without a word, the brute turned from the window, not sparing her a glance as he trudged past her.

She whirled around to follow him, but he stepped into the hall and closed the door, turned the key in the lock, closing her in. She grasped the doorknob and pulled, but it held fast. She ran to the window, testing the nails that held it shut. It wouldn't budge. Again, she turned, her gaze searching for something—anything—to use to pry the nails from the window. She found nothing.

She was trapped.

A scream rose from her chest but she swallowed it down. She bent double and inhaled slowly, trying to contain her panic. She could not lose control. She had to escape before the earl forced her to marry Tony. And he could. She knew he could.

She had to find a way out. She could not let a locked door and a few nails in the window stop her. Something slammed behind her, throwing her chamber into darkness. She jerked upright and whirled about, realizing that the shutters on her window had been closed. "Oh God," she said on a broken sob as she again heard the dull thump of a hammer. The brute was nailing them shut as well.

Her tears ran freely as she groped in the darkness for flint to light a candle. But even light in the room and a fire in the grate was denied her. She felt along the wall until she reached her dressing table and yanked the drawer open, pulling it out all the way and scattering the contents on the floor. Falling to her knees, she fumbled through the clutter. Her scissors were gone. She opened another drawer and found it empty of hairpins. With short, panting sobs, she crawled into her dressing room and reached for her jewel box.

It was empty, with not even a stickpin or hair comb with which to pick a lock. She sat with her back against the bureau and drew her knees up to her chest, trying to accept the unacceptable. The earl had taken everything.

The freedom she had dreamed of would remain a dream.

There was no escape.

# Chapter 11

❧ ⟨◯◯⟩ ❧

**D**amien sprang into his saddle and kicked the hired horse into a full gallop, riding toward Blackwood Manor as if the hounds of hell were on his tail, though in truth he was riding toward them.

The Earl of Blackwood and Tony Edgewater.

He'd never been so enraged as when he'd listened to Smithy's tale.

That the earl intended to force Kathy to marry Edgewater was reprehensible. That he intended the ceremony to take place tomorrow was inconceivable. How in hell had Edgewater met the earl in the first place, much less gained his permission to marry Kathy? It was all too bloody convenient, as if they'd been plotting the whole thing for months.

Remarkably, Kathy had tried to thwart the earl's plans by announcing she was betrothed—to himself, of all people. That more than anything else, told Damien how desperate she was. He knew how she felt about him.

As if all that wasn't enough, the earl had ordered Smithy off the premises, effectively isolating Kathy and leaving Damien as good as blind with just his imagination to conjure visions of what was happening to Kathy.

His imagination had been running rampant since Smithy had opened his palm to show Damien a clump of bright auburn hair.

103

Kathy's hair, torn out by the roots.

He shouldn't have left her.

He leaned low over the horse's neck and urged the gelding to turn off the road. His mount bunched his hindquarters, cleared a fence, and galloped across a field. It would take him minutes longer to reach Blackwood on the winding road.

He had to get Kathy out of there.

Now he understood her terror. He felt it, too.

The manor loomed up in front of him, looking sinister when just hours before he'd admired the untamed beauty of the grounds. They'd made him think of Kathy with the flowers that were planted in no particular design and left to grow as nature dictated along pathways that meandered in unexpected twists and turns. Now the whole place looked wild and dangerous, mazes with no escape.

Something seemed wrong, out of place, yet he couldn't put a name to it.

Damien cursed Bruce and Max as he slowed the gelding to a trot on the cobbled drive and reined in directly in front of the house. Why hadn't Kathy's brothers foreseen the possibility that the earl might someday return? he wondered as he vaulted from the saddle. Why hadn't Bruce told him that the earl was dangerous? Surely, Damien couldn't be the only one to recognize it.

He wasn't, he reminded himself as he took the stone steps two at a time. Kathy obviously knew it. So did Smithy.

"Blackwood!" Damien shouted and raised his gloved fist to pound on the solid oak door. "Open the goddamn door or I'll break it down!"

The door swung open. The Goliath filled the space, his legs wide apart, his massive arms folded over his chest.

"Get out of my way," Damien ordered.

The Goliath neither moved nor spoke.

"He answers to no one but the earl."

Damien's gaze jerked to the small private verandah outside the study and found Tony Edgewater sitting on the balustrade idly swinging his leg.

The earl strolled out the French doors holding two glasses of whiskey. "You're not welcome here, Westbrook."

"I want to see Kathy," Damien gritted.

"I can't allow you to have an audience with my fiancée," Tony said and glanced at his nails. "In any event, she is preparing for our nuptials."

"There aren't going to be any nuptials," Damien said, and decided in that moment to exploit the excuse Kathy had used to avoid marriage to Edgewater. "She's mine."

"No," the earl said as he handed a glass to Tony. "She is my daughter. Only I decide who will have her."

"And you would rather she wed this filth than a duke?"

It gave Damien immense satisfaction to see Tony's face pale at the dig, to see something like panic widen his eyes and lead his gaze to his hands—

"I would rather wed her to Freddie than to a Duke of Westbrook." The earl turned at Tony's sharp intake of breath. "Edgewater is a fine man," he said with a conciliatory tone. "A father couldn't ask for more in a son-in-law."

Tony's chest expanded and color returned to his face.

Damien kept silent long enough to absorb the implications. The earl wasn't simply looking for material gain as he'd first suspected. He wanted revenge. His constant and calculated references to Kathy being his daughter and his plans to doom her to a life with Edgewater confirmed that she was his immediate target.

Hoofbeats clattered on the drive behind him. He turned slightly, keeping Edgewater and the earl within his sight. From the corner of his eye, he saw Smithy pull up his horse beside the gelding and dismount.

"Your Grace," Smithy called loudly.

"Not now, Smithy," Damien said, irritated by the interruption.

"But, Your Grace—"

"Shut up," Damien snarled and turned his full attention back to the verandah. "How did you get the earl to agree to this, Edgewater? What did you give him?"

Tony frowned. "Why nothing. All I did was promise to sign over Kathleen's fortune to her father. She won't need it." He planted both feet on the stone floor of the verandah and drew up to his full height. "I am, after all, perfectly capable of providing for her in lavish style."

A new wave of cold anger washed over Damien. It would make her completely dependent on her husband and completely helpless to protect herself. He raised his head to glance around, to find the best way to reach the verandah and beat both men senseless. He would get Kathy out of there if he had to knock down every man in the place to do it.

Damien heard Smithy mutter behind him, but paid no attention as his gaze snagged on the second story and skimmed the row of windows. All but one were dark with drawn draperies. He clenched his fists and his stomach churned as he realized what had disturbed him earlier.

One window was shuttered and the paint was chipped around the edges, as if struck by a hammer. It took little imagination for him to know that the door to that room was barred as well.

"You goddamn bastard," Damien snarled as he lunged toward the verandah, crashing through foliage and trampling flowers. "You locked her in." He leapt the balustrade and grasped the earl by the collar.

Tony stepped forward. "Lady Kathleen is locked in? Why?"

Damien swung the earl around and folded his

forearm over the earl's throat. "Stay back, Edgewater, or I'll break his scrawny neck."

Tony stepped back.

"Good," Damien said, barely able to keep from carrying out his threat. "Tell your trained ape to let her out, Blackwood. *Now!* Or so help me God, I'll make fertilizer out of you and your *friends*."

He heard a dull thud inside his head. Pain shot from the back of his skull to his forehead. His knees buckled and he pitched forward, taking the earl with him, down . . . down to the stone floor.

Lights exploded behind Damien's eyes and then he saw nothing as darkness swirled around him, through him, swallowing him whole.

The light blinded Kathy, a wedge reaching for her from the opening door. Resisting the urge to throw up her arm and shield her eyes, or even to blink, she scrambled from her bed to the nearest corner and pressed her back against the wall. She didn't have to wonder who had unlocked her door. She'd known the silence and the darkness would have to end.

She'd known she wouldn't be left alone for long.

She kept her gaze fixed on the doorway, on the hulking figure that took shape as her eyes adjusted to the light. Another figure moved in, small and compact and infinitely more frightening.

The brute stepped aside and admitted the earl.

She could not cower. She could not tremble in fear. She could not allow him another victory over her.

"Edgewater is most concerned about you," the earl said as he strolled into her room. "He fears that you are not marrying him of your own free will. Of course, it was quite easy to convince him otherwise. All he cares about is taking possession of you."

"Then he will be disappointed," Kathy stated, feeling ill with the effort to keep her voice calm, her body straight and proud. "I will not marry him."

"Of course you will. In fact while I'm here I'll help you choose something to wear for your wedding." He yanked open the double doors to her wardrobe and riffled through her gowns, carelessly tossing those he rejected onto the floor. "Your fiancé wants to see you walk down the aisle rigged out as a bride should be." He held up the white gown she'd worn at her come-out ball. "This will do."

Kathy folded her arms across her chest. "Why are you doing this?"

The earl shrugged. "Because someone has to pay and you're convenient."

"It was your choice to enter into that arrangement," Kathy said, knowing he referred to the bargain he'd made with Bassett and her mother. "Mama and the old duke are both dead now. It is time to put the past to rest."

The earl laughed. "I'm afraid your mother made that impossible by leaving you a fortune that is rightfully mine."

"Take the fortune. All I want is my freedom."

"It's not that simple. You see, I find I cannot tolerate you bearing the Palmerston name."

"And what of Bruce? He also carries the name."

The earl sighed. "I have learned patience these past years. Just as fate presented me with the opportunity to rid myself of you, so I must rely on fate to take care of your brother. In the meantime, I shall be content with stripping you of my name and my money."

Kathy did not miss the subtle threat against her brother. But for the time being, Bruce was safe. She was not. "And what of Damien?" she asked, again using the lie she'd told earlier. "Why not allow my marriage to him next spring? It would accomplish the same thing."

The earl chuckled. "How amusing. He asked the same thing an hour ago."

"Damien was here?" Kathy asked on a slow intake of breath. He had come back. And, astonishingly, he had gone along with her fabrication. Hope leapt in her breast.

*If I should die, then my son will protect you.* Her mind spun until she was dizzy with it. Had she been wrong? Was it possible that the promise made by the father could be kept by the son?

The earl's gaze narrowed. "You seem surprised."

"No," she said quickly. "But I am surprised that you would rather see me wed to Tony Edgewater than Damien."

"I cannot exact retribution from the old Duke of Westbrook for his role in having me exiled." The earl shrugged. "But, I can be content with denying his son what he wants. It's a paltry revenge, but better than no revenge at all." He stepped away from the wardrobe. "And now that you understand that you have no recourse, I trust I can rely on your cooperation tomorrow. Otherwise I'll have to punish you. Do you understand?"

*Tomorrow.* She still had time . . . Damien had time. All was not lost. "Yes, I understand," Kathy said, fighting to keep the tremor from her voice.

He reached out his hand to her.

Warily, she placed her hand in his, keeping as much distance as possible between them. She had a feeling he'd spent the last fifteen years perfecting new ways to hurt her.

His fingers closed around hers like a steel trap. She gasped at the sudden pain shooting from her wrist to her shoulder as he spun her around and bent her arm behind her back. A silent scream of terror welled in her throat as he propelled her toward the wardrobe and shoved her inside.

She fell to her knees and her shoulder rammed into the back of the wardrobe. More pain arrowed down her arm and up her neck as she tried to push her hair from her face.

"I don't believe you," he said silkily.

Kathy made no reply as she realized he meant to lock her inside the wardrobe. In spite of the pain that was slowly subsiding to a miserable ache, she almost laughed. Was this the best he could do? She was not afraid of small dark places; they offered a sense of safety. And here, she could wait in peace and pray that Damien would come back, that he would take her far away where the earl could not find her.

The brute appeared and handed something to the earl.

"Do you like wasps, Kathy?" the earl asked as he held out a jar crawling with what had to be hundreds of the stinging insects.

She recoiled in horror, shoving herself into the farthest corner of the wardrobe.

"I thought not," the earl said.

The brute threw down another jar that shattered at her feet.

The doors slammed shut, closing her in with a swarm of agitated wasps.

They flew at her, pelting her face and her arms and tangling in her hair. She batted at them and clawed at the door. She was going to die.

That had been his plan all along.

She screamed and they seemed to fly at her faster, irritated at her frenzy. One brushed past her mouth. She slapped it away and pressed her lips together, willing herself to keep silent, to remain still. But, her skin prickled as if they had alighted on every inch of her. Her scalp crawled. With shrill whimpers, she slapped at her arms, her face, her head as panic ruled her. She couldn't stop her muffled cries as she felt more and more of them diving at her, swarming over her, overwhelming her.

*Damien,* her mind cried out. *Help me. Save me. . . .*

"It is your choice, Kathy," the earl shouted. "Marry Edgewater or die."

"Let me out," she screamed, feeling as if the wasps were in her ears and her nose and on her eyelids. "I'll do it!"

"Swear to me on your mother's grave."

"I swear," she cried.

The door opened. Kathy pressed against the back wall of the wardrobe as the insects flew out into the light in a cloud of brown, fluttering wings. She blinked at the earl's grinning face looming before her.

In his hand was a jar of wasps. "They were only moths, Kathy. But if you try to defy me again, I *will* turn the wasps loose on you."

Hysteria buffeted her mind on a wind of outrage and renewed fear. She felt violated by his deception, by the way he'd so easily reduced her to the mewling terror of her childhood. She clenched her fists against the need to claw at him, to tear the smile from his face. But the buzz of the wasps in the jar held her still.

Her gaze whipped around the room and to the doorway, seeking help, seeking a means of escape. Her heart seemed to shrivel as the truth of her situation descended over her in a smothering blanket of despair. There would be no help. Like Frances, the servants would be too afraid to interfere. Even if one of them went for help, it would do no good. The law would support the earl.

Her shoulders slumped as she accepted her defeat. Even Damien could not protect her.

"What the bloody hell . . . ?" Damien gasped and shuddered as cold wetness splashed over his face and chest, shocking him back to awareness. Pain was a jolt behind his eyes as he snapped them open. More pain throbbed and stabbed in his neck and the back of his head.

"Begging your pardon, Your Grace, but there ain't no time for me to cosset you."

Though the voice sounded fuzzy and dim, he recognized it as belonging to Smithy. He tried to focus but could make out only a blurred outline leaning over him.

"You'd best get your wits about you, Your Grace. Lady Kathy needs us."

A memory swamped him—of shutters nailed shut, of a Goliath barring the door and Edgewater and the earl lounging on the verandah with drinks in their hands, of fury such as he had never known propelling him over the rail to loose his wrath on them.

Kathy locked in her chamber. Kathy suffering from the earl's brutality. Kathy condemned to marry Tony Edgewater. . . .

Kathy needing him.

He'd given his word to Bruce and Max that he would protect her.

Damien sat bolt upright and gritted his teeth against the pain that nearly blinded him.

Smithy handed him a snifter of brandy.

Nausea rose as he downed it in one gulp, then subsided as it hit his stomach. His thoughts righted themselves and Smithy came into focus. He was in his room at the inn. "Who bludgeoned me?" he asked.

"I did," Smithy said with no sign of remorse. "You were about to get yourself killed, Your Grace."

"I was?"

"Begging your pardon again, Your Grace, but you're too blooming hot-headed," Smithy said. "You didn't notice that the earl's goon was coming after you. You can't help Lady Kathy if you're splattered all over the cobbles."

Damien snorted. "The man wouldn't have dared touch me, just as the earl never dared touch my father and Bassett."

Smithy gave an aggrieved sigh. "The bloke is from the colonies, and wouldn't know a duke if one bit him on the arse," he muttered. "And your father and the old Duke of Bassett always stuck together." He walked away, continuing to speak over his shoulder, as if he thought it would be prudent to get out of Damien's reach. "Meaning no disrespect, Your

Grace, but they always took time to think before they jumped their traces."

Damien wanted to cuff Smithy for such impertinence, but reason nudged outrage aside. Smithy was right. His father and Max had always stood at one another's backs, creating an image of power few dared to challenge. He and Max had always done the same. And it was always Max who tempered Damien's impulsive actions with caution and logic.

But Max wasn't here, and much as he'd like to deny it, one duke was not as powerful as two. He didn't even have the advantage of Bruce's conniving mind.

He *was* hot-headed. Somewhere along the way he'd forgotten that this was not a battle to be settled with fists.

With a groan, he swung his legs over the side of his bed and sat on the edge, cradling his head in his hands. "A lady in distress with a fiancé who is as stubborn as he is repulsive and a father bent on vengeance. I don't need this."

"Father," Smithy scoffed. "We know better than that."

Damien peered up at him through his fingers. Outside of the immediate family, no one had spoken of Bruce's and Kathy's parentage, yet Smithy's comment implied otherwise. "We do?" he asked carefully.

"I was there when the truth came out and threw the whole family into an uproar." Smithy handed him a damp towel. "The earl beat Lord Channing within an inch of his life, then the old dukes came and packed off the earl right and tight. Never heard from him again until now."

"I should have known that my father was involved in banishing the earl to America." Damien wiped his face with the length of linen. "Someone should have foreseen this."

"Should have, considering how much the earl hates Lady Kathy and her brother," Smithy agreed.

Damien lowered his hands to dangle between his outspread knees. He couldn't comprehend the kind of hate Smithy spoke of. The image of Kathy's hair being torn from her head by the roots came back to haunt him. He couldn't fathom what drove a man—any man—to abuse a woman.

Smithy straddled a chair and propped his elbows on the straight back. "If your head has cleared enough, we should be talking about how to save Lady Kathy from marrying that dandified lunatic."

"The idiot is deluding himself by thinking that Kathy will fall in with his plans. Docile she is not," Damien stated firmly, needing to believe it, needing to banish the image of how Kathy had run to him rather than face the earl, how she had held onto him and trembled until he thought she couldn't stand without leaning into him for support.

"She won't be given a choice," Smithy said.

"If she isn't given a choice, she'll take one," Damien said, needing to believe that, too.

Smithy shook his head. "Not this time. If the earl has his way, she'll be paying for what the others did for the rest of her life just like she did when she was a little girl."

"Blackwood has hurt Kathy before," Damien stated, acknowledging the suspicions lurking in the back of his mind.

"If he'd do it now, he'd have done it then," Smithy said.

"It would explain why she was so afraid of him when he arrived," Damien said, controlling a shudder as he remembered how she'd been paralyzed with fear. Never again did he want to see her as frightened as she'd been when the earl arrived.

As frightened as she surely must be now.

"It explains why she'll do what the earl tells her to do," Smithy said, "even if it means marrying a man she can't stomach." He swiped his hand over the back of his neck. "Too bad she didn't tell the earl she hated *you*. Then he'd likely force her to marry you out of spite." He grinned. "No offense, Your Grace, but it ain't no secret that there's no love lost between you."

No, Damien thought, there was no love lost between himself and Kathy. But, for the first time since he'd met her, he realized that he respected Kathy's strength and spirit. Oddly enough, he thought that she might respect him as well. Why else would she have run to him and clung to him as if she actually trusted him? Why else would she have named him as her fiancé in an attempt to defy the earl?

He couldn't betray that trust.

"Smithy," he said as he rose to his feet and retrieved a box containing a brace of pistols. "Have my coach readied, and hire three fast horses." He checked the pistols and his supply of powder and ball. "You might clean your musket also."

Rising, Smithy stood in front of him, his fists clenched pugnaciously at his sides. "Not if you're planning to go off half-cocked again."

Damien gave him an innocent smile. "I am simply planning to attend a wedding tomorrow."

Smithy's eyes narrowed. "And what else?"

"I haven't decided yet," Damien admitted as he considered one possibility after another in an effort to dismiss the only one that made sense.

He had to think, to plan.

# Chapter 12

Time seemed to crawl as Damien watched the house, waiting for Kathy and the earl to appear. There wasn't a servant or a gardener to be seen. Nothing but birds and insects stirred from gatehouse to stables. Not even a curtain fluttered behind closed windows.

One would think a wake was about to commence rather than a wedding.

Damien settled his backside more firmly on the high branch of a massive oak while Smithy crouched behind a fallen log on the ground below him, using a dead bramble bush for cover. The height of Damien's perch gave him a panoramic view of the only path leading from house to chapel while shielding him with masses of leaves. With narrowed eyes, he studied the area between Blackwood Manor and the chapel nestled in the woodland abutting the gardens. No one would see him even when they passed along the flagstones directly beneath him.

Edgewater had arrived a good quarter hour ago. The earl's man, Freddie, stood guard at the doors, his huge hands dangling at his sides like clubs.

Damien hoped his head was not as hard at it looked.

He glanced down at Smithy. "You remembered to bring your cudgel?"

Smithy reached behind him and produced a

wicked length of age-darkened wood that had vicious-looking knobs protruding from the stout end.

"Good God," Damien murmured. "Is that what you hit me with?"

"Of course not, Your Grace; I hit you with this one." Smithy produced another cudgel half the size of the one in his right hand. "I wasn't trying to hurt you none," he added.

"How magnanimous of you," Damien said dryly as he ran his finger around the edge of his neckcloth. The air was thick and heavy, though not a cloud marred the summer sky.

A small beetle fell past his face and landed on his arm.

Where was Kathy?

Damien began to wonder if the earl had changed his mind. Apparently Edgewater had the same concern as he anxiously peered out the arched chapel doors and muttered something to Freddie. The Goliath grunted and shifted from foot to foot as if he might need a trip to the necessary. His scrubbed-clean features pleated by a frown, Edgewater ducked back inside.

"Easy now, Your Grace," Smithy whispered as he scooted down on his belly behind the log. "They're on their way."

Forcing himself to move with care, Damien drew up his legs and focused his attention on the path. His hackles rose as he watched Kathy and the earl step from garden to woodland and pass beneath him.

The earl strolled over the flagstones that wound through the gardens, a benign expression on his face. Kathy walked beside him, her hand on his arm, her steps slow and dragging, her shoulders slumped and her head bowed so low her chin seemed to be connected to her chest, like a puppet whose joints were worn from too many performances.

Midmorning sunlight streamed through the treetops and fell over the white silk of Kathy's gown. A gown Damien recognized as the one she'd worn at her come-out, a stunning confection he'd admired for the way it had enhanced her tall and slender form with gossamer folds of iridescent silk and lace as fine as cobwebs draped around the neckline from shoulder tip to shoulder tip. But now the fabric hung unevenly from her stooped figure and the laurel of flowers encircling her head outshone the hair that hung limply down her back, the fire and life gone out of it.

Just as the fire and life seemed to have been drained from Kathy as she obediently climbed the steps to the chapel and disappeared inside without a single protest or fulminating look at the earl.

This was not the proud and elegant Kathy he knew.

What had the earl done to her?

The doors of the chapel swung shut and the Goliath adjusted the two pistols stuck in his waistband then stood with his arms crossed, his feet wide apart.

Damien swung his legs over the branch and shimmied down the tree. "Bring the horses," he bit out as his feet touched the ground.

Smithy nodded and disappeared through the woods.

He clenched his fists at his sides, struggling to contain his rage and the urge to rush in and throw caution to the wind. He had to keep to the simple plan he had devised to solve the problem with the least aggravation possible, though it had taken some time to convince Smithy of its practicality.

He hoped Kathy would see things his way as well.

Regardless, it had to be done. He'd vowed to Bruce and Max that he would protect their sister. They would do the same for him under any circumstances. But more than that, Damien knew if he failed, he would never again be able to close his eyes without seeing images of his Kathy broken and defeated as she walked into the chapel and the arms of Tony Edgewater—

*His Kathy?*

The thought caught him by surprise, stunning him with how easily it had rolled from his mind. Yes, by God, *his. His* to watch over and protect. *His* responsibility. He would take any measure, no matter how drastic, to protect what was his.

And what was hers. He would take everything from the earl that the earl had conspired to take from Kathy. Nothing that belonged to Kathy would remain at Blackwood.

The wheels were in motion. There would be no turning back.

He turned at the rustle of grass and gentle whuffling noises as Smithy appeared with three horses in tow. From the corner of his eye, Damien watched the Goliath to see if he'd heard.

The man didn't move.

"Here you go, Your Grace," Smithy whispered, and handed him the reins. Again, he reached for his cudgel—the large one—and slapped it against his palm. "I'll have the giant sleeping like a baby in a few minutes."

"No doubt you will," Damien said.

Smithy smiled roguishly and slipped away.

Frustrated that he would not be the one to dispatch Goliath, Damien mounted his gelding and waited. But Smithy had held fast to his weapon and insisted that he had more experience in wielding blunt instruments.

Damien rubbed the lump on the back of his head. He certainly couldn't argue the point.

In spite of his dark mood, he smiled as he watched Smithy creep up the side of the chapel, move in behind Freddie, and bring the club down on his head.

The man's eyes widened and he seemed cast in stone for a moment as he maintained his stance, his suddenly blank gaze fixed straight ahead. He didn't so much as blink as Smithy reached over and relieved him of his pistols.

Freddie fell forward and sprawled facedown on the steps.

Damien spurred his horse forward, tugging the two other mounts behind him. He reached the chapel steps, tossed the reins to Smithy, and dismounted with a fluid leap. Drawing his own pistols from the waistband of his breeches, he nodded to Smithy.

Smithy pulled his musket from the sling over his back.

Together they strode up the stone steps.

Damien kicked open the double doors, sending them crashing into the stone walls.

Edgewater spun around.

The earl rose from his seat in the first pew.

The vicar smiled in what could be construed as relief as he backed into the altar.

Damien's gaze settled on Kathy as he stepped inside and pointed the pistol in his left hand at the earl.

She turned slowly, a puppet still, seeming to move because the others had. Her skin was deathly pale and her normally brilliant eyes were dull and glazed, as if her body was present, but her spirit had flown away. She stared at him, yet did not cry out in relief nor did she run to him.

Goddamn the earl to hell for doing this to her.

"Westbrook, you intrude where you have not been invited," the earl snapped, his gaze riveted to the pistol aimed at his chest.

"Have you no decency?" Edgewater said indignantly, his hand clasping Kathy's arm.

"Apparently, more than you," Damien said. "Move away from her." He cocked the pistol in his right hand and sighted it between Edgewater's eyes.

"You wouldn't dare shoot an unarmed man in a church," Edgewater sputtered, releasing Kathy and stepping away as if he weren't quite certain.

"If I must." Damien's gaze flickered to Kathy. "Come to me."

"I can't," she said in a flat, dead voice.

Damien wanted to shout at her, to insult her, to do anything that would bring her back to life.

"Consider yourself jilted, Westbrook," the earl said smoothly.

"Yes," Edgewater said. "She loves me, not you. Don't you darling?"

Kathy's gaze skipped to the earl as he deliberately turned his back on Damien. "Yes," she said in the same monotone.

Tony's chest expanded as he smiled with a pleasure so intense he seemed to glow.

A chill crept up Damien's spine. What had the earl done to her to make her so submissive as to utter rehearsed lies and stand as if she were bound to the pulpit? Swallowing down a surge of vicious anger, he fixed his gaze on Edgewater and lowered his voice to a dangerously soft level. "Would you be so kind as to join the earl in the pew?"

Edgewater sullenly complied.

"Good," Damien said. "Now sit, both of you."

Tony dropped like a rock. The earl's mouth tightened as he slowly lowered himself to the bench.

"Smithy would you please see that neither one of these toads move?" Damien tucked the uncocked pistol back into his waistband.

"My pleasure, Your Grace." Smithy sauntered forward with his musket trained on Edgewater and the earl.

"You'll regret this, Smithy," the earl said. "I'll see you in Newgate for your complicity."

"I'm shaking in my boots, your lordship."

"No, Smithy, don't antagonize him," Kathy said frantically as her gaze shot to Damien. "Please, both of you, just leave."

Damien gritted his teeth, hating Kathy's panic almost as much as he'd hated her apathy. Reaching her in three long strides, he grasped her around the hips and tossed her over his shoulder while still holding one pistol on the men in the pew.

"Please don't," she said in a frightened whisper as her hands dug into his waist. "You don't understand."

"Be silent," he ordered and winced as she sobbed once, then quieted. "Vicar," he said to the silent man at the altar, "if you wish to leave, I suggest you do so now."

"Bless you, sir," the vicar whispered to Damien as he edged past him, "and take good care of Lady Kathleen, if you please." Without missing a step, he walked swiftly out the door.

"Come along, Smithy," Damien ordered as he turned and strode down the aisle, distinctly aware that Kathy sagged over his shoulder in a dead, unresisting weight, yet her grip had tightened even more on his waist, holding onto him as she'd held onto him the day before.

"I demand that you put Kathleen down at once," Edgewater called.

"Don't concern yourself," the earl said. "I'll notify the authorities at once, and have her back before nightfall."

Damien ignored them, trusting that Smithy backed up the aisle behind him, keeping his musket leveled on Edgewater and the earl.

Holding his pistol steady on the front of the sanctuary, he cleared the doors and skirted the still-prone Goliath. Behind him, Smithy hauled the unconscious body into the vestibule, slammed the heavy doors shut, and slid the crossbar into place, trapping the earl, Edgewater, and Freddie inside the chapel.

Damien set Kathy on her feet and checked the stained glass windows of the chapel, satisfying himself that their height would make them a difficult means of escape.

He turned back to Kathy.

She stood exactly where he'd placed her, staring at him with neither outrage nor gratitude. "Why?" she asked quietly.

Damien plowed his hands through his hair. "Because I told your family I would look after you," he grated. "And I never break my word."

"But it won't do any good," she said, a note of hysteria in her voice. "He'll follow us. *They'll* follow us."

"Then we had best get moving," Smithy said and mounted one of the hired horses.

Damien glared at her in irritation and handed Kathy the reins to a mare. "They can follow us to hell and gone if they wish," he said, carefully spacing his words to keep from shouting at her. "But they will not have you. Now mount up."

She stared back at him, neither moving nor speaking.

Damien grasped her waist and lifted her, holding her at eye level for a moment. "You will do as you're told!" he ordered as he roughly plopped her in the saddle, hoping to see even a glimmer of spirit return to her eyes. He'd rather deal with her anger than her apathy.

Yet still, all she did was stare at him.

He eyed the way her gown constricted her seat on the men's saddle Smithy had decreed would be more practical, and impatiently yanked it up to expose a long expanse of her shapely calves. Annoyed beyond reason that he should be tempted to take a longer look at such a time, he reached up to tear the wreath of flowers from her hair and toss it on the ground, ignoring the urge to run his fingers through the strands. He wanted them wild and alive rather than limp and tamed.

She did not react.

Damn her.

He bolted into his saddle and spurred his horse into a reckless gallop through the forest without looking back to see if she followed, refusing to entertain the notion that she might not. Smithy would see that she did.

Muttering a curse to the wind that rushed past him, Damien wondered what kind of madness plagued him that he should be so bloody fascinated by a pair of legs and a mane of hair when the one who owned them was not only an unwanted responsibility, but far more trouble than she was worth.

The promise made by the father had been kept by the son. The thought marched through her mind to the thundering beat of hooves as Kathy leaned low over the saddle. Damien knew nothing about that promise, yet it seemed as if it had become a legacy of fate.

Panic churned in her stomach and her heart hesitated on a beat. She glanced anxiously over her shoulder as she rode at an all-out gallop behind Damien, expecting the earl and Tony to overtake them at any moment. She knew the earl too well to believe that he would let her go. Even if he did, she knew that Tony certainly wouldn't. His look of possession as she'd entered the chapel had felt like a hundred snakes crawling over her flesh.

She urged her horse to go faster, to gain more speed, to put as much distance between herself and Blackwood as possible.

"Slow down, Lady Kathy," Smithy shouted as he came abreast of her. "Don't want you to go breakin' your neck so soon after getting it out of a noose."

She glanced back again and saw nothing but the trees of the forest seeming to close ranks behind them. A rational thought crept into her mind. *The trees.* She and Damien and Smithy were riding at a dangerous pace. Instinct took over and prompted her to tug on the reins and slow her pace. Smithy did the same.

But Damien rode on as if he were being pursued by demons.

Suddenly the trees thinned out and there was nothing but a flat meadow ahead of them. They were off Blackwood land.

"We'll be long away from here before the earl and his familiars get free of the chapel," Smithy said beside her.

The words sank in as she dimly recalled Freddie's unconscious form being dragged into the chapel, the heavy iron bolt slamming into place over the doors, the way Damien had studied the narrow windows of the chapel set so high on the stone walls.

She fixed her gaze on Damien riding ahead of her, his hair gleaming ebony black in the sun, his broad back wedging into narrow hips that sat so well in the saddle, his long legs pressed into his horse's sides with absolute control. Just then she could almost believe that Damien could and would save her from the earl.

And as the moments collected with no sign of pursuit and the meadow opened out before her, she began to feel free.

She urged her chestnut to greater speed over the flat meadow. She thought she saw Damien's lips curve in a smile as she flew past him. Sweet sensation uncurled inside her, filling and warming her from her toes to her head. The same sensation that had awakened the first time she'd seen him standing so proudly on the steps of the cathedral. A sensation of awareness and trust that had again stirred within her when he'd protected her from her own fear by tossing her over his shoulder, removing the burden of an impossible choice from her.

She'd known it was Damien the moment she'd heard the chapel doors crash open. Only Damien would announce his presence and his displeasure with a blatant physical act rather than words. Only Damien would storm a place when he could have simply walked in. Only Damien would dare to kidnap her from under the earl's nose. Damien, whose temper was exceeded by his arrogance in assuming he could protect her from both the law and the earl armed only with a sense of honor and a brace of pistols.

He had been magnificent.

All she'd wanted to do was run to him as she had before. But she'd been paralyzed by fear, convinced that the earl's power over her could not be broken, even by a duke.

"Ride to the left," Damien shouted as he pulled up beside her.

She obeyed without hesitation, the sound of his voice filling her with the same sense of comfort and safety she'd felt yesterday when she'd so fearfully clung to him in the hope that he could shield her from the earl. While she'd been able to touch him and feel his presence, an odd feeling of strength had seemed to flow from him and into her. The same strength she felt now as he rode so closely beside her. And suddenly she knew that Damien really could and would help her, that because of him, she could again help herself.

She *was* free.

She intended to stay that way.

They veered toward the main road bordering the far edge of the meadow and the black coach bearing the Westbrook coat of arms, its team of six—six!— powerful horses stomping the ground and restlessly tossing their heads. A driver sat on the box and two footmen stood stationed by the open doors.

She drew on the reins, stopping her mount. Beside her, Damien pulled up at the same time, his gelding rearing at the abrupt halt, then snorted at his master with a baring of teeth at such treatment. Obviously Damien preferred his horses to be as ill-tempered as he was.

Smithy reached her other side and brought his horse to a sudden stop and leapt from the saddle.

Another footman joined his comrades from the other side of the coach, and all three hurdled over the fence and took charge of the three horses, snatching the reins from her hands.

Damien encircled her waist, dragged her from the saddle, and set her firmly on the ground.

Her heart raced at his touch and her waist tingled with the memory of his fingers as he jerked his hands away. Unsettled, she stared at him, at the way he frowned in bemusement then turned away from her. She glanced up and saw Smithy take a seat beside the driver in the high box at the front of the coach, and cradle his musket in his hands.

Again Damien gripped her waist and swung her up over the fence and set her onto the road, then cleared it himself with a fluid leap. Barking orders to the footmen, he rushed her toward the coach and lifted her inside, then followed her in, filling the space even though he sat on the seat facing her.

The coach lunged forward as the horses immediately broke into a run. Dust rose outside the windows and enveloped them in an obscuring cloud. The coach rocked from side to side and pitched Kathy from one end of the seat to the other as they rounded bend after bend on the twisting country road.

Damien braced his shoulders against the squabs and bracketed her feet with his.

She grabbed for a hand grip, caught it, and held on for dear life. "Where are you taking me?" she shouted above the thunder of hoofbeats and the crack of the driver's whip.

"Scotland," Damien said succinctly.

"Scotland?" she echoed in confusion. "Whatever for?"

Damien met her gaze squarely. "There is no other place we can marry without the earl's permission."

"Marry?" she cried. "You can't be serious."

Damien nodded firmly, his green eyes filled with steely resolve. "It's the only way I can protect you from the earl."

*Protect.* The word hit her like a ghost slipping through her thoughts, renewing the promise his father had made to her, becoming Damien's promise as well. Yet, she didn't think marriage was what the old Duke of Westbrook had in mind and it certainly wasn't an option she'd considered. She refused to consider it now. Enclosed in the coach and off Blackwood land her courage returned to her.

"I won't do it," she stated emphatically.

"Would you rather be leg-shackled to Edgewater for the rest of your life?"

"Of course not, but I don't want to be leg-shackled to you either."

"Nor do I wish to marry you," Damien snapped. "But have no fear; it will be only until you reach your majority and your brothers return home, at which time we will have it annulled."

She didn't care if it lasted only until the middle of next week. "You're insane. There are other ways to circumvent the earl. Put me on a ship to the West Indies or America. It shouldn't be too difficult to locate Bruce or Max."

"Out of the question. You can't travel alone."

"I can look after myself."

Damien snorted. "Oh yes, we all know how well you can look after yourself." He braced his legs more firmly against the jarring of the coach. "I suggest you get some rest. We've a long way to go and we won't be stopping except to change horses. It won't take long for the earl's servants to free him from the chapel. No doubt he'll be hard on our heels by nightfall." He closed his eyes and folded his arms over his chest as if the subject were closed.

And it certainly was not. While the earl may have the power to make such decisions for her, Damien certainly didn't. He was just too stubborn and too arrogant to recognize that fact. And he was entirely too fond of going to unnecessary extremes. "You can accompany me," she said with a patience she didn't feel.

He opened one eye. "If I did, you *would* find yourself leg-shackled to me for the rest of your life. Imagine how your brothers would react should we arrive and inform them we've just crossed three thousand miles of ocean together and unchaperoned." He closed his eyes again. "I know how I'd react."

*With flared nostrils and hammering fists, no doubt,* she thought acidly. "Then hide me away somewhere and send Smithy."

He sighed. "I don't want to be constantly concerned with the earl's whereabouts over the next few months. If we're married, I won't have to bother."

"How convenient for you."

"Exactly," he said. "A marriage of convenience is the best way to inconvenience myself as little as possible until your family returns to take you off my hands."

"Stop this coach and let me out this instant," she said evenly.

"Nothing would please me more. Unfortunately if I allowed anything to happen to you, your family would see me drawn and quartered."

"Sir Galahad," Kathy spat.

Damien's mouth slanted in a parody of a smile. "Hardly. That worthy knight had the privilege of choosing his responsibilities."

"I won't do it," she said firmly. "Marriage is out of the question."

Damien's mouth tightened and a muscle bunched at his jaw. "It's not as if I were asking you to share my bed and bear my children," he grated.

Her heart thudded once and then seemed to stop. She pressed her back more firmly against the cushions and drew her feet in as close as she could to the bottom of her seat, horrified at the idea of sharing a bed with Damien, of making love—something she wanted no part of . . . ever.

"Do you understand?" Damien asked, his expression smug and more than a little mocking.

"Perfectly," she bit out as she remembered the way her mother had gone all misty-eyed when she'd spoken of the physical bond shared between men and women. She understood how that bond rendered a woman helpless and far too trusting. And although she didn't know specifics, she knew that such a bond could hold a woman in a man's power long after he had gone from her life.

Never would she allow herself to succumb to a man in such a way.

A queer sensation shivered from her scalp all the way down her body as she unconsciously slipped her gaze to Damien's mouth, to the perfect shape of his upper lip and the lower one that was slightly squared off on either side of the curve.

She clamped her mouth shut, tore her gaze away from him and glared at the landscape outside her window. How on earth could she be so intrigued by Damien's mouth? And how could she endure marriage to him when she could barely tolerate the control he had over her now?

She couldn't.

Kathy's chest tightened and the walls of the coach seemed to close in on her as she admitted to herself that she was drawn to him in ways she didn't want to understand. She didn't want to know why he made her feel more protected than she'd felt in her entire life. She didn't want to feel safe with anyone but herself, didn't want to depend on anyone for security of any kind.

She'd made too many plans for a future gloriously free of entanglements. She intended to buy a house she would have to share with no one, least of all a husband.

Least of all Damien.

She intended to be free.

Her breath stalled as the thought grew and took on a new prominence in her mind. The house, the fortune her mother had left her, the bid for independence—all were merely symbols of what was truly important to her. Freedom. It was what she'd always wanted. What she'd always needed. To be on her own, bound by nothing but her own rules and answering to no one.

To belong only to herself.

She could not do that as Damien's wife. She would belong to him, and no matter how short the time they would be together, she feared that he would take possession of a part of herself that could never be retrieved. He was too unpredictable, taking her to task one moment and taking her to safety in the next. Her feelings for him were too erratic, as she thought him a wretch one moment and utterly magnificent in the next.

Anxiety dried her mouth and brought heat to her face.

Marriage was definitely out of the question. There *had* to be another way to thwart the earl.

By the time they reached Scotland, she intended to make sure Damien felt the same way.

# Chapter 13

**T**he next time anyone waxed enthusiastic about the high romance of a runaway marriage, Damien would be sure to acquaint them with the horrors of spending two days in a coach without benefit of a bath or shave or a decent night's rest in a decent bed. Not doubting that the earl was in pursuit, he hadn't risked stopping except to change horses and procure whatever food this innkeeper or that could wrap in a napkin.

He could manage the problems associated with food and transport. He could certainly accept the discomforts of their present situation. But sharing such a confined space with Kathy was another matter entirely. Ever since he'd brought up the subject of sharing a bed, the coach had seemed to become smaller with every mile they traveled, forcing his awareness of Kathy to acutely sensitive levels.

Awareness of just how long her legs were as they accidentally brushed against his, and of how beautifully formed they were when she'd fallen asleep curled up on her seat and kicked her skirts free as if they were an annoying blanket. Awareness of her hair that reflected the fire of her personality, alive again as she was alive again, fighting and defying him and tempting him to bury his fingers in the vibrant strands. Tempting him into fantasies of silencing her with his mouth on hers, of slowly baring her until she was clothed only in the flame of her hair, her legs wrapped around him, creating a tempest in him with the movements of her body.

He stifled a groan and shifted in his seat. For two days, he'd spent agonizing minutes—or had it been hours?—trying to find a position that would conceal the erections that plagued him at such visions. And he would recall what she had said—that she understood perfectly what it meant to share a bed. Given her background and the frequent visits of her mother's lover to Blackwood, he imagined that she did understand . . . perfectly.

That more than anything else fueled his imagination and the persistent ache in his groin. As a result, his mood was decidedly black, his manner toward Kathy decidedly choleric. As a result, Kathy had given new meaning to the word churlish, reminding him of all the reasons why he'd spent the last two years trying to avoid her.

How was he going to protect a woman he both disliked and desired?

"What about my inheritance?" she asked waspishly.

"I assure you your money is quite safe. Until your birthday, Bruce is in control of your inheritance," Damien said as he rubbed the back of his knuckles over the heavy growth of beard covering his face, thankful that Bruce had told him that much at least. "Our marriage will ensure that Blackwood can't touch it."

Kathy lifted her chin a notch. "I don't want you to control my fortune."

"And I don't want control of your bloody fortune," Damien gritted, noting the paleness of her fair skin and the dark circles that ringed her eyes. If only she were as fragile as she looked.

"We have no license," she argued.

"We have no need of one. A legal marriage in Gretna Green requires just the consent of the bride and groom and a blacksmith."

*"A what?"*

Under any other circumstances, her frown of consternation might have amused him. But, being a less than happy groom, he found no entertainment in the peculiarities of a runaway marriage. "Anyone in the village can marry us," he explained grimly. "And those who regularly perform the ceremonies are often referred to as blacksmiths."

"A blacksmith indeed," she said, her mouth flattening mutinously. "It can't be legal."

"It is quite legal," he replied, beginning to enjoy her outrage in spite of himself. "We are about to join the many other impulsive and mismatched couples who have indulged in a marriage performed 'over the anvil' . . . a rather colorful phrase, don't you think?"

She glared at him and clamped her mouth shut and then squirmed into the corner of her seat, curling up into a ball with her knees drawn to her chest and her head buried in her arms. Whether she sought to shield her eyes from the light or to keep from looking at him, Damien neither knew nor cared.

He had finally rendered her speechless.

With a sigh, he leaned his head back and closed his eyes, grateful for the silence, knowing it would last for just a little while. Unless he was lucky and she slept the remainder of the way to Scotland.

But that was wishful thinking. She would surely awaken when they stopped in Carlisle for fresh horses, where once again, she would assault him with a thousand new reasons why marriage between them was a bad idea.

He'd stopped listening an hour after they had begun their journey. It was far more satisfying to silently curse Kathy's brothers for listening to her in the first place. If they had exercised good sense rather than indulging her flighty whims, she would be safe and sound in America with Max and Jillian.

Damien wasn't going to make the same mistake.

The more she protested, the more he was convinced that marriage offered the best temporary solution for them both. He couldn't spend the next four months guarding Kathy every minute of every hour.

Ironically, marriage would allow him to pursue his own life once again.

And, ironically, marriage vows would free him from the constant indispositions caused by the obligation Max and Bruce had foisted upon him.

And though he wouldn't admit it to anyone else, he would rather be married to Kathy for the rest of his life than see her suffer more at the earl's hands. What Anthony Edgewater would do to her made his skin crawl.

His fists clenched as he reminded himself that Edgewater wasn't the real threat. The earl was. Damien didn't know what exactly Blackwood had done to Kathy, but sooner or later he would find out.

In the meantime, convincing Kathy to cooperate had to be his immediate concern. They were nearly to the border and running out of time. He had to convince her that marriage was the only solution. Logic certainly hadn't worked. Neither had anger and threats. He was beginning to wonder if anything could make her see reason.

The coach slowed and rolled to a halt before a posting inn.

"Why are we stopping?" Kathy demanded as she scrambled to an upright position. "And where are we?"

"We have to change horses, and we are at Carlisle," Damien said, pinning her with a hard stare, "the last stop before we reach the border and Gretna Green."

The color drained from her face. "Don't you care in the least how I feel about this?"

Suddenly he was there—at the end of his rope and losing his grip. "Goddammit," he shouted. "My name is the best protection you can have against Blackwood." He shoved open the coach door. "Ei-

ther stop tossing my help back in my face and accept
my solution with good grace or take your chances
with the earl."

Her eyes widened as she pressed back in her seat.

He bit back a smile and wished he had thought to
use such an approach with her before. "Your choice,
Kathy," he said, his voice softening with something
that felt very much like tenderness for her vulnerability as she stared at him with parted lips and a chin
that trembled slightly.

Tenderness for Kathy?

He tore his gaze from her. Absurd! This whole
situation was absurd. He was tired and out of sorts.
He was more impatient and more annoyed than he'd
ever been in his life that he should be so neatly
caught in the parson's mousetrap with a woman who
abhorred the idea as much as he did.

"Your choice, Kathy," he repeated. "I suggest you
make it before I withdraw my offer."

He was serious.

Kathy stared at Damien, awed by the realization
that he was indeed offering her choices. That with a
word from her, he would let her go.

There was an odd comfort in knowing that.

Dust rose and hooves clattered in the yard outside.

Scowling fiercely, Damien abruptly retreated back
into the coach, his gaze fixed on the yard outside.

Kathy leaned forward and peered out the window.

A man dressed in Blackwood livery reined in his
horse in front of the posting stage, his eyes narrowing on the mud-splattered markings on the side of
Damien's coach. As quickly as he'd appeared, the
man turned and charged back in the direction from
which he came.

"The earl," Kathy choked.

Damien nodded. "One of Blackwood's outriders,
which means the earl has caught up with us sooner
than I anticipated." He cocked his head at her.
"Well, are you going to get out?"

She couldn't speak for the terror strangling her.

He cupped her chin in his hand. "Kathy, do you wish to go elsewhere?"

*Elsewhere?* There was no elsewhere. There was nowhere to go, nowhere to run. Nowhere to hide. She shook her head, words still beyond her reach.

He smiled slightly and his thumb caressed her cheek. "Would you prefer to remain with me and under my protection?" he asked so gently that tears stung her eyes.

All she could do was nod. She had to stay with Damien. Only with him did she feel safe from the earl.

"You're quite certain?"

Again, she nodded and felt tears slip down her cheeks.

"Your Grace!" Smithy appeared in the window.

"We saw," Damien said. "Get inside with Kathy. I'll ride on the box."

"What do you have in mind?" Smithy asked.

"To slow the earl's team down," Damien said tersely as he reached beneath his seat and drew out the box containing his pistols.

"Lady Kathy don't need me," Smithy said. "I can do more good riding on top of the coach." He pulled first one and then a second pistol from his waistband to check their loads. "The way I see it, the more discouragement we can send the earl's way the better."

"As always, your vision is quite acute," Damien replied, then turned toward Kathy. "Will you be all right?" he asked in that disturbingly tender voice.

"Yes, I'll be fine," she croaked. "Please . . . discourage the earl any way you can."

Damien smiled and thumbed away a tear. "It will be all right, Kathy." With a wolfish grin, he climbed from the coach and shouted orders to the driver.

"There now," Smithy crooned as he secured the door. "His Grace ain't such a bad sort." He was gone before she could reply.

Her tears doubled. It was not what she wanted to know, not what she wanted to admit.

The coach lurched ahead and rumbled over the road. Landscape rushed by in a blur.

Tasting fear and dust, Kathy sat braced into her corner of the coach, fighting the hard squeeze of panic and trembles of fear, forcing herself to direct her energy toward something more worthwhile, like remembering how confident and calm Damien had been as he checked his pistols. How tender he'd been as he'd cradled her chin and skimmed her cheek with what had seemed like a comforting gesture. She'd hadn't known he could be calm in a crisis, much less gentle. She hadn't known he could look so magnificent and so dangerously exciting with his tousled hair and piratelike growth of beard and hopelessly rumpled clothing.

How she wished he would be overbearing and awful all of the time.

She didn't understand him, didn't understand how she could dislike him and yet be so intensely aware of him. She understood only one overwhelming fact.

She was going to marry him. She was going to hand over her freedom and her life to him. She had no choice.

It would just be for a short while, she reminded herself.

She knew she couldn't bear it even as the thought sparked an odd thrill inside her.

Her shoulder crashed into the wall as the driver shouted and cracked his whip and they moved faster and faster.

A shot exploded in the air, then another and another. Her heart slammed into her ribs as one of Smithy's legs dangled over the edge of the coach and thudded into her window.

The leg disappeared, replaced by Smithy's face grinning at her upside down. "Hah! His Grace got the earl's team dancing a jig and his rig is about to go over," he shouted down to her. "The earl will never catch us in time."

"Thank God," Kathy shouted back. "I think," she murmured, feeling as if she had escaped the earl's cage only to walk into the panther's lair.

The ten miles to Gretna Green seemed more like ten thousand.

# Chapter 14

**"A**re you both here of your own free will?"
Mr. Isdale inquired in a rolling Scottish brogue.

"Yes," Damien said forcefully.

Kathy's reply stuck in her throat. It was all moving too fast. They'd stopped at the first cottage they'd seen, a dark confining house with small rooms and too much furniture. A place that looked as clandestine as the marriages that took place here. And judging from Mr. Isdale's matter-of-fact manner as he'd ushered them inside, his sole interest was in the full purse Damien had produced.

She hadn't taken Damien seriously about any citizen being able to perform marriages until then, but the avaricious gleam in Mr. Isdale's eyes and the efficiency he displayed in placing them at the one place in the parlor that caught the sunlight from a narrow window—all without a word being said—had convinced her. So had Smithy when all he'd done was give her a nod before climbing onto the seat next to the driver and following Damien's orders to take the coach to the other end of the village in an attempt to misdirect the earl and gain a few more minutes of time.

"Are you here of your own free will, lass?" Mr. Isdale inquired again, his beady eyes narrowing as

140

he sat behind a small table, waiting for her reply before he filled out the marriage certificate.

The man made her skin crawl. He looked like an undertaker with his pasty complexion and somber demeanor.

"Answer him," Damien prompted. "We haven't much time."

"Yes," she said, weakly, knowing there was no other answer she could give.

Mr. Isdale laid his quill aside. "I don't perform marriage rites unless both are in agreement. The young lass seems reluctant."

"She is tired," Damien said evenly.

The Scotsman folded his arms across his chest.

Damien laid twenty more guineas on the table.

Kathy was appalled. Mr. Isdale knew time was of the essence and he was using it to extort money from Damien.

"I'm quite ready," she said, nearly gagging on the words. "Please proceed."

Grunting, Mr. Isdale picked up his quill and filled out the marriage certificate, then opened the book near his elbow, glanced up at them and cleared his throat. "Do you, Damien Forbes, take this woman, Kathleen Palmerston, to be your lawful wife?"

"I do," Damien said.

"Do you, Kathleen Palmerston, take this man, Damien Forbes, to be your lawful husband?"

"I do," she said, trying to steady the wobble in her voice.

"Have you a ring?" Mr. Isdale asked.

"No, I'm afraid we left in rather a hurry," Damien said, placing another twenty guineas on the table. "We are *still* in rather a hurry."

Kathy blinked. That brought the total up to ninety guineas.

"I now pronounce you man and wife," the Scotsman said in a staccato voice. "What God joins together let no man put asunder."

Kathy blinked again. That was it?

Mr. Isdale snapped his book shut and pocketed the coins. "Have you need of a wedding chamber?" he asked as he handed Damien the marriage certificate. "I have a nice room in the back for ten more guineas."

Damien gave him a steely look. "We'll be on our way."

Mr. Isdale nodded curtly. "You can show yourselves out," he said and disappeared through a curtained doorway.

"Greedy sod," Damien muttered as he stuffed their marriage papers in his coat pocket. "There's an inn just over the border. I could use a bath and a decent night's sleep."

Kathy's mind reeled as she stared at the corner of the parchment sticking out of his coat. This couldn't be real. It was a parody of a marriage ceremony just as she and Damien were a parody of a bride and groom—her in her white dress, grimy from days in the coach and Damien in dusty black pants and coat and with a heavy overgrowth of beard.

"Are you sure we're married?" she asked.

"Positive," he said as he grasped her upper arm and steered her toward the door.

Before they had taken two steps, it swung open and Smithy stepped inside. "Your Grace, the earl and Edgewater are in the village. They're telling everyone who crosses their path that they'll pay three hundred guineas to the man who brings Lady Kathy to them before—before—"

"Well they're too late," Kathy said with a measure of relief. Caught between the devil and the deep blue sea, she would rather drown in Damien's annoyance than burn alive in the earl's hell. "It's done, Smithy."

Smithy's brows shot up, his gaze snapped to Damien. "It is?"

Damien raked his hand through his hair and shook his head. "It is not."

"But you just told me you were positive we were married," Kathy said on a burst of sudden panic.

Smithy flushed and glanced away.

"We are," Damien reaffirmed. "Guard the door, Smithy. If the earl and Edgewater arrive here, delay them as long as you can." He tightened his grip on Kathy's arm and dragged her toward the curtained portal at the opposite end of the room.

"Where are we going now?" she asked, her confusion mounting by the second. "You said the earl couldn't touch me after we were married."

"We have no time for questions," Damien said grimly as he yanked her through the curtain.

Mr. Isdale blocked the narrow passage, his hand outstretched. "That will be ten guineas, if you please."

The man was a thief, Damien thought as he all but slammed the money in Isdale's hand and watched him turn on his heel and disappear down the hallway. And if Isdale was a thief, he was probably a liar as well. For enough money he might even say that Kathy had not been here of her own free will. A minor point, but one that could be used to contest the validity of the marriage.

*Bloody hell.* There was nothing for it but to leave no doubt in the earl's mind that Kathy was well and truly beyond his reach. Yielding to the inevitable, Damien tugged Kathy into the crude but adequate "bridal chamber" and latched the door.

Barely adequate, he amended as he quickly surveyed the amenities. It didn't take long. All the room contained was a bed and a single wooden chair in the corner. Even with the sparse furnishings, there was scarcely enough room for himself and Kathy.

"Why are we here?" Kathy asked, her expression blank.

"We are going to pretend this marriage has been consummated," Damien said, bracing for the argument that would surely follow.

Her brows pleated as she continued to stare at him in confusion and . . . *innocence?*

No, it couldn't be. She'd told him in the carriage that she understood "perfectly" about the physical relationship between a man and a woman. He hadn't doubted her. How could she be aware that her mother had been a man's mistress for nearly thirty years and not understand what a mistress's duties included? Especially since she was a product of that liaison. She *had* to know, but suddenly he wasn't so sure. And if she didn't know, he was going to have a devilish time getting her to play her role in the farce he planned.

There was not enough time to debate the issue with Kathy, nor with himself.

Deliberately, he slipped out of his jacket and began unbuttoning his shirt. "We are going to convince the earl that our marriage is irrevocable."

Kathy's face flamed bright red and her hands clenched at her sides as if it took all her effort to remain where she stood. "No," she said flatly. "We wouldn't be able to have it annulled."

"We're just going to *pretend*," he repeated, convinced by her reaction that she *did* understand the carnal aspects of marriage. For a moment, he'd been uncomfortably afraid that he would have to spell it out for her. Relieved, Damien released the breath he'd been holding and finished unfastening his shirt and loosening the laces on his breeches.

Her gaze dropped to his open shirt and partially open pants. "What are you doing?" She stumbled back a few steps and flattened herself against the wall, her eyes wide with outrage . . . or was it shock?

Perhaps she *didn't* understand. He gave her a hard stare, having neither the patience nor the time for her sensibilities and his doubts. "Kathy, what do you know about making love?" he asked bluntly.

She pressed her back closer against the wall, as if she were trying to become a part of the plaster.

"That it is as close as a man and woman can get and that if they love one another it is beautiful . . . and that is how Bruce and I came to be."

*Jolly wonderful,* Damien thought. That told him precisely nothing and he hadn't time to question her further. He expected the earl to bang on the door at any minute. "Do you trust me?" he asked as he ripped the covers back on the bed.

She stared at her feet. "Sometimes," she conceded after a long pause.

Annoyance took a bite out of his control. After all they'd been through in the past few days and she had to think about it. "This had best be one of those times. If you don't do exactly as I say, there is still a chance that the earl can take you away."

"But you said we wouldn't—" She swallowed as her gaze darted to the bed.

He pulled his knife from his boot. "I know what I said and I meant it." He slashed his finger and smeared the sheet. "Remove your dress."

Kathy gasped. "I will not."

Damien's patience frayed to a thin strand of reason. "Do it, Kathy. Or would you rather argue with me until the earl arrives to take you back to Blackwood?"

"He can't!"

"Unless you do as I say, he can and he will. And so help me, if the earl invalidates this marriage, I won't come to your rescue again. Now take off the god-damned dress."

She jumped and quickly reached behind her back to work at her buttons.

Damien yanked off his shirt, then sat down the bed to tug off his boots. Why did she always insist on pushing him to his limit? She was the most obstinate, the most—

His thought broke off and focused on the rustle of silk whispering through the room.

He jerked his head up, startled at how much noise

a gown made when it hit the floor, and at how deficient his imagination had been when conjuring images of Kathy.

The dirty white silk piled at her feet was a husk that had been peeled away to reveal beauty in its purest form . . . exquisite . . . arresting . . . sensual.

She stood before him in her shift, her body trembling, her eyes skipping everywhere but at him. Her hair fell over one shoulder, a wild, curling, mass of brightness against creamy arms and shoulders. Dusky shadows beneath the delicate fabric captured his stare. The circles at the center of her breasts and the points of her erect nipples tantalized him. The lithe contours of her waist and hips and the blurred wedge above her thighs tortured him. The graceful length of her legs—oh God, they were long—incited him to swell and harden and rise up to meet her. He wanted to kiss her, to see if her breasts would fit perfectly into the palms of his hands, if her body would be an exact fit for his—

Muffled voices penetrated the solid barrier of the door. Angry, demanding voices.

"Come lie on the bed, Kathy," Damien murmured.

She shook her head fiercely.

The voices grew louder and Damien could hear Smithy's implacable refusal to move away from his post in front of the door.

Damien reached out, grasped Kathy's hand, and jerked her onto the bed.

With a quick, short, yelp she tumbled onto the mattress, squirming beneath him as he quickly covered her mouth with his hand and pinned her down with his body.

Several forceful raps sounded. "Westbrook! I demand you leave my betrothed untouched," Edgewater shouted.

Kathy's struggles ceased.

"Open the door, or we'll break it down," the earl added.

Damien stared down at Kathy. "Don't make a sound," he ordered.

She nodded, then lay still, looking more like a statue frozen in fright than a well-loved bride.

He lifted his hand, satisfied that her fear of the earl would keep her still. "You intrude where you have no right," he called.

The voices seemed to fade as he stared down at her mouth, at the way her lips parted and her breath seemed to be as frozen as the rest of her. Every thought he'd ever had about kissing her drifted through his mind and sank to his groin.

Dimly, he heard something slam into the door. A shoulder probably.

"Touch that door, again, Mr. Edgewater, and I'm going to have to shoot you," Smithy said.

Kathy lay beneath Damien, her breasts rising with the breath she had found, pressing into his chest, then falling and rising again as her whole body began to tremble.

He had to do something to make Kathy look warm and tousled and glazed with passion.

And just then, with his erection overruling his sanity, he cared about nothing but bringing his fantasies to life.

He took her mouth in one swoop, his tongue thrusting between her lips, swallowing her gasp.

She squirmed beneath him and flattened her palms against his chest, pushing at him, fighting him.

Her legs drove him insane, first bending up on either side of his as she bucked her hips, then straightening abruptly at the pressure of his hardness against her belly. She pushed her hips down into the mattress, trying to escape him.

"Kathy, be still," he groaned against her mouth as he captured both her hands above her head with one hand and cupped her breast with the other. It fit his hand perfectly, and responded just as perfectly to his touch in spite of her struggles.

She raised her knees again, and tried to twist her face away from his. Her hips cradled him, her movements a rough caress through the fabric of his breeches. He plunged his tongue deeper into her mouth, tangling with hers, stroking, exploring, dueling with hers as she fought him . . .

Incited him.

He rotated his hips and felt Kathy's breath quiver. He outlined her nipple with his thumb, over and over again, and felt it tighten and thrust upward, seeking more. He cupped her breast, stroked and teased it and felt her sigh whisper into his mouth. Her lips softened and opened wider and her tongue retreated, then brushed his and retreated again. Her hips arched upward, not in protest but in need. Her hands fought free of his hold on her wrists and gripped his shoulders, digging into him, not to deny him but to pull him closer.

He broke the kiss to string small hungry nips along her jaw, her neck, and collarbone and farther to the center of one beautiful, fabric-covered breast, to kiss it and draw it into his mouth.

She cried out and slid her hands into a frenzied hold on his head, not to fight his caress, but to ask for more.

She whimpered and her breath became hard and fast as she yanked on his hair and drew his head up to seek his mouth, to open hers in demand. He ground his lips over hers in desperation and frantic desire. Her tongue matched the movements of his and then boldly thrust into his mouth.

He buried his fingers in her hair and the strands seemed to cling to him. Her hips danced with his in a hard, driving rhythm and her legs—oh God, her legs—were a vise around his thighs, holding him.

She wanted him as fiercely as he wanted her.

Damien tore his mouth from Kathy's as the voices outside the door became a roar in his ears, growing louder, more threatening and insistent. But then he looked down at Kathy and saw her closed eyes and her hair falling over her cheek as she tossed her head.

To hell with them. To hell with the whole bloody world outside this room. He levered upward, desperate to remove the barriers of her shift and his breeches, to plunge into her, to complete their passion, and drive them both mad with pleasure.

But the whole bloody world was battering the door down.

"What is the meaning of this!" Mr. Isdale demanded in the hallway.

Kathy stared up at him, her blue eyes glazed, her lips swollen and red, her cheek abraded from the roughness of his whiskers. She looked confused and dazed and ravished.

Damien gritted his teeth at the pain of frustration.

Fear overtook Kathy's features as the earl's voice boomed.

Damien's erection sagged in defeat.

He turned onto his side and rolled off the bed, then leaned over Kathy, careful not to touch her. "I'm going to answer. Remain in the bed. Do not say a word," he said, every word an agonizing exercise in control.

She opened her mouth, then shut it and nodded slowly. His gaze swept her body lying so limply on the bed, her arms crooked on either side of her head and her legs still splayed where they'd fallen when he'd pulled away from her.

Damn.

He straightened and drew the counterpane over her, careful to arrange it so the small smear of blood from his finger was properly displayed on the white sheet.

The door burst open. The earl and Edgewater crowded in the doorway. Smithy's and Mr. Isdale's faces loomed behind them.

"Don't take another step," Damien snarled as he retrieved his pistol from the chair and leveled it on them. "I need little to convince me to shoot all of you."

The earl turned a mottled shade of red as his gaze swept over the room, over Kathy's dress crumpled on the floor, over Damien's shirt in the chair and his partially opened breeches . . . over Kathy lying so still on the bed and the small, red stain near her leg. "Goddamn you, Westbrook," he said.

Edgwater stepped into the room, his hand outstretched toward Kathy. "Oh, my darling—"

"You forget yourself, Edgewater," Damien said as he tracked Edgewater with the pistol. "*Your* darling happens to be *my* wife."

Edgewater halted in his tracks his gaze riveted on the stained sheet.

Satisfied that everyone had gotten an eyeful, Damien casually reached over and arranged the counterpane to conceal everything but Kathy's face. She looked ravished, and she looked dazed.

"You best be getting along," Smithy said, waving his musket. "The Duke and Duchess of Westbrook be needing their privacy."

The earl gave Smithy a stony look. "You presume much to give me orders, Smithy. And you may rest assured that I intend to bring criminal charges against you for your part in this."

"Well now," Smithy said. "I'm thinking you won't. I work for His Grace now and a duke beats an earl any time."

The earl gave a bark of laughter. "Am I supposed to feel threatened by that?"

"You should," Damien said as he waved his pistol toward the hallway. "I believe I told you and Edgewater to leave."

"Not without my daughter," the earl said.

"You weren't listening, Blackwood," Damien said. "Kathy is now my wife."

"A claim," the earl replied smoothly, "that is dubious at best—a fact I intend to prove beyond doubt."

"Dubious? Really?" Damien drawled as he leaned his shoulder against the wall, still holding the pistol at the ready.

"It will be easy enough to prove that you abducted her and forced this marriage on her," the earl said.

"Yes," Edgewater agreed. "I'm sure the courts will agree." His gaze skipped to Kathy. "Look at poor Lady Kathleen. She appears quite unhappy for a bride."

Kathy struggled to sit up, leaning her back against the headboard while holding the covers high around her neck. "A bride," she said in a strained whisper, "is rarely happy when her wedding night is so rudely interrupted."

"There you have it," Damien said, surprised that she had managed to find her voice, much less give him an opening to elaborate on the lie they'd begun the day the earl had returned. "And Blackwood, should you entertain further doubts, let me make it clear that my marriage to Kathy has the blessing of her brother, Viscount Channing."

The earl drew in a sharp breath and stiffened, his gaze suddenly wary. "The wishes of her brother are of no consequence."

He was suddenly weary of it all. It was time to fire a cannon and end the confrontation. He knew of one name which might inspire fear in the earl. "This marriage also has the blessing of the Duke of Bassett," he said. "He is quite fond of Kathy and takes a *highly personal* interest in her welfare and happiness." He arched his brow. "In fact, one might say his affection for her is quite . . . *filial.*"

A red flush stained the earl's cheeks and he tugged at his neckcloth as if it were suddenly too tight.

Smithy grinned and pulled Mr. Isdale out of sight farther down the hall.

Kathy shot a frantic look at him and drew her knees up under chin.

Edgewater's puzzled gaze volleyed between the earl and Damien and Kathy.

"Extraordinary, isn't it, how close we have all become?" Damien said, making sure the earl understood that he knew everything about Kathy's true parentage. Making sure that the earl believed he would use it against him if he had to. Of course he never would, but that was his secret. "With the birth of Max's and Jillian's child we now have a bond of blood as well as one of friendship . . . and you might say that my marriage to Kathy makes her an *official* member of Bassett's family."

The earl's face darkened until it was almost purple.

"I see that you understand," Damien said. "Understand this as well: It was your actions that precipitated our runaway marriage. If either of you breathe one word about what has transpired here—if the slightest scandal should be attached to my name or Kathy's—I'll see to it that your names will suffer twofold." He pushed away from the wall. "Now get out before I lose my patience entirely."

"Come along, Edgewater," the earl said as he turned sharply on his heel and strode toward the door.

"But, we can't just leave Lady Kathleen with this—this animal," Edgewater sputtered to his back. "Look at the marks on her face. God knows what else he has done—"

The earl paused and glanced over his shoulder. "He can do anything he pleases to her. She is his wife."

"But he burst into the church and abducted her against her will," Edgewater said frantically. "You heard her protests. There are laws."

"It is consummated," the earl snapped. "It is possible that she already carries Westbrook's heir."

"Entirely possible," Damien agreed.

Edgewater blanched and stumbled backward. "Lady Kathleen, tell me it isn't true."

"It's true," she said dully. "It is . . . consummated. I am his wife."

His head shaking in denial, Anthony Edgewater backed out of the room.

Smithy appeared, gave Edgewater a jaunty nod as he passed him, and began to whistle as he righted the door and set it across the threshold. "The coach will be ready whenever you are," he called from the other side.

Damien set the pistol down and watched Kathy, waiting for her to say something, to do anything. But then what did a counterfeit bride say after she had just entertained her counterfeit father and former suitor from a dingy wedding bed? For that matter what did the counterfeit groom say in such circumstances? Hell, Edgewater was the only one in the whole farce who was exactly who he said he was.

With a shake of his head, Damien picked up her dress and tossed it on the bed. "As soon as you're presentable, we will leave."

Kathy flinched, looked down at herself and shuddered. Without a word she rolled to the opposite side of the mattress, turning her back to him as she sat on the edge and reached behind her for her dress.

Raking his hands through his hair, Damien wondered what in blazes was wrong with her. He'd effectively dispatched Edgewater and the earl. She was safe. She had the protection of his name and his title. She could do what she bloody well pleased. What more could she want? Tender words and pretty declarations to soften what had happened between them? He glared at her straight back and stiff, mechanical movements.

Surely not. It wasn't as if she entertained any romantic notions toward him or anyone else for that matter. It wasn't as if they entertained anything but a passing lust for one another. And Kathy wasn't the romantic sort. All her fond thoughts were centered around *her* money and *her* house and *her* independence.

And why in bloody hell was he standing there worrying about *her* feelings when he was the one who had been well and truly trapped by *her* dilemma? A dilemma created solely by *her* obstinacy.

Wanting nothing so much as to plant his fist in the nearest wall, he snatched up his shirt and jerked it on. What had possessed him to allow things to go so far with the earl beating down the door?

He knew the answer. Kathy had possessed him.

He bunched his jacket over his arm and strode from the room. The sooner they arrived at Westbrook Castle the better. At least there, they could wander about for days without running into one another.

# Chapter 15

❦❦❦

"**N**o! No! No!" Tony wailed, the words he struggled to contain slipping out, sounding pitiful to his own ears and adding humiliation to the indignities he'd suffered at the hands of Westbrook. He had to compose himself, had to do something to reclaim his beloved Kathleen.

He grasped the earl's arm to stop his rapid retreat down the hall.

Blackwood calmly looked down at his hold, then up at his face with a contemptuous glare.

Tony released his grip on the earl's arm and snapped his gaze to Mr. Isdale. "You, sir, have committed an unpardonable sin by wedding Lady Kathleen to the Duke of Westbrook," he said with as much calm authority as he could muster. "She was promised to me."

"A duke, eh?" The Scotsman's gaze turned stony. "And who might you be?"

"I am Mr. Anthony Edgewater—"

"Mr.," Isdale snorted. "Seems she got a fair trade."

"My Lady Kathleen is not the mercenary sort," Tony said, ignoring yet another blow to his pride. "But she is, alas, just a woman at the mercy of a man who takes what he wants without regard to her wishes." He examined his hands and frowned in distaste at their gritty feel. He really did hate travel-

155

ing. It was such a filthy business. "I, on the other hand, am willing to pay handsomely for what is rightfully mine."

An avaricious gleam crept into Isdale's eyes. "It may be that the lass wasn't willing," he said carefully.

"And you would swear to this in a court of law?" Tony asked.

The Scot shuffled on his feet. "Depends. I'm a busy man—"

"It is over," the earl interrupted. "There is nothing to be done." He pinned Isdale with a hard stare. "Do you understand?"

Isdale licked his lips as his gaze passed from the earl to Tony. "If the girl's father says it's over, I canna argue."

"The earl is distraught," Tony said. "I'll pay—"

"You'll pay nothing," the earl said coldly. "And you, blacksmith, will say nothing."

Isdale's gaze sharpened on the earl. "Well, now that is another matter," he said. "Silence is golden as they say."

For the second time that day, Blackwood's complexion turned an angry, mottled red. "How golden?" he asked with controlled force as he removed a purse from his jacket.

"They say you offered three hundred guineas as reward for your lass. It seems a fair price to save her reputation . . . and your own." Isdale shrugged. "'Twould be a shame if word got out that your girl had slipped away from you . . ." He smiled at Tony. ". . . or that she threw you over with no regret that I could see."

"Enough!" the earl gritted as he tossed the purse to the Scotsman.

Mr. Isdale deftly caught it and without another word, proceeded down the hall and disappeared into the parlor.

"I am leaving, Edgewater," the earl said. "If you

wish to ride back to England in comfort I suggest
you come along now."

Startled out of his thoughts, Tony stared at the
earl's back and then followed hastily behind. He
couldn't even imagine what horrors he might suffer
if he had to take the common post coach back to
London.

Isdale stood at the front door, holding it open as if
he'd been waiting to see them out all along.

Tony waited until the earl was outside, then
leaned close to Isdale. "I will give you a thousand
guineas to say that Lady Kathleen was an unwilling
bride."

"You don't ken, do you, laddie?" he said. "What
God has joined together let no man put asunder."

"Two thousand."

Isdale shook his head and set his jaw. "I don't
mind taking money to be silent, but I'll not lie
against a duke and an earl for a mere mister. The girl
was a wee bit scared but she was standing on her
own two feet when she spoke her vows."

Tony clenched his fists against the urge to drive
them into the Scotsman's face, to force him to
comply with or without a bribe. But as seconds
passed his mind drifted onto a new path and
wrapped around a single word.

*Scared.*

Yes! Kathleen had been coerced into the marriage.
And she had looked so pale and . . . and . . .
cringing as she'd scooted back in the bed. And there
had been a look of horror on her face as she'd
admitted that the marriage had been consummated.

Westbrook had forced her. He'd taken sweet Kathleen and violated her. Tears pressed behind his eyes
as images formed in his mind of Kathleen being
ruthlessly raped. Of her pleading and calling for
help. She might even have been calling for him.

It hadn't been her fault—not her fault at all. She
was as much a victim as he himself was.

If he and the earl had arrived a few moments sooner, they could have saved her. He could still save her.

Yes!

Tony smiled in triumph as he edged past Isdale without comment. The validity of the marriage could be contested. And surely after being brutalized by Westbrook, Lady Kathleen would be quite happy to place herself into his far more tender and adoring care.

Yes!

With his spirits revived, he strode jauntily toward the earl's coach. But his step faltered as he saw the earl's rigid profile through the window, and recalled the exchange between him and Westbrook in that wretched little bedchamber. The earl had been visibly upset in those few moments before he'd recovered himself. Tony had sensed then that something of vital importance was being said, yet he could not fathom what it might be.

He did, however, understand quite clearly that the earl had no interest in rescuing Kathleen. That, in fact, the earl appeared to want as much distance as possible between himself and his daughter . . . and her reprehensible husband.

Husband. Hah! Not for long, Tony vowed. He didn't need the earl. He had the marriage contracts for evidence and his wealth for any inducements he might have to offer. He would reclaim his beloved and take her to the country. Yes! The country would be perfect. She could hide away from the world that had treated her so harshly. He would see to it that nothing touched her except himself, that she never suffered more than the full magnitude of his love for her, that she never knew another harsh emotion. Of course he wouldn't touch her right away. Not for a few months at least until she was free of Westbrook's taint on her. In the meantime, she would languish in luxury, be purified by his forgiveness—

A larger, mud-bespattered coach drove up in front

of the cottage. Tony scrambled out of the way but not soon enough to avoid the cloud of dust that rolled over him. He stood paralyzed as the grit and grime settled on his clothes, his shoes, in his hair. He could taste it, feel it permeating his very flesh. He raised his gaze to the driver. Smithy. It was Smithy and the insignia obscured by dried mud on the door was surely the Westbrook coat of arms.

Nausea rose in his throat and it was all he could do not to shed his befouled clothing right there. His knees trembled and his legs felt like liquid as he proceeded to the earl's coach, reciting over and over again that his Kathleen had endured worse, that he could endure this, that it wasn't all that far to a decent inn where he could bathe.

Smithy jumped down from the driver's box and loudly cleared his throat. Spittle landed on the ground beside Tony's once glossy shoe. It was more than he could bear, more than he would countenance. Damien Forbes had ripped his darling Kathleen from his arms and Damien Forbes had stripped Tony of his dignity. Even now he strove, through his coarse servant, to sully Tony's world and make it uninhabitable.

He would endure for Kathleen and the future they would share.

# Chapter 16

*T**he marriage had been consummated. There might be a child.*

The earl had said so. And Damien had agreed with such firm conviction that Kathy believed him.

Now, she would never be free.

For three days, the thoughts followed Kathy as tenaciously as the cloud of dust that billowed behind the coach since they'd left Scotland behind and rumbled across England toward Damien's castle. She hadn't been able to sleep at the inns they'd stopped at for the nightmares that visited her. She'd barely been able to choke down food for the lump of misery that had settled in her stomach and clenched with every thought of being forever trapped in marriage to Damien. She could find no ease even when the coach didn't jar over ruts and rocks for the tension Damien created with his cold and constant silence. She could barely breathe for Damien's closeness in the coach, could barely move for fear of brushing her knee or her foot against his and perhaps experience again the sensations that stirred and warmed her with every glance at him, with every memory of what had happened between them in Gretna Green.

She'd learned quickly after they'd left Mr. Isdale's cottage to be afraid to look at Damien much less touch him.

Now that she knew that clothing only concealed his true beauty, she could not view him in the same light again—as a friend of the family, and a nuisance to be borne with as much grace as possible. Now she could see beneath the surface of elegant nobleman to the man himself. A man of plated muscles and heated flesh. A man who had seduced her away from herself, and her visions of freedom.

No, not seduced. He'd made love to her, overwhelming her with sensations, drowning her in urgency like a flash flood during a hard rain. Hard. Damien had been so hard—his mouth on hers, his bare chest pressing against her breasts, his hips wedged between her legs and moving so insistently against her, sweeping away her resistance.

Mama had told her that making love was as close as a man and a woman could physically come to being one.

Kathy couldn't imagine being any closer to Damien than she'd been in the bed at Mr. Isdale's cottage. She couldn't conceive of anything being more physical than Damien taking advantage of a response she hadn't wanted to give, exerting a mastery over her that still quickened the blood in her veins whenever she thought of it.

Kathy tensed her muscles, refusing to give in to that swift thrill of pleasure that shivered through her as she sat in the corner of the coach, her body perfectly straight, her knees and ankles together, her hands folded in her lap. And as it always did, panic followed on the heels of that momentary pleasure, squeezing every feeling from her but anger and despair.

How could she have allowed it to happen . . . without a single coherent thought, without more than the briefest of struggles? How could she have allowed Damien to take advantage of her fear of the earl and bully her into his mad scheme?

And now because of Damien's manipulations and

her own weakness, she might be with child. Trapped in marriage to the most arrogant man on earth with no hope of annulment. Doomed to live according to his dictates, his wishes . . . his arrogance. The tears that had been so close to the surface for the past three days rose higher, threatening to blind and choke her. She dug her nails into her palms to still the trembling of her hands.

Oh why had she allowed him to make love to her?

Mama had told her about conception, presenting it as if a child resulted only if the two people involved loved one another deeply. But Kathy wasn't stupid. She knew that most marriages in the ton were cold-blooded affairs designed to join estates rather than hearts, and to produce heirs rather than nurture children. If love were a requirement for conception, most of the marriages in England would be childless.

Now, she wondered whether Mama had truly been in love with Bassett or merely been ensnared by the force of her own need? As Kathy had been ensnared by the pleasure of Damien's touch. Had she and Bruce been conceived out of passion rather than love?

Need or love—what did it matter? Mama had borne Bassett's children and lived for him rather than for herself. She had never been free.

Just as Kathy would never be free of Damien if there was a child.

Dimly, she heard a rustle of cloth and instinctively shrank back to avoid Damien as he leaned forward to look out of the window of the coach.

Kathy glanced up at him, then slid her gaze away, unable to look at him without wanting to scream in frustration, or stare at him in fascination to see if he had changed as she knew she must have changed. She couldn't define it, other than she was more muddled than she'd ever been in her life. She could not order her thoughts, could not make them go in any direction other than back and forth over old ground.

She had wanted what Damien had done to her.

Yet she hated him for doing it.

She was grateful he'd saved her from the earl's cruelties and Tony's sickening adoration.

Yet she could not forgive him for making her forget her dreams with his touch, for proving to her that she was no stronger than her mother had been.

"Look through the trees," he said softly. "There's a deer."

Startled to hear his voice after three days of silence, she again glanced at him, again jerked her gaze away, following the direction of Damien's extended arm and finger. Those parts of his body seemed safe enough. But then she realized that they weren't. Not when she knew how strongly muscled that arm was, how it joined his broad shoulder attached to an equally broad chest. Not when she recalled the touch of his hand on her so vividly it seemed to be happening all over again.

She had to gain control of herself and the workings of her mind. She had to remember why they were here, why they were together. Damien had told her family that he would look after her, and his skewed sense of honor demanded that he keep his word. He had made it quite clear that he would do so with as little inconvenience to himself as possible.

She was here because she didn't know what else to do.

"Do you see it?" he asked.

See what? she wondered, trying to recall what he had said and why it should matter. A deer. Yes, he'd said there was a deer. She narrowed her eyes, forcing herself to concentrate on the landscape sweeping past her window, needing to see something—anything—but the confusion that riddled her mind. She blinked and tried to focus but it was all a blur of green woodland and blue sky. The deer, she reminded herself. He wanted her to look at a deer. She couldn't see one, but nodded anyway.

"We're on Westbrook land now," he said, and it sounded like a deep purr of contentment. "The castle isn't far."

How pleased he sounded. After days of grim silence he deigned to speak to her now of his deer and his castle.

She hated castles. They were all great, ugly piles of stones. She imagined Damien's castle was black and forbidding and cold and so massive that she would have to be constantly on her guard. One wrong turn and she could become lost forever. Just as she'd become lost in Damien's logic as to the convenience of their marriage.

Just as she'd become lost in his lovemaking.

Mama had told her that to make love was to lose yourself to the moment. Kathy should have realized that one moment was enough time in which to lose a future.

"I'm looking forward to getting out of this coach," Damien said. "I imagine you're feeling the same way."

Yes, she was, but she kept her reply firmly behind her teeth as she continued to stare out the window, uninterested in his attempts at conversation. She didn't want him to be congenial or nice. It wasn't as if he was actually concerned about her comfort or her feelings.

Her chest tightened. She felt so alone.

"We'll be home in few hours," he continued in a conversational tone.

*Home.* She lowered her gaze to her lap to hide her quivering chin. She had no home. She did not belong at Westbrook Castle any more than she had belonged at Blackwood Manor. Tears stung the back of her eyes as she wondered if she would ever have a home of her own, a place where she belonged.

"Imagine," Damien said lightly. "We'll be able to change our clothes every day."

A painful lump stuck in her throat as she stared down at the dirty white gown she'd been wearing for five days. Not only did she not have a home, but she didn't have any clothes. Everything she possessed was still at Blackwood and in the earl's hands. With a sudden, agonizing twist of her heart, she thought of the portrait of her mother that hung above the fireplace in the drawing room.

How could she have forgotten the portrait?

"I can't say that I'll be sorry to see you in a different gown."

Her gown? She didn't care about her gown. She just wanted her mother's portrait. The earl would most likely destroy it.

"I doubt the laundress at Westbrook will be able to get the stains out," he said. "It's probably ruined."

Her whole life was ruined and Damien was prattling on about a dress she never wanted to see again. Burning was too good for it and there would still be ashes to remind her of her downfall.

A tear spilled from her lower lid and fell to the back of her hand, then another and another, until they flowed in rivulets down her cheeks. Vaguely she was aware that Damien would notice and she didn't care. Perhaps when he realized she was crying, he'd cease his inane chattering and leave her alone.

He chuckled. "I believe if you were forced to wear that gown one more day, you wouldn't need to hang it up at night. It's so stiff with dirt, you could stand it in the corner."

She gasped as his amusement penetrated the haze of misery surrounding her. How could he be so insensitive? Had it not occurred to him that she was wearing the only clothing she possessed?

Had it escaped his attention that in the space of a week, she'd lost everything?

Had it not even crossed his mind that she might be with child?

Her spine stiffened with a jolt of panic.

*Oh wonderful.* Now she was back to that. Sniffling, she dashed her tears away with the back of her hand and glared out the coach window. She drew in a deep, shuddering breath. She could not weep her way through these next few months and she certainly couldn't weep her way through the rest of her life.

She lifted her chin. No matter what the future held, she would survive. No matter what, she would find a way to have her dreams. She would have the freedom she longed for.

She was not her mother!

She lifted her chin another notch and squared her shoulders.

"Good girl," Damien said softly. "Buck up."

Buck up? *Buck up?* she thought hotly as she realized that he'd been tormenting her on purpose, taunting her into gaining control of herself. She should have known. She'd seen him tease Jillian out of the doldrums or a fit of pique. For that matter, Bruce was quite adroit at teasing and tormenting himself. It was the way of older brothers, he had once told her, to save their sisters from drowning in self-pity over a lost ribbon or a crushed hat.

But Damien was not her brother. And she had lost . . . everything.

Still, her tears had vanished and anger was an excellent source of energy. Energy to endure whatever awaited her in his great ugly pile of stones. Oddly she did feel better. Warmth curled inside her, thawing her mood. Once again Damien had rescued her by goading her into becoming herself again, just as he had outside the chapel at Blackwood and in the coach at Carlisle, and in so many other ways she was beginning to lose count. Memories of each incident flickered through her mind like flames licking at a log.

"It is good to see you smile again," Damien said with satisfaction.

She frowned and stared at her folded hands. Had she been smiling? Why was she smiling? She was furious at Damien's neat-handed manipulation of her.

He gave an exasperated sigh. "I grow weary of addressing the side of your face or the top of your head. You could at least do me the courtesy of looking at me."

She studied a stain on her skirt. She couldn't look at him. She was too close to losing her hold on her emotions.

"Now that I think about it," he persisted, "you haven't met my gaze since we left Scotland. Is it because I kissed you?"

Her face flamed. *Kissed her?* He knew as well as she that they'd gone far beyond kissing. He'd tasted her. She'd tasted him. They'd shared a bed. They'd made love.

She lifted her gaze from her lap and again stared out the window.

"Ah," he said, in a knowing tone. "It *is* the kiss that has you so upset. So sorry. There really wasn't any other way to convince the earl it was too late to retrieve you."

He didn't sound sorry at all. And she wasn't a parcel to be retrieved. The slender thread of her control snapped. She jerked her gaze to his so hard pain shot up her neck and into her head. "A kiss? A kiss is simply a pressing together of lips or a peck on the cheek or forehead. You made love to me!" She grimaced at the term she loathed; there must be another way to refer to what they'd done. "I could be with child. You said so yourself."

The color drained from his face.

Oh, so now it occurred to him. Now, his amusement gave way to shock and perhaps fear. She hoped so. She wanted him to feel the same fear and anxiety that had gnawed at her every minute since they'd left Gretna Green. "What if we can't get this marriage annulled." Her voice fractured and gave way to a strangled sob. Tears overflowed again, harder and faster than before. She buried her face in her lap, hating herself for breaking down, hating Damien for being there to see it.

"Kathy look at me," he said with a sigh.

She shook her head and buried her face deeper into her skirt, trying desperately to muffle her sobs.

"Look at me," he demanded.

"No."

She heard him move on his seat and his knees bumped into hers. He pried her hands away from her face and cupped her chin, forcing her with gentle strength to raise her head.

She sobbed and closed her eyes, unable to look at him, unable to bear the touch of his hands on her. Hands that had transformed her into a woman without dignity or shame.

His fingers threaded through the hair at her temple and sifted through the strands, stroking and caressing, calming her in spite of herself. "Look at me."

"I can't," she croaked. Didn't he understand? Why didn't he understand?

She felt his lips on her forehead, a touch of butterfly wings. "Look at me, Kathy." A wave of heat rippled through her.

He placed a kiss high on her cheek, and then another along her jaw.

Air seemed to elude her lungs and roar in her ears instead.

"Open your eyes, or the next one will be on your lips," he threatened hoarsely.

Her eyes flew open and her gaze collided with his, a sea of green, pulling her down into that place where a now familiar need waited to drown her. How did he do that to her? Why did she allow it?

"There is no child," he said, his breath warm on her face.

She blinked. Her heart stalled. She tried to pull away from him, suspicion overcoming sudden hope. But he moved with her, framing her face with his hands. "How can you possibly know there is no child when I don't?" she asked.

"Because I *didn't* make love to you," he said.

She batted his hands away from her face. Just how far would he go for the sake of "convenience"? she wondered. How could he be so cruel as to make her consider, even for a moment, that his absurd statement might be true? "You're lying to me."

"No, I'm not," he said simply.

"I understand about making love," she stated as she scooted back against the squabs.

Damien leaned back and propped his chin on a closed fist. "Really?"

"Yes, I do," she said, indignant at his condescending tone. "We shared a bed and we were as close as two human beings can be."

"No, we weren't," he said, his heavy-lidded gaze studying her. "We can get closer. Much, much closer."

A bolt of excitement shot down her spine and exploded like a crack of lightning low in the pit of her belly. "Impossible," she said weakly. "You're making it up."

He gave her a lazy smile.

"I'm so pleased that you find this amusing," she snapped. "But I do not and I assure you that if I am with child, I'll make your life miserable."

"More miserable than usual?" He rolled his eyes and chuckled. "Do let me know."

"You can be certain that I will," she grated and sat on her hands. She had never wanted to slap anyone so much in her life.

Yet, doubt niggled at her. Could he be right? Did he know something she didn't? She gripped the edges of the upholstery and swallowed the last of her pride. She had to know what he meant. She had to know whether to give in to anger or to hope. Most importantly, she needed to know whether he was lying to her.

Damien was overbearing and hateful and hot-tempered, but she had never known him to be a liar.

"How will I know if I have conceived?" she asked haughtily, refusing to wince as humiliation took a sharp bite out of her.

Damien dissolved into laughter.

Kathy dissolved into fury, helpless against the onslaught of emotions confined for too long. How could he find amusement in such disastrous circumstances? How could she have believed him, even for a moment? She lurched forward and reached for his face, determined to claw that damned smug smile from his loathsome mouth.

In one smooth movement, he caught her wrists and yanked her across his lap, pinioned her arms to her side, and scissored her legs between his. His chest still shook with laughter.

She struggled against him, twisting her body and tossing her head. But he held her fast and pressed her cheek to his shoulder while his other arm held her firmly around the waist, his legs like steel rope around hers. Yet still she pushed at his chest and bowed her head, resisting him as her breath came in heaving pants and her mind darted in a dozen directions at once, heaping misery upon misery into a great pile of confusion.

He had taken over her life, marrying her when she hadn't wanted any such thing. He'd ignored her for three days. He managed to look well groomed while she wore a tattered gown that had refused to come clean despite her best efforts. He ate and drank heartily while she could barely choke down a morsel or two and no doubt he slept soundly while she tossed restlessly and battled a pervasive sense of dread. He might have gotten her pregnant.

He had lied to her and now he laughed at her as she fought him.

He had forced her to abandon her mother's portrait.

She couldn't stop fighting him.

His arms closed around her like shackles. "Enough of your hysterics," he snapped.

*Hysterics?* Strength deserted her. Frustration and anger fled. It was true. She was hysterical. She shuddered and gulped in air and her head fell onto his shoulder as she wept for all her dreams that would never come true, and for the freedom that would never be hers.

Wept, too, for the loss of the hero she'd thought Damien to be in spite of his shortcomings.

She hated him even as she clung to his jacket and trusted him with her tears.

"Kathy? Can you hear me?" he asked.

"Of course, I can hear you," she sobbed, wishing that she was someone else, somewhere else, with anyone else but Damien.

"It is impossible for you to be pregnant. I give you my word of honor."

*His word of honor.* He always kept his word. It was his one redeeming quality.

"Kathy, are you listening? We did not make love. Not completely. You cannot possibly be with child."

Not completely? Not possibly? She gulped back a sob and peered up at him, seeing the intensity of his solemn expression. Suddenly, she knew he was telling her the absolute truth. Suddenly, she realized that there had to be more than what they had done, though she couldn't imagine what. Suddenly, she recalled what she had banished from her mind for three, long, horrible days. She recalled the sense of disappointment she'd felt when Damien had released her and left her on the bed alone, still craving his touch, still in the grip of whatever power he'd had over her. And every time thoughts of what they'd done on that bed returned to plague her, she'd wanted it to happen again except that she'd wanted it to be more . . . *complete.*

He *was* telling the truth.

Relief caught her in mid-sob and she hiccuped as the carriage hit a bump in the road.

Damien tightened his arms around her even more, keeping her from falling to the floor. "Do you believe me?" he asked gently.

She nodded as all the anxiety and fear of the past week drained out her, leaving her feeling weak and more exhausted than she'd ever been in her life.

"Good, then also believe that I would never do anything that would prevent an annulment of this marriage."

She could not doubt the utter conviction in his voice. She hadn't the energy to wonder why it hurt and saddened her. Her head slipped from his shoulder to his chest and for the first time in days, she felt calm and content. . . .

Shock stiffened her back. Never had Damien inspired peace in her. Not Damien, whose volatile disposition maddened her. She angled her head back to stare up at him and her gaze landed squarely on his mouth. Something splintered inside her and her heartbeat thundered in her ears. His beautiful, wonderful mouth. She ached with longing just to look at it.

She squeezed her eyes shut as she realized she was very close to lifting her lips to his. It was happening again. He was seducing her, trapping her, with nothing more than his presence. She couldn't allow it. She had to be strong, had to fight herself as well as Damien. She would not become enslaved to . . . what? A craving? Yes, a simple, mindless craving.

The carriage rounded a bend in the road and she leaned more heavily into Damien. Again, contentment began to unfold inside of her, a welcome peace that held her close to him as surely as the strength of his arms.

She could stay here forever.

She renewed her efforts to break free of him.

He released her and set her on her seat, placing her in the corner as if he knew she wanted to hide from him.

He sprawled back in his own seat and laced his

hands on his flat belly. "And by the way," he said, "if you ever find yourself in a position where you might wonder if you've conceived a child, one of the first signs is missing your monthly course."

"Oh," she murmured, too weary and peaceful to be embarrassed by his bland mention of the subject, and her ignorance of such a fact. Nothing was important anymore. Nothing but the certainty that they hadn't made love.

Mama had told her that making love was beautiful. She should have remembered that sooner.

What had happened between herself and Damien had been exciting, urgent, intoxicating. But beautiful? Beautiful was a soft watercolor or a bed of flowers. Beautiful inspired a gentle pleasure rather than a dangerous one.

Yet what they had done had convinced the earl as well as herself that the marriage had been consummated. Could there be more to making love than beauty?

She didn't think she wanted to know.

She yawned and her eyelids grew heavy. It seemed like forever since she had really slept. Closing her eyes, she drew her legs up on the seat, nestled more snugly into her corner, and wondered what else Mama hadn't told her.

# Chapter 17

**N**othing had gone as he'd planned. But then when did anything involving Kathy go as planned?

With his chin propped on his fist, Damien stared at Kathy as she slept restlessly on the opposite seat, her feet tucked up under her skirts and her hand flattened under her cheek. Every now and again she murmured something incoherent like a child praying away demons in her sleep. The combination of innocence and cynicism that was so much a part of Kathy boggled his mind. *She* boggled his mind.

She'd actually believed they'd made love, and worked herself into a frenzy of fear over the possible consequences.

"Amazing," Damien muttered as he stretched his legs out at an angle and crossed his ankles. He'd known since leaving Scotland that their encounter in the bed at Gretna Green had left her in a state of shock. He'd assumed that she was furious with him for taking advantage of the situation, and furious with herself for participating so enthusiastically. Her response to him had convinced him that her mother had indeed told her of such intimacies.

How could he have known that she was completely ignorant or that she would react so violently to his deliberate goading? But he couldn't tolerate her silence and her obvious misery another moment.

Given her scathing looks, he'd anticipated a good tongue lashing, but not that she would pounce on him in a fury.

He shouldn't have provoked her. If he'd left her to mope, perhaps she wouldn't have attacked him and she wouldn't have wound up in his arms again, reminding him of all that he hadn't done to her in that bed. Of all that he wanted to do to her over and over again.

Having Kathy in his arms was dangerous regardless of how she got there.

But he hadn't thought of that when he'd set out to make her angry enough to face him and talk to him again, and in the end, return their relationship to its earlier status of open dislike. Once that was done, they would have been able to discuss how they would go on with one another until her brothers returned to sort things out.

It might have worked if she hadn't been so stubborn, and if he hadn't laughed at her haughty but earnest question of how she would know if she was with child. That question had cost her much in pride and even as he'd laughed, he'd felt badly about indulging in such cavalier amusement.

Why couldn't he have had the sense to let her pummel away at him rather than using kisses, of all things, to force her to look at him and listen to his explanation that there was no possibility of a child? All that had done was spawn an overwhelming urge to correct her misconceptions with a physical demonstration. In that moment the prospect of a child between them had held a certain appeal—

Kathy's body jerked suddenly, startling him from his thoughts. "Hide," she mumbled. "Never find."

Damien raised a brow. This wasn't the first time she had talked in her sleep, but normally he could make no sense of her babble. This time, the words were clear and urgent and he thought she must be dreaming of the night she'd hidden from Edgewater in Max's study.

How different things would be now if he had told Max and Bruce about that incident. But he hadn't thought it necessary at the time, and it was too late to indulge in hindsight now.

Kathy stirred and shook her head. "Must hide. China cabinet," she said even more clearly.

For some reason it irritated Damien to know that she still had nightmares about Edgewater. "Desk," he corrected softly. If she was going to dream about her first near catastrophe with Edgewater, she might as well get it right.

"China cabinet," she said firmly.

The urge to laugh displaced his annoyance, but he swallowed it down. "If you insist," he murmured. She even disagreed with him in her sleep.

Kathy's contrary nature aside, the next few months were going to be difficult. He had to keep the marriage as quiet as possible; the fewer people who knew about it, the fewer complications there would be in getting an annulment. Yet the servants at the castle had to know about it, and servants talked. They would expect him to visit his bride. They could not exist in a constant state of discord, yet friendship was not something he and Kathy had been able to achieve in the two years they had been thrown together at family gatherings and social events. He doubted they ever would.

He'd never disliked a woman so thoroughly in his life, yet it was becoming more difficult to remember why. He'd never worked so hard to avoid a woman until he'd met Kathy, yet now he was desperate to make love to her, a state that confounded and annoyed him.

He rested his head on the back of the seat and stared at the ceiling of the coach, forcing himself to think of anything but Kathy's body, the touch of her hands, the hot urgency of her kisses.

Even the memory was enough to start a fire in his belly.

He cursed under his breath and shifted on the

seat, and then for good measure he cursed Edgewater for setting his sights on Kathy and on the earl for returning to torment them all.

He had to admit a certain satisfaction at having routed Blackwood with a few implied and obliquely phrased threats. Damien hadn't planned to use the truth of the earl's marriage to Kathy's mother and the true parentage of the heirs who carried his name as a weapon, but it had been effective.

He should have realized sooner that the earl would fear being exposed and would not want disgrace to fall upon his name and title. Why else would he have perpetuated the sham of his purchased marriage to the countess and claimed Kathy and Bruce as his own children if not for appearances? Why else would he have gone off to America if not to save himself from disgrace?

Bloody hell! Kathy had been right. There had been a way "to circumvent the earl" as she had so succinctly put it. He had rushed headlong into an unnecessary situation.

Smithy had been right as well. He was too hotheaded. If he'd thought rather than acted, he could have done exactly as old Bassett and his father had done and used his knowledge to blackmail the earl into letting Kathy go. After a few well-placed threats, he could have simply removed her from Blackwood, installed her at the castle, hired a companion, and waited for her brothers to return.

"Giant," Kathy breathed and shuddered.

Damien's gaze narrowed on her. Apparently, the earl's man, Freddie, had just entered her dreams. He frowned as he wondered once again what the earl had done to her besides tear out her hair and lock her in a dark room. Had the earl used Freddie to terrorize her as well?

Suddenly, he didn't want to know. To know would involve him even more in Kathy's life. It would draw him closer to her and prompt a sympathy he did not want to feel for her. To know would obligate him by honor to exact retribution. It was not his place to do so and he would not make it so. He had done all he could for her. The rest was up to Max and Bruce.

He wanted to feel nothing for Kathy but the old, familiar annoyance that kept a solid wall between them.

"Ogre," Kathy cried out. "He's coming."

"Shhh," he whispered. "You're safe. I won't let them ever hurt you again."

"I know," she stated clearly, then mumbled and burrowed deeper into the cushioned seat.

The note of confidence and trust in her voice disturbed him. Even though he would never allow anyone to hurt her, her acknowledgment of trust felt like a millstone around his neck. He straightened and crossed an ankle over the opposite knee. "Wake up," he said roughly.

She started and bolted upright, swiping the hair from her face and pressing herself into the corner, her gaze wide and wary on him.

He hated that, hated the way she had begun to watch him as if she feared him as much as the ogre in her dreams. He was beginning to take it personally, as if her opinion of him mattered. And much as he hated to admit it, her suspicious behavior hurt him in a way he didn't want to examine too closely.

It had to stop. They had to find a way to live together during the next few months that would create as little strain on them as possible.

Kathy could not mope about and burrow into corners. He damn well wouldn't have her hiding from him.

Nor would he allow himself to be provoked into touching her again.

Deliberately ignoring the way she huddled in the corner of her seat, he glanced out the window and felt the first real pleasure he'd known since his family had so neatly maneuvered him into playing nanny to Kathy.

"Look there," he said, forgetting everything but the sight ahead of him. "The turrets of Westbrook Castle."

# Chapter 18

Kathy yanked her gaze away and stared out the window, grateful for something else to look at besides Damien. He'd seemed angry when he'd awakened her, and in the aftermath of the dream that had distressed her sleep she hadn't the energy to face such an emotion. Still she wondered why Damien was cross when all she had done was fall asleep. It seemed to her that she should be the one to be miffed.

How strange that she wasn't angry with him for forcing her into marrying him. But then why should she be? She wasn't with child, and in due time she would be free. Nothing had happened between them, nor would it in the future.

Yet, something had happened. Something turbulent and consuming—

She blinked and focused on the view outside the window. She couldn't think about all that; she was confused enough as it was.

She scanned the woodland and saw nothing. She lifted her gaze to skim the treetops.

Awe swelled and caught in her throat as she stared at turrets rising into the sky like the jeweled points of a majestic crown, their conical roofs glinting sapphire in the afternoon sunlight.

The carriage slowed and rounded a bend and the

land opened up to reveal a sight so beautiful she felt as if she'd stepped into a painting.

Westbrook Castle stood atop a hill, a graceful queen overlooking her domain rather than the grim tyrant she'd envisioned. It was not the largest castle she'd ever seen, nor was it the smallest, though it was the most beautiful with its robe of pale gold sandstone, its rounded towers studded with sparkling mullioned windows, and the train of white and yellow daisies that covered the hillside and rippled like embroidered velvet in the breeze.

Westbrook Castle, as overwhelming as the master it served . . . and as breathtaking. "It's like something out of a fairy tale," she whispered.

"I'm beginning to believe you're quite fanciful— what with giants and ogres chasing you in your dreams," Damien said with an odd note in his voice.

"Pardon me?" she said, her voice unsteady.

"You talk in your sleep."

Alarm spiked through her at the memory of the earl chasing her through her sleep and Damien's father appearing to rescue her, then changing into Damien as he reassured her that he wouldn't allow anyone to hurt her again.

"I take it you were dreaming that you were a damsel in distress?" There was a hard edge to his tone, as if he were taking the concept personally.

"I don't remember," she said, feeling vulnerable and peeled back to the soul. She'd never spoken of her dreams with anyone. To share them would be to share the nightmare of her childhood. To share them with Damien would be to expose herself to him, to expose the part he'd always played in her dreams.

The carriage rolled to a stop. She had to tighten every muscle to keep from vaulting out of her seat, to escape Damien and the answers he seemed to be waiting for.

A grinning Smithy pulled open the door. "I would've never thought it, Your Grace. It looks like something out of a fairy tale," he said as he let down the steps.

"That's precisely what your mistress said," Damien replied as he climbed out of the coach and held out his hand to her. "Do you feel like a princess?"

"Yes," she said in mock sweetness as she reluctantly took his hand and stepped down on shaking legs. She couldn't look at him, couldn't look even at Smithy. "One about to be sent to the dungeons."

"Now there's a thought," Damien said dryly.

The great double doors of the castle flew open and a butler emerged. "Your Grace," he sputtered. "I hadn't expected you for hours. I haven't assembled the staff to greet the new duchess."

"It's quite all right, Peters," Damien said. "I'm sure the new duchess would like some time to freshen up before meeting the staff."

Shock flickered on the butler's face as he glanced at her, then faded into blandness as he stared at a point above her shoulder.

Acutely aware of her tangled hair and dirty gown, Kathy marched past Damien. "Yes," she said briskly. "I should very much like to be shown to my chambers."

"Yes, of course, Your Grace," the butler said as he caught up with her.

"Princess," Damien called.

She paused but did not turn to face him.

"I should like to see you in the library after you've changed. We've a few things to discuss."

"As you wish," she replied and continued on, her head high and her tattered gown draping sluggishly about her. Damien would be waiting a very long time before she presented herself. He had forgotten she hadn't a gown to change into, not to mention that she hadn't an inkling of where the library might be. A minor point to be sure, but one she intended to use.

She stepped through the doors of the castle into

the great hall, not at all surprised that it was as elegantly whimsical as the exterior of the castle. Tapestries featuring mythical beings covered the walls and ancient suits of armor gleamed brightly in the corners. Beams of sunlight slanted through high stained glass windows and splashed on the marble floors with an ethereal shimmer of color.

She followed the butler without comment, refusing to be enchanted.

Naturally, the castle had a charming curved staircase and a maze of long, winding corridors. It was as she had suspected earlier; one wrong turn and she'd be lost forever.

The butler halted before gleaming walnut doors. "Your chamber, Your Grace. The duke's rooms are through the next set of double doors."

Kathy glanced down the corridor, noting the long distance between the doors of her chamber and his. Apparently they didn't connect from the inside. Good. She didn't want him to have the freedom to waltz into her room whenever he wished.

*Freedom.* The word lay like an invalid in her mind.

The butler pushed open the doors.

Rather than the bedchamber she'd expected, Kathy stepped into a small formal drawing room, furnished with chairs and a settee, some upholstered in deep rose damask and others in ivory and wine striped silk. The same silk covered the walls above polished walnut wainscoting and the ceiling was slightly domed and bordered by bas relief carving.

"If there will be nothing else, Your Grace," Peters said.

"Hmm," she murmured, too steeped in reverence for the magnificence around her to respond properly. She jumped as the door clicked shut.

She whirled about and yanked open the door. "Wait," she cried, looking one way and then the other down the hall.

The butler halted and turned sharply on his heel in well-practiced respect. "May I be of service, Your Grace?"

"Yes," Kathy said. "Are you certain you've delivered me to the right place?"

The butler drew himself up straight. "Yes, Your Grace. Are the chambers not to your liking?"

"No, they're fine," she said weakly, realizing the man had said "chambers" in the plural. Of course a castle such as this would house its master—and mistress—in apartments rather than a mere suite. "That will be all." With her face flaming, she retreated. One would think she'd never been in a grand house in her life, much less grown up in one. Still, there was a vast difference between a castle and a manor.

She walked deeper into the room and studied the closed door on her right and the two others to her left. She pushed open the one on her left and peered into a bathing room fitted with a marble tub. Inside, she skimmed her hand over the surfaces of marble walls and leaned over to inspect the painted and gilded flowers on the most magnificent chamberpot she'd ever seen. Another door was set into the far wall.

She pushed it open to find a dressing room almost as large as her bedroom at Blackwood. A teak chest occupied one wall. A large, framed looking glass that appeared to be of Italian design was hung on another. Watercolor landscapes filled a third, framing a large window draped in ivory lace and rose silk.

She approached a dressing table to look more closely at the perfume bottles lined up in neat rows beside a silver tray holding brushes and combs.

*Her* perfume bottles. *Her* brushes and combs. *Her* dressing table.

Heart pounding, she ran to yet another door across the room and peeked inside.

It was a closet lined with racks of gowns above shelves of shoes.

She darted around, touching silken frocks and woolen spencers, opening drawers to find chemises and petticoats and nightdresses and stockings, ribbons and hankies. In a concealed nook, she found her own jewels as well as those left to her by her mother.

*Her* gowns. *Her* shoes. *Her* things . . . all of them. *Damien had done this.*

A familiar warmth uncurled inside her, of comfort and pleasure and safety. How had he managed it? When had he managed it? Why would he go to such trouble?

She glanced down at her dirty dress, wanting to focus on anything but Damien's consideration, Daamien's kindness. She had to keep her distance from him, even in her thoughts.

The fabric was gritty and sticky with grime. The hem was ripped in the side and almost black from trailing in the dirt of half a dozen innyards. Damien was right; it was beyond saving.

Damien again. The warmth inside her boiled into fury. Damn him! It didn't matter how he had managed to bring all her belongings to Westbrook. Didn't he always manage everything, including her? He could have told her. She stalked back to the sitting room toward yet another closed door and yanked it open. What else had he not told her?

She was in the center of the room before she realized it was a bedchamber. Blankly, she studied a paneled wall, the wood gleaming deep and rich like candy in a confectioner's shop. The other three walls were covered in pale pink silk that matched the counterpane on the high tester bed as well as the hangings on the windows. Even the thick carpet beneath her feet was pale pink.

She felt as if she were standing in room made of spun sugar and chocolate. A room that was decidedly female and from the look of it, newly refurbished. Suddenly, she wondered if Damien had been entertaining the idea of marriage and had prepared this chamber for another bride. The thought disturbed her.

Out of the corner of her eye, she noticed that another door stood ajar at the far end of the room. She wandered toward it and found a second sitting room, but this one was small and private, the only entrance through the bedchamber. Flanking a large bay window were two overstuffed chairs upholstered in pink and gold stripes with matching hassocks. Against one wall stood a desk and behind it were recessed shelves filled with books.

*Her* books.

Her chest tightened. How could this seem so familiar and so foreign all at the same time? Vaguely she remembered how Jillian had once told her about how she had moved herself into Max's home and his life in much the same way. At the time, Kathy had thought the story charming.

Now, she wondered if Max had felt as confused and helpless and angry as she did now. Damien had simply moved her things into his castle as abruptly as he'd stormed into the church and whisked her away to Scotland.

She'd had no more time to prepare for this than she'd had to marry him.

The dull thud of a door closing echoed softly through the air.

Kathy spun around and froze as her gaze landed on the fireplace . . . on the painting hung above the mantel.

On the portrait of her mother.

She couldn't move, couldn't take her eyes from the painting. Emotion clogged her throat. She had believed it lost to her forever. But how and who? The servants at Blackwood would never do such a thing. They were too frightened of the earl.

"My lady!" a familiar voice cried out.

Kathy jerked her head around to see Frances, her maid, standing in the doorway with a wide smile lighting her face. She had never thought to see

Frances again after the maid had dressed her for her aborted wedding.

"Frances, how did you get here?" Even as she spoke she realized it was Frances who had brought her treasures from Blackwood.

The maid stared at her feet. "I came with the footmen the duke sent to Blackwood to collect your things."

Dimly Kathy remembered the three men who had taken their horses after their escape from Blackwood. How thoroughly Damien had planned. How completely he taken control of the situation and of her.

"I tried to bring everything that meant something to you," Frances said.

"Yes, you did a fine job," Kathy said, appalled at the resentment she felt. How could she feel this way when everything she valued was here? "Thank you."

Frances ventured closer, her expression solemn. "I'm sorry I couldn't help none before that, but that father of yours threatened to string us all up if we so much as spoke to you. When the duke's men came, I knew I had to help. The rest of the staff just stood around watching, the blooming cowards."

Kathy's resentment slipped away, nudged out by admiration for the Damien who not only kept his word but embellished it with broad gestures of caring. Admiration and something else. Something like tenderness.

Impossible, she told herself. He didn't deserve it. Everything he'd done was to serve his purpose and his honor, not to please her. And certainly not because he cared.

Frances clasped her arms beneath her breasts. "I never saw anything so romantic in my life as when the duke and Mr. Smithy stormed the church and rescued you. I'm so happy for you, my lady—I mean Your Grace." She raised her hands to her face. "Oh my, you're a duchess now."

Kathy turned away to stare at the portrait. She was

no more a duchess than she was a Palmerston. The title was borrowed just as her surname was borrowed. Neither she nor her possessions belonged here any more than they'd belonged at Blackwood.

She was tired of living her life as a fraud.

"Are you feeling all right, Your Grace?" Frances asked. "Your face has gone all red."

"I'm fine," Kathy replied briskly as she shook off her self-pity. "I suppose I'm a bit overwhelmed."

Frances clicked her tongue. "I should say so. You've had quite the week. What you need is a nice hot bath and then right to bed with you."

Kathy couldn't agree more, but Damien had commanded her to come to the library as soon as she'd made herself presentable. He could wait, she thought numbly. She was in no mood to see him, not until she sorted through the confusion muddling her thoughts.

On the one hand, she was grateful to him for having her possessions and Frances removed from Blackwood. On the other hand, she cursed him for so arrogantly claiming control of her life right down to her hairbrushes and ribbons.

It was churlish to be angry with him after all he had done.

Yet, the price had been her freedom.

She took a deep breath and reminded herself that she would only be here for a short while. Only until she reached her majority. Then she would be free to live as she wished, in her own home, as her own mistress.

Damien would be out of her life once and for all.

Oddly enough, the thought brought sadness rather than comfort.

# Chapter 19

*. . . The Earl of Blackwood has returned. He attempted to take control of Kathy's inheritance by forcing her into marriage with Tony Edgewater. I saw no other course of action but to marry her myself. Advise you return at once.*

*Damien*

**D**amien tossed down his quill after signing his name with hard slashes. He hadn't bothered with adding formal closings and titles. Bruce and Max knew who he was and the message he'd written to each of them was clear enough. He'd spent hours writing and rewriting, searching for a diplomatic way to inform Kathy's brothers that he'd temporarily married her. Finding none, he'd settled on discreet bluntness. It would not be a good idea to commit his plans for an annulment to writing.

He shook sand over the parchment and sealed it. In the next few days he would have to go to London and arrange for a trustworthy agent to deliver the letters to Bruce and Max. By his estimation, it would take approximately two months for his messengers to find Max and Bruce and another two months for them to return, depending on weather. They would have just arrived at their destinations when his news reached them.

It served them right.

He glanced at the clock on the mantle. It was past noon and Kathy had been in her rooms approximately twenty-four hours, blatantly ignoring his instructions to come to the library yesterday afternoon.

He would have been disappointed had she done otherwise, especially after he'd goaded her about her appearance and called her a princess, perversely reinforcing her opinion that he was an insensitive bounder. He'd known that she'd expected to be left without clothing and possessions and had deliberately refrained from telling her otherwise. He had hoped that finding all her own things in her chambers would have been a nice surprise for her after such a grueling journey.

She could have thanked him for a change.

It had been bloody difficult setting so many plans into motion in the space of one day.

Obviously a wasted effort if she was going to hibernate in her quarters. He couldn't very well return their relationship to its previous footing of an armed truce if she wouldn't come out of her rooms.

He was vastly uncomfortable knowing she was in the chambers next to his, unseen, but nevertheless a presence that haunted him. Last night, he'd gone to bed feeling as if a ghost was in the castle.

He slumped back in his chair as reality slammed into him. Kathy, settled into the rooms next to his with all her possessions about her. His responsibility.

His wife.

It had been easy to ignore the consequences of his actions until he'd brought her to Westbrook Castle, his home, his retreat. Here, he'd enjoyed solitude while doing what he enjoyed most, running his estate and dealing with the tenants. Here, he was absolute master of his own life.

And now, the castle had a mistress, no matter how

temporary. Whether he liked it or not, he had someone else to think about.

He had a wife. A woman who was everything he didn't want in a wife. Once, he'd told Jillian he would choose a woman who was kind and gentle, honest and courageous. Beauty would be an added prize rather than a necessity.

Yet, with the exception of being beautiful, Kathy was woefully lacking in the other qualities. She reserved her kindness and gentleness for those she loved. She resorted to honesty when it suited her. And as far as courage went, he hadn't a clue. She had displayed no such strength at Blackwood. But then, he admitted, it was hardly fair to judge her based on the situation in which Edgewater and the earl had forced her.

It didn't matter. Nothing did except getting through the next few months. He would have to exert strict control over himself or Kathy Palmerston Forbes would remain Kathy Palmerston Forbes, Duchess of Westbrook. Much to his dismay, he had learned that dislike did not discourage passion.

Damien ran his hand over his face. He'd procrastinated long enough. Matters between them had to be settled. He rose and strode from his private study, crossed his bedchamber and stood before the connecting door, his hand poised to knock.

He lowered his arm and frowned.

Entering through her bedchamber seemed far too intimate, and far too dangerous. If he couldn't trust himself with her in a dingy room with half the world pounding on the door, how could he confront her with a bed standing like temptation itself in the room? For that matter how was he to find any peace at all with Kathy occupying the apartment adjoining his?

He should have specified that she be housed in a separate wing of the castle, preferably in a tower where she could hide to her heart's content.

He turned on his heel and wound his way through his chambers to his sitting room and stepped into the hall. Reaching the formal entrance to Kathy's chambers, he rapped impatiently on the door.

Nothing.

He counted to ten and knocked again.

"Yes," she called.

"I require a word with you," he said, hearing a strained edge to his voice.

He counted to twenty.

"Perhaps tomorrow."

"Today," he snapped.

The key turned in the lock; the door remained shut.

His pulse pounded in his temple. No one locked him out of a room in his castle.

He returned to the door connecting their bed-chambers. There was no lock on that door. Apparently some long-ago ancestor had decided he'd never be denied entrance to his wife's bedchamber. Damien had never appreciated that until now.

He pushed the door open and stepped inside, studiously avoiding looking at the bed. Stealthily, he made his way toward the private sitting room, instinctively knowing she'd prefer its intimacy to the larger salon designed to receive guests.

Kathy sat curled up in a chair, her gaze fastened on something within the room, oblivious to his presence.

His footsteps dragged to halt and his breath snagged in his throat. Yesterday, he'd mockingly called her a princess. Today, she looked like one.

The dirty and tattered gown she'd arrived in was gone, replaced by an ice-blue morning dress that fell in graceful folds to the floor. Her hair was caught in a loose bun with wildly curling tendrils framing her face. He'd almost forgotten how vibrantly red her hair was and how it contrasted with her fair and finely textured skin. He had forgotten how distant her expression could become or how cool and unapproachable she could appear, like now—an ice princess, sequestered by choice in an ivory tower.

Well, he'd be damned if she'd hide from him before he'd had his say. After that she could bloody well live in a mouse hole if she wished.

She turned her head and the sun streaming through the window behind her seemed to ignite her hair into flame.

*Ice princess indeed,* he thought sourly. He knew there was fire in her, was intimately acquainted with it. He felt it now, rushing through his veins, gathering and sizzling in the pit of his belly.

Perhaps she should hide herself away.

They'd both be better off.

He was tempted to leave her in her ivory tower and let her fend for herself as best she could. Tempted to retreat to the farthest corner of the castle to nurse his anger until it became strong enough to quench his desire for her.

But his sense of responsibility wouldn't allow it. He had to know she *could* fend for herself before he left her to it. She had yet to be introduced to the staff. She needed to learn her way about the castle and grounds. He needed to make sure she understood that nothing in their lives had changed.

Maybe then he would understand it as well.

He strode into her line of vision. "Enough, Kathy," he said, not bothering to control the annoyance in his voice. "We have to live together for the next four or five months. During that time I expect you to treat me with a modicum of respect."

She started, glanced at him, averted her gaze, and offered no reply.

A muscle began to tick in his jaw. "You will look at me when I address you."

Her hands clenched in her lap as she bowed her head, refusing to look at him as if he were an insect not worthy of being slapped away.

He stepped closer. "I can force you to meet my gaze," he said in a deliberately low voice. "Shall I take you into my arms and kiss you?" Just then he wanted her to ignore him, to give him a reason to do just that.

He burned with the need to touch her.

Her head snapped up, her face washed of all color as she stared at him through blue eyes glazed with frost.

His blood cooled. "Thank you," he said, stung that his threat had worked so well. "That pleases me greatly."

"How else might I please you?" she asked tightly.

Desire returned, hotter and brighter than before as he envisioned taking her hair down . . . disrobing her . . . making love to her on the chair . . . on the floor . . . in her bed . . . making her writhe beneath him. . . .

It would be disaster. It would be doom.

He was losing his bloody mind. "Pleasing me is not a requirement during our time together."

"Apparently it is," Kathy spat. "Otherwise you would not bully me into capitulation."

*Bully her?* Of course he bullied her. How else was he to command her attention? Yet he would not say so, would not defend his actions to her or anyone else. "It is also not my responsibility to please you. But there are a few things you should know that may make your stay here less trying."

"Rules," she said, matching his sarcasm as she folded her arms across her chest.

"If you prefer to see them as such," he said evenly. Had there ever been a woman who annoyed him so much? he wondered as anger and desire melted together and sat like an aching lump in his groin. It was an effort to continue speaking with a clipped voice and perfunctory manner. "While I am in residence at the castle I keep no particular hours. I rise early and work late. Some days, I visit tenants; others I spend closeted in my study. If you wish to see me, inform Masters, my secretary."

"I am to make an appointment to see you?"

"No," Damien said as he raked his hand through his hair. "I am merely stating that days may pass without our seeing one another, and Masters might be the only one to know where I am." He would see to it, he added silently.

"Good," she said.

It felt like a punch to his midsection. Still, hostility was preferable to the physical tension that seemed to crackle between them in quieter moments. "All meals are served whenever I wish to eat," he gritted, impatient with Kathy, impatient with himself.

"And am I to schedule my meals around yours?" She was deliberately twisting his words. "Eat whenever you like as many times as you like. Grow fat for all I care," he replied.

Her brows shot up. "I'll try to restrain myself."

She was impossible. Conversation with her was impossible. There had to be another way to make his point. A way that wouldn't require her to speak. "Come," he ordered, "it's time you had a tour of the castle and then a ride into the village."

"I don't wish to see the castle nor do I wish to ride into the village."

"Too bloody bad," he snapped. "You may change into your riding habit now or after we tour the castle. Your choice."

"I am not going."

His hackles raised at her open defiance. Still, he understood that Kathy's refusal was nothing more than a reaction to his having ordered her—bullied her—into obeying him. Once she was acclimated to her surroundings, he would not be so quick to order her about. He pinned her with a sharp gaze. "Now, Kathy."

She lifted her chin and remained seated.

He had no choice but to use the tactic that had worked so well a few moments ago. Yet, the alternative of threatening her with his touch was fraught with dangerous consequences.

Enticing consequences.

"Shall I help you change, Kathy?"

She surged to her feet. "No! I'll change as soon as you get out."

He nodded, inexplicably peeved at her obvious aversion to his touch. It was too bad that aversion did not extend to the moments when he actually did touch her. It was maddening that he did not experience the same aversion when he looked at her, thought of her, wanted her. "You have fifteen minutes," he rapped as he strode from the room without a backward glance.

Surely there were better ways to deal with Kathy. He had only to find them.

So that was how he'd gained entrance, Kathy thought as she watched Damien disappear through a door skillfully covered with the same paneling as the wall surrounding it. She ventured closer and turned the recessed handle carved from the same wood, pushed the door open and stared into a bedchamber as masculine as her own was feminine.

She gasped in horror as she realized Damien stood in the middle of the room, hands braced on his hips, his brows raised. "Boo," he said dryly.

With a squeak of outrage she backed away and slammed the door shut.

Panic and anger mingled and burst in her chest. Their bedchambers adjoined. There was no lock on the door. She couldn't lock him out. She couldn't escape him.

She wanted to laugh. She wanted to scream.

She'd spent the morning trying desperately to come to terms with her situation.

Instead, she had become more confused.

Every time she had looked at her mother's portrait, she'd thought Damien to be wonderful.

Every time she remembered how he'd taunted her on their arrival, she thought him horrible.

Every time she thought of him kissing her in Gretna Green, she thought him exciting . . .

magnificent. Yet every time she recalled how cold he'd been afterward, she thought him despicable . . . inhuman.

It was rather like plucking petals from a daisy.

He was wonderful. He was horrible.

He was wonderful—

Suddenly, the door opened again and Damien's head popped through. "Ten minutes," he barked.

He was horrible.

Kathy fled to her dressing room. There was no time to call Frances to assist her, and she had no doubt that Damien really would help her dress if she didn't hurry.

All she could do was please him by bending to his will.

She yanked open the closet door, easily spotting her collection of riding costumes. A claret-colored habit beckoned her with a mischievous twinkle of abundant silver braid trim. It clashed monstrously with her hair, but she'd had it made up deciding it was just the thing to discourage the suitors who seemed to lie in wait for her in the park.

She'd never had the nerve to wear it. Her pride hadn't allowed it.

She reached for the habit, changed clothes quickly, and shoved her hair under the matching and equally garish hat.

Thwarting Damien and gaining some control over her life was more important than pride. Perhaps he would be so ashamed of her that he wouldn't want to be seen in her company.

He was waiting in her sitting room, his long, elegant body sprawled in a chair as if he had every right to invade every corner of her existence.

She swept into the room, her chin in the air, her gaze cold and haughty . . . she hoped.

He blinked and threw up his arm to shield his eyes. "Good God, that's hideous."

Kathy felt her lips twitch and turned her face away, stifling the sudden urge to giggle. Upon seeing the habit, Jillian had gently suggested that a deep blue would be a much better color for her. Bruce had lied outright by telling her it was splendid.

Damien's was the first honest reaction she'd ever had to the riding habit.

He was wonderful.

"You're not actually going to wear that are you?"

"Yes, actually, I am," she replied smugly. Her ploy had worked. Surely, Damien would not want to be seen with her like this.

His jawed tightened and his eyes glittered. "I've changed my mind," he said and rose to his feet. "We'll tour the castle after we return from the village." He strode to the door and motioned for her to precede him with a courtly bow and an elegant flourish of his hand. "After you, *Princess*."

She lifted her chin and swept past him, sickeningly aware that she had cut off her nose to spite her face. Would she never learn that once Damien made up his mind to do something, he always had his way?

She nearly had to run to keep up with him as he led her through a series of winding hallways and down a set of steep stairs that abruptly ended at a closed door.

She blinked against the bright sunlight as he pushed it open and stood aside for her to pass, once again with a mocking bow.

She stepped out onto a small stone path bordered with tiny purple flowers.

"Come along," Damien said curtly as he brushed past her, leading her through a small courtyard and an iron gate set into the outer wall of the castle.

She was captivated by the beauty of terraced gardens falling away to a cliff bordered by another stone wall, and enchanted by the field of daisies that studded the hillside on three sides like white pearls and canary diamonds.

It felt good to be outside and anticipating a ride. She glanced down at herself and cringed. Oh, why hadn't Damien ordered her to change her clothes?

He was horrible.

The subtle scent of horses and hay drifted through the air as they approached a fenced meadow that stretched between two stables. She counted fifteen thoroughbred mares and geldings and an equal number of grooms exercising them within the confines of the pen. Kathy paused and searched for a path leading to the buildings.

"This way," Damien said, never breaking his stride. "There's a shortcut."

Her spine prickled with unease as he approached the corral. Unease became outrage as Damien climbed over the fence, then turned and raised an expectant brow.

"You don't actually expect me to scale a fence, do you?" she asked rigidly.

"Yes, actually I do." he replied and folded his arms across his chest.

"N—" She bit off her refusal, realizing he expected it and was waiting for yet another opportunity to exert his power over her.

He was behaving like a child.

Well, she would not.

Grinding her teeth, she hoisted her skirt and hauled herself over the rails with as much grace and dignity as she could manage. Once her feet were on the ground, she straightened her shoulders and met Damien's bland stare with one of her own.

He unfolded his arms.

"Do not bow," she snapped, knowing if he did, she would kick him.

Damien made no reply, but simply turned and sauntered toward the center of the meadow, unmindful of the horses scattering as gaping grooms guided them out of his path.

Ignoring them, Kathy held her skirt as high as decently possible and followed him, skipping to avoid piles of steaming droppings, and flinching when her hem occasionally dragged through the manure.

Damien looked as if he were taking a stroll in the garden.

The beast.

He smiled as he reached the other side of the meadow and opened the gate.

She swept past him, her nose in the air.

He was beyond horrible.

A groom appeared.

"Are Goldie and Sorcerer saddled?"

"Yes, Your Grace," the groom replied. "I'll bring them around." He loped toward the planked door of the stable.

Kathy felt the blood drain from her face. Her horse? Had she heard him correctly? "Goldie is here?"

Damien nodded and slapped his crop against his thigh. "As is Bruce's mount."

She stared at her feet, speechless and oddly numb, yet the anger and confusion she'd felt when she'd arrived to find her other possessions here was absent.

She rushed forward as the groom reappeared leading Damien's blood bay and Goldie, her coat gleaming from a recent brushing, her nose warm and comforting as she nuzzled Kathy in welcome.

Tears stung Kathy's eyes. How could she have worried about her clothes and a painting and not given thought to flesh and blood?

Yet, Damien obviously had thought of everything, including Oscar, Bruce's favorite horse.

He was wonderful.

No, he wasn't, she reminded herself weakly. He'd just forced her to climb a fence and trudge through a corral.

*How inconsequential.* The thought shamed her in the wake of all the good Damien had done, making her feel as if she were shrinking in on herself, becoming smaller in the face of his many kindnesses.

She mounted in silence as Damien did the same.

And in silence she rode beside him at a leisurely pace down a winding dirt path, dense with trees.

Absently, she reached down to stroke Goldie's neck, thankful that her mare was safe. She shuddered to think what might have happened to Goldie and Oscar if Damien had left them at Blackwood.

Kathy's breath froze in her chest as she wondered whether she was thinking of the horses or of herself.

Suddenly, Damien trotted past, sitting tall and proud in the saddle, leaving her behind and feeling lost in the chaos of confusion.

A low-hanging branch caught her hat and ripped it from her head. "My hat," she cried, not because she cared, but because she needed to say something, anything.

"Leave it. It's no great loss," Damien growled as he spurred his horse into a full gallop.

She charged after him, the sound of Goldie's hooves loud in the dense forest. She didn't know where she was or how far they had come from the castle. A branch caught in her skirt, ripping a hole before she could snatch it free.

The land opened up and she urged Goldie to pick up speed, to catch up with Damien and run abreast of him. Suddenly, he veered to the left and rode through a wide stream.

She reined Goldie to an abrupt and rearing halt. But there was no way to avoid the wake of water flying up behind him, no way to avoid being drenched in the ice-cold spray. . . .

No way to avoid the truth that had been hard on her heels since Damien had taken her and her possessions into his keeping.

Damien could have left her at Blackwood. She would have married Tony. Her life would have been destroyed.

Because of Damien, she would eventually have the life and freedom she craved. What was answering to him for the next few months compared to a lifetime of submission to a man who repulsed her? And what had Damien really asked of her other than to look at him when he spoke to her, to treat him with respect?

He was not behaving like a child; she was. A spoiled, ungrateful child.

She watched Damien as he rode back to her, trotting sedately through the stream.

"So sorry," he said. "You can't go to the village looking like that." He sighed dramatically. "I'm afraid your habit may even be ruined."

As if that hadn't been his intention, she thought as she glanced down at the large water spots marring the fabric, the glops of green silt dotting the front, the manure staining the hem. "Actually, I believe it's much improved," she said.

His brows drew together, then a smile tugged at his lips.

Laughter bubbled in her throat and she let it go. It felt so very, very good to laugh, to let go of resentments and accept the truth. So very, very good to meet Damien's gaze and see the amusement that sparkled in his green eyes and widened his often stern mouth.

Yes, he was an overbearing bully. An arrogant scoundrel. A fiendish manipulator.

Yet, he was an honorable man. An engaging rogue. A magnificent protector.

He was beyond wonderful.

# Chapter 20

The last thing Damien expected from Kathy was amusement. That it was aimed at herself was a complete surprise. But then, he hadn't expected her unwavering resolve to wear such an unflattering riding habit. Nor had he expected to be so illogically determined to see it ruined. They had both succeeded.

His lips twitched. Laughter rumbled out of him at how comical she looked and how ridiculously he'd behaved . . . how alike they were. No wonder they'd always been at odds.

They were both stubborn and willful, their emotions often overruling good sense, clouding judgment and precipitating actions that were not easily called back. As a result, he had married Kathy out of anger and she had gone along with him out of fear.

The thought sobered him. His laughter trailed off, yet he held her gaze, reluctant to break the tenuous bond their shared laughter had forged.

The woodland fell silent as Kathy's mirth faded and disappeared. She snapped her gaze away from him and sat quietly in her saddle, staring at the sleeve of her ruined coat as she ineffectually brushed away bits of green slime from the fabric.

Suddenly, he wanted to call the moment back, to again witness how dramatically laughter enhanced her beauty, warmed it. He wanted to again see her eyes sparkle like sunlight dancing on the ripples of a clear blue pond. He wanted to laugh with her again and share that short breath of pleasure with her in a more intimate way.

How could he be so weak as to fall prey to what was surely a momentary lapse in Kathy's cold and intractable disposition?

He dismounted, preparing himself for Kathy's true nature to assert itself. Any moment, she would no doubt let loose with a scathing tirade or attack him with fists flying—yet another trait they shared. And unless they declared some sort of truce, it would be a miracle if they survived these next few months together.

His mouth flattened. He supposed he should begin with an apology, although she'd probably toss it back in his face. He cleared his throat. "I—ah—apologize for ruining your habit."

A frown pleated her brow, yet she did not look up at him. "Accepted," she said quietly.

*Accepted?* He hadn't expected that.

She, too, dismounted and reached up to stroke Goldie's muzzle. "Thank you for seeing that Goldie and Oscar were removed from Blackwood."

*Thank you?* He hadn't expected that either. Never had Kathy expressed gratitude to him. Bemused, he stared at her, searching for signs of mockery.

She inhaled deeply. "And thank you for seeing to it that Frances and my belongings were here waiting for me."

Another thank you? It rocked him. Although he'd seen this side of her before, she'd always reserved it for Bruce or Max or Jillian. Never for him. The new softness in her manner fascinated him as her laughter had fascinated him.

It made him vastly uncomfortable.

He had the urge to make some stinging remark, to force the familiar and acerbic Kathy out in the open. Yet, he'd wanted peace, and apparently so did she.

"You're welcome," he said and the words seemed to scratch his throat. Had it been as difficult for Kathy to express her gratitude as it was for him to accept it?

Suddenly, she stilled and her eyes narrowed. "Did you hear that?" she whispered, her gaze searching the foliage around them.

"What?" he asked, wondering if she was reverting to the caustic repartee they normally exchanged. "The sound of arrogance shattering beneath so much abject humility?"

She shook her head as if to clear it, then gave him a soft, tentative smile.

The familiar fire ignited in his belly. It would be so easy to lay her down and cover her mouth with his, cover her body with his, fill the air with cries of passion.

He was deranged.

It was her smile, he told himself. A smile that beckoned him with its uncertainty and lack of guile. He didn't want to see that side of Kathy. He didn't want her to be nice to him.

He didn't want to want her.

"I'm leaving for London in the morning," he said tersely. "I need to hire agents to take letters to Bruce and Max. While I'm away you're not to venture out or explore the castle alone."

Her eyes reflected confusion as she glanced away from him, exposing her long neck and proud and elegant profile. "I hope you instructed Bruce and Max to return posthaste," she said, her voice cool and distant.

"Of course," he clipped out, stifling a groan of frustration. He had broken the tenuous truce between them for nothing. The fire in his belly still burned, no more, no less. Warm and sweet, or cold and hostile—it made no difference how she conducted herself toward him. He still wanted her.

"May we go now? I should like to change my clothes," she said with a quiver in her voice.

Damien raked his fingers through his hair. He was behaving like an ass. It was not her fault that he lusted after her. He had no right to punish her for his weakness by snapping her head off. "I apologize. I did not mean to order you about. The castle is very large—"

"There is no need to explain," she interrupted. "I understand perfectly."

Damien grimaced. Whenever Kathy said she understood something "perfectly," she generally understood nothing at all. "Exactly what is it you understand?"

She shrugged. "Your expectations of me in the coming months," she said with resignation.

"Which are?" he prompted.

"I am to remain here under constant supervision while you are *free,*" she spat the word out as if it were bitter on her tongue, then swallowed and took a deep breath before continuing more calmly, "while you are free to come and go as you please."

The brittle quality of her voice troubled him. If he comprehended nothing else about Kathy, he understood her need for freedom. He'd just attained it himself with Jillian's marriage. He recalled how fiercely Kathy had fought her family for the right to live her life as she chose. But she hadn't been able to fight the earl or his scheme to marry her to Edgewater. And though she'd tried, she hadn't been able to repel his own invasion into her life and the freedom she valued so highly. A needless invasion that could have been easily avoided if he had listened to her, and thought before he'd acted. If he had they would both be free.

Thanks to him, Kathy had won the battle and lost the war.

He could not bring himself to admit to Kathy that he'd made a mistake by marrying her, but he could give her what she craved most.

"You are also free to come and go as you please, Kathy."

"As long as I am escorted," she murmured.

"As I tried to explain a moment ago," he said patiently, "there are no less than a dozen paths that lead to the village, and another half dozen that lead into the woodland. The castle itself is a maze of corridors. An escort is necessary only until you become familiar with your new surroundings."

"I have a keen sense of direction," she said. "I doubt it will take me more than a day to learn my way about."

"Then I will concern myself no further," Damien said. "You're free, Kathy, as I am free."

Stone-faced and obviously unconvinced, she eyed him suspiciously. "Free to search for my house?"

"Yes," he said in exasperation. "I'll even help you if you like."

She stared at him thoughtfully. "You really mean it, don't you?"

"Not all of it," Damien said honestly. "I really don't want to trail along behind you looking over properties."

She grinned at him. "And I really don't want you trailing along—" Her grin faded and her hand flew to her heart as she stared at something behind him, her eyes wide with fear.

He glanced over his shoulder. "What is it?"

"I thought I saw someone lurking in the trees."

Damien tensed and half turned to search the dense foliage, finding nothing.

"Listen . . . do you hear it?" she whispered.

He cocked his head at the distinct sound of branches crunching beneath bootheels. "A hunter," he replied softly.

"A hunter?" Kathy echoed. "Are you certain?"

"Positive. The tenants know they are not supposed to hunt this close to the castle, but they no doubt do so."

She didn't look convinced.

"Who did you think it was?"

She shook her head. "No one."

He didn't believe her for a moment. Her fright was evident in her shaky laugh and too-wide eyes. He knew of two people who had the power to rattle her. One was Edgewater, but he was a nuisance rather than a threat. Only one person inspired fear in her. "The earl?" he asked.

She stared at her feet.

"What did he do to you to make you so afraid? Is he the ogre in your dreams?"

She flushed crimson.

"Blackwood can't hurt you anymore, Kathy."

Her eyes seemed to cloud as if she had turned her vision inward, seeing what Damien could not imagine. "He can always find a way to hurt me."

Rage clenched in Damien's chest at the images her certainty conjured in his mind of the earl looming over her, threatening her, hurting her.

He wanted to shake her until she told him every cruel thing the earl had done to her, feeling that if she talked about it, perhaps it would free her. He shook his head, banishing the rage, dislodging the images, reminding himself that it was not his business to know.

Yet, he could turn his back neither on her fear nor the reasons behind it.

God help him, he needed to know.

Perhaps one day she would trust him enough to confide in him. In the meantime, he could have Smithy discreetly watch over her to ensure her safety. More importantly, he could give her freedom from her fears as he'd given her the freedom to do as she pleased.

"There is no need to look over your shoulder." Damien swept his hand through the air. "You are the Duchess of Westbrook, mistress of all you see. No one enters here without your permission or mine. This is sanctuary, Kathy."

"Sanctuary," she breathed as if she were absorbing the word, making it a part of herself, her expression so solemn on him, he felt as if she could see right through him. "Thank you for marrying me," she said quietly.

His knees nearly buckled. He hadn't expected yet more gratitude. He certainly didn't want to be thanked for what had turned out to be a foolhardy act. Or was it? he wondered as he studied her face, awed by the way her features smoothed out, transforming her beauty, intensifying it with qualities of both wisdom and peace . . . serenity. Suddenly it occurred to him that in the two years he'd known Kathy, her gaze had always been watchful, her brow creased with anxiety, her manner itself always cautious and alert.

He thought then that perhaps the marriage had been worth it if the protection of his name could bring about the softer look in her eyes, the relaxed curve to her mouth, the calm way in which she gazed at him. It would be worth it if he could help her defeat the fear that ruled her. He reached out to stroke the back of one finger down her cheek. "My pleasure," he said.

And her small trembling sigh provoked in him a sensation that was far more poignant than mere protectiveness, far more powerful than lust.

If he weren't careful, he might actually grow to like her.

Something had happened between them. Something that made Kathy ache all over and wonder what it would be like to have him kiss her now.

Now, when she almost liked him.

*Stop it,* she told herself as she watched Damien lead their horses to the stream and allow them to drink.

Nothing had happened other than they'd actually spoken with civility to one another. Nothing had happened other than she'd allowed herself to express her gratitude to him. Nothing had happened other than he'd been reasonable and understanding of her need for freedom.

Nothing at all.

Yet, she couldn't deny the sense of comfort and safety Damien had given her as he'd made her believe that she was indeed part of his private kingdom. A kingdom that no one would dare invade, not even the earl. Nor could she deny how much she'd wanted to pour her heart out to him when he'd asked about the earl.

That frightened her more than the thought of the earl watching her, waiting for the opportunity to exact his retribution from her.

"We should return now," Damien said as he led the horses to her and held out his hand. "I still haven't given you a tour of the castle."

She glanced down at herself and blinked as the sun glinted off the silver braid of her grime-coated habit. "Do you mind if I change first?"

"Good lord no," Damien said as he lifted her into her saddle. "In fact I insist upon it."

"It is awful, isn't it?"

"Truly," Damien agreed as he mounted and gathered his reins. "Whatever possessed you to purchase such an abomination?"

A chuckle escaped Kathy. "I grew weary of being accosted in the park by overeager suitors. I thought perhaps if I were dressed garishly enough, they wouldn't want to be seen with me."

"And did it work?"

"No," she said, refraining from telling him that he was the first one she'd worn it for.

"I'm not surprised," he said as he kicked his horse into a trot.

A flush climbed up Kathy's neck as she clicked her tongue at Goldie and set off behind him. Surely he hadn't just paid her a compliment. Yet, it had sounded like one.

He slowed his horse and waited for her to catch up with him. "Is there anything you need me to bring you from London?" he asked.

"No, nothing that I can think of," she said, caught

off guard by the question. She was beginning to feel very awkward with the consideration he heaped on top of a compliment on top of amiability, not to mention his easy acceptance of her plans to search for a house. It felt very peculiar to realize how much she liked his new manner toward her.

Surely it wouldn't last.

She glanced over at him, deciding to test the matter. "Actually, there is something. Bruce's solicitor is compiling a list of properties for me to look over. Will you collect it for me?"

"I think I can manage that," he said. "Unless you'd like to come with me and see to it yourself?"

Come with him? She didn't want to. Everything seemed to be moving too fast suddenly. For two years they'd been at odds with one another, yet within the space of a few hours they had gone from barely veiled animosity to open and spontaneous camaraderie. Never in her wildest imaginings would she have thought Damien would be so easy to talk to, to be with. It was all too confusing . . . and far too appealing for comfort.

It couldn't possibly last.

"Actually, that's not a good idea," Damien said abruptly. "It's best that we keep our marriage quiet as long as possible. I want nothing to complicate our annulment proceedings."

Kathy nodded in agreement, too relieved to take umbrage at his change of mind. "How long will you be away?"

"Three days, four at most," he said.

She wished it was longer, but she would take it. She did not trust the familiarity that had so precipitously sprung up between them. She didn't even want to think about the intimacies they'd shared and the cravings she had for more.

She needed time away from him. Enough time to regain her equilibrium, to remind herself that nothing had really changed between them until she believed it absolutely. She needed time to convince herself that when their marriage ended he would again become disapproving and intolerant of her.

She needed to convince herself that he was not beyond wonderful at all.

# Chapter 21

**B**itch!
  Tony chanted it over and over again as he lurked near the disgusting scene in the copse. The scene of his disillusionment. He'd followed her from Scotland, intent on rescuing her from Westbrook, only to find her smiling up at him and laughing with him.

Tony hated Kathleen with every fiber of his being as he watched her laugh and smile at Westbrook, watched as Westbrook helped her mount her horse, watched as they rode away side by side and chatted as if all was right with the world.

Kathleen had played him false.

Humiliation writhed inside him like a living thing. How could he have been so fooled by her? How could he have believed so ardently that she was everything he wanted in a wife? Why hadn't he seen before that she was a mercenary bitch who'd rather wed a duke than a mere mister?

He shuddered in revulsion. She'd been so filthy and dressed so vulgarly, showing her true colors. Well, Westbrook could have her in all her slovenly glory. He'd certainly gone to great lengths to have her.

Tony swallowed down gorge at the realization that he might have married Kathleen and taken her into his home before discovering how vile she really was.

Kathleen didn't deserve him, nor the pristine elegance of his home.

Home. Yes! He would go home, wander about the house where he and Julia had been so blissfully happy. He would revel in his memories and offer thanks that he had been spared the misery of being tied to an ill-kempt hag.

Besides, it would be a very long while before he could face the world and its inhabitants again.

As he mounted his horse, Tony cursed his indiscretion in announcing to more than one acquaintance his plans to wed Lady Kathleen. No wonder they had snickered behind their hands.

They had known all along how fickle she was . . . a deceiver of the most calculating kind.

Tony spurred his horse to greater speed. He had to get off Westbrook land. He had to escape the taint Kathleen had left on his heart.

# Chapter 22

**D**amien clenched his fist under his chin and stared broodingly out at the meadows and fields as the coach rolled inexorably toward Westbrook Castle.

Toward home.

It seemed like forever since he'd journeyed to London, leaving Kathy behind. In reality it had been just a fortnight. A wasted fortnight spent trying to put his relationship with Kathy into perspective.

All he had accomplished was to see that his letters to Bruce and Max were in the hands of reliable men. And when he'd gone to see Kathy's and Bruce's solicitor to collect Kathy's list, he'd warned him that the earl had returned and might try to seize control of Kathy's inheritance. He'd instructed Goodman to contact him immediately should that occur. It had been nerve wracking to speak with the man without revealing his marriage to Kathy, but it had been worth the strain to know that he'd done all he could to tie up loose ends.

Kathy was the only loose end he hadn't been able to grasp. He'd thought that if he stayed away long enough he'd be able to convince himself that Kathy was as mercenary and self-absorbed as all the other unmarried women in the *ton*.

Especially after the day they'd spent together, conversing and laughing together as if they had always done so. Damien remembered his parents sharing just such moments together before his mother had died giving birth to Jillian. And then his father had changed, withdrawing his emotions and his presence from the home that held so many memories. The thought caught Damien unaware, stunning him with a truth that seemed so obvious now.

His father had traveled so much because he couldn't bear to live in a house occupied by only his memories of happier times. He had separated himself from his children for the same reason. They were a living part of his memories.

As Kathy was now a living part of Damien's memories, interrupting every waking thought and every dream in the depths of night, cluttering his mind and his life with unwanted responsibilities, uncontrollable desire.

He had to control it, dammit! He couldn't live under the same roof with Kathy otherwise. That had become evident the day before he'd left. The day he'd begun by goading her into slogging through manure. She'd taken it—his callousness and disregard, his apologies and offer of peace. And then she'd thanked him.

An extraordinary occurrence considering Kathy's usual disposition. Even more extraordinary was the way they'd talked and laughed as if amusement had always been a harmony between them. With the exception of his sister and his aunt, there had never been a woman he'd enjoyed conversing with. Except for making love, he found the company of other women tedious.

Except for Kathy.

He'd enjoyed being with her that day. In fact, he'd enjoyed it so much, he'd wanted to take her with him to London. Thank God, he'd had the presence of mind to discourage her from agreeing. For every moment spent in her company was a painful exercise in carnal temperance. It had been all he could do to keep from dragging her off her horse and making love to her by the stream, to enjoy the body beneath the hideous riding habit, to make them both forget past grievances and remember only passion.

Thank God, he'd managed to restrain himself.

For all the good it had done. For the last fortnight, all he'd thought about was Kathy as she'd been in the woodland, carefree and filled with laughter. It was a side of her he'd observed from a distance, yet had never bothered to take seriously. He didn't want to take it seriously now.

Most likely he wouldn't have to. Old resentments didn't just disappear. And Kathy had many resentments toward him. From the day of their first disastrous meeting two years ago, she'd disliked him for his quick temper and arrogance. For all he knew she disliked him for the way he parted his hair. Surely he'd given her enough time to review every one of his shortcomings in lurid detail.

He would find out as soon as he arrived home.

But, he discovered on his arrival that first, he had to find Kathy.

No one seemed to know her whereabouts. The butler thought she'd gone out riding. Frances, her maid, said she had gone for a walk. Smithy also was nowhere to be found, unsurprising since he had strict orders to keep an eye on Kathy—discreetly of course.

Damien gnashed his teeth and stifled the urge to order the entire staff to search for her.

"Your Grace," one of the downstairs maids eventually offered, "I saw the duchess in the gallery while I was dusting."

*Finally,* Damien thought in exasperation and swiftly made his way toward the gallery. He halted at the entrance to the long, narrow room, furnished with portraits and busts of his ancestors.

Kathy stood in the dim room, staring up at a portrait on the wall, her beauty a living flame amidst ashes of the past.

Desire rose inside him, demanding that he give her a greeting befitting a wife, or a lover.

But she wasn't really his wife.

He could take nothing from her but the companionship she had offered. But not now, when need was the only voice he heard. Need to watch her and take with his mind what he dared not take with his body.

Who was she?

As she had every day since Damien left, Kathy gazed raptly up at the portrait of an exquisitely beautiful woman with hair so fair it was almost white and eyes as vividly green as Damien's.

Kathy had seen this same woman before, in a painting at Bassett House, a curiosity in itself. Why would Bassett have a portrait of a woman who was so obviously a Westbrook ancestor? She would have to ask Damien when he returned from London.

If he ever decided to return. He'd said he'd be gone for four days at most, yet he'd been away a fortnight. She'd been anxious for him to leave, and had wished he would stay away longer, yet she was annoyed because he had done just that.

She'd enjoyed the ease that had developed between them before he'd gone away, yet she hoped that he'd had enough time to revert to his old domineering self. She'd rather fight Damien than the unruly emotions that underscored her every thought. She even dreamed of him at night, a sleek panther standing over her, warding off predators, protecting her even as she struggled to avoid the dangers of being trapped in his warm, seductive lair. A lair surrounded by daisies, of all things.

She was beginning to understand that sanctuary held its own dangers, and that disliking Damien had been far more safe than . . . what? She didn't know exactly. She was grateful to him, of course. She could even concede that he had some redeeming qualities like his sense of fairness and lack of duplicity. He hid nothing, not his amusement nor his indifference, and certainly not his temper and his passion.

He hid nothing but himself.

*Good,* she told herself. She wanted him far away from her, where he couldn't touch her or make her smile, where she couldn't see him and find pleasure in his laughter. His absence was a relief, a blessing. His failure to return at the appointed time confirmed his indifference toward her. No doubt he was having a marvelous time in London.

Well, she was having a marvelous time, too.

For the first time in her life, she did as she wished, when she wished. There were no big brothers to answer to, no drunken companion to deal with, no earl to lock her away and use her as a tool for his revenge. If she wanted to go into the village, she went and stayed as long as she wished.

Alone.

If she wanted to go for a walk, she did.

Alone.

If she wanted to ride for hours, she did.

Alone.

Well, not exactly alone. Occasionally, she caught brief glimpses of Smithy lurking about, never intruding but simply watching her from one vantage point or another. She tolerated it because Smithy had always been near, and was one of the few people in her life whom she trusted.

Truth to tell, she'd been vastly relieved to discover it was Smithy who followed her. Until then, the hair on the back of her neck prickled at odd times and she'd had an overwhelming urge to run and hide, to escape whomever followed her, watched her. Now she ignored those momentary bursts of panic, determined to trust in the safety Damien had promised.

She wished she could ignore her feelings for Damien, and forget how he'd appeared at her door to say goodbye, how his smile had turned her legs to pudding.

Her hands clenched. She couldn't allow herself to

think about it. Within a few months Damien would be a part of her past. What was there to think about?

Nothing. Nothing at all.

Except that she would miss him.

She was losing her mind.

Determined to think of anything but Damien, she leaned back against the wall and slid down to sit on the floor. She stared up at the painting and told herself that it was wonderful to have nothing more to be concerned with than a portrait and the mystery it presented.

"Who are you?" she asked as she stared at the green eyes and widow's peak that were so like Damien's.

"Fair Alyce," Damien replied.

Her gaze jerked to the entrance of the gallery. She raised her hand to her chest as her heart lurched, stalled, then pounded faster than before.

"I'm sorry," Damien said from the arched threshold. "I didn't mean to startle you."

"It's quite all right," she said, wishing she didn't sound so breathless. But he looked so handsome and imposing in his buff breeches and navy blue superfine. His black hair was disheveled, as if he'd plowed his hands through the strands. There was an expression on his face she couldn't quite define. His jaw was clenched as if he were angry or frustrated, yet his mouth was relaxed and gentle as if a softer emotion edged out the more desperate ones. His presence was more disturbing than she remembered.

She should rise but her legs seemed to have turned to liquid and she couldn't trust them to hold her. "When did you arrive?"

He shrugged and strolled toward her. "A quarter hour ago."

Her mouth was suddenly dry. She said the first thing that popped into her head. "Are you certain?"

Damien cocked a brow at her. "Pardon me?"

Her mind was so full of Damien, it refused to function in any logical way. She was relieved that he was back. She was embarrassed to be found sitting on the floor, talking to a piece of canvas on the wall. "Well, you told me you would be away four days at most and you've been gone a fortnight," she babbled. "Obviously you have no concept of time."

Damien grinned, his tension fading away. "You're teasing me," he said with an exaggerated note of disbelief.

Heavens! She was. Aside from her brothers, she'd never teased a man in her life. "Maybe just a little," she admitted and lowered her gaze, trying to collect herself before she started tittering like a schoolgirl or worse, interrogate him as to what he'd been doing for a fortnight. Though she badly wanted to know, his activities were none of her business.

Besides, she might not like the answer.

She swallowed and glanced up at him. "Did you send the letters to Max and Bruce?"

"Yes," he said absently, his gaze intent on her. Too intent for comfort.

Kathy folded her fingers into her palms, stifling the urge to wring her hands. There was something about the way he stared at her, something that both stirred and frightened her. Something exciting and dangerous.

He shifted on his feet and her heart jumped in panic. Was he leaving? She didn't want him to leave. "Who is Fair Alyce?" she asked, reaching for anything that might hold him here for a while longer.

His glance shifted to the portrait then returned to her as if it were on a string that allowed no diversion. "The woman who began the Forbes and Hastings tradition of guarding one another's backs."

"Really?" Kathy said, fascinated, telling herself it was Max, the half-brother she'd known only for two years, who piqued her curiosity. "Is that why her portrait hangs at Bassett House?"

"No," Damien said. "Do you want to hear the story? You'll find it interesting."

"Yes," Kathy said with a vigorous nod.

He lowered himself to the floor beside her, his shoulder almost grazing hers, his thigh almost brushing hers.

She stiffened to keep from scooting closer to him.

"Fair Alyce," he said, "was the wife of the second Earl of Westbrook."

"Oh," she said and wished he had remained standing.

Damien bent his leg and propped his forearm on his knee. "Theirs was an arranged marriage, and neither of them cared for the other at the onset. But after a few years and the birth of a son, Alyce came to love the earl so desperately that she declared she would die for him."

A chill crept up Kathy's spine, radiating outward until she shivered. "She was a fool then. I wouldn't die for anyone." *As my mother died for love of the late Duke of Bassett,* she silently finished the thought.

Damien chuckled. "The earl felt the same way. He told Fair Alyce it was a pity, because he didn't love her."

"And he certainly wouldn't die for her," Kathy supplied. "I can guess the remainder of the tale. Alyce dedicated the rest of her life to the earl in the hope that he would fall in love with her."

Damien bumped her shoulder with his. "Will you keep your comments to yourself until I'm finished?"

She smiled in spite of the dark mood that threatened her. The ease they'd had with one another the day before he'd left had not been a temporary aberration. It was real, becoming more natural and spontaneous with every moment they spent together. "I'll try," she said.

He sighed in exasperation. "As time passed, Alyce came to believe that the earl did love her because he seemed very content and chose to spend most of his time with her."

"Of course he was content," she said, controlling

her urge to snap. "He had a wife who adored him and was always at his beck and call."

Damien slanted her a quizzical look as he continued. "One day, they were set upon by bandits in the forest. As an arrow was about to strike down Alyce, the earl threw himself in front of her and the arrow pierced his heart. His last words to her were, 'I love you. I would die for you.'"

Kathy winced at the sudden pain of her nails digging into her palms. "Surely he wasn't so big a fool. Such tales are often embellished as they're retold."

"It's the absolute truth. I have her diary if you would you like to read it."

"I believe you," Kathy said, feeling hollow and angry at the tragedy that always followed love. "No one could make up such an outlandish tale."

He leaned his head against the wall as if he too were impatient with such a senseless waste of life. "Shall I tell you what happened next?"

"She grieved herself to death," Kathy spat. "A high price to pay for loving a man who couldn't or wouldn't love her until it was too late."

Damien shifted to give her a thoughtful look. "No, she didn't. She lived a long and full life. She fell in love again and wed and had another son."

Oddly, the ending pleased Kathy even less than her supposition of what had happened. Fair Alyce had done what her own mother could not. She had gone on, truly leaving her first and supposedly undying love buried in the grave.

"You seem disappointed," Damien said quietly.

"No," she said though she knew she sounded weak and inexplicably frightened. She didn't want to know that love could grow from nothing. She didn't want to know that it didn't have to destroy.

"After our marriage is annulled, do you ever plan to marry again?" he asked, changing the subject.

"No!" she said vehemently.

Damien sucked in his breath as if he had not expected such brutal honesty. "Why?"

"Because I don't wish to be ruled by any man," she said as she raised her knees and wrapped her arms around them.

He smiled slightly and tucked a stray tendril behind her ear. "And if you should fall in love?"

Something quickened in the pit of her belly at his touch. "I won't," she said, unsettled by the flush of warmth he could so easily evoke in her.

"As I understand it, love is not something you can control."

"Precisely," Kathy said, feeling the warmth fade. "Love controls you. It rules and destroys you."

"A rather cynical notion for someone who has yet to experience love."

"It's not a notion. I watched my mother grieve herself to death over Bassett." She smiled bitterly. "She loved him so much she died for him."

"But Bruce said your mother died from a wasting disease."

"The onset of which coincides with Bassett's death."

"If that is true, then I think it was a matter of choice," he said gently.

"Exactly," she said. "She chose to allow her life to be consumed by Bassett and her love for him."

"I see," he said. "So you will lock yourself away rather than risk meeting a man you might love, and perhaps making what you consider a foolish choice."

It sounded wrong when he said it, as if it were *her* beliefs that were foolish, as if her course was skewed and might lead her astray. Sudden doubts collided with long-held convictions, shaking and confusing her. She pressed her back against the wall, bracing herself against them, willing herself to trust her convictions. "As you said, it is a matter of choice. *My* choice," she said firmly.

"You fear becoming like your mother," he said

softly, as if he knew how fragile she was, how easily she would shatter just then.

*Yes!* she wanted to shout as the truth slammed into her. More even than the earl, she was afraid of that. Afraid of caring too much, of needing too much. Afraid of losing herself to an emotion, to a man . . . to *this* man. Afraid of wanting him more than she wanted freedom. But she couldn't admit that to Damien, who made her feel more vulnerable and exposed than she'd ever felt in her life. He knew too much about her fears, her weaknesses, her dreams. If he could see such things he could touch them, use them against her.

Only to herself could she admit that, more than anything or anyone else, Damien was the reason she was frightened.

Damien had thought that the story of Fair Alyce would entertain Kathy, yet it had clearly distressed her. He hadn't meant to allow his curiosity to impose on what should have been a light moment, yet he hadn't been able to stop himself. Somewhere along the way he'd discovered a soft center beneath her brittle exterior. He'd discovered the real Kathy, a woman who intrigued him. A woman he felt compelled to know better.

He turned to study the vulnerability in her profile, the way she held her head so stiffly erect as she stared straight ahead and pressed her lips tightly together as if to still a quiver.

There was so much pain in her, so much bitterness. The words "love" and "marriage" were anathema to her.

And while he felt that a healthy distrust of both was advisable, he knew that a very few people like Jillian and Max were fortunate enough to find love with one another. It disturbed him to know Kathy would deny herself even the possibility of finding that kind of happiness and sharing.

She shuddered slightly and squared her shoulders.

"What about you, Damien?" she asked abruptly. "Do you plan to marry again?"

He blinked, amazed at how she always recovered herself so quickly, repairing the cracks in her shell and neatly turning the tables on him before he could avoid stumbling over them. He thought to avoid her question but Kathy had been candid and deserved a like honesty from him. "I do."

"I suspected as much," she said with a firm little nod of her head, as if she were conducting a separate conversation with herself.

He frowned. "How so?"

"Because my chambers have been newly refurbished," she said matter-of-factly. "Does your lady know about me?"

"No," Damien said carefully. He hadn't discussed his plans with anyone. In fact he'd given little thought to them beyond the decision to take a wife within the next year or two.

She stretched out her legs, giving Damien a glimpse of trim ankles. "Who is she?"

"I don't know yet," he said suddenly feeling strangled by so much honesty and refusing to admit that it didn't matter who he married as long as his requirements were met.

Kathy leaned away from him and propped one elbow on the floor. A slow grin spread across her face. "You hypocrite. You don't plan to fall in love either, do you? You plan to marry for convenience."

He grimaced at how contrived and unnatural it sounded when she said it. "It's different for a man," he said as stretched out his own legs, needing a moment to come up with a good defense. There wasn't one.

She slanted him an arch look then shifted again to lie flat on the carpeted floor with her fingers laced beneath her head, her pose a study in artless provocation with her breasts rising and falling with every breath she took and her legs enticingly outlined beneath her skirt.

"Why don't you want to fall in love?" she asked as she stared up at the ceiling.

He wished he could end the conversation and slide his body over hers and kiss her. He averted his gaze from her breasts and yanked at his cravat. "Frankly, I don't want the responsibility of it."

She turned her head toward him, her brow pleated. "I don't understand."

It was the one thing he did understand, though he'd never spoken of it before. He'd never felt the need. He felt it now. In light of her comments, he knew Kathy was the one person who would understand and not try to convert him to the ranks of the romantics. "Until Jillie married Max, I played the role of father and brother to her. I worried over her future. I protected her. I gave her everything that was in me to give."

"And now you're free to love her without being responsible for her," Kathy supplied with a soft, knowing smile.

"Exactly. I'm selfish," he said.

"As am I." Kathy chuckled and raised to a sitting position. "We are a pair. I believe love destroys and you think of it as a responsibility."

Yes, they were a pair, he thought. So much alike in so many ways. Yet, hearing their respective ideas of marriage summarized so dispassionately left him feeling as hollow inside as the suit of armor gracing the entry hall. "There are those who build dynasties with love," he said nodding toward the portrait of Fair Alyce and wondering why he felt the need to provide arguments for his own beliefs. "I never finished my story. Don't you want to know what happened to Alyce's sons?"

"Only if it's good. If they died tragically, I don't want to know."

Damien smiled at that. Apparently there was a bit of the romantic in Kathy after all, though he had the sense to keep his observation to himself. "Her son by her first marriage to the Earl of Westbrook became the first Duke of Westbrook. Her son by her second marriage became the first Duke of Bassett."

Kathy's eyes widened as she stared up at the portrait. "You mean we're related?"

"Hardly," Damien said. "The lines have been so diluted over the centuries as to be nonexistent. Until Max and Jillian, Hastings and Forbes had never intermarried . . . for obvious reasons initially, but as the generations passed and the connection became more distant, it became tradition."

Kathy's eyes sparkled. "As did the guarding of one another's backs," she mused then sharpened her gaze on him. "And that is why you felt honor bound to look after me while the family is abroad, isn't it?"

"Yes, that's why," Damien said, irritated that she would continue to believe he was so cold as to be motivated solely by tradition and honor. Irritated, too, that he should feel the need to promise her that for as long as he lived, and no matter what direction their lives took, he would always be there to guard her back.

He ran his hand over the back of his neck and mentally cursed his own lapse into romanticism.

Kathy would drive him mad yet.

# Chapter 23

**S**he shouldn't be doing this. The thought came as it had every afternoon for the past two weeks, filling Kathy with apprehension, warning her that she was establishing a ritual that could not last. A ritual that she would miss. Yet every day, she remained sitting on a wrought iron chair in the small nook at the edge of the gardens, waiting for Damien to stroll down the path, knowing that if he did, it would be because he knew she was there and wanted to spend time with her.

She'd discovered the garden within a garden after leaving the gallery the day Damien had told her the story of Fair Alyce. Bordered by arched stone walls draped with climbing vines, carpeted with velvety grass and artfully arranged flower beds, and furnished with wrought iron chairs, the place had an atmosphere of peace and solitude that appealed to her. She'd needed refuge from Damien and his disturbing insights.

This had become "her place," where nothing intruded on her thoughts but birdsong and rustling breezes. Her place, until Damien had wandered in two days later.

He'd clearly been preoccupied as he'd strolled through the arched entrance, his gaze skimming past her as if he hadn't seen anything beyond his own thoughts. His step had faltered then halted, and he'd blinked and glanced around as if something were out of place and he had only to find it. He'd found her, staring up at him, both dismayed and strangely thrilled that he was there.

Since then, she came every day at the same time. Damien joined her soon after, sauntering in to sprawl in the chair opposite her as if they had agreed to meet by silent consent.

"Her place" had become "their place."

She looked forward to this time and dreaded it.

Damien had a way of getting her to speak of things she'd never wanted to share with anyone. She'd certainly never considered sharing her views on love and marriage with him. Yet, she found herself speaking freely with him, though the conversations left her anxious, as if pressure was building inside her. Nevertheless, she still came here. Still she waited for Damien to come, hoping he would not, fearing he would not.

She clenched and unclenched her hands in her lap, battling the tension that seemed especially sharp today.

Last night, she'd dreamed of wasps and awakened with a silent scream trapped in her throat as she batted at her face and arms. When she had finally fallen back to sleep, she'd dreamed again—of watching her mother and Bassett laugh in the dining room at Blackwood while she hid in the china cabinet with fear and loneliness crowding her, smothering her.

She shivered and rubbed her arms, feeling chilled. She should go inside, break the ritual that brought both pleasure and pain.

Perhaps today, she and Damien would speak of the weather or the book she was reading. Perhaps they would speak of Damien himself.

At that thought, warmth radiated inside her, chasing away the cold. He'd been doing a little sharing of his own.

He'd spoken of his mother and father and how happy they'd been together. He'd told her how his father had grown cold and distant after his wife died giving birth to Jillian, and of how Damien had never been able to break through his father's wall of grief.

Damien wondered if his father had been proud of him.

Kathy had assured him that his father must have been and went on to point out all his admirable qualities. Strength, courage, unwavering loyalty, a sense of honor that was second to none. And when he'd tugged at his neckcloth in embarrassment, she'd added that he wasn't bad to look at either.

She had meant it sincerely. She had wanted to tell him of the promise his father had made to her, but then, she would have had to speak of the earl and that she could not do. And to acknowledge the promise was to acknowledge how she'd always felt connected to Damien since that day so long ago. It would make her feel even closer to him now. They were becoming too close as it was.

She had to constantly remind herself that life with Damien was not life at all, but an interlude that would end all too soon.

A twig snapped. She glanced up, and her heart jumped in anticipation.

Damien strolled down the cobbled path toward her, wearing black trousers, white shirt, and brocaded waistcoat. His stock was perfectly centered and tied, yet his sleeves were rolled up as if he had been working in his office all day and had forgotten to shrug into his jacket on his way out the door.

She stared at him, at the way his trousers tightened over his thighs as he walked, at the way his wide shoulders extended beyond the edges of his waistcoat, at the way the sun burnished and shadowed the planes of his face.

Even casual and distracted, he was imposing, breathtaking, magnificent.

"This became lost on my desk," he said as he sat

in the chair opposite her and held up a sheet of parchment. "It's from Mr. Goodman."

"My list of properties," Kathy said, more dismayed than excited. *My house,* she thought. It hadn't entered her mind in days.

A month to be exact.

Damien said nothing as he handed her the parchment and stretched out his legs, crossing them at the ankles.

She reached for it as if it were a lifeline, quickly breaking the seal, hoping desperately that Mr. Goodman had good news to impart. News that her dream had become a reality. She badly needed reality just then. She needed a tangible reminder that her life awaited her beyond the castle walls. That she had a stronger purpose than waiting in the garden for Damien every day.

Her heart sank as she read the brief message. Willow Cottage was not for sale.

"Why so glum?" Damien asked.

"Mr. Goodman hasn't been able to locate any properties that meet my specifications," she said, not knowing why she avoided mention of the property.

"What are your specifications exactly?"

"Well," Kathy said, eluding Damien's gaze and fixing the vision firmly in her mind. "I don't want an excessively large house, twenty rooms at most. It must have lovely gardens and a stable."

"Is that all?" Damien said with a wry smile.

"No," Kathy said. "It must be no more than three hours' ride from Bassett House."

Damien raised his brows. "That's rather a limited area to choose from."

"I know," Kathy said. "But I don't want to feel too cut off from my family."

"I can understand that," Damien said slowly, his forehead pleating. "Why does the description of the house sound so familiar to me?"

Kathy decided there was really no reason to keep

it a secret from him. "Most likely because you've seen it before. It's Willow Cottage, the small estate north of Westbrook Court. It's been vacant for sometime. Mr. Goodman inquired about it, but it's not for sale." Damien glanced up at the sky and cleared his throat. "I assumed you'd want to be near Blackwood."

"Why would I want to do that?"

"It's been your home all your life."

"Home?" She shuddered. "No, it was never that. Blackwood was a hiding place for my mother and Bassett."

Damien pinned her with a penetrating stare. "How long are you going to be bitter and angry with your mother?"

"I'm not," Kathy said defensively.

"Then who are you angry with?"

"Bassett," she hissed. "Because of him, my mother wasted her entire life."

"Did she say that?"

"Of course not. She never allowed anyone to see her unhappiness."

"Perhaps because she wasn't unhappy."

Kathy pressed back in her chair and folded her arms across her chest. "How could she have been happy? Her life was never her own."

"Her life was always her own and she lived it exactly as she chose," he said gently.

"You know nothing of it," she snapped as her mind groped for a way to change the topic. She didn't want to talk about Mama and Bassett. Suddenly, she didn't want to talk of anything that was remotely personal.

"I know that your mother is to be admired—"

"Admired," Kathy burst out as a wave of hot fury washed through her. "She sold herself to Bassett as surely as the earl sold himself. She was just as selfish in her own way as the earl and Bassett." Her gaze shot to Damien, horrified at the intensity of an anger she hadn't known existed. An anger that kept coming, welling in her throat, spilling out before she could stop it. "What kind of woman would agree to become another man's wife in order to keep her lover? What kind of a woman would allow her lover to treat their children as if they were puppies or kittens he didn't want underfoot?" She clamped her mouth shut before she said more, before she brought the earl into it and looked too closely at her mother's blindness to his cruelties.

Damien watched her closely, his brows knitted in thought, his posture calm and still, as if he knew any sudden movement would scare her away. "Unfortunately," he said so softly she was compelled to listen. "There are some choices in life that have their roots in selfishness. But, as near as I can ascertain, your mother did her best to make it up to you."

"Really," Kathy said. "How?"

"By leaving you a fortune."

"You believe money can make up for what she did?"

"Most women must either marry or live as poor relation." His voice was casual, offhand almost, as if he were discussing the weather. But then he leaned forward, catching her off guard as he took her hand, held it with a tenderness she could not reject. "The fortune your mother left to you was merely a means of leaving you a far more important legacy— choices. Choices that many men do not have."

Yes, her mother had ensured that she'd have choices, and for that Kathy was grateful. But something cold and horrible squirmed inside her, a question that took shape in her mind. Had Mama known about the earl's cruelties and done nothing? She tried to banish it, but it wouldn't disappear, and she knew then that it would never disappear, never be silent. She would always wonder.

With a shuddering breath, she focused on Damien's hands, which still held hers between both of his, his thumb caressing her wrist in what seemed to be an absent gesture. He gazed at her with concern and pity . . . no, not pity, she amended. It was sadness she saw in his eyes.

Sadness for her. Concern for her.

Just then she wanted nothing so much as to close the distance between them, to tell him everything about the earl, her suspicions about Mama, and the promise his own father had made to a frightened child hiding in the china cabinet.

She eased her hand from his and rose from her chair, determined to escape his knowing gaze, his soothing words, his stirring touch. She *did not* want his concern nor his sadness. She *did not* want this closeness between them nor did she want to know why it existed at all.

She could not want anything from Damien but her freedom.

Damien watched Kathy walk away, knowing she wouldn't welcome his escort back to the castle just then. Her straight back and stiff gait confirmed that he had touched a nerve. Just because he'd found some release and comfort these past weeks in speaking of his relationship with his father, didn't mean the same would be true for Kathy.

He rose quickly and reached her side unwilling to allow one of their afternoon encounters in the garden to end on a discordant note. "Shall we walk?" he said wryly and placed her hand in the crook of his arm to lead her down the winding path through the gardens rather than the more direct route to the castle.

She nodded and swallowed as if she couldn't speak, and she kept her gaze firmly on the path ahead as if she couldn't bear to look at him.

He shouldn't have pushed her.

The extent of her anger toward her mother had surprised him as much as it had obviously surprised her. Still, her questions were valid.

He wished he could give her some answers.

But, given the little information he had on the

subject all he could do was point out that the countess had tried to make amends. But it had sounded feeble even to his own ears especially when he'd seen how deeply the past had wounded her. What made it worse was the real reason behind his probing. He'd seized upon the only subject he knew that would divert her from the subject of the house.

Of all the houses in England, why had she set her cap for this one? It was so bloody ironic as to be laughable.

Apparently Kathy had never mentioned to her brothers that she had her eye on a certain house. If she had, they would have told her Damien owned the property. Nor had Goodman informed her of the owner's identity. But then Goodman hadn't revealed to Damien the identity of the proposed buyer. Damien had never cared enough to ask.

He had to admire Goodman's discretion, though in hindsight, he would have preferred some warning.

If he were extremely lucky, the subject would never come up again. He wasn't sure how he could explain to Kathy that for her to live so near to Westbrook Court was to invite disaster. It was all he could do now to keep from seducing her and risking their chances of annulment. Once their marriage was ended, he wanted Kathy as far away from him as possible.

On the other hand, if she lived close to Westbrook Court, secure in her coveted independence, there would be nothing to stop him from trying to seduce her. The thought crept in and took a place beside the temptation that had lurked in his mind since that day in Gretna Green.

Damien groaned at the twisted logic of it.

Kathy wanted no man in her life.

And he needed a wife in the near future. A willing wife who was kind and gentle, honest and courageous.

Had Kathy not been kind and gentle of late? Did her honesty not take courage?

He turned his gaze on her to watch as the breeze molded her muslin gown to the contours of her body. His breath stalled at the beauty of her in profile, at her fine straight nose and firm chin, at her graceful neck and rounded breasts, at her long legs that seemed to go on forever, her hair that curled and drifted around her, a thousand shades of fire in the sunlight.

So beautiful.

His belly tightened and desire flared.

He jerked his gaze away.

He'd been right not to tell her he owned the house she wanted. For without doubt, if she remained close to him, he would take her to his bed and damn the consequences. And if they continued to go on as if they were building a relationship and a life together, they might end up with a child rather than an annulment.

Impatient with the silence, and the confusion that riddled his mind, he guided her around the corner and toward the front of the castle. "Max and Bruce will return before we know it," he said, forcing himself to speak aloud of the time to come when she would be gone from his life.

"I know," she said on a trembling breath, then gasped as she stared straight ahead.

A man on horseback galloped away from the front of the castle, passing so close to where they stood at the edge of the path, Damien could smell the sweat of overworked horseflesh.

It was the earl's man Freddie.

Kathy broke into a run.

Damien stared after her and saw the abandoned wagon, the bed covered with canvas, concealing whatever lay within. *He can always find a way to hurt me,* she'd said of the earl.

He raced after her. "Kathy, wait," he shouted, knowing only that he had to catch her, had to stop her from looking into the wagon.

But he was too late.

Kathy reached the wagon and tore away a corner of the tarp, exposing the corner of something made of mahogany. She screamed and backed up a step, then fell to her knees. "Mama," she cried out in horror.

He lurched to a stop beside her and glanced at the wagon, at the corner of gleaming wood and cursed under his breath.

It was a coffin.

# Chapter 24

"**M**ama," Kathy cried again, a whisper that echoed like a dirge through every part of her. She felt as if she were falling into a chasm, felt as if she would never stop falling. Out of hatred, the earl had removed Mama's body from the crypt at Blackwood and sent it to her. So much hatred that he had to take his revenge out on the dead.

Hands gripped her arms and urged her to stand, cradled her against him, pressed her cheek to his chest so she could not see the wagon. Damien's hands. Damien's strength and warmth and his deep voice vibrating against her ear, giving orders to someone—Smithy, she thought—as he stroked her hair and her back.

"Now, Your Grace? Are you sure?" Smithy said.

"Now," Damien said firmly. "It's best to get it over and done with."

Kathy listened without comprehending. Without caring. Fear and grief numbed her to the world around her, separating her from it all, from Damien.

Only the earl and his cruelty were real. Only the coffin existed.

Some part of her mind recognized that they were moving, not into the castle but alongside it toward a stately companion building of old stone walls and arched stained glass windows and solid doors that were never locked. Daisies of gold and pearl stood still and reverent in the yard.

*The chapel,* she thought. They were going into the chapel where the sun burst through the windows and fell on the stone beneath their feet in tranquil pools of color. She stared at every detail, concentrating on each nuance, finding comfort in the atmosphere that was like arms enfolding her, protecting her. Arms stronger than the world that she no longer felt a part of.

And then she knew that they descended a stairwell because the light changed to a soft glow cast by candles set into the walls where images of angels were carved into the stone.

She walked where Damien led her, his arms still around her shoulders, never releasing her, never letting her stumble or fall. They entered a room as large as the chapel above. She stood still when he halted and leaned into him. She stared at the marble vaults set into deep niches, and she watched as Smithy entered with four footmen carrying her mother's coffin.

Her teeth began to chatter with the cold inside her. Cold like spikes impaling her, holding her upright, holding her together.

The footmen placed the coffin inside a crypt and retreated.

Smithy stepped forward and she saw that he held something yellow and white and alive. He stood with his back to her and Damien and sniffed as he sprinkled daisies over the mahogany. He cleared his throat and slid the lid over the vault with a soft whisper of sound that spoke of well-fitted appointments.

Everything fit well here, the castle, the field of daisies, the color and light that flowed even into the burial chambers from the chapel above.

Even her mother seemed to fit in . . . to belong.

Smithy backed away to stand next to her.

Kathy blinked and turned her gaze from one side

to the other, to Damien and Smithy standing beside her, *with* her, caring for her and providing another kind of sanctuary in their silent, undemanding presence.

Smithy, a friend who had always been there.

She looked up at Damien, seeing his concern, his compassion, his goodness, that had always lain beneath his fierce temper and quicksilver moods. Damien, who had been a part of her life long before she had known him, the knowledge of his existence giving her hope and the strength to stand when she would have fallen beneath the onslaught of fear.

He strengthened his hold around her shoulders. "That was to be my father's vault," he said in a low, soothing voice. "Your mother rests beside mine now, Kathy. Neither of them will be alone now."

Warmth crept through her, melting the ice in her soul, bringing her to life. Senses awakened in her body, awareness burning her. Awareness of cruelty and hatred and fear. She inhaled deeply, past the lump that grew larger in her throat and the ache that was like a vise around her heart. She shivered and winced at the sudden pain of her nails digging into her palm. Her fingers ached at being clenched so long.

It hurt, becoming part of the world once more.

"Are you all right?" Damien asked.

She nodded, a lie she could not voice as she wondered if she would ever be all right.

"If you wish, we can move your mother later . . . to any place you choose."

She blinked and focused on the crypt, on the mellow candlelight caressing cold marble. "No," she said. "Leave her be. She is safe now."

Damien seemed to tremble for a moment, but then he was steady once more as he turned her and guided her up the stairs. And as they left the chapel, he drew her to a stop and tipped up her chin with his forefinger. "You're safe, too, Kathy," he said hoarsely.

She nodded, willing herself to believe him, needing to believe him.

Damien stood at the door connecting his bedchamber to Kathy's, waiting for the sound of sobs, hoping for it, needing to know that her grief had found its voice.

But there had been nothing but silence since they'd returned from the chapel two hours ago and she'd entered her room, shutting herself away from him with a quiet click of the door.

What the earl had done was unspeakable.

What Kathy suffered as a result was unimaginable.

Damien swiped his hand over the back of his neck as he paced the length of his bedchamber and back to the door. He paused and listened. Still nothing.

Kathy suffered as she lived—alone, showing nothing, sharing nothing.

He could stand it no more.

Determined to shake some emotion out of her if necessary, he pushed open the door and stepped inside.

The sight of her nearly brought him to his knees.

She lay curled in the center of the bed in a small lump, her hair wild around her as if she'd torn it loose from the ribbon and combs that had held it back. She was asleep, yet tears ran down her face and soaked into the counterpane beneath her cheek. Unrelenting tears that had no voice of outrage or protest. Tears that were silent, as defeat was silent and submissive.

She turned, her arms upraised, her hands frantically batting at the air around her face. Her chest rose and fell in breathless pants and her mouth opened in a soundless scream. She bolted upright, slapping at her face and tearing at her hair.

A nightmare surely.

He strode to the bed and sat down, hauling her into his arms, restraining her, afraid she would hurt herself as she continued to bat at her head. "Stop it, Kathy."

"Wasps," she gasped as her eyes opened. "Get them off of me!"

The hair on his nape prickled. "There are no wasps," he said in a calm voice.

She stilled, yet her body was stiff, her gaze frantic, searching for danger.

"It's a nightmare, Kathy. Just a nightmare," he said over and over again as she sagged against him.

"*Just* a nightmare." She gave a wild laugh. "It won't go away. *He* won't go away. Ever. He'll come back with his wasps and his pins—" A harsh, dry sob cut off her voice.

"Who, Kathy?" he asked, though he was sure he knew the answer. The earl. It all had to do with the earl. It had to.

"Him . . . the earl. He'll do it again," she stammered, and her body trembled so hard, Damien felt the vibrations down to his bones.

"Do what?" he asked.

She trembled harder and leaned into him. "He'll lock me up with the wasps . . . make me do what he wants." Her voice was small and breathless as if fear were squeezing it out of her, making more room for itself.

He rested his chin on the top of her head and held her more closely, holding himself closely as well, controlling his own shudder at the implications of what she'd said. "When—" he swallowed to clear the harshness from his tone. "When did he lock you up with wasps?" he asked, trying to envision such a thing.

"The day he came back . . . he wanted me to marry Tony and I wouldn't . . ." She spoke into his chest, as if she sought to stop the words from tumbling out, to hide them from him.

He couldn't allow it. Not now. The visions of what she'd suffered were too horrifying, too unthinkable.

If he didn't get some answers from her, they would both have nightmares. "Kathy, you weren't marked by welts or stings. Are you certain it isn't just a dream?"

"No!" she said in a short, panicked shriek. "He shoved me into a wardrobe, held up a glass jar filled with wasps while Freddie tossed another jar inside. He shut me in with them, and all I could hear was the flap of wings . . . all I could feel were these *things* landing on me, crawling on me."

Damien's temple throbbed. "What was in the jar?"

"Moths," she said with a harsh laugh. "They were only moths."

He could not speak for the anger that came alive inside him, a roaring beast filling him, demanding release from the control he exerted over it. "Shh," he whispered and rocked her back and forth as she shuddered and buried her face in his shirt. "It will be all right." What else could he say to banish her fear, to keep her memories at bay?

She whimpered and tried to curl herself into a tight ball. "No, it isn't all right. You don't know. No one does," she choked, "and now he won't let any of us have peace, not even Mama."

He unfolded her fingers to loosen her hold from around her knees. She suddenly became limp and unresisting, like a doll made of cloth.

"Mama," she said in an anguished whisper and her shoulders heaved with silent sobs. "I had all those awful thoughts," she babbled, "that Mama knew all the things the earl had done to me . . . that she knew and turned a blind eye . . . angry with her . . ."

He listened, sorting through the scattered bits of information and their implications. If Kathy felt guilty for suspecting that her mother knew, then there had to be more than a jar of wasps invading her dreams. "What else did the earl do to you?" he asked, unrepentant at taking advantage of Kathy's vulnerability. She was so seldom pliant and yielding, and he had to seize the opportunity regardless of what form it took.

It was bloody well time that he knew what power Blackwood had over her and why.

He waited for her reaction, expecting her to retreat back into silence as she always did when his questions involved the earl. He tightened his arms around her, securing his hold on her lest she try to bolt. "Kathy, tell me," he whispered into her ear. "What did the earl do to you?"

She shuddered as if she were struggling with herself rather than with him. And then the words spilled from her as if she could control them no more than she could control the tears that continued to soak his shirt. "He did everything he could devise to frighten me. He'd sneak up behind me and stick me with a pin or come into my bedroom at night and put a pillow over my face and smother me or he'd pull out clumps of my hair. He hurt me, but never left marks anyone could see."

Fury such as Damien had never known demanded that he find the earl and tear him apart, make him suffer a thousand times for every cruelty he'd committed against Kathy. Insidious cruelty, calculated to linger long after the pain, to feed fear until it was larger than the victim.

But, Kathy lay in his embrace, sharing with him, holding him back with her trust and need, making him listen to the small voice of reason in a corner of his mind.

His anger settled in a hard inert lump in the pit of his belly. An anger with which he was becoming too familiar of late. Merciless anger at the earl. Unreasonable anger with the countess and Bruce for not seeing or knowing what torment Kathy suffered. They should have known, damn them. Smithy had seen it. If nothing else he should have told them.

"Why didn't you tell your mother?" Damien gritted.

"The earl said he'd kill Bruce and Mama if I told." She sounded like a child just then, telling secrets she'd kept to herself for too long.

"And you believed him?" he asked, forcing himself to regain control of his temper, to see to Kathy's immediate needs rather than his own.

This was a matter best left to Bruce and Max. They would see to the earl.

Kathy angled back away from him, her gaze steady through eyes haunted and frighteningly resigned. "I still believe him," she said calmly, as if having confided in Damien, she was determined to make him understand. "He sent Mama's body here to hurt and frighten me . . . to let me know he isn't finished with me yet. He'll find a way to hurt me again at first opportunity. And I'm afraid he'll hurt Bruce. He said as much the day he came back."

"No, he won't," Damien said harshly. "Remember what happened at Gretna Green? He knows he will have to deal with Max and me if . . ." He trailed off, realizing how empty the words were in light of what had happened today.

"You begin to understand," Kathy said softly. "The earl's hate always overcomes his fear. And he is patient. He'll always be out there waiting for me or Bruce."

A chill washed over Damien. It was the truth. The earl had proved that today. "Do you still wonder if your mother knew?" he asked, leading her away from the subject, wanting to ease at least one of her torments.

"No. It was wrong of me to think it when I know she didn't."

"How do you know?"

Kathy was silent for a long moment. "Because Mama summoned Bassett immediately after the earl lost his temper one day and beat Bruce." She breathed deeply. "He left marks that could be seen."

*And she summoned Bassett.* It explained so much—why the earl had returned from America only after the old Duke of Bassett and his own father had died, and why he had so aggressively taken over everything to do with Blackwood, including Kathy. As she said, the earl had waited patiently for the right time to strike.

He smoothed her hair with his hand, then slid a finger from her ear to her collarbone. So silky and fragile, yet so courageous. He lightly caressed her cheek.

She turned her head to gaze up at him, her eyes liquid and drowsy and so trusting.

Trust that filled him with a sense of poignancy and awe. It drew him, urging him to cradle her cheek with his hand, to lower his head, and drown in the beauty of her eyes as he grazed the tip of his nose over hers.

She released a whispering sigh.

He brushed his lips over hers, once, twice, and again, barely touching her, barely tasting the sweetness of her. She did the same, following his movements, gently, not holding him yet not letting him go.

Weakness overcame him, a lassitude and a pleasure that drifted through him like a soft melody as he settled his mouth on hers, slowly rubbing back and forth and skimming the outline of her lips with his tongue.

Her breasts brushed his chest as she turned into him, the movement of her hips a caress on his groin. She opened her mouth and met the tip of his tongue with the tip of hers, sharing with him the taste of her tears.

He deepened the kiss, lingering and savoring with a tenderness he'd never felt before.

Tenderness that seduced his mind rather than his body, his heart rather than his flesh. It filled him with peace rather than need.

He had to let her go.

He lifted his head, yet his arms tightened around her, cherishing the closeness, refusing to let her go.

Regret thickened in his throat as he pressed her cheek against his shoulder, not wanting her to see his vulnerability, not wanting her to know how easily she'd captured him with her trust.

A trust that could take far more from him than he was willing to give.

"Do you remember the day James was born?" she asked, the words wafting around him, penetrating his awareness.

"Yes," he said, wondering why he remained, why he continued to hold her and absently stroke her hair and her cheek and the soft side of her arm.

"I was so excited about the baby that I slipped into Max's room early that morning. I understood that Max would want his heir to be born in his bed, but I had no idea he would be there. It was so beautiful the way he lay with Jillian, just holding her while she slept. He kept stroking her hair or her cheek or the back of her hand as if he *had* to touch her, as if he weren't complete unless he was touching her."

Damien blinked and fixed his gaze on the far wall.

"Would you stay with me like that now if we were really married?"

He shut his eyes and willed away the sudden temptation. A few moments ago he would have said that if they were married he would have done more than hold her. That "just holding" her would never be enough for him.

That he would have been wrong scared him witless.

"We're not really married," he said roughly, yet still he cradled her against him. Still he could not leave her, did not want to leave her.

He had to leave her.

She didn't resist as he eased her out of his arms and laid her on the mattress, but stared up at him with sadness and resignation.

He couldn't leave her.

He stretched out beside her and rolled to his side

to face her, to pull her into his arms and hold her close, to inhale the scent of her hair and feel the warmth of her breath on his neck and savor her presence in the silence.

She slowly relaxed against him, her body curling into his as her hand found his chest, resting there, holding him with that slight weight.

He held her as the late afternoon sun fell to earth and the light turned soft and silver, as Kathy's maid tiptoed in and lit the fire when he did not wave her away, as the sounds of servants scurrying about soothed Damien with a sense of normalcy.

A normalcy Kathy had never really known.

He curled his lip in a silent snarl as the memory of all she'd told him reared in outrage. A thrashing would be too good for the earl, too honorable. The man deserved to feel the same terror he'd inflicted on Kathy.

He couldn't wait for Max and Bruce. The man had to be stopped . . . *now.*

Darkness filled the sky and his anger lowered into a menacing crouch as his mind whispered commands to plan, to act decisively . . . effectively.

The moon would be a mere sliver by tomorrow, casting little light for the next week, giving him more than enough time to carry out the plan that had begun to form in his mind. The darkness would serve him well as would Smithy and his pair of cudgels.

Damien smiled grimly as he stroked Kathy's hair and inhaled her scent while his thoughts narrowed to a single purpose. . . .

Revenge.

# Chapter 25

Nature had cooperated beautifully, Damien thought as he studied his surroundings with satisfaction. Not a shred of light from the new moon reached beyond the clouds hovering listlessly in the night sky. The air was thick and heavy with moisture. In the distance, thunder growled in menace as more clouds lumbered in from the sea.

The trees of Blackwood forest loomed about the clearing like demons waiting for their pound of flesh, their limbs twisted and gnarled, their leaves nothing more than dark shadows against the night. A single owl hooted above them, its eyes iridescent and unblinking as it watched the doings of man from a safe height.

Flames snapped and cackled in the silence and licked at the small iron cauldron set above a fire built in a nest of rocks, as if it anticipated its part in Damien's scheme with relish.

"There you go, Your Grace," Smithy said as he rose and stepped back. "Ready to wake him up?"

Damien stared coldly at the earl's slumped form lashed to the trunk of a tree, one half of his face underlit by the fire before him with an evil glow.

"As soon as the water boils," Damien said as he watched the liquid in the pot steam and simmer. As his anger had simmered for the past two days.

Oddly, he had felt no intolerance for the time it

had taken to summon Smithy and make prepara-
tions. Nor had he chafed as they'd traveled to
Blackwood and waited for just the right moment to
strike. The only impatience he'd suffered was at
having to leave Kathy.

He hadn't wanted to leave her . . . ever. Yet, while
he'd lain with her, an annoyed restlessness had
begun to take hold of him. Restless because he'd
been anxious to put his plan into effect. Annoyed
because he'd never found appeal in sharing anything
with a woman but pleasure. He'd never remained
with a woman after their passion was spent, yet all
that had been spent in Kathy's bed was her grief.

He hadn't cared. Kathy had given him satisfaction
of a different sort, and just having her near had been
enough. Women had come and gone in his life and
he would be hard pressed to remember any of them
in any detail. Yet, he doubted he'd ever forget the
wild silk of Kathy's hair tangled in his fingers as he'd
held her, the sweep of her lashes on her cheek as she
slept in his arms, the weight of her hand on his chest
such an eloquent gesture of need.

No, he would never forget, and that was the
greatest annoyance of all.

He didn't want Kathy or anyone else to need him.

The earl stirred against the ropes holding him
upright with his back to the tree.

Damien sighed wearily. After tonight Kathy
wouldn't need anyone.

It still surprised him that his abduction of the earl
had come off so smoothly. Yesterday, he and Smithy
had watched Blackwood Manor from a perch in the
same tree they'd used the day they'd liberated
Kathy. It had quickly become obvious from the
earl's habits that he felt safe at Blackwood. He
walked alone in the morning and the afternoon.
Freddie was rarely seen. Today, they'd simply waited
for the right time to strike.

They hadn't needed Smithy's large cudgel. The

small one had been most efficient in assisting the earl into unconsciousness. So effective that the earl had been oblivious of time and discomfort as they'd slung him over the back of a horse, brought him to the clearing, tied him to the tree, and waited for darkness to fall.

"The water is boiling, Your Grace," Smithy said. He nodded toward the earl. "It's time to wake his lordship up for our little tea party."

He answered Smithy's grin with one of his own, picked up the bucket at his feet, and doused the earl with cold water.

Smithy snorted in amusement as he stood by the fire, his body still and watchful.

Blackwood opened his eyes and coughed and sputtered and frantically glanced around. His gaze raced past Damien, then returned with a narrow-eyed glare. "Westbrook," he gasped.

Damien strolled closer and looked down at his prisoner. "I wanted to personally thank you for the wedding gift you had delivered to Kathy."

The earl slanted him a malicious smile, as he raised one knee and sat back as if he were entertaining guests in his drawing room. "I take it that you and *your wife* accepted the gift in the same spirit with which it was given," he said mildly.

"How could we not?" Damien replied just as mildly. "And now that I've thanked you, I offer a gift of my own . . . one that will ensure that you will live past the night."

"How kind," the earl said.

"Not kind at all," Damien said, "a fact that will become painfully clear to you if you come near me and mine again, either in word or in deed."

"Threats, Westbrook?" the earl spat. "How predictable of you."

Damien ignored him. "If you see Kathy on the street, you are to cross to the other side. If you are in her presence at a social function, you will bow and scrape to her and then politely excuse yourself from the proceedings."

"Go to hell."

Damien reached down to retrieve a pottery jar sitting on the ground at his feet, and then leaned forward. "I understand that you have a fondness for wasps."

The earl's brows jerked together.

"Oh, yes," Damien said. "Kathy told me everything—how you coerced her into agreeing to marry Edgewater, how you hurt her and never left marks anyone could see."

Blackwood tightened his jaw and turned his face to the side.

"I, however, do not care if I mark you," Damien continued as he held the jar close to the earl's ear, close enough for the earl to hear the frantic batting of wings. "Think of it, Blackwood. Think of what it will be like to be stung over and over again, to have your eyes swell shut and your body burn with fever." He picked up a sharp twig and brushed it over the earl's temple, then the vein that visibly pulsed in his neck. "Here and here, stingers in your flesh, poisoning your blood." He smiled. "How will it feel to see your own agony approaching from every direction and know you are helpless against it? How does it feel to know you are preyed upon by someone stronger than you are?"

Tearing the cloth covering off the top of the jar, Damien released a hundred angry insects into the earl's face.

The earl stiffened, but barely flinched when a moth flew into his chin. "Moths," he said with a curl to his lip. "You'll have to do better than that."

"I didn't think you would be fooled by your own trick, Blackwood . . . not for long." Damien waved a wayward moth away from his face.

"You don't frighten me," the earl said.

"You should be frightened of me," Damien said

softly as he stared pointedly at the cauldron bubbling over the fire, then returned his gaze to the earl and pretended to examine the scratches the twig left on Blackwood's flesh. "I've marked you. A pity you won't have scars. But then we both know that the places we cover on our bodies are the most vulnerable. I haven't any pins but I've no doubt Smithy carries a knife."

"That I do, Your Grace," Smithy said and pulled a wicked blade from the waist of his pants and held it up, allowing the firelight to shimmer on the polished metal. "The point is so fine it will leave scarcely a mark on the outside while slicing the insides to ribbons. Could cripple a man for life, it could."

The earl's eyes widened, yet still he remained composed. "An amusing game, Westbrook. I wonder if you will find it so entertaining when I bring you up on charges."

Damien smiled as he held out his hand for the knife.

Smithy handed it to him hilt first, then peered into the steaming cauldron.

"You're a fool if you think I will buckle under your threats." Blackwood stared at the kettle as if mesmerized. "You wouldn't dare to harm me."

"Would I not?" Damien asked as he dipped the knife in the water, holding it there until he was sure it was hot. "Have you not yet learned that a Westbrook will dare anything to protect what is his?" He pressed the flat of the blade against the earl's throat. "Don't move, Blackwood, lest my hand slips."

Perspiration beaded the earl's forehead and upper lip.

"The anticipation of pain is the worst, is it not? Of course, you know what torture it is to always wonder and wait for your fear to become reality. You used that knowledge often enough on Kathy."

With the tip of the knife, Damien traced a line from beneath the earl's ear to his temple. "Your flesh cringes in spite of your defiance." He tested the edge of the knife and drew a spot of blood on his own finger. "Smithy is right. This is a fine blade. Fine enough to sever a muscle in the arm and render it useless." He leaned over the earl and ruffled the knife over his head. "Most men your age have a bald spot or two. Perhaps I should relieve you of some of your hair as you relieved Kathy of some of hers."

"Have your fun, Westbrook," the earl said as he tried to angle his head away from the knife. "And then I will have mine when you are brought to trial in the House of Lords."

"Tell your tale to the Lords if you wish," Damien said as he shaved a small area above the earl's ear free of hair. "Tell all of Parliament. It will be interesting to see how your power stands against mine." He set the knife aside, pulled on his gloves and picked up the cauldron. "I tire of this. You've already taken too much of my time."

Damien tipped the pot, but not enough to spill its contents. "Let's see," he mused. "Where should I mark you? Here?" He held the pot over the earl's lap.

"The earl is right vain about his appearance, Your Grace," Smithy offered. "He's too proud by half of his pretty face."

"Too proud by half," Damien mused as he moved the pot closer to the earl's face until the steam beaded his face. "That can be remedied." He drew the pot back.

Blackwood closed his eyes and his feet dug into the ground as he tried to shrink against the trunk of the tree.

Smithy picked up a second cauldron and dashed its contents over the earl.

Blackwood screamed, a bloodcurdling sound of agony and terror that seemed to bounce off the dark ceiling of clouds and rebound from the trees.

The scream broke off abruptly. The earl shook the

water from his face gasped for breath. His teeth chattered uncontrollably as his body registered that he'd just been doused with frigid water.

"The mind is strange," Damien said conversationally. "It accepts what it is told until the body registers that it is a lie. But then you know that, too, don't you Blackwood? On the other hand, threats are insidious things, terrorizing the mind, taking it over until there is no other truth but fear and morbid anticipation."

Blackwood's jaw worked as he stared straight ahead, defiant even in the aftermath of terror.

"You're a spineless coward," Damien said in disgust, "creating nightmares for helpless children and beating boys and hiring thugs to make others believe you are strong." He dropped the pot.

The earl winced as hot water splashed onto his boots and soaked into the ground.

"I've decided not to kill you, by the way." Damien crouched down in front of him. "And I've decided not to drive you out of England as Bassett and my father did. I want you here, where I know what you're doing. Do you understand?"

"Yes," the earl said, hatred gleaming in his eyes.

"No," Damien said. "I don't believe you do." He picked up Smithy's small cudgel and idly tapped the earl's knees, one, then the other. "If Kathy ever gives me the slightest indication that you've harassed her in any way, I will make you wish that I had killed you tonight. If harm comes to either one of us, or to Bruce, whoever is left will exact the appropriate revenge."

The earl's face turned paste white, a macabre mask of fear in the glow of the flames.

But Damien knew that within a day or a week, the earl would again feel secure in his malevolent world. He wanted the earl to live in fear, to eat it with his meals, to feel surrounded by it in his house, and sleep with it in his bed. He lowered the cudgel and removed the bonds from the earl's feet and from around his middle, leaving the ropes that tied his wrists together. "You'd do well to pray that we all remain in good health, or that we aren't struck down by a stray boulder falling from the sky. If a freak injury should befall any of us, you'll be held accountable. There will be no place on earth where you can hide. Enemies will lurk in every corner, ready and willing to take you through the tortures of hell before you're allowed to die."

Damien stretched a length of rope between his hands, wrapping it around his knuckles as he rose. "Of course you are aware that any threat I make will be honored by the Duke of Bassett as well."

The earl gave a jerky nod, but otherwise did not move or speak.

"Send this piece of offal on his way, Smithy," he ordered and turned away, the ugliness of his own words a bitter taste in his mouth, the cruelty of his own actions a creeping sickness in his soul.

He stared down into the fire, watching from the corner of his eye as Smithy hauled the earl up and shoved him in the direction of the manor house a good night's walk away.

"A right good bit of work, Your Grace." Smithy's voice trailed off and his smile faded as Damien rounded on him and fixed him with a hard stare. "What, Your Grace?" he said, glancing around as if searching for evidence of some mistake he might have made. "Did I forget something?"

"You forget your own role in the earl's schemes, Smithy," Damien said, his voice as cold as his disgust. Disgust of the fury he could not seem to control and of the cruel streak threaded through every man and how easily it strangled his sense of decency. Yet he could not stop himself, could not march his thoughts past the persecutions Kathy had suffered. He could not see beyond the outrage that ruled him over her suffering.

"I did nothing, Your Grace." Smithy faced him, meeting Damien's anger with consternation.

"Yes, you did nothing," Damien said wearily. "You suspected Blackwood was hurting Kathy and said nothing." He rubbed his hand over the back of his neck, knowing he had to get it out, to purge the fury and find reason once again. "Your silence was the earl's accomplice."

"I know," Smithy said, his voice thick and hoarse, his expression stricken.

Smithy's response defeated Damien, defeated his need to place blame, and to punish. Smithy had suffered enough in his silence, as had Kathy.

Damien walked toward his horse, leaving Smithy standing by the dying embers of the fire, his head lowered, his arms limp at his sides. He glanced at the servant, seeing a man who had been victimized by the hierarchy of master and servant and done what he could, protecting Kathy and Bruce when he could, however he could.

As Damien had done what he could, committing upon the earl acts which he abhorred, transferring Kathy's terror to her tormentor, ensuring her safety. It was enough.

Damien mounted his horse.

Smithy looked up at him, a gleam of moisture tracking down his weathered cheek. "It won't happen again, Your Grace," he said simply.

"I know," Damien said and reached for the reins of Smithy's horse and held them out to him. "It's over. It's time for us to return home." He turned his horse toward Westbrook Castle, leaving his anger behind in the ashes of the fire set within a ring of stones.

# Chapter 26

❦

They had been the longest four days of Kathy's life. Nothing appealed—not the gallery where she'd just been, and not here in the walled garden. The colors seemed flat, the sound of the birds mocking, the scents of the flowers stale.

Never had loneliness felt more acute as she sat in the garden every afternoon, waiting for Damien to appear as he always had.

Where was he? Why hadn't he told her he was leaving? All she could think of was that he'd been disgusted by what she'd told him about her childhood.

But then why would he have remained with her, holding her with such compassion and listening as she'd spoken of her mother and the earl? Why would he have kissed her with such tenderness? She could have lain in his arms forever, believing that nothing and no one could hurt her if Damien was near.

Yet, Damien had been gone for four days, and every time she thought of the confidences she'd shared with him, fear jumped in her stomach.

She had told. The earl would hurt her. He would kill Bruce. She had told and now she was alone and waiting for the worst to happen.

The earl would come. He would have his revenge. And his evil would not stop at her. He would strike

259

at anyone he could reach. Bruce was across the sea, untouchable for the moment.

He would try to hurt Damien.

She bent over double in the chair and buried her face in her skirt, trying to still the trembles that shook her body, trying to think of what to do through the panic that chased her thoughts.

Why didn't Damien return?

Suddenly, the birds fell silent and even the breeze seemed to still. Something touched her—an awareness that she was being watched, studied. She raised her head and lunged to her feet, ready to bolt.

Her gaze flew around the garden, searching for escape, then skidded to a stop at the arched entrance and swept over the man leaning against the lattice, his riding clothes dusty, his crop dangling from his fingers, his eyes dark with fatigue.

Damien. He'd returned. He'd come here, straight to their place.

She wanted to run to him, throw herself at him and laugh with the sheer joy of seeing him. She wanted to shout at him for leaving without a word. But she felt suddenly shy as she watched him, unsure whether to laugh or cry or do nothing at all.

As the silence stretched thin between them, the expression in his eyes changed from weary to alert. "You were afraid," he stated.

She swallowed and nodded.

"Why?"

He could ask that, after what she'd told him? "The earl," she croaked, unable to voice the fear she'd had for herself and for Damien.

"He will not harm you again," Damien said tersely and glanced away as if he were suddenly uncomfortable.

"Don't say it." She shook her head as anger burst like a bubble inside her. Anger that he would be so cruel as to try to give her false hope. Anger that for the space of a thought, she blindly accepted Daamien's words as truth. "It's cruel of you to expect me to believe such a thing."

He swiped his hand over the back of his neck. "Believe it."

"Why should I?" she asked, grasping for the same conviction she heard in his voice, wanting it.

His jaw clenched and unclenched, giving her the odd sense that he was groping for words. "Suffice it to say that Blackwood and I have been in negotiation and have reached acceptable terms."

"Is that where you've been? With the earl?"

He nodded with a jerk of his head. "He will bother neither you nor Bruce again. In fact you might think of him as our guardian angel from now on."

She stared at him, at his apparent discomfiture, at the flush that climbed up his neck and almost convinced her that he spoke the truth. "What did you do to him?"

"He is whole," he said, then sighed heavily. "It is over." He approached her, his expression dark and intense and strained. "Ask me no more," he said harshly as he stopped in front of her, grasped her elbows and held her at arm's length. "He will never hurt you again, Kathy. This I promise you."

She reeled with the force of hearing Damien make the same promise his father had made to her. Yet it was more because he had already protected her from the earl more than once. He had stopped the earl. She could see it in the grim intensity of his eyes.

Oh dear God, it was true. Weak with relief, she wrapped her hands around his forearms, gripping him tightly. Bruce was safe. They were all safe.

Damien had promised. She had no need to know more.

"Now," Damien said as he set her away from him. "I am going to bathe and change into fresh clothing." The tightness around his mouth relaxed into a lazy smile, and his eyes softened into drowsy perusal of her from the top of her head to the tip of her toes.

"I suggest that you make use of the time to have Cook arrange a basket for us. I rather fancy a picnic."

"A picnic," she echoed dumbly, forgetting everything but the way he looked at her and the tingling trail his gaze left wherever it touched her, the pleasure that radiated through her like heat as he continued to smile, the lurch of her heart as he turned and sauntered across the lawn and through the arbor.

"Three quarters of an hour, Kathy, or I'll go without you," he called over his shoulder as he disappeared from view.

She recovered her equilibrium and raced to the kitchens, breathlessly ordering certain foods to be packed into a basket and rifling through the pantries in search of delicacies. Then she raced to her room to fuss with her hair and change into a simple muslin skirt and embroidered blouse with flowing sleeves and dab scent beneath her ears and, shamelessly, between her breasts as well. She paced restlessly, waiting for Damien to bathe and change. Every few moments she paused before the looking glass on the wall to fret over whether to loosen the ribbon at her neckline to expose the tops of her shoulders or pull it demurely tight to show only her neck and collarbone. And then she resumed her pacing, angry at herself for contemplating such coquettish nonsense.

Finally—only an hour really—he knocked on her door and stood in the threshold when she jerked it open.

He looked amazingly refreshed and stunningly handsome and far too magnificent to be real. Yet he was real, and he was hers for the entire day.

She knew she shouldn't feel so flustered and happy and carefree. She shouldn't be so mushbrained as to ogle him as if he were the only knight in a world full of dragons.

Yet she was happy. And, Damien was her knight

of legend, possessing the honor and strength to free her from fear and suspicion with the power of a single promise.

It was heady stuff, being free. Free even to be mushbrained if she wished.

"The day passes," he said. "Shall we go?" He offered his arm in courtly fashion and escorted her from the room and down the grand staircase.

Kathy caught their reflections in a window on the landing and marveled at the picture they presented—the duke and his lady, quite worthy, she thought, of such admiration.

As they reached the bottom of the stairs, the butler paused in the midst of a conversation with a footman to stare at them. The footman fell silent. A parlor maid sighed as she, too, glanced at them.

Cook rushed in from the kitchens and held out a large covered basket to the footman.

Damien shook his head. "I'll take it," he said and turned toward the butler. "Her Grace and I are officially indisposed for the remainder of the day, Peters."

"Of course, Your Grace."

Kathy stifled a giggle at that and cocked her head in bemusement. How odd. She was not given to giggles, yet the urge bubbled inside her like champagne.

More freedom—to behave as she wished, to be however she wished to be.

With a light step, she walked beside him with her hand on his arm as they left the castle, not knowing where he led her and not giving a fig if he took her to a cave.

He took her to a pond set like a sapphire in the center of a meadow studded with flowers of topaz and amethyst and pearl. The Westbrooks seemed to have a particular fondness for daisies and pansies and forget-me-nots.

She seemed to have developed a particular fondness for fairy tale castles and dark, handsome knights.

Ripples expanded outward in the pond and lapped at the grassy bank as Damien skipped stones one after the other in mindless activity. Thinking was proving to be a dangerous occupation.

Spending time with Kathy was equally dangerous.

She sat on the blanket he'd spread beneath an old oak tree whose branches cast patterns of shade and light out over the water and offered some shelter for her delicate skin.

That was the problem. Despite his assertions that he didn't want Kathy to need him, he felt compelled to shelter her in small ways as well as large. He threw a stone with unnecessary force, aware that something had changed inside him since he and Kathy had been together. Somewhere along the way, he'd stopped thinking of her as an unpleasant but necessary duty. He hadn't wanted to leave her.

He'd felt compelled to return to her as quickly as possible, to share more moments with her in the walled garden, listening to her rich voice and seeing her brilliant smile and her beauty that seemed to become more vivid and arresting, more provocative with every moment that collected between them.

Dangerous indeed.

As dangerous as her gaze on him as he stooped to carefully choose a handful of stones, then straightened to skip them, one at a time, across the water.

He never should have brought her here. It was too intimate, sharing a meal with her on a blanket under a tree. Too intimate being close to her and finding his hand on her arm or his fingers absently playing with a strand of her hair as if it were a habit he couldn't seem to break.

Even their conversations seemed intimate. Conversations that were too easy, followed by silences that were too comfortable. Underlying it all was the awareness rippling beneath the surface until lust spiraled and threatened to pull him under.

No, not lust . . . desire. Lust was impersonal, indiscriminate. His desire had a name and a face, a voice and a body.

Kathy . . . *her* face, which was beginning to freckle in the sun and invited a kiss on the cheek, the tip of her nose, her lips damp with the wine she still sipped. *Her* hair that flamed in the afternoon light and tempted his fingers to play amidst the strands. *Her* voice blending so well with the bird song, lulling him into absurd, poetic fantasies of their naked bodies joined and rolling in the grass, the scent of their passion a heady mix with the scent of fertile earth and flowers.

He could not continue this way, with his body perpetually alert when Kathy was near, and his mind fogged to everything but her presence.

He transferred a stone to his left hand and launched it across the water with a decisive snap of his wrist. It skipped four times before it sank beneath the surface.

"Very impressive," Kathy said as she appeared at his side.

"Nothing to it," he replied with a frown as he caught a whiff of her scent. He hadn't noticed that she'd risen from the blanket, hadn't heard her footsteps as she approached. It seemed that the only time he wasn't aware of her every move was when she filled his thoughts to distraction.

Goddammit! He'd come to the bank to escape her nearness. The only place left to go was into the water—a thought that held a certain appeal as well as the prospect for momentary relief.

"May I try?" she asked.

He poked through his remaining stones, chose one, and dropped it into her outstretched hand. At least he hadn't had to touch her.

He wanted to touch her. Badly. He resented her for it. Deeply. Never had his mind been overruled by his body. Never had he been so driven by need for a woman.

She grasped the rock and raised her arm.

"You're holding it wrong," he said as he stood behind her and grasped her wrist, arranging her thumb and forefinger until they were curled in a half circle around the flat stone. Her bottom was round and soft against him, her hair silky and sweet smelling as it brushed across his face.

Her blouse slipped down, baring one shoulder and revealing a rise of flesh that betrayed her rapid breathing. It seemed natural to sweep her hair over her shoulder, then place his free hand at her waist. The nape of her neck looked infinitely kissable.

She stiffened and her breath caught. Her wrist became limp in his hold. She turned her head, presenting her graceful and elegant profile and baring her neck even more. He had the strangest feeling that she was as aware of his body as he was of hers.

He had to get away from her. Far away.

Damien released her and laced his hands behind his back. "Now, flick it, moving only your wrist," he ordered brusquely.

She didn't move.

"What are you waiting for?"

"Don't hurry me," she snapped breathlessly, then flung the stone. It skipped once and sank. She whooped with delight. "There! Look, I did it!"

Damien frowned and gave her another rock. His body was fast rising to the occasion of her nearness and all she could think of was skipping stones.

Her next one skipped three times.

"I believe you have a knack for this," he said, striving for a normal tone and pure thoughts all at the same time. He cleared his throat. "Jillie never could master the art of skipping stones."

"Did you and Jillian come here often?"

Seizing on the subject of his sister with alacrity,

Damien sat on the bank and raised his knees to hide his lack of control. "Not often. She rarely came to the castle when she was a child. Neither did I, for that matter. We spent the majority of our time at Westbrook Court."

Kathy dropped down beside him and folded her knees to the side. "Why?" she asked.

Damien shrugged as he fought the urge to ease her onto her back in the grass, to flip up her skirts and satisfy the craving that grew with every moment he spent with her. "Our father always found one excuse or another to keep us away. When I look back, I believe he thought I'd be too overwhelmed by it all, that I wasn't man enough to fill his shoes."

He glanced away. Where had that come from? Why in blazes did he always find it so easy to speak candidly with Kathy as if it were another habit he couldn't seem to break?

She frowned. "And did you believe it as well?"

"No." He lowered himself to his side and propped his head in his hand—a move that added a good hand's width to the space separating them. "I knew I could fill his shoes."

Her lips twitched. "Of course you did," she said matter-of-factly. "But you wanted him to acknowledge it."

Had he? Damien wondered, uncomfortably aware of the emptiness he'd felt when his father had died, as if something weren't quite finished. "Perhaps," he admitted, wishing he could think of another subject to introduce.

"He acknowledged it to me," she said softly.

His brows jerked together. "You knew my father?"

"I met him once," she said. "It was the day your father and Max drove the earl from England for beating Bruce. But I didn't know the earl was gone and I'd hidden in the china cabinet. Your father found me and I screamed because I thought he was the earl come to murder me then and there."

He absorbed what she revealed to him and wondered why he was surprised that she'd met his father. Still, he couldn't have anticipated their conversation would take such a turn, nor that it would unleash so many questions. Why would his father have discussed him with a seven-year-old child? Why would Kathy remember it unless it was too significant to forget? Something inside him dreaded what she might reveal.

Still, he had to know and told himself it was because he needed to fit all pieces of her past together. "What happened?"

"He demanded that I stop screaming and frowned so fiercely at me his eyebrows ran together. I thought he was an ogre."

Damien winced. Of course his father would have had no patience nor understanding for an hysterical child. "He is the ogre in your dreams," he guessed.

"Yes," she murmured.

"So, my father added to your nightmares."

"Oh no. He comforted me and made me feel safe."

"How?" Damien asked, bemused by the image she presented of his implacable father.

"He told me the earl would never return, though I didn't believe him at first." She swallowed. "I knew the earl would come back if for no other reason than to keep me from telling what he'd done to me. Your father convinced me otherwise."

"How?" he asked again, unable to conceive that his lofty parent would stoop to persuading anyone about anything.

She lowered her gaze to her lap. "He promised me that as long as he lived he would protect me from the earl."

"He promised," Damien said in disbelief. She couldn't be speaking of his father, a man known for his terse explanations and arrogant assumptions.

She nodded and stared out over the water. "I believed him. I'd never felt so safe, yet I couldn't help but be afraid that something would happen to him." A ghost of a smile tipped up the corners of her mouth. "I asked him if he thought he would live long."

"And he stood for it?" Damien asked, amazed at Kathy's gall.

"Not only that, but he promised that if he should die, his son would protect me." She turned and fixed her gaze on him. "And so you have."

"My God," Damien said, realization a rush of blood in his veins, a prickling on his flesh and a pounding of his heart. He'd never believed in such things as providence or destiny, yet it seemed as if the future had been foretold in that promise. He shook his head, impatient with the thought. It was coincidence, nothing more. "How reassuring to know I didn't fail him," he said lightly.

She gave him a knowing smile. "He knew you wouldn't," she said with a small catch in her voice. "I also asked if his son was like him."

Damien blinked and then stilled, waiting for her to continue.

Kathy reached out and covered his hand with hers. "He said you were very much like him. Your name was the last word he ever spoke to me, and it was the only time his voice was not harsh." She tilted her head to squarely meet his gaze. "He promised in your name," she said urgently as she leaned toward him. "Damien, he *knew* you could guard my back with all the honor and strength of the Forbeses that preceded you."

Pressure built in his chest as he absorbed what Kathy was telling him. His father *had* been proud of him. Even though Damien had been only sixteen at the time, his father had faith in him, enough faith to make a promise in his name. His father had known that Damien could and would fill his shoes. Damien hadn't known that it mattered to him until now. Until Kathy had reached down inside him to un- earth a secret he'd kept so long he'd forgotten it still lurked in a corner of his mind.

Somehow she had known that it would matter.

And, it seemed appropriate somehow that it had come from Kathy. Kathy, who shared neither herself nor parts of her life lightly. Kathy, who had so clearly seen his need when he had not. . . .

Kindness, gentleness, honesty, courage, and beauty. Oh God, such beauty . . . in flesh and in spirit.

He tried to force his gaze away from her face before she read the emotions battering at him from the inside out. Before he wrapped his arms around her and told her what an inestimable gift she had given him. But he could not. If there was one thing he had learned in these months with her, it was that he could not touch her. Not when he was laden with emotion and prey to his own vulnerability. Not when she trembled and caught her breath every time he came near her.

Her presence in his life had become the source of his greatest pleasure.

The realization shook him to his soul.

# Chapter 27

She had no more secrets. There was nothing she hadn't told Damien, nothing he did not know about her. And with each confidence they'd shared in the past two months, she'd felt a little more relieved, a little more free. Free from all the doubts and fears of a lifetime. Because of Damien.

She'd wanted to give him something back, yet all she'd had to offer was her memory of a promise. In spite of his cavalier attitude, she'd heard the pain in his voice when he'd spoken of his father. She'd done the right thing. She saw it in his expression, and in his stillness as he sat beside her on the bank, his gaze fixed on something only he could see.

Yet, there had been a price in the telling.

As she had feared, acknowledging the promise made her feel more bound to him, as if they were becoming a part of one another. It had not been what she wanted, yet now she wanted more.

Closer . . . she wanted to be much closer to him. He'd told her it was possible, and she knew it was so by the need that grew more insistent with every thought of him, with every moment she sat next to him, aware that nothing more lay between them but cloth and restraint. She knew that he was holding back as much as she, in the way he avoided playing with her hair or touching her arm when he'd been touching her all afternoon.

271

She couldn't think of that, not when the mere memory of his body against hers was like a caress inside her.

Distance . . . she needed distance between them.

She shoved to her feet and walked to the edge of the water before she leaned closer to him, rested her head on his shoulder, lifted her mouth for his kiss.

She stared up at the oak tree, frantic to find something, anything, to distract her from the hollow ache in the pit of her belly. "Is that a rope tied around that tree branch?"

"Yes it is," Damien said from where he still sat on the bank behind her. "When I was a boy I used to swing on it and then drop into the water."

"What fun," she said, feeling his gaze on her back, desperate to escape it. "I want to try it."

"I doubt it's sturdy enough."

"Of course it is." Kathy kicked off her shoes, shimmied up the tree, released the rope, and climbed back down. "It's not even frayed," she said, giving it a hard tug. "I'm certain it's strong enough."

"You're not dressed for swimming," Damien pointed out. "If it breaks, you'll drown in that skirt."

She gathered the rope in her hands and backed up a distance. "If it breaks, I'll drown regardless," she babbled, knowing there was less peril in the water than in remaining on the bank where it would be so easy to give in to the temptation to throw herself into Damien's arms and drown in his embrace.

She took a run at the bank. Her feet left the ground and she swung into the air.

The rope snapped.

"Kathy!" Damien shouted as she plunged into the water.

Her thoughts scattered into chaos as water closed over her head. Her skirt twisted around her legs, binding her in a sodden shroud, dragging her down. She couldn't seem to make her arms work right. Her lungs burned for lack of air.

If she didn't get rid of her skirt, she was going to drown.

She had survived the earl and a runaway marriage to Scotland. She absolutely refused to drown.

The last of her panic faded. She forced herself to be still, to move her arm down, to make her fingers ease open the buttons at the side of her skirt, to drift without kicking as the yards of fabric began to unwrap and slide free of her. She scissored her legs and shot upward.

Something wrapped around her neck, pulling her. She reached up trying to tear it away, but it held fast.

It was an arm—Damien's arm. He was towing her to the surface.

"Don't fight me," he snapped as they broke into air and sunlight.

She went limp, allowing him to tug her to shore and wondering how she could escape the wrath that was sure to come.

But he didn't even give her a chance to catch her breath.

"You bloody little idiot," he roared as he dragged her up the bank, dropped her to the ground, and fell down beside her.

"I didn't expect the rope to break," she gasped.

"I warned you that it wasn't sturdy enough."

"I thought it was."

"You thought!" Damien rose up on his knees and grasped her shoulders, giving her a hard shake. "And did you think you'd learn to swim once the need arose?" He dug his fingers into her arms and locked his elbows, as if he struggled to keep himself from shaking her more. "You could have drowned!"

He thought she couldn't swim. She saw it in the fear clouding his eyes and bleaching his skin. She felt it in the way his hands trembled and weakened their hold on her, heard it in the way he drew in a breath and released it slowly. His mouth was a tight, thin seam above his chin, as if he were forbidding himself to continue shouting at her.

She stared up at him too awed by his restraint to form an immediate reply. Never had she seen Damien exert control over his temper. Never had he so impressed her.

She reached up and cradled his face between her hands, speaking softly as her thumbs caressed the planes of his cheeks. "Damien, I was never in any danger. I can swim."

He pulled back and swiped the water from his face. "You can swim?" he said in a dazed tone.

"Like a fish. I knew what to do, you know. I would have been out of the water in a thrice."

He grabbed her and jerked her to his chest and held her so closely, she thought she would drown in his strength, his warmth, his fierce display of caring.

"Don't ever do that to me again," he said as he angled back to stare down at her. "Do you hear me?"

"I hear you," she said, flinching at the fury in his voice.

"Get out of that wet blouse," he said gruffly as he began to work the buttons of his shirt free.

Excitement flared from her belly to her throat and it was all she could do to remain upright as her gaze slipped from his face to his chest. It seemed to take forever before he peeled the shirt from his body, revealing plated muscles, and the dark, silky mat of hair that covered his chest and wedged into a narrow pelt that disappeared into his trousers.

So beautiful. So sleek and full of power—

She moistened her lips with her tongue.

Damien inhaled sharply.

Her gaze snapped up to his face.

He glanced down at her legs clothed only in stockings and the thin chemise plastered to her thighs, then back to her face, his green eyes glittering, smoldering . . . burning her.

She shivered.

"You're cold," he said softly.

She nodded dumbly, unable to speak just then. *Yes, she was cold,* but it was a different sort of cold. A cold that came from empty arms and too much space between them.

"Shall I help you remove your blouse?" he asked.

Heat rose in her face and slowly moved down her neck, flared in her breasts, then radiated lower. This was what she'd tried to escape. She'd wanted distance from Damien. Yet, now, with him kneeling in front of her, temptation was like an enchantment around her, binding her to the moment, binding her with the need to know just how close they could become.

Still, she couldn't answer, didn't know how to answer.

His mouth curved into a slow smile, as if he knew her silence was a consent she could not voice. Never taking his gaze from hers, he slid his hands up her shoulders to her neck and his fingers stroked her flesh beneath the edge of her blouse.

She gave a little jerk as his knuckle grazed the sensitive place at the base of her throat. Her back arched as his hand moved lower, his fingers deft as they unfastened her buttons. She stilled as he separated the front of her blouse . . . pushed it from her shoulders and down her arms. The air touched her through the wet lawn of her shift and it seemed that she could feel every thread of the fabric against her breasts, and then he slipped that down too, baring her to her waist.

A flush burned hot through her entire body as she raised her arms, crossed them over her chest, and turned her head to the side.

"No." He grasped her wrists, urged her arms to her sides, then crooked his forefinger to tip her chin up. "Let me see you as I've imagined."

It was all she could do to hold herself upright as she remained kneeling before him, her arms lowered. "You've imagined me like this?"

"Oh yes," he said softly. "Many times."

Pleasure seemed to melt inside her and become liquid, flowing through her as she followed the path of his gaze. Her breasts seemed to grow firmer before her eyes, the nipples tight and puckered and tingling.

He covered them with his hands and rotated her nipples in his palms. He pulled her to him and lowered his head, covered her mouth with his, plunged his tongue inside, dancing with hers in a rhythm that lured her to respond, to follow wherever Damien led.

She should resist, but her limbs were warm and languid. . . .

She didn't want to resist.

Damien groaned as he broke the kiss and lowered her to lie on her back on the grassy bank, his gaze intense and unfathomable as he stared at her, as the damp cloth of her chemise became another texture of his touch as he stroked and caressed her. And then it was flesh against flesh as his hand slipped beneath the shift and covered the place between her thighs.

She arched her hips as he nudged her legs apart, urging them to open for his touch. Sensation throbbed a staccato beat as he found a deeper layer of her. And then it stabbed through her, writhed inside her, rising and rising and then he slipped his finger inside her a little, driving her mad with pleasure and wanting.

She wanted to touch him but didn't know how or where. She could only lie on her bed of grass and stare up at him, needing more and more of his caresses. . . .

He took her mouth again in a hard, demanding kiss that plundered and ravaged and left her gasping. He slid down her body slowly and opened his mouth over her breast, taking the nipple into his mouth, his tongue engaging in a slow waltz with the pebbled flesh as his finger thrust into her and his hand pressed against her, driving her to arch her back and rotate her hips and pant with the wildness of reaching for more . . . more . . . more. . . .

Pleasure leapt high within her and whirled and whirled and transformed into exquisite agony suspended high. She reached for it, held it, felt it explode into sound and movement inside her as vibrating spasms shook her until she knew nothing but a crescendo of sensation.

She cried out and stiffened, then collapsed and lay still beneath Damien, shattered into a thousand pieces floating on a sigh.

He rested his head on her shoulder and stroked her hair as she stared up at the sunlit sky and slowly searched for the scattered parts of herself.

"We made love, didn't we?" she asked as she lay very still, bracing herself for the truth that would seal her fate.

Abruptly, Damien left her and sat with his back to her, his shoulders heaving and his head lowered. "No, we did not make love," he gritted.

No? How could that be? How could something so . . . so profound be anything else? "Then what did we do?"

"Something we shouldn't have."

"I don't understand," she said, understanding only what she'd wanted, what she'd felt in the having.

"I'm bloody well not going to explain it to you," he said, his voice strained as he rose to his feet. "I've already done enough. Forget it, Kathy. Forget what we just did." He strode to the water and dove headlong into the pond.

She stared after him, watching as he swam toward the far bank.

They hadn't made love, he'd said.

But then what had they done that could give her a pleasure she hadn't known existed. Yet, she realized that Damien had not found such pleasure. It was obvious that he did not feel limp and satiated and strangely content.

She watched him plow through the water as he had plowed through her life, leaving spumes of confusion in his wake.

He'd told her to forget what had happened.

She feared she would never forget.

A cold swim had not cooled Damien's passion. Never had he felt so undone as he stalked through the woods ahead of Kathy, holding his coat as casually as possible in front of his erection. An erection so full and hard, agony jarred through him with every step.

His thoughts were equally tormenting. Thoughts of how wonderful it had been to stroke her and know he was the one to give her a pleasure she had never experienced. He didn't want to dwell on how he'd been compelled to give without thought to his own satisfaction. But now all he could think about was his lack of satisfaction.

How was he going to keep his hands off her?

He could have Smithy lock him in the tower for the night and guard the door. Better yet, he could have Kathy locked in the tower and have Smithy guard the door.

But what of the nights yet to come? After what had just passed between them this afternoon, any high-flown notions he'd had of controlling his baser instincts had quickly turned to compost. He knew too well how passionately she responded to him, how easy it would be to slip into her bedchamber, and find the release his body demanded.

Kathy's presence had become a double-edged sword, sharp and poignant with companionship and jagged with a desire that tore through him at every sight and thought of her. A desire he could control no more than he could control Kathy herself. And like Kathy's presence, desire had become a living part of him, a contrary thing that he could no longer view as a minor irritation to be dispatched in the most convenient manner possible.

The only chance he had of preserving her chastity and his sanity lay in putting her out of sight and therefore hopefully out of mind.

He'd leave Westbrook Castle in the morning and

stay away until her brothers arrived to take her away. If there was any mercy in the world it would work.

Silence interrupted his reflections. He paused and listened for the rustle of leaves underfoot or a telltale feminine grumble at his rapid pace. He heard nothing.

What was Kathy up to now? he wondered sourly. Climbing another tree? Swinging from a vine? He glanced over his shoulder and searched the woodland behind him, then released a short impatient sigh as he spied movement to his left. Of course it was his erstwhile wife, bending over to pick a flower. Of course her wet skirt clung to the exquisite curve of her derriere. Of course he had to remember in taunting detail that derriere fitting as perfectly into his hands as her breasts.

His erection throbbed and seemed to lean in her direction. "Don't dawdle," he snapped.

Kathy jerked upright and whirled; the daisy in her hand fluttered to the ground. "I'm sorry," she said.

Damien glanced away. He was sorry, too. Sorry that he'd given in to the temptation to touch her and that she'd looked so panicked when she'd once again believed they made love. Sorry that he couldn't stroll hand in hand beside her. Sorry that the idea of having a husband was so abhorrent to her.

With a disgusted snort, he resumed his pace back to the castle and the solid barriers of twelve-foot-thick walls.

Why should he care whether she wanted a husband or not?

Why indeed? He shouldn't care. It shouldn't matter.

Yet all he could think of was how eminently suitable she was to be his wife. How perfectly she seemed to fit into his days. How her responses to his touch both sweetened and spiced his lust until it became something else. Something he craved with mindless fervor, a rare delicacy he could not refuse.

He didn't want to refuse.

Kathy appeared beside him and grasped his arm. "Damien."

He jerked away from her and stepped out of reach. "What?" he barked.

She drew back. "Your shirt," she said. "It's buttoned wrong."

"Well, your hair is a mess," he shot back as he made the necessary adjustments.

Hurt clouded her eyes as she lowered her gaze.

He was being a cad, punishing her because he could not control his lust for her. More than that, he was punishing her for not wanting what he wanted. How ironic that he didn't know what he wanted either.

"Here," he said as he stepped toward her. "Let me help you." He combed his fingers through her hair and brushed it away from her upturned face. He searched her expression, seeing nothing that provided any answers, seeing just her confusion and lack of guile and the blankness she employed to defend herself from being touched too deeply.

He hated it when she hid herself away in a cubbyhole of dark silence and cold pride.

He turned her around and gathered her hair at the nape of her neck. Alive—the strands were so alive, holding the warmth of the sun and curling around his fingers as if they would absorb any warmth they could find. Like Kathy herself. "Have you anything to tie it back?" he asked with a catch in his throat.

She fished in her pocket and produced a soggy ribbon, reminding him of his fear when she'd fallen into the pond, his panic at the thought of losing her, his fury at feeling so helpless against the onslaught of such emotions.

He had to get away, to find his balance. "I'm going to London," he said, the decision made as he said it. "I won't be back until Bruce and Max return."

She didn't move, didn't react at all. "Because of what happened at the pond," she stated.

"Yes," he clipped as he finished tying the ribbon. "I should never have allowed it to happen."

She turned to face him, to look up at him with a desperate intensity. "I don't understand. It was wonderful. What I felt—" She broke off and flushed. "What did I feel?"

He raked a hand through his hair. "Must we discuss this?"

"Yes," she said, "we must. I need to know what it was I felt. I need to know what we did if we did not make love."

"It was a prelude, Kathy. Nothing more." He swallowed and glanced away. It had been far more than nothing.

It had been disaster.

"A prelude," she echoed. "Then I take it we have not ruined our plans for annulment."

What he could not see in her expression he heard in her tremulous sigh. Relief, no doubt. It could be nothing else. A relief he should feel, yet didn't. Even the sagging of his erection gave him little ease.

"I'd be a fool to allow it to go that far," he said with a conviction he was hard pressed to believe. At the moment, he was feeling very much the fool. An hour ago, he had behaved like one, arbitrarily discarding common sense in favor of more irrational instincts.

Kathy certainly seemed to have no trouble maintaining her grip on practical matters regardless of diversions. He could do the same. He had to get on with his own plans for the future.

He turned back on the path. "Shall we get back? I'm anxious to prepare for my departure."

"Why must you go tomorrow?" she asked.

"The Little Season begins soon and I'm not of a mind to miss it." He scowled at how lame it sounded, how lame it was. He hated the Season, little or otherwise. Kathy had robbed him of imagination as well as reason.

"Yes, of course," she said crisply. "You're bored. I should have realized. . . ." Her voice faded as she took off toward the castle at a brisk pace, leaving him to stare at her back.

She'd assumed he was bored, and Kathy was as positive of her assumptions as she was of her "understanding" of things she knew nothing about.

He would, of course, allow her to believe it.

He shook his head as he followed her at a safe distance. It would be all too easy to catch up with her and convince her that he'd never been less bored in his life.

# Chapter 28

**D**amien was leaving.

Kathy sat cross-legged in the middle of her bed furiously raking a brush through her hair. Not so long ago, she'd found Damien's presence irritating in the extreme and would have been ecstatic to have him gone from her life. Yet, now the prospect brought sadness and a melancholy sense of loss.

Never again would they meet in the walled garden and speak of things great and small. Never again would they share intimate confidences laced with comfortable silences.

*Intimate.* More than their confidences had been intimate. More than their minds had touched and spoken to one another.

She trembled at the memory of being immersed into sensation, of frantic strokes and a driving need for more, of drowning in a pleasure so intense she'd thought she would surely die from it. Her breasts throbbed and swelled at the memory. Desire spread in the pit of her belly, a hot knife of need, a gathering pool of urgency.

She would never feel that way again—never feel the stroke of his hands or the press of his body against hers. Never again would she feel the bittersweet need to reach out to him, to touch him as he'd touched her.

And now it was too late. Damien was leaving. He would not return until Max and Bruce came back to take her out of his life.

She tossed the brush aside. She'd wanted to touch him so badly this afternoon, but she'd been too overwhelmed by the sensations Damien had evoked in her, unable to do anything but feel.

A flush washed over her and she raised her hands to her suddenly hot face. She still wanted to touch him, to explore the heat and texture of his skin, the curve of hard muscle, to discover the nature of the hard ridge she'd felt beneath his clothes.

She left the bed to pace the floor, as if she could outdistance the terrible ache of wanting. But it followed her, casting its shadow over her.

She stared at the wall separating her room from Damien's as yearning quickened in her blood and urged her toward the connecting door, as decision gave her the strength to push it open and step inside his bedchamber.

Now more than ever before, she had to touch him. Just once.

On trembling legs she made her way to his bed, her gaze fixed on him.

He slept on his back, his head turned to the side, his arms outflung. The counterpane and sheets were pushed down to his waist and tangled in his legs, exposing one bare calf and foot. His chest, too, was bare and rising and falling in a gentle rhythm.

Her breath shuddered in and out as she reached out and stroked his jawline, down his neck, and lower to his chest.

His eyes opened with a snap.

She froze, waited for him to speak, to act on her intrusion.

But he said nothing as he lay so still and watchful, as if he, too, were waiting.

She swallowed, struggling against the instinct to flee. It was too late to run. Her need to touch him as he'd touched her had become compulsion. Compulsion to share all that she could with him, to try to give him the same pleasure he had given her beside the pond.

She splayed her fingers over his chest, caressed his nipples, followed the silky line of hair down his midriff and belly, then paused, staring as the part of him that had so intrigued her this afternoon became alive beneath the sheet. Her hand inched downward and paused again, her courage faltering.

Still, Damien said nothing as he grasped her hand and pushed it beneath the covers, down past his navel, down over his groin, down to close her fingers around his shaft, encouraging her to explore the smooth texture and bold shape of him.

She moistened her lips with the tip of her tongue as she dragged her gaze up to his, caught her breath at the pleasure she saw in his eyes. Desire became breathless excitement as she held him more tightly, stroked him more urgently.

He groaned and pulled her down beside him into his arms.

And suddenly the enchantment was there, surrounding her, banishing the world beyond Damien's embrace. This was all that mattered.

She turned her face toward him, seeking his lips. Just once more she wanted him to kiss her.

He framed her face in his hands and his mouth captured hers. And it was like nothing she'd ever known before as she thrust her tongue into his mouth, kissing him with demand and urgency, becoming a part of the kiss, giving as well as taking.

He broke the kiss and stared down at her, his eyes a turbulent green. Every breath seemed torn from him and his chest heaved as if a storm raged inside him. He opened his mouth, about to speak, his gaze piercing her with awareness, with panic.

He was going to send her away. She couldn't let him.

Forsaking all but need, she raised her hand to his lips, pressed her fingers there, willing him to understand.

Just once more, she wanted him to touch her.

Damien shuddered and lowered his mouth to hers, driving his tongue between her parted lips as his fingers ripped the drawstring from her nightrail.

Liquid fire flowed through her veins and gathered in her belly at his urgency. She felt it too as she pulled her arms out of the sleeves and bared her breasts for his touch. He shifted and leaned over her, opened his mouth over her breast, drawing on the nipple as he shoved her nightgown down over her hips and legs.

Thrills of pleasure sparked from every place he touched—the sides of her breasts, her ribs, her stomach. Anticipation flared as he turned her over and explored the nape of her neck, her spine, the sensitive flesh of her bottom. Passion burned as he rolled her over again and brushed his hands over her legs, behind her knees, down to her toes, and back up again to the insides of her thighs. Need ignited a hot flame deep inside her as he stroked her as he had by the pond, his fingers entering her and withdrawing.

She wrapped her arm around his neck and drew his head down, parting her lips, inviting another kiss.

It felt good having his weight on top of her, his hands moving over her as wildly as his mouth moved over hers. But it wasn't enough.

Closer. She wanted him closer.

Instinctively, she opened her legs wider, bent her knees on either side of him, inviting him to do what he would . . . urging him to do it now.

Her heart seemed to stop as his shaft pressed against her. She arched against him, seeking more.

And then she stilled as he eased inside her, slowly . . . so slowly . . . felt herself accept and close around him as if she had been waiting for him, needing him to fill an emptiness she hadn't known existed. An emptiness that diminished as he penetrated deeper, farther inside her. An emptiness that became pain and pleasure and an emotion so profound she could think of just one word to describe it.

Beautiful.

He paused and she felt something inside her, barring his way, preventing her from having all of him.

His breath came in short, gasping pants as he withdrew from her, leaving emptiness and need.

"Damien, no," she cried as she wrapped her legs around his waist, holding him, pulling him toward her again.

He drove into her, tearing through the barrier in her body, filling her completely.

A sob caught in her throat at the pain. Yet still, she arched to meet him, to feel the pressure of him inside her, to meet his thrusts over and over again as he drove faster and faster into the very heart of her.

*Her heart.* He had found her heart. "No," she sobbed.

"Shh," he whispered against her lips as his mouth swallowed her protest and his body arched into her and thrust again and again, leaving no part of her untouched. He was everywhere—around her and inside her. Ripples of ecstasy became a storm inside her, sweeping her away, giving her flight without wings as she felt herself tighten around him, drawing on him with spasm after spasm until she didn't know where she ended and he began.

She gasped and shuddered and cried out as he stiffened and poured heat into her.

He had penetrated her heart and touched her soul. He was a part of her.

She loved him.

He didn't want love.

She whimpered and sagged into the mattress as Damien eased out of her and lay on his side facing her. She turned her head away, avoiding his gaze as her mind spun with visions of her mother and Fair Alyce. She'd trapped herself just as they had. Doomed herself just as they had doomed themselves to love men who took devotion without giving it back.

Married to Damien forever. A convenience.

Loving Damien forever. A fool.

She couldn't bear it.

Kathy lunged from the bed and stumbled blindly from the room.

Damien would have caught Kathy's hand if he'd been quick enough. If he'd been expecting her to flee in the first place. All he had expected was her usual questions.

But, apparently, she hadn't needed to ask if they'd made love. Some things were self-explanatory, like her tears. . . .

Her obvious regret.

Apparently, she had found enlightenment to be more than she'd bargained for.

He raised up to punch his pillow into shape, then sprawled on his back to glare up at the canopy of his bed. Goddammit! She had come to him. She had to have known what would happen.

He wished he had known what would happen. He wished he'd known that it would be something so incredible it defied description. Something that went beyond need, touching him in places that had nothing to do with sensitive muscles and hot blood, a need for her that transcended desire.

*Something mindless . . . consuming . . .*

*Beautiful.*

Snorting with impatience, Damien layered his hands behind his head and ordered himself to think with his head rather than with his less than logical appendage.

He could not lay the entire blame on Kathy. He'd been the one to introduce her to the pleasures and mysteries of the flesh during their picnic this afternoon. He had known that Kathy was not one to allow a mystery to go unsolved. And when it was over, he'd been too preoccupied with the release he hadn't felt to consider the consequences of the release he'd given her. He should have known she'd want it again.

That was the way of it once desire was awakened.

He'd done a splendid job of awakening Kathy.

The marriage had been consummated. The marriage was irrevocable.

He frowned. For the life of him, he couldn't summon up any sense of frustration or fury at the situation. Instead, he felt an odd sense of relief, as if a difficult question had just been resolved without a battle between common sense and instinct. As if nature had taken its own course in spite of his—and Kathy's—best efforts to muck it up.

He'd wanted to marry for convenience. What could be more convenient than to keep Kathy? What could be more pleasurable than to make love to her every night?

What was there to stop him?

It wasn't what she wanted.

It wasn't what he'd wanted either. Not in the beginning. Not when he'd been sane and rational. He shouldn't want it now. He and Kathy were too much alike to live in harmony for any length of time.

Sooner or later, familiarity would breed contempt . . . again. And while he'd known nothing so satisfying as Kathy's body, he would soon tire of her resentment.

It was easy to cry *pax* on their animosity toward one another when they both still had choices. It was equally easy to place blame when those choices had been removed.

He rolled out of bed and grabbed his dressing gown. He was a duke. He had enough wealth to buy all the choices he wanted.

Shrugging into his robe, he strode to the door and pushed it open.

Kathy was huddled in the middle of her bed, her head buried in a pillow to muffle her sobs, her hair a tangle of curls over her shoulders. She'd put her nightgown on wrong side out.

He raked his hand over the back of his neck, irritated that she should be so devastated over something she had asked for and enjoyed.

He knew she'd enjoyed it. Her responses had been too spontaneous to be feigned.

"Enough, Kathy," he said gruffly as he walked toward the bed. "Nothing is lost." He winced at the absurdity of such a statement.

She sat up and shoved her hair away from her face to reveal an expression of disbelief. "Nothing?" she asked with a note of hysteria. "What will you tell me next? That we did not make love? That I did not . . . do not—" Swallowing, she shook her head and buried her face in her hands. "Oh God, how could it have happened?"

Indignation rose as his pride fell into the bog of her misery. Next she would be denying the pleasure she'd found in his bed. Next, he would be shaking the truth from her and then proving it all over again. "I believe you came to me," he gritted.

"I know," she said baldly.

He narrowed his eyes on her and struggled to find the anger he ought to be feeling. She had no right to twist him in so many knots that he didn't know where one emotion ended and another began. She had no right to look so provocative in her tears and disarray.

He had no reason to feel so damned disappointed at her regret.

"The marriage can still be annulled," he said, ignoring how each word seemed to echo in a part of himself that had suddenly become hollow and dark.

She peered up at him from the shelter of her hands. "It can?" she asked in a small voice. "How?"

"By claiming a prior marital contract," he all but

growled and took a deep breath in an attempt to soften his voice. "I'm sure between Max, Bruce, and myself, we can find someone among our discreet friends willing to swear he had a prior contract to marry you."

"I don't know," Kathy said doubtfully. "It sounds very shaky to me."

Baffled by her response, Damien jerked his brows together. He'd expected her to be so relieved she would snatch at any straw he offered. For that matter, he ought to be pleased at finding enough composure to present such a sensible solution to her. "It is a sound plan," he said.

"Is it reasonable to ask your friends to do something that's most likely illegal? Is it fair to expect them to keep silent about it for the rest of their lives? Do you really trust any of your friends to be that discreet?"

"No," he snapped, annoyed that she should sound so bloody rational when his own mind was at odds with itself. If he didn't know better, he'd think Kathy was searching for reasons not to end the marriage. She hadn't said it outright, but she'd made it clear with her escape from his bed. If that wasn't enough, he could not doubt the evidence of her red and swollen eyes and the tears tracking down her cheeks.

Yet, he had to be sure. "Unfortunately, there is no choice but to risk it," he said tersely.

Kathy stiffened and met his gaze with a level one of her own. "Then why take any risk at all? There is a prior contract with Tony. I'm sure he'd be more than happy to produce it."

"No," Damien said hoarsely, the word snagging in his throat. He had his answer. Kathy was so desperate to get away from him that she would go to Edgewater for help. The knowledge ripped into him, hollowed him out. "I don't want Edgewater brought into this."

"Nor do I," Kathy said with a tremor in her voice. "But if we're found out, we may become the only couple in history whose annulment is annulled."

"You can rest assured that I'll see this marriage well and truly dissolved." The hollowness inside him yawned wider, deeper at the thought.

Kathy turned her face away from him. "What if there is a child? Please don't tell me there's no possibility of one now."

A child. Why hadn't he thought of that? Why wasn't he appalled at the prospect? "The chances of it are slim," he said, unable to deny it, not even if he wanted to.

Why didn't he want to deny it?

"But there is still a chance," she said in small, pleading voice.

"Yes," he said. "But if there is a child we can always divorce." The word tasted vile in his mouth.

"Divorce? That would mean complete ruin, would it not?"

"For you, yes. But you've made it more than clear that you hate society and planned never to marry anyway. The course you have set for your future is just as scandalous as divorce."

"True," Kathy said. "But what of your reputation?"

Why would she be concerned with his reputation? he wondered as he again felt the vague sense that she was searching for reasons to remain with him. He dismissed it as absurd. He was tired and out of sorts, nothing more. "I'm a duke," he said as if it answered everything, knowing it sounded arrogant. Still, it was the truth.

"Oh," she said. "Of course." She took a shuddering breath and captured her lower lip with her teeth. "If there is a child, would you allow it to remain with me?"

He stared at her, not knowing how to answer her. He had not carried his thinking that far.

Her body stiffened and her eyes widened. "Please Damien, don't take my child from me."

"Our child," he corrected softly, unstrung by her distress. "A child I would not deprive of its mother."

The tension seemed to drain from her as her eyes fluttered shut.

Damien could almost believe Kathy hoped she was with child. She adored Max's and Jillian's son, James. It stood to reason that she'd want children of her own. Children she would be denied once their marriage was dissolved. But if a child had been conceived tonight, she would have it all — independence, a home, a family.

It struck him then, what conflicts she suffered, how hard she had to fight against herself, her instincts. He knew she feared becoming like her mother. Feared it so much that she would deny herself a full measure of life, sacrificing her chances for a family of her own in favor of independence.

Now, he understood why she wanted the house near Bassett House. She would be close to her nephew and any other children Max and Jillie might have. She would live vicariously through their family.

Yet it would not be necessary if they remained man and wife. They could both have what they wanted. Kathy, a home and family as well as her precious independence. For himself, a wife who expected nothing from him.

Why didn't she see it?

He would make her see it.

Yet, he knew better than to bully her into an agreement. Experience had taught him that Kathy must be allowed to make her own decisions. Her brothers would return within two months, three at most. That should give him enough time to ensure she reached the right one.

He would have to manipulate Kathy into remaining married to him. And he knew just how to accomplish it. He would take a page from his sister's book. Jillian had manipulated Max into marrying her. He would do the same with Kathy.

"Why don't you accompany me to London?" he said as he idly strolled toward the bed. "It's time you began your search for a house in earnest."

Her back stiffened. Her gaze flew to his, startled and flickering with something he couldn't identify. "All right," she said. "If you wish it."

"I thought it was what you wished."

"It is," she said weakly.

Damien nodded. "Well then, I suggest that you get some rest.. I'd like to depart by mid-morning." He turned toward his own chambers. "Good night, Kathy."

He strode from the room without a backward glance, feeling inordinately pleased with himself. He'd handled that rather well, though he didn't fool himself into believing Kathy would be easily taken in. Until she realized she should remain his wife, every word he spoke to her would have to be strictly calculated and carefully delivered.

Tomorrow, he would begin the second assault.

# Chapter 29

**D**amien could not be rid of her soon enough.
The thought marched through Kathy's mind as the footmen marched in and out of her chambers with the trunks Frances had hurriedly packed early this morning.

Her eyes felt dry and feverish as she stood in the middle of her receiving room, feeling helpless against the tide of events that had swept through her life. She had not slept at all, kept awake by a confusion so intense, she felt as if she were going insane.

Last night, the realization that she was in love with Damien had terrified her. Yet, when he'd come to her and reassured her that all would proceed as planned, she'd felt a profound sadness rather than relief.

He didn't want to remain married to her and would go to any lengths to see it ended—even divorce if there was a child.

She flattened her palms over her belly willing herself to feel some movement, some sign that life quickened within her. She wanted a child. Damien's child.

What was she thinking?

"Kathy?"

She jerked her gaze toward her open door.

Damien stood there, sleek in his black clothes,

remote with his stiff posture, disturbing with his watchful eyes.

"May I come in? I've something to discuss with you," he said, his expression solemn, as if what he was about to say was of great import.

Her heart turned over and swelled with hope. "Yes," she whispered, wanting him to say he loved her, to ask her to stay with him.

"It is important that we continue to keep our marriage quiet," he clipped out. "Therefore I think it best for you to stay at Bruce's townhouse."

Her heart sank and writhed with anguish. "Do you think it safe to leave me alone? The earl . . ." she trailed off. What was she doing? She knew how he felt about love—about her—yet still she tried to remain with him. Still she hoped that his heart might be as stubborn as hers, offering no choices as it listened only to its own needs.

"You're not still worried about Blackwood, are you?"

*Let him go,* she told herself. She shook her head miserably.

"Good. I'll send Smithy with you and I'll be nearby should you need me. And then, before you know it, Bruce and Max will return." He glanced around the room. "I'll leave instructions to have all your things packed and have them sent to you when you're ready for them. That way, you won't have to come back here."

She swallowed convulsively and nodded.

"Are you ready to leave?" Damien asked.

*No!* She never wanted to leave here. Sometime in the past few months the castle had become more than her sanctuary, giving her a peace and content-ment she'd never dreamed possible. It had become home. "Will you give me a few moments? I'd like to go the gallery one last time and see Alyce."

"If you like, I'll have a copy of the portrait made for you. She's your ancestor, too."

"Yes, I would like that," Kathy said.

"I'll see to it," he said and disappeared down the hall.

Kathy made a slow circuit through the chambers she'd come to think of as her own, taking one last look. With a heavy heart she made her way down the winding spiral staircase. A bittersweet smile curved her lips as she said a silent goodbye to the fairy tale castle, to the memories that would always seem like magic to her. Like the dining room where she and Damien had shared so many meals, at first sitting formally at the head and foot of the table and later together in the center. It had been Damien's idea for them to meet in the middle. And like the parlor where she and Damien had sipped wine and watched the fire in the grate in intimate silence or lively conversation. It had been her idea to join him there after the evening meal rather than retreating to separate rooms, he for his brandy and cigar, she for a cup of chocolate and the companionship of a book.

She rather liked the smell of his cigars mixed with woodsmoke and his own unique pine scent. She far preferred trying to read him rather than the pages of a book.

And then there was the private garden. . . .

Kathy squeezed her eyes shut and swallowed at the vision of it, of patches of daisies and forget-me-nots and pansies, of marble urns full of annuals and the roses climbing the old stone walls. Of the wrought iron settee where she'd sat while Damien lounged in the chair next to her or on the ground at her feet, plucking her secrets from her as easily as she plucked the petals of a daisy.

She could not go to the garden, could not face the memories it would evoke and the roots of happiness she had planted there, knowing they would never flourish and multiply.

Opening her eyes, Kathy willed herself to put such maudlin thoughts from her mind. She stepped into the gallery and stared up at the portrait of the beautiful fair-haired Alyce, marveling at how the artist had managed to so clearly capture Alyce's serenity.

How had she endured loving a man whom she knew hadn't loved her? How had she endured the pain of losing him at the very moment he finally declared his own love? Yet, Alyce had endured. She'd gone on with her life. She'd loved again.

*She's your ancestor too,* Damien had said.

She would be like her, Kathy thought. She, too, would get on with her life. She would go to London and resume the search for a house.

She would put Damien from her heart, but unlike Alyce, she would never love again.

Now, more than ever, she believed that love destroyed.

She felt destroyed.

Damien propped his shoulder against the outside of the coach as he waited for Kathy and idly watched a second coach rumble toward the gates, bearing Frances and Smithy and sundry baggage.

His conversation with Kathy had gone much better than he expected.

She had reacted to his intention of installing her in separate residence from him as he had believed she would. Just as she had last night, she'd tried to fabricate a reason why he shouldn't. Nor had she been happy when he'd told her she would not be returning to Westbrook Castle. Her reluctance to leave had become quite evident in her desire to make a last circuit of the castle. He'd watched her from a distance, noting which rooms she visited, gratified that she lingered in the ones in which they'd spent the most time together.

Now he was certain the key to keeping Kathy was to send her away from him.

Suddenly, the second coach halted at the gates and Smithy emerged and stalked back up the drive with a ferocious frown on his face. "There's a thing or two needs settling, Your Grace," he said as he drew to a halt in front of Damien.

"What things?" Damien asked, wondering what had put Smithy in a froth.

"Yours and Lady Kathy's marriage."

"What of it?"

Smithy took a deep breath. "You said the marriage wasn't going to be a real one."

Damien's jaw tightened and he glanced at the coach stalled by the gates. Kathy's maid took a quick glance out the window, then ducked back inside. "I see you and Frances had a nice chat. How did she know?"

"The upstairs chambermaid among others. Sheets got to be washed. It's clear what went on last night and now you're sending her to Lord Channing's house to live." Smithy propped his fists on his hips and glared at him. "What's going on?" he asked, an underlying threat in his voice.

Damien massaged his temple. If it were any servant but Smithy, he would not tolerate such insolent questioning of his personal affairs. In any case, he had no intention of explaining himself to Smithy or anyone else. "Nothing that is any of your concern."

Smithy drew himself up pugnaciously. "I say it is. And it'll be a big concern to Lord Channing and the Duke of Bassett when they return."

Damien ground his teeth together until his jaw ached. How dare Smithy threaten him with Bruce and Max? But since he had brought it up, Bruce and Max would just have to live with it. "Have a care, Smithy. This is a private matter between my wife and myself. I will countenance no interference from you or anyone else, including Lord Channing and the Duke of Bassett."

Smithy's brows jerked together in surprise for a moment, then his expression became thoughtful as he stared at Damien. "You know what you're doing, I'm thinking."

"It will serve you well to remember that, Smithy," Damien warned.

Smithy's gaze slid toward the front doors of the castle as they swung open and Kathy stepped out, her face pinched and drawn, her posture straight and resolute.

"I forbid you to speak to her of it," Damien said under his breath.

Smithy gave a quick nod and walked back toward the other coach.

Damien frowned. It wasn't like Smithy to give in so easily. But there was no time to consider it further. Kathy was ready to leave and he was looking forward to the journey.

She would not be able to avoid him in the coach and he fully intended to make the most of his last day with her. In view of how stubborn she was, it could be quite some time before he saw her again, depending on how long she took to decide to continue their marriage. In the meantime he would give her a taste of the independence she sought by keeping his distance.

Stubborn nature or not, Damien had no doubt that in time, Kathy would come to him.

# Part 3

# Chapter 30

**H**ow curious!

Tony urged his horse into the shadowed alley down the street from Bruce Palmerston's townhouse. Curiosity had been driving him mad since Kathleen and Westbrook had returned to London a month ago and settled into separate residences across town from one another

The only reasonable explanation Tony could think of for their living arrangement was that they were keeping their marriage a secret.

But why? Oh, Tony understood very well why Westbrook had threatened him with retribution if he bandied about the details of what had transpired in Scotland. As if Tony would ever divulge to anyone his part in that humiliating fiasco. He shuddered at the thought.

Still, that did not explain why their marriage had not yet become common knowledge. Tony had not heard a whisper about their runaway match from his acquaintances at the club. Normally, the entire city would be buzzing with gossip. Yet, there was nothing.

More curious still were Kathleen's outings. She ventured out almost every day with a solicitor to visit vacant houses in town, as if she was searching for a residence of her own.

Yes! Separate residences. Had Westbrook tired of Kathleen?

Yes! They were estranged! All was not lost.

Hope swelled inside him. In that moment, Tony knew he still loved Kathleen, would always love her. He wanted to run to her now and speak to her and comfort her, yet he could not. Not yet. He must be patient. He must watch and wait. He would not rush in as he had last time. He would not make the same mistakes.

And in the end he would have his beloved Kathleen.

Forever.

# Chapter 31

I t had been a very long month.

A little more than a month actually, Damien corrected himself as he lay his head back against the squabs of his coach. One month and two days, to be exact, since he'd left Kathy at Bruce's townhouse and dragged himself through each day, his patience stretched beyond its limits as he waited for Kathy to come to him.

She hadn't.

He felt as if he'd stepped into a different world since coming to London, and often caught himself wondering if the time they'd spent at Westbrook Castle had been an elaborate dream that grew more distant with every passing hour. He and Kathy had created such an isolated and idyllic world for themselves, full of discovery and contentment, empty of boredom and loneliness.

He missed her.

His plan wasn't working. A plan fraught with misplaced nobility and short on practicality. Nobility would be lost on Kathy. How could she admire his patience when she'd become accustomed to action rather than caution from him, much less appreciate it when she was every bit as impulsive and demanding as he?

How could she spare him a thought when she spent every minute of daylight traipsing about either in search of a house or shopping for domestic trappings? Without doubt, she'd viewed every available piece of property in the city and surrounding countryside. And when she wasn't inspecting houses, she was purchasing linens monogrammed with the letter "P."

It rankled that she so easily thought of herself as a Palmerston rather than a Forbes.

It rankled that she could so easily become engrossed in her freedom while he seemed to spend an inordinate amount of time either waiting for Smithy's twice daily reports or watching his wife from a distance.

*His wife.*

He never should have left her to her own devices. It wasn't natural for a man to pander to his wife's whims to such an extent, much less concern himself with her sensibilities. He should have locked her in the tower and kept her there until she saw things his way—a thought that appealed greatly to *his* sensibilities.

She'd reduced his mind to treacle. He'd left meetings with his solicitor early and ignored his mail, unable to concentrate on anything but Kathy. Thoughts of her filled his every waking moment, and he felt the press of time like a weight on his shoulders.

At this rate things would never be settled before her brothers returned.

How arrogant he'd been to believe that Kathy would miss him enough to come back, that she would crave his kisses and caresses and the urgent slide of their bodies against one another. He should have known better. Her pride was equal to his.

On second thought, his pride seemed to have shrunk considerably, while his erections grew more insistent with every memory of the passion they'd shared.

It had to stop.

He'd have to go to Kathy.

The carriage lurched to a halt, startling Damien from his preoccupation. He glanced out the window, bemused that he should have traversed the city without noticing a single sight or sound.

He left the coach and climbed the steps to his townhouse, determined to see this impasse come to an end once and for all.

It was time for action.

The butler greeted him at the door and helped him off with his coat. "A Mr. Goodman is waiting to see you in your study, Your Grace," Jacobs informed him as he took Damien's hat. "He insisted upon seeing you the moment you returned."

He frowned as he stripped off his gloves.

"Shall I send Mr. Goodman away, Your Grace?" the butler asked.

Damien shook his head. "I'll see him."

He strode down the hall and into his study, shutting the door firmly behind him before turning to the man standing respectfully in the middle of the room. "Goodman, what brings you around?" he asked, ignoring the usual social preambles.

Goodman blinked at Damien's abrupt greeting, but otherwise maintained his composure. "It's about the property you own to the north of Westbrook Court, Your Grace. My client has asked that I again inquire if it is for sale. She is becoming quite insistent."

Damien smiled in satisfaction. "No, it is not for sale," he said as he took a seat behind his desk. If Kathy ever found out that he owned the house she wanted so desperately, he'd never convince her to—

The thought stalled and was nudged aside by an intriguing notion that gave rise to all sorts of possibilities. She had just presented him with the perfect opportunity to push her into the direction he wanted her to take.

He pinned the solicitor with a steady gaze. "I know who your client is. The question is: Why have you not told her that I own the property?"

Mr. Goodman flushed. "Considering your friendship with her brother, Lord Channing, I did not wish to put you in an awkward position."

Damien nodded, marveling at Mr. Goodman's discretion. "Perhaps it would be best if I spoke to her."

"I would be most grateful, Your Grace," the solicitor said. "I've done all I can to divert her interest in the property. Lady Kathy is quite stubborn."

"Yes, she is," Damien agreed, chafing with the need to inform the solicitor that Kathy should now be addressed as "Her Grace." But it was too soon for that, a fact that chafed him even more. He cleared his throat. "Tell *Lady Kathy* that the owner will meet her there tomorrow at precisely two o'clock. The house will be unlocked."

The solicitor rose. "Yes, Your Grace."

"And Goodman, tell her nothing else, particularly not my identity."

Goodman didn't bat an eye at the order. "I will leave all disclosures to you." He bowed and headed toward the door. "I bid you good day, Your Grace."

"Good day, Goodman," Damien replied as he sat back in his chair and propped his feet on his desk, turning his thought back to the conversations he'd had with Kathy over the months, searching for anything he could use to persuade her to see things his way.

And if all else failed, there was always the tower at Westbrook Castle that was conveniently high and fitted with a sturdy lock.

Kathy stood in the center of the parlor at Willow Cottage gazing at the cold grate in the fireplace and remembering how many times she'd pictured a fire casting a mellow glow over the room. The windows were bare, yet she'd always seen welcome in the small diamond panes set into frames of rich dark wood. How many times had she peered in the windows and imagined carpets on the floors and paintings on the walls?

Yet now, the rooms seemed empty and cold. Now, she could find no excitement in the possibility that she might actually be able to purchase the house, could find no comfort in knowing that in having her dream, she would be living on the outskirts of Damien's life.

She should flee before the owner arrived. She should find a residence at the farthest corner of England where she would not see Damien coming and going, would not be tempted to steal into the neighboring Westbrook Court and slip into bed beside him.

No, she thought with a hard shake of her head. She would not give Damien such power over her life nor her dreams. This was the house she wanted. The one she must have.

The note Mr. Goodman had sent to her yesterday had been the answer to a prayer. She had looked at house after house in London and the surrounding countryside, trying to find one that might suit. But, she'd been only able to imagine living here, close to Max and Jillian. And it was close to London where she could visit Bruce when the solitude of rustication palled. She could go to the theater and the opera by night and to the shops by day.

She sighed impatiently at the reminder of her own behavior in the last month. She'd never cared for shopping in the past, finding it tedious and frustrating. Yet now, she browsed the shops daily and purchased items for a household she didn't have.

That would soon change, she told herself firmly. The owner was coming to meet her—a good sign, surely. She would have her house, her freedom, and still be near her family. For the first time since Damien had deposited her on Bruce's doorstep and drove away, she felt a glimmer of happiness.

Or so she tried to believe.

She clenched her fists against the melancholy that hovered over her thoughts and swooped down on her without warning.

She had made no progress in putting Damien from her heart, but suffered renewed sensations of desire with every memory of his hands on her flesh, his breath mingling with hers in a kiss, his body merging with hers until she was sure he would always be a part of her.

Nor had she been able to put him from her mind, but remembered with longing and loneliness their companionship as they shared secrets and dreams until she was convinced they were kindred in soul and spirit.

She missed him as desperately as Fair Alyce must have missed her first love.

She frowned at the thought. Why was it that every time Damien entered her thoughts, Fair Alyce was never far behind?

More and more she wondered about the expression on Alyce's face in the portrait, the small shimmer of sadness in her eyes mingling with the aura of serenity that gave her a look of strength and courage . . . and acceptance. More and more Kathy wondered if Alyce had found happiness in simply being able to share her life with the man she loved.

More and more she wondered how Alyce had won the love of her earl.

The sound of footsteps intruded into her musings. She began to turn toward the entrance but something stopped her. Something she sensed, a quickening in the air, a subtle scent, a feeling of being watched and studied.

She turned slowly. Her breath froze in her throat. Her heart lurched, then thumped madly.

Damien stepped into the room, his eyes glittering green fire as his gaze slowly swept over her, missing nothing, revealing nothing.

"What are you doing here?" she stammered.

"I came to see you," he said.

"How did you know where to find me?"

"Mr. Goodman told me you would be here," he said, slapping his gloves against his thigh. "Do you know . . ." He paused and glanced away, as if he suddenly felt awkward, then cleared his throat. "Do you know yet if there is a child?"

"No, there is no child," she replied in a monotone as she struggled against the cold pierce of the disappointment that had added gloom to her days. Her monthly course had come the day after they'd arrived in London, ending her hope for a child. Until Damien had appeared, she'd consoled herself by believing that it was just as well, that she would not wish to be bound to Damien, nor he to her, by duty and obligation to a child.

But now, with Damien so near, she wanted to cry out her disappointment, to tell him of the emptiness she felt with no part of him to hold and to love.

Now, the hope that Damien had come for her shriveled and turned to dust. He wanted only to know if she had conceived. No doubt he was pleased that she had not.

His gaze narrowed on her. "I'm sure you're relieved."

She didn't want to speak of it. She wanted him to go away once and for all. "I don't want to appear rude, but I'm here to meet the owner of this property."

"And so you have," he said softly.

It took her a moment to absorb what he had said, to understand it. And when she did, it was all she could do to keep from doubling over from the blow. "You?" she said, not wanting to believe it. "You're the owner?"

He nodded. "I am."

She stared at him as she thought of the times she'd inquired about the house and been told the owner wasn't interested in selling, not once being told who the owner was. Mr. Goodman was *her* solicitor, yet he had protected Damien. And she'd confided in Damien, telling him of her plans for the house as if there were no question that she would succeed in having what she wanted. He'd listened, saying nothing, revealing nothing.

"I see," she said in a near whisper, the best she could manage in the face of such disillusionment.

His mouth quirked in wry amusement. "I wonder if you do."

Anger shouted inside her at his evident mockery. Her face burned and her ears rung. "It seems clear enough," she said as she clenched her fists and leaned forward, glaring at him. "You knew all along how much I wanted this house. You knew I wanted to live near Max and Jillian." Unable to stand still under the fury that kept building and building inside her, she whirled and paced to the hearth and then back again. "Did it amuse you to hear me prattle on about this house? Did it satisfy your twisted sense of humor to know that you literally held the key to my future?"

Her muscles screamed with tension, forcing her to pace again—to the opposite wall, to the window, and back to the hearth again. "Did it feed your sense of power to manipulate me? To listen with such thoughtful interest while withholding the truth?" She whirled on him so quickly her skirts wound about her legs, and she felt as if she were drowning again. "You deceived me . . ."

*Betrayed me.* She pressed her lips together and glanced away, unable to say it aloud, afraid that she would betray herself, her devastation.

"That was not my intention, Kathy," he said as he took a step toward her. "My silence was a result of indecision, nothing more."

She backed up a step. "What was there to decide? You have estates all over England. Surely you would not have missed this one. It has been vacant for years. What possible reason could you have for wanting to keep it from me?"

He swiped his hand over the back of his neck. "I do not want you living so close to me."

She swayed with the force of his statement, delivered so matter-of-factly and with such cold rejection. If she'd had any doubts before, she had none now. He'd been tolerating her because he had to. Once their marriage was dissolved, he wanted nothing more to do with her.

Nothing had changed for him. Nothing at all.

With careful and deliberate movements, she smoothed her skirt and adjusted her pelisse. "Well then, there is nothing more to discuss," she said evenly. "If you will excuse me, there are several other properties I must inspect."

"You understand then?" he asked casually.

"Perfectly."

He shifted slightly, his body blocking her path, continuing to speak as if she'd said nothing. "You understand that within the year I intend to take a wife. I spend too much time in residence at Westbrook Court, and would spare her the awkwardness of having you live nearby."

Feeling as if she'd been slammed against a wall, she stilled, willing herself not to reel, not to gasp at the shock of it. She had known he planned to marry again. Yet, hearing him say it, here in this house, hearing him speak of his future wife and herself in the same sentence made it despairingly real, hopelessly final.

It brought a fresh spasm of pain to know that her place in his life could be so easily filled, that he wanted nothing more than to forget her, that he cared more for the feelings of an as yet faceless, nameless woman than he did hers.

"And what will you tell your wife of me?" she blurted. "Or do you plan on telling her? After all, our marriage is a secret, and if I am out of sight, there would be no reason to—" She choked off the rest, horrified that she felt so put upon and full of self-pity.

"I see no need for such drastic measures," Damien said with galling patience as he sauntered further into the room, his footsteps a hollow echo in the unfurnished house, his expression seeming a little too smug for her liking. "I'll explain to her that ours was only a brief marriage of convenience gone awry."

How could he reduce the pleasure they'd taken in one another to "only" convenience? Had it all been so trivial to him—the companionship, the sharing, the passion that had shaken her world and turned it upside down? "Just as you will explain to her that you are marrying her for the sake of convenience?" she lashed out before she could humiliate herself by voicing the thoughts that tortured her.

"Yes," he said, staring at her intently. "I take it you disapprove."

"I do," she snapped. "If you don't want the responsibility of love, why take on the responsibility of marriage?"

He turned his face away from her. "Because it's my duty to see that Westbrook has an heir."

An ache welled in her throat as she gazed up at his profile. His entire life was composed of duty. He had married her out of his sense of duty to his family and friends, and he would marry yet again out of duty to his name and title. It wasn't fair for her to object to what he must do, especially when she knew her objections stemmed from her love for him. Love he had not asked for and did not want.

The ache in her throat grew larger, more painful, and tears burned at the back of her eyes. She'd been forced on him and he'd accepted the responsibility, asking nothing of her but congeniality. That he'd gotten a great deal more was her doing. She'd welcomed conversation with him and made herself available. She'd reveled in his caresses and asked for more, blatantly, thoughtlessly, stupidly.

She wished that she had conceived, sparing him the necessity of taking yet another a wife he did not want. She would at least have had a bond with him then, a measure of closeness.

Lifting her chin, she struggled to maintain some semblance of dignity and graciousness. It was all she could do, all that he would want from her. "I wish you well, Damien," she said quietly, shocked to realize she meant it. She wanted him to be happy. "I hope that the wife you choose will be someone you like." She stepped past him. "I must go."

His hand closed around her arm in a firm grip, jerking her to a halt, yet not forcing her to face him, not pulling her close. "Goddammit, I like *you*," he said fiercely.

She barely moved, barely breathed and even her heart paused as the strain and sincerity of his tone slid over her and through her, filling her with hope. But then the actual words sank into her, a knife shredding her. She exhaled and locked her knees to keep from sagging in disappointment. She pressed her lips together to keep from crying out in protest.

*Like,* not love. He did not love her.

"I like you, too," she choked, fighting the pain.

"Then stay with me," he said from behind her, the heat of his body reaching out to her as he drew nearer still. He slid his hands up her arms to rest lightly on her shoulders, his fingers leaving a trail of sensation on her flesh. "Nothing has to change between us."

Such simple words to create such temptation. Yet everything had changed and could not be changed back.

"I can't," she said raggedly, wishing she could be like Fair Alyce, content to be liked and wanted rather than loved and needed. But she could not. She could not be his wife of convenience, living bittersweet days of being near him and spending nights holding him inside her, taking pleasure from him, yet wanting so much more. Wanting everything.

"You will not lose your freedom, Kathy," he said as beams of sunlight slanted in through the window behind her and splashed their shadows onto the bare floor, each separate and pointing toward the outside, pointing toward escape.

Yet, there was no escape from loving a man so much that she could not even take a step away from him. Like Fair Alyce. Like her mother.

She would never be free.

She stared at the floor, at Damien's shadow moving closer to hers, merging with hers.

"We can go on as we have, each of us living our life as we please," he said, his breath a warm caress on her ear.

*Go on as we have,* she thought. It might have been possible once, when all they had exchanged were words of disapproval and anger; there had been a certain challenge and dignity to that. It might even have been possible when she'd been content to talk and laugh with him, when she had merely liked him; there had been happiness in that. But where was the challenge in loving a man who did not love her? How long would her dignity last in such a situation? How could she find happiness knowing that she would be like her mother, living each day for Damien instead of herself?

"It won't work," she said as she took a step away from him, away from the heat of his body.

His grip tightened on her shoulders, pulling her back. His hand slid up her neck and gently covered her mouth. "Yes it will," he whispered, his lips brushing the side of her neck, sending a shiver down her spine.

"Please don't," she said against his hand still pressed to her mouth, acutely aware that he'd moved closer to her, though only his hands touched her, only his words reached out to her, beating down her resistance.

"Why?" he asked as he traced the outline of her lips. "Are you so afraid to admit that you don't really want to live out your life alone?"

"I won't be alone," she said as he caressed her

cheek and the curve of her ear. "I have Bruce and Max and Jillie."

"What of children? You want children, do you not?" His hand slid down to rest lightly on her abdomen, creating warmth, yearning.

Her heart twisted and she again felt the keen sense of loss and emptiness she'd experienced when she'd realized there would be no child. Yet, she could not admit that to Damien. "No," she denied.

"Then why were you disappointed that you hadn't conceived?"

"I wasn't," she said quickly, feeling as if she were a block of ice being chipped away, falling apart under the assault of his arguments, melting under the heat of hands on her belly and his breath on the side of her neck.

"I know you too well, Kathy. I could see the disappointment in your eyes. Think long and hard of the life to which you condemn yourself," he said, seducing her convictions as surely as he seduced her body. "You will live alone with no one save servants for companionship." He caressed her stomach. "You will never have children to fill your house. I've seen you with Jillie's baby. You love children. You want them."

She closed her eyes against the vision of a cold and lonely future where she would have her freedom and nothing else. Unless she chose to build another kind of life.

With Damien.

She opened her eyes and focused on the door. Escape was so close, yet something inside her resisted, encouraging her to stay with Damien, to listen and believe him.

"We can have everything we want, Kathy. We can have children as well as freedom." His hand moved lower and touched her through her dress. "We can have the companionship as well as the pleasure of one another's bodies night after night." His arms entrapped her as his other hand cupped her breast, his fingers circling the nipple through her clothing, then moving to the buttons of her pelisse, working them free . . . parting the edges . . . finding the shoulder of her gown and sliding it down. . . .

She trembled as his hand slipped inside the square neck of her bodice . . . beneath her chemise . . . over the center of her breast. *Pleasure.* She wanted it now, wanted to turn in his arms and feel his mouth on hers, his body against hers, inside hers.

As if he read her mind, he pulled her back against him, molding their bodies together, his erection hard and urgent as it pressed against her bottom. "You can even have this house if you stay with me," he said and laved her ear with his tongue.

*The house.* Realization swept through her, cracking the ice inside her, crumbling resolve around her. She'd been lying to herself. She'd wanted Willow Cottage, not because she would be near Bassett House and Max and Jillie, but because it was near Westbrook Court. Because it was near Damien. It had always been Damien she'd wanted.

Scarcely aware of what she was doing, she turned in his arms. "I want—" She broke off as she saw the intensity of his gaze on her, felt the sudden tightening of his hands as they gripped her arms.

"What do you want?" he asked in a low, gruff voice.

"I want to stay with you," she said, knowing it was true, knowing that she wanted whatever he offered.

She was more like Fair Alyce and her mother than she knew.

It didn't seem to matter as she saw him exhale slowly as if he'd been holding his breath, as she watched his eyes darken and his mouth curve into a gentle smile. He lowered his head and rubbed his lips over hers again and again—

Suddenly, he plunged his tongue inside her mouth as his hands sought the fastenings of her dress, found them, released them, and pulled her bodice to her waist. He tore his mouth away and lowered his head, taking one nipple into his mouth, drawing on it, sending a rush of pleasure to the pit of her belly.

Her knees weakened and she sank to the floor. Damien sank with her, covering her body with his. His fingers tangled in her skirts and drew them up, skimming over her legs, between them, seeking her.

She parted her thighs, urging him to wedge his hips between them, to come into her and become a part of her. She gasped as he thrust inside her, cried out as he withdrew, wrapped her legs around his waist to hold him, to arch upward as he thrust again and again, taking her beyond thought and breath and pain to where only ecstasy reigned. Where only she and Damien existed in a perfect world.

She arched again, cried out again, feeling him stiffen and spill into her, feeling herself fly beyond light and sound, beyond everything but Damien. Everything but the beauty of that single moment when nothing mattered but being with Damien.

It was enough.

# Chapter 32

**T**hey were together!

From a small grove of trees Tony stood beside his horse, his gaze burning as he watched the front door of the small house. Westbrook and Kathleen were together for the first time since they'd returned to London.

He rubbed his hands over his breeches, trying in vain to wipe away the film of dust and grit. In his haste to arrive at Kathleen's, he'd forgotten his gloves. He would have gone back for them but Kathleen had come out of her townhouse and he hadn't wanted to lose sight of her.

It had alarmed him to see that she was heading in the direction of Westbrook Court, but then her coach had veered north to arrive at yet another vacant property. A property owned, Tony knew, by Westbrook.

And then Westbrook himself had arrived, a short while later, his expression grim, as if an unpleasant task lay ahead. He'd gone inside and shut the door and they'd been in there for over an hour.

An hour of agony for Tony as he watched and waited, tortured by visions of what might be going on inside the empty house. Westbrook was Kathleen's husband; he could do anything he pleased with her whether it be beating or banishment.

His heartbeat quickened. Banishment!

Yes! Westbrook was banishing her. It was the logical explanation for their meeting here at an estate Westbrook owned, an estate that neighbored Westbrook Court. He wasn't even going to allow Kathleen to live at one of his primary residences, but planned to exile her to a house that was little more than a hovel with twenty rooms at best.

Oh, Westbrook was vile, Tony thought in outrage.

He longed to venture closer and peek into the window, yet he dared not for fear the two coachmen, assorted footmen, and that hideous servant, Smithy, would see him. He had to rely on his imagination to envision what must be going on between Kathleen and her odious husband.

Westbrook was probably shouting and Kathleen was probably weeping.

Yes! She was weeping and her heart was breaking because Westbrook had used her and cast her aside.

Tony's vision blurred. When the time was right, he would help mend her broken heart. He would love her and comfort her and worship her.

A low rumble of masculine laughter split the air. Tony's gaze narrowed on the door as it opened. He gasped in disbelief as Kathleen and Westbrook stepped outside and walked hand in hand down the steps of the house.

Kathleen's hair was down—Tony distinctly recalled it being in a neat chignon when she'd arrived. A smile tipped the corners of her mouth. Her cheeks were flushed and her eyes sparkled—not at all the pinched look she'd had of late.

Westbrook's smile was drowsy, relaxed . . . satiated.

There had been no shouting and weeping. They'd been making love!

They had reconciled.

Tony's ears roared as he stared at them through unblinking eyes, transfixed by the loathsome sight of Westbrook and Kathleen strolling across the lawn

toward the coaches standing in the drive. The coachmen and footmen discreetly averted their gazes. The
servant, Smithy, stepped forward with an insolent
scowl on his face as his gaze shot from Kathleen to
Westbrook, yet Westbrook's expression was placid as
he spoke to the servant.

Westbrook was a fool for tolerating such behavior,
Tony thought on a jolt of renewed outrage and
disgust. He cocked his head and listened intently,
but all he could hear was a murmur. His outrage
increased when Smithy broke into a grin and turned
on his heel, striding toward the coach Kathleen had
arrived in. He climbed on top, spoke to the driver
and they were off, leaving Kathleen and Westbrook
behind with the ducal coach.

Together. They would be leaving together.

In spite of his disgust, Tony could not stop staring
at them in morbid fascination.

Westbrook gazed down at Kathleen with a tender
smile. She spoke and returned his smile, so warm
and beautiful. Westbrook stroked her face, then
lowered his mouth to hers as she wrapped her arms
around his neck.

Tony's hands clenched into fists as envy burned in
his belly.

How dare they keep toying with him!

How dare they torture him with such a display!

How dare they look so happy!

They did not deserve happiness. They deserved to
hurt as he hurt, to feel the pain of betrayal, to have
their newfound happiness shattered as his newfound
hope had been shattered.

He raised his chin a notch. It would come to an
end. How could it not?

Tony knew, as Kathleen did not, the true character
of the Duke of Westbrook. He was a man without
morals or conscience. He would cast her aside again,
as easily as he had cast aside his mistress of five
years.

Poor Vicki. Tony had met her on the street last

week and discovered that she was not aware that her erstwhile lover had returned to London. Tony had not enlightened her either. Perhaps he should have.

Yes! How easy it would be to destroy the harmony between Kathleen and Westbrook. How easy it would be to create dissension and distrust. How easy it would be to help Kathleen see her husband's perfidy.

His heart fluttered. She would turn away from Westbrook and Tony would be waiting for her, ready and willing to console her and cherish her.

No! It was a ludicrous idea. Every man of wealth and position kept a mistress.

Yet, what if Kathleen was like Julia and she held faithfulness above all else in marriage? Tony raked his hands down his face, then snatched them away. They were filthy. He could not bear the filth. He shuddered and scrubbed the sleeve of his coat across his face.

Kathleen did not care for Tony or she would have never married Westbrook in the first place. Bitch!

Still, Westbrook had stolen her away and forced her into marriage.

He could not bear the way his thoughts bounced back and forth between love and hate.

*Kathleen!*

He would have her yet.

# Chapter 33

**K**athy was his.

The thought came with the sunlight slanting in through the window, penetrating Damien's sleep-fogged senses. He became aware of the early morning silence and the scent of passion lingering in the air of his bedchamber. Aware that his head and body ached as if he was suffering from the effects of a long night of overindulgence . . . with Kathy.

His wife.

Their marriage was finally out in the open and would continue. After they'd left Willow Cottage yesterday he'd wasted no time in bringing her to his townhouse and making a great show of formally introducing her to the staff as the Duchess of Westbrook. By now belowstairs gossip should have spread to every household of consequence in the city.

He should be satisfied with himself, yet unease rippled through his thoughts as if something were not quite right and there was more to be done. He dismissed the feeling. The only thing wrong was that he could not feel the press of Kathy's body against his.

He slid his hand across the vastness of his bed.

The sheets were cold, the space beside him empty.

He jerked his head to the left, focused on the form lying curled in tight ball on the opposite edge of the mattress, her hair splayed across the pillow, her back turned away from him.

Irrationally he resented the distance she had put between them in her sleep. As irrational as the depths to which he'd been willing to sink to keep her with him, as if he'd been driven by some unfathomable emotion.

He snorted his disgust at even entertaining such nonsense. He'd been driven by logic alone in his determination to remain married to Kathy.

His jaw tightened as he remembered in humiliating detail the scene between them at Willow Cottage. He'd gone to her after vowing that he would wait until she came to him. He'd literally begged her to stay with him and when that hadn't worked he'd resorted to bribery and finally, seduction.

The thought angered him as he continued to stare at Kathy's huddled form, at the line of her back turned to him and the covers she had drawn close around her body.

Even now he was irrational in his need to pull her to him, to tease and torment her until she begged him to bury himself inside her and take her over and over again. Beg as he had begged her yesterday to stay with him. But the thought soured and anger died. He did not want to contaminate the passion he and Kathy shared with churlish attempts to restore his pride.

What he really wanted was to make slow, patient love to her, to linger with each stroke and caress, to draw out each moment. He wanted to savor the nuances of lovemaking rather than give in to the fire and storm of it.

He turned to his side and reached out for her, rolled her to her back, drew the covers away from her bare breasts, cupped one then the other, stroking the petal-soft areolas with his thumb.

Kathy stirred and murmured as she opened her eyes and blinked them shut again.

"Kathy," he called softly as he traced a line from her collarbone to her navel, nudging the covers down until they concealed nothing but her hips and the fiery curls between her legs.

"Damien?" she sighed sleepily as she trembled beneath his touch and her nipples puckered into tight nubs.

"Who else?" he asked and shifted to accommodate the desire that was already rising, hot, hard, and insistent.

"It's morning," she murmured.

"What an astute observation," he said as he slid his hand between her and the sheet and found her moist and ready for him.

She arched her back and gasped as he stroked her. "Now, Damien," she said as she reached for him. "I can't wait."

Goddammit. He couldn't wait either. He levered up on one elbow and hooked her waist with his arm, pulled her beneath him, eased her legs open and sank into her. He clenched his teeth and reminded himself to go slowly, even as his hips moved in a fast, driving rhythm.

She wrapped her legs around his waist and matched him stroke for stroke. Her hands seemed to be everywhere at once, skimming down his arms and back and buttocks, tangling in his hair and pulling his head down, parting her lips for him and plunging her tongue into his mouth as he plunged into her body, once, twice, three times, each time harder and deeper than the last.

He bit back a groan as his heart thundered and his blood boiled. The air itself seemed to ignite around them as she closed around him in tight little spasms, driving him toward release.

He tore away from the kiss, arched his neck, gave her all of himself until he died in her arms and came back to life again.

Exhausted, he rolled to his back and lay still . . . and frustrated. So much for lingering over Kathy's body. So much for patience and control. With Kathy patience and control were always overwhelmed by need.

He hadn't realized until now that he resented it.

"It *is* beautiful," Kathy murmured as she lightly caressed his belly.

"What?" Damien asked, amazed that even now, he could be aroused by her touch.

"Making love. My mother told me it was beautiful. Now, I understand," she mused. "Promise me that you will awaken me so every morning."

The request slammed into him, and knocked the breath from him. *Every morning.* She wanted him to promise that he would relinquish control every day for the rest of his life. "That may become wearisome," he said tightly, feeling as if he were changing and he was helpless to stop it. As if he was helpless against Kathy, helpless even against himself It had always been this way with her. She compelled him to behave in ways that were new to him, confusing and confounding him. He had to stop it. He had to regain mastery over his own needs. "I have no doubt you may wish to sleep in your own bed at times. There's a connecting chamber for you."

She caught her breath and reached for the sheet. "Yes, yes, of course." She raised up on one elbow and stared over his shoulder. "My chamber . . ." Her voice faltered, then gathered strength. "Is it through that door?"

"Yes," he said, hating the sound of hurt in her voice, hating that he was responsible.

In one swift movement, she rose and gathered the sheet around her. "Do you mind if I avail myself of the privacy of my chamber now? I should like a bath."

His arm shot out toward her, reaching for her, then paused in midair. He jerked it back and shoved his hand beneath his head, aware that he'd instinctively reached out for Kathy, as if it were a habit of many years. As if something deep inside him depended on her in some intangible way, needing to know she was always within reach.

To know that she was his. He had what he wanted—a wife who didn't need him. It had never occurred to him that he might need her.

Suddenly, he felt naked and exposed. "You live here," he said as he rose, shoved his arms into the sleeves of his robe, and headed toward his dressing room. "You may do anything you like." Acutely aware of the distance that had grown between them, he paused at the door and glanced over his shoulder, unable to allow it to end this way. Not after making love with Kathy. This was no way to begin their marriage. Not when they'd both agreed to the terms. "Shall I have a tray sent up or would you prefer to breakfast downstairs?"

She gathered the sheet closer. "Actually, I haven't time for breakfast," she said briskly. "As soon as I've made myself presentable, I must go."

He tensed and gripped the door frame. "Where must you go?"

"I need to collect my things from Bruce's town-house."

"Send the footmen."

"I'd rather attend to it myself," she said avoiding his gaze.

"Very well," he said with curt nod of his head as he stepped into his dressing room and closed the door firmly behind him. He'd tried to close the distance between them and failed. A distance that had grown so fast, he hadn't had time to understand why it existed, much less why it rattled him to the point that he couldn't think it out. He gave the bellpull a vicious yank and waited for his valet, fighting the urge to accompany Kathy, to be with her every second of the day.

*As if she held a power over him.* He frowned and bit back a snarl at the thought. He had shared many a bed with a woman, but never his own. He had reached out for many a woman in the night, but only in lust, never in need. Never for the simple comfort of knowing she was beside him.

He twisted his mouth in self-mockery. What trick of imagination was this? Kathy was a friend who happened to be his wife, a woman who inspired an inordinate amount of desire in him. Nothing less and nothing more. For the moment she might control the responses of his body but she held no power over his mind and heart.

With a muttered curse, he did what he had never done in his adult life. He poured a draught of brandy and downed it in one gulp. He shuddered. Brandy for breakfast. Were there no limits to the depths he would sink?

Yates arrived subdued and cautiously efficient, as if he sensed Damien's foul mood. Not a word was exchanged as he shaved Damien, then left him to his bath.

A bath that Damien rushed through, then donned his clothes without calling for Yates to help him. He strode through his bedchamber and lifted his hand to knock on the door to Kathy's room, then changed his mind and entered her quarters as if he had every right to invade her privacy unannounced.

He did have the right. The house was his.

By her own choice, Kathy was his.

It was done and there would be no going back.

He scanned the room and found it empty. Surely she hadn't had the time to dress and be gone.

He took the stairs two at a time and slowed his pace at the entrance to the morning room. The sideboard was laden with serving dishes. The table, set with informal china and crystal undisturbed.

Kathy was nowhere to be seen.

One of his coaches rumbled by outside the window and turned onto the street. He caught a glimpse of Kathy's red hair inside the conveyance.

She was gone, taking advantage of her freedom.

He walked into his study and shut the door, sank into the chair behind his desk, and closed his eyes, telling himself that he didn't care what she did. That he had his own work to do, his own life to live. All was as it should be. As he wanted it.

Where the hell was Kathy? Damien wondered as he shoved his luncheon tray aside and attacked the pile of correspondence on his desk. If she did not return within the quarter hour, he would go to Bruce's and retrieve her himself. She'd had ample time to pack her belongings and return.

A light knock sounded on the door.

"Enter," Damien called on sigh of weariness and relief. It was about time.

Jacobs stepped in. "A young lady has arrived with several trunks. She says she is Her Grace's maid and requires a word with you."

"Send her in," Damien said, strumming his fingers on his desk.

Frances entered the room, bedraggled and looking as if she had put in a week's work in one morning. If she had packed all of Kathy's things, he supposed she had. If Kathy had rushed her so, he could assume that she was just as anxious to take up residence with him as he was to get this business of shuffling about over and done with. He needed order and routine and there had been precious little of that the past few months.

"Where is the duchess?" he asked tersely.

"She asked me to tell you that she was going to search for fabric for new bed hangings for her chambers. She took Mr. Smithy with her."

Apparently, Kathy did not care for the furnishings in her new chambers. Now that he thought about it, he couldn't say that he blamed her. The room hadn't been refurbished in years. Still, she could have asked if he wanted him to accompany her on her shopping expedition—

"Um, Your Grace?" Frances said, interrupting his preoccupation. "Where should I put Her Grace's trunks?"

He frowned at the reminder that Kathy was indeed moving into his life, lock, stock, and barrel. "Jacobs will show you the way. Thank you for delivering the message, Frances. You may go now."

The moment she pulled the door shut, Damien dismissed the maid from his thoughts, and rummaged through the pile of invitations on his desk. Surely there was some social gathering he could attend tonight. Surely he could find some antidote to the restlessness that broke his concentration and frayed his nerves.

He perused the invitation to the Torrington's musicale, then rejected it. The next time he appeared in society, Kathy should be with him. In fact, it would be wise to make a formal announcement in *The Post.*

Another knock sounded on the door. Damien snapped a call to enter.

Jacobs stepped inside, bearing a silver tray. "A note just arrived for you, Your Grace." He gingerly placed a heavily scented piece of parchment on the desk, then backed out of the room.

Damien scowled at the decidedly feminine handwriting on the envelope. Another message from Kathy? Had she found yet another mindless diversion to keep her away from home? He reached for the note and tore it open, his frown deepening as he read the brief missive.

*Darling,*

*Meet me in the park at three o'clock.*

*V.*

Damien stared at the "V" and drew a blank for a moment.

"Vicki," he murmured. God, how could he have forgotten golden and voluptuous Vicki—a poor actress and his most talented mistress for the past five years? Yet, she hadn't crossed his mind in months. His mind had been too full of Kathy. It was still too full of Kathy.

A ride in the park was just what he needed. His mistress was just what he needed.

Yet, he felt compelled to end his liaison with Vicki.

But, why should he?

He did not owe Kathy faithfulness.

He rose from his desk and strode toward the door, then halted and retraced his steps to pick up the note and toss it into the fire.

He stepped from his office and called for his horse to be saddled, then took the stairs two at a time, anxious to change his clothes and be gone, to do something—anything—to assert control over his own life.

# Chapter 34

**A**dulterer!

Tony chanted the word over and over again under his breath, feeling them vibrate with outrage as he watched Westbrook escort Vicki Hatherton into her house. How easy it had been to lure Westbrook back into the arms of his mistress. Aside from tracking Vicki down at Covent Garden last night and mentioning to her that he'd seen her duke, he'd had nothing to do but wait for Westbrook to show his true colors.

Vile, disgusting colors.

How could he want a woman who had defiled herself in the bed of whoever offered to keep her when he could have sweet, innocent Kathleen?

Allowing the corner of the curtain covering the window of his coach to slip through his fingers, Tony sat back in the seat. With trembling hands he withdrew his handkerchief from his pocket and blotted the perspiration from his palms. He had to do something before Westbrook returned to his wife. He couldn't allow Westbrook to touch Kathleen's purity after dipping into such a fouled well.

Yes! It was time to act.

How would Kathleen react to the news of Westbrook's faithlessness? No doubt, it would devastate her, considering that last night was the first she'd spent with her husband since her return to London.

His chest tightened and his breath shortened as images taunted him. Images of *his* Kathleen, *his* love lying beneath Westbrook suffering his touch as he drove into her, battering her with his beastly lust. He shuddered and wiped his hands again as he remembered how Kathleen had looked yesterday when she'd arrived at Willow Cottage, so beautiful and dignified, and later with her hair rippling down her back as she'd returned Westbrook's embrace, the passionate kiss they'd shared.

How could she have done that to Tony? How could she have allowed Westbrook to touch her, to know her?

Hate! Hate! Hate!

He hated her.

But no, he couldn't hate her. She was young and trusting. Too young to understand the nature of the fiend she had married. Too trusting to believe he would not treat her with honor and respect.

He rapped his walking stick on the top of the coach. His driver's face appeared in the window. "Number two, Park Lane," Tony ordered. It was up to him to tell Kathleen, to make her believe. And after he'd told her of Westbrook's betrayal, she would see her folly in rejecting the humble suit of Anthony Edgewater, a man who truly adored her.

She would trust *him* and know that *he* would be faithful to her. Always faithful.

The coach lurched into motion.

Tony straightened his waistcoat and neatly folded his handkerchief into precise fourths, then set it aside and felt his pocket for the spare he always carried. He would need it later, for Kathleen. He would watch her pain with relish; she did deserve to suffer for her poor judgment. He hoped she wept. He hoped she would seek comfort in his arms. He touched his fingers to his own lips. Yes! He would kiss away her tears, taste her remorse, satiate himself with her regrets.

He raked his fingers though his hair, then snatched

them away. What was he thinking? He must not feel any tenderness toward her. She had betrayed him. He must remember that.

On a deep sigh he raised his hands to gingerly pat his hair, searching for any wayward strands and finding a stray lock at his temple. Carefully, he smoothed it back and pressed down hard to force it back into place. He held his head very still, lest it escape again.

Kathleen always had tendrils of hair framing her face, yet instead of being offended by such dishevelment, he thought of an angel with fire for a halo. He frowned. Angels did not consort with fire . . . unless they had fallen.

Had Kathleen fallen? he wondered. Had he been beguiled?

Of course not. Kathleen's soul was pure.

Wasn't it?

He closed his eyes and breathed deeply, slowly, trying to still the chaos in his mind.

Confused, he felt so very confused.

# Chapter 35

**T**he first official day of her marriage was nearly at an end.

And Kathy had spent it alone. She was still alone, though the sun had slipped below the city horizon, the fiery splash of sunset color slowly fading behind a curtain of evening fog. She'd arrived home to discover that Damien had gone out hours ago and had not yet returned.

She stood at the window of the drawing room, her gaze drifting to the street, hoping to catch sight of Damien riding through the gate.

He had been in a strange mood this morning as he'd awakened her and pulled her close to him with a now familiar gleam of need in his eyes. Need that had barely given her a chance to emerge from her dreams. It was always that way between them— urgent, hard, fast—with no time to exert control, no opportunity to think of why it should not be.

Yet, he'd moved away from her so abruptly as he made a point of mentioning her quarters. She'd understood then that he expected her to occupy her own bedchamber. It had been all she could do to keep from showing the hurt he'd inflicted, to keep from blurting out how she felt about him, to ask if he felt anything for her beyond liking and desire.

If she had, the first official day of her marriage would have likely been the last.

Damien had no use for love. He had made it perfectly clear what he wanted from their union. It was she who had so quickly lost sight of the terms of their marriage.

Convenience. Separate lives and separate beds. Moments shared on a whim of passion.

A chance that he might one day love her. A chance that would be no chance at all if she spoke her thoughts aloud.

She blinked as a coach rumbled up the drive. Her heart leapt in her throat and her senses reached out, seeking sight and sound of Damien, anticipating his nearness, needing it to feel alive. But it couldn't be Damien. He'd taken his horse rather than the coach.

A man emerged into the waning light of dusk, straightening his waistcoat and smoothing his hair as he walked toward the front entrance, avoiding any fallen leaves and spots of dirt in his path.

It was Tony.

She instinctively backed away from the window before he caught sight of her. She'd forgotten the strength of her revulsion for him, how it permeated her awareness like a stench in the air.

She took a deep breath and sank into a chair, staring at the open doorway, waiting for the butler to announce Tony. She was in Damien's house—her house now. There was no earl to force her to see Tony. She was at no one's mercy but her own.

"Mr. Anthony Edgewater requests to see you, Your Grace," Jacobs announced from the threshold.

"Tell him to leave his card," she instructed with the slightest falter in her voice.

"As you wish, Your Grace," Jacobs replied and backed out of the room.

Kathy grinned as she settled deeper into the chair. How easy it had been to state her wishes and have them obeyed. It felt good to have the authority to dismiss the undesirable from her life—

"I beg your pardon, Your Grace," Jacobs interrupted her thoughts, "but Mr. Edgewater insists he must speak to you on a matter of utmost urgency. He says it concerns His Grace."

*Damien.*

Her gaze darted to the clock. Half past six. Damien had left five hours ago—far too long for a turn about the park. Sharp, paralyzing fear gripped her. Had he met with an accident? Was he hurt? Before she could think further, she nodded to Jacobs. Yet, as she pressed her hand to her breast, fear gave way to awareness of her heart beating calmly and the steady flow of blood at the pulse in her neck.

Damien was all right. He was too much a part of her for her not to know it, to feel it, if he weren't.

If he weren't, Tony Edgewater would be the last person entrusted with the news. If Damien needed her, Tony would be the last person he would send for her.

Why hadn't she remembered Tony's penchant for bad melodrama?

Preferring to meet Tony on her feet, she rose from her chair.

He strode into the drawing room ahead of the butler, his expression rigid, his posture so stiff he seemed more statue than man with his immaculate clothing and the scrubbed clean polish of his skin. The only thing that made him seem human was the wing of hair that drooped over his ear.

"Mr. Anthony Edgewater, Your Grace," Jacobs announced with a look of apology, then bowed and pushed the door fully open on his way out of the room. Kathy had a feeling that within seconds, several footmen would be assigned duties nearby.

Yet, anxiety washed over her at the unnatural light in Tony's eyes, and the way he seemed to tremble though he did not move a muscle, as if he were in the throes of ecstasy and controlled his manner by sheer force of will.

By sheer force of will, she defeated the urge to

shudder and turn away from the sight of him. Instinct held her still and calm, told her to stand fast and keep him from seeing her alarm.

"Hello, Tony," she said in a monotone.

"Your Grace," he said coldly. "How kind of you to finally consent to receive me."

That he was angry at her initial refusal to see him was obvious. She'd never seen Tony angry before. He'd always been the soul of politeness and good grace, taking her rebukes and insults with a patience and indulgence that was . . . odd.

Why hadn't she seen before how very odd Tony was?

She forced a polite smile. "What is it you wish to see me about?" she asked, adopting the same curt manner she'd used when he'd been pursuing her.

Keeping his head perfectly still, he slanted a glance at the settee, a ghost of a smirk curving his marblelike mouth. "Perhaps you should sit down. I fear what I'm about to impart concerning your husband will be most distressing, what with your being a new bride."

Unease crawled up her spine as she stood her ground, the vindictive pleasure in his voice chilling her. "Since this concerns Damien, I suggest that you wait until he is present to hear it."

He showed no reaction to her implied threat as he frowned down at his fingernails. "I doubt he will return for hours yet. He's with his mistress."

Kathy felt the blood drain from her face. Her vision blurred. Damien had a mistress. He was with her now. She tried to dismiss it as more of Tony's histrionics, but could not ignore the ring of truth in his voice and his obvious relish in being the one to inform on Damien.

He would not dare to invade Damien's home, unless it served his own ignoble purpose. Unless he knew that Damien would not be present.

Unless what he said was true.

"Ah," Tony said, with a slight inclination of his head, the wayward lock of his hair flopping from his ear to his temple. With a quick swipe of his hand, he smoothed it back into place. "From your shock, I can see he hasn't told you of his liaison with Vicki."

"No," she choked, betrayal a hot knife in her belly, thawing her shock too quickly and painfully for her to dissemble.

"Then, allow me to enlighten you further. She's an actress, a very inept actress, but she is oh, so beautiful. So beautiful that she's managed to keep your husband enthralled for the past five years."

*Five years.* A long time for a man like Damien. She choked back a hysterical laugh, forgetting that Tony was still in the room, forgetting everything but that Damien had kept the same mistress for longer than she, Kathy, had known him. It was Bassett and her mother all over again, except that she was the wife. The convenience.

The one left behind.

Damien was with his mistress now after spending the entire night making love to his wife.

Kathy wrapped her arms around her middle, feeling violated, ravaged, her thoughts racing in circles, clamoring for escape.

Did Damien feel the same way about his mistress that Bassett had felt about her mother? Was this woman someone who would always be in his life, someone with whom she could not compete? An actress would not be worthy of marriage to a duke, but the heart recognized no rank or title. He could be devoted to Vicki. He could love her.

Was that why he was so certain he could not love a wife?

Tony gasped.

Kathy blinked and focused on him, then followed his gaze to the door.

Damien stood just inside the room, his body still and tense though he propped one shoulder against the wall. His arms were folded across his chest in a relaxed posture, but the muscles flexed as he clenched his fists over and over again. His green eyes gleamed with calculation and menace as he pinned Tony with his stare.

He was furious . . . dangerous . . .

A panther ready to pounce.

"Are you quite finished, Edgewater?" Damien asked through clenched teeth, taking grim satisfaction in the terror in Edgewater's eyes. He was right to be afraid.

It was all Damien could do not to tear him apart. "You always were foul," he said as he pushed away from the wall. "I would do society a service in eliminating you."

Edgewater straightened and pointed his quivering chin to the air. "I merely speak the truth."

Kathy straightened and stepped forward and grasped Edgewater's arm. "Leave him alone, Damien," she said on a high note of fury.

"Stay out of this," Damien said.

"No," Kathy spat. "You will not punish him for telling me what you should have told me long ago." She gazed at Tony. "Go home."

Tony shot a wary glance at Damien.

"He will not accost you," Kathy said as she took her hand from Edgewater's arm and glared at Damien. "Will you?"

Tony took a hesitant step, then halted, as if he expected Damien to attack him the moment his back was turned.

"Oh, for God's sake, Edgewater, get out before I change my mind," Damien snapped.

"Go," Kathy whispered.

Edgewater's gaze lingered on her for a moment as he smoothed his coat and ran a trembling finger around the edge of his neckcloth. "Very well, Kathleen. I will go because you ask it of me," he said with a slight quake in his voice, then turned and strode from the room, carefully keeping out of Damien's reach.

Damien smiled grimly as he faced Kathy. "I see you've wasted no time in judging me."

Kathy remained rooted where she stood, her chest heaving. "What is there to judge? It's true, isn't it?" she said, looking as if the world had collapsed around her.

*Tell her,* his conscience prompted.

He opened his mouth to tell her he'd ended the affair with Vicki, but sudden panic smothered the words inside him. There was something in the way Kathy stared up at him, her fixed gaze a deep chasm of pain, as if her entire life depended on his dispelling her belief in Edgewater's poison.

She looked destroyed. . . .

She'd once said that love destroyed.

Realization descended, a crushing weight that held him immobile, unable to function beyond a single thought.

Kathy loved him.

His hackles stood on end. He hadn't expected that from her. He'd been convinced that they were indeed a pair. A perfect pair, compatible in all ways, including their shared cynicism.

He'd been a blind fool. Blind from the moment she'd come to his bedchamber at Westbrook Castle. He should have seen it then. Kathy never would have offered herself to him unless she loved him.

She'd loved him even then, yet he'd had to plot to keep her with him. He'd had to beg her not to walk away from their marriage.

He'd trusted her not to love him.

She'd betrayed him, violated their pact. And now as he saw the bitter condemnation in her eyes, he knew that she had changed the rules they'd agreed upon.

He raked his hand through his hair as he watched her back up and sink into a chair, again struck by her devastation. The knowledge that he could ease her mind did nothing to ease his.

This wasn't what he'd bargained for. He would not allow it. Whatever it took, he would remind her of the rules until she understood them. . . .

Perfectly.

"Aren't you going to defend yourself?" she asked.

"There is nothing to defend," he said with a mildness he didn't feel. "Vicki is none of your concern."

"It is my concern when you leave me to go to her. It is my concern that you might leave her and come to my bed, expecting me to receive you after—" She swallowed and looked away from him.

"I expect you to honor the terms of our agreement," he said tersely as he strolled to the sideboard and splashed brandy into a snifter.

"It had not occurred to me that our arrangement included lovers." She stared up at him, her blue eyes dark, bleak. "Damien, I cannot be so sanguine about such things. I do not possess such sophistication." She shook her head. "I cannot share you with another woman," she stated firmly and laced her fingers so tightly her knuckles whitened.

*She didn't have a wedding ring.* The observation broke through all else, inconsequential yet seeming infinitely important. Damien tossed down his drink, willing the fire in his gullet to burn away the errant thought. "Just as how you spend your days is none of my affair, how I spend my days is none of yours."

"None of my affair?" Her face flushed and she raised her hands to her cheeks, her long tapered fingers caging her face. "You've been with her for five years. You must care for her. How can you expect me to live with you knowing that?"

"It is what we agreed upon yesterday—both of us free to come and go as we please, to do as we please."

From the corner of his eye, he saw her mouth work and knew she struggled for words.

"I made a mistake," she said finally.

"How so?" Damien asked and loosened his cravat.

"I was wrong to think it would work. I want to dissolve our marriage," she choked.

Her bald statement stunned him with its finality. Knowing that she loved him, he should be anxious to let her go. But the thought of losing her prompted only confusion and panic. He couldn't let her go, and the realization gutted him.

She'd become too much a part of his life.

He'd become too accustomed to her husky laugh echoing off the stone walls of Westbrook Castle, the whimsical softness of her eyes as she studied the portraits in the gallery, the flame of her hair bringing new life to the garden as her conversation filled the shadows cast by late afternoon sunlight.

And, God help him, he wanted no one else in his bed. Kathy made him feel more alive than he'd ever felt before.

"Did you hear me?" Kathy said, her voice reaching through his confusion. "I want an annulment . . . a divorce . . . whatever is necessary."

"No," he barked as he turned his back to her, refusing to take her seriously and reminding himself that Kathy was as impulsive as he, and as quick to anger. She needed time to think, to fully understand how completely she belonged to him.

To accept that he would not release her. That it was too late.

Too late to ignore emotions that grew larger with every moment he spent with Kathy. Too late to fool himself into believing that his only obligations were to sire an heir and to see that Kathy had comfort and protection. Too late to believe that life could go on as it always had.

He, too, needed time.

He needed time to understand why.

# Chapter 36

Tony had been wrong. Kathleen did love him. Why else would she have protected him from her lunatic husband?

His legs trembled violently as he collapsed in the seat of his carriage. Westbrook had wanted to tear him apart. He had seen it in the feral gleam of his eyes, heard it in the savage undertone in his voice.

The coach lurched into motion, slamming Tony into the seat, the race of his heart slowing with each turn of the wheels away from Westbrook and his fury.

On the other hand, he'd acquitted himself quite well, Tony thought. Surely Kathleen had seen the difference between his civility and her wretched husband's appalling lack of it. The man was a barbarian.

And oh, how courageous his darling Kathleen had been, standing up to Westbrook, defying him. Never would he forget the gentle pressure of her hand on his arm and the hopeless anguish in her eyes as she'd sent him away.

He frowned as he recalled how she'd looked, realizing that it was more than anguish. He'd seen fear in her eyes. . . .

Hadn't he?

He was certain of it.

She had to be terrified of Westbrook. He was obviously mad.

Yes!

How could he have forgotten how afraid Kathleen had been in Scotland?

Tony understood at last. Westbrook was mad and everyone had known it but him. No wonder the earl had beat such a hasty retreat when they'd confronted Westbrook in that ramshackle room in Gretna Green. Upon recollection, Tony could see now that the earl had tried desperately to wrest Kathleen away from Westbrook. After all, hadn't the earl initially refused to leave without his daughter?

Westbrook had threatened him.

It all came back to Tony—every vivid detail of Westbrook waving his pistol around, threatening to shoot them like a raving lunatic. He had even invoked the name of the Duke of Bassett. Everyone knew that no one man could stand against those two.

Yet, Bassett was still out of the country. At present, Westbrook was only one.

And, Tony thought as his chest expanded, the earl was no longer one man. Tony would stand at his side. Together they could defeat Westbrook. The earl had not had the opportunity to realize what a steadfast and powerful ally he'd had in his future son-in-law.

Yes!

They could help Kathleen. Together, they could find a way to free her from her disastrous marriage. Even if it meant stealing her away, as Westbrook had stolen her away from him.

Yes! He would use Westbrook's methods against him. He would take Kathleen far away where Westbrook would never find her while the earl contested the marriage.

Tony had misjudged the situation completely. The earl would want what was best for Kathleen. Had he not demonstrated that months ago by agreeing to a match between Tony and Kathleen?

The earl was her father. He loved Kathleen—not as much as Tony of course. No one would ever love her as much he did, and the knowledge that she returned his love filled him with indescribable joy.

Nothing would ever stand in the way of their love again.

Soon Kathleen would be his.

The words played over and over in Tony's mind, keeping rhythm to the jarring of his coach as it rumbled down the drive to Blackwood Manor, anticipation a celebration inside him.

The coach rolled to a halt.

Tony shoved open the door and bounded out without waiting for assistance from his footman. He drew up short as he caught sight of the earl standing on the small balcony that led from the study, the tip of his cigar glowing red in the evening light. The same balcony that Westbrook had leapt over the day Tony had brought the earl home. Tony shuddered at the memory. Westbrook had been like a rabid animal—more proof of his madness.

He jerked on his coat and walked proudly toward the earl.

"Edgewater, why are you here?" the earl asked.

Tony halted at the edge of bushes surrounding the balcony and frowned at the earl's rudeness in not inviting him inside. Still, the earl had spent many years in America, a primitive place at best. He could be forgiven his lack of manners. "I've come to assist you in freeing Kathleen from her disastrous marriage to Westbrook," he said as he brushed a twig off his sleeve.

The earl's brows shot up. "Have you now?"

"Yes," Tony said. "Something must be done. Westbrook is cruel to her—"

The earl raised his hand, cutting Tony off . "How Westbrook treats his wife is none of my affair," he snarled.

It shocked Tony, the earl's rude interruption, but

even more shocking was his lack of concern about Kathleen. Apparently, Tony had not made himself clear. "My lord, she is your daughter. Do you not care—"

"No, I do not," the earl thundered. "I wish to never hear her name, nor that of her husband's, spoken in my presence."

Tony drew himself up. The man was beyond rude. He was a beast. He didn't care about Kathleen at all. It seemed no one did, but Tony. "Very well. I shall see to this matter myself."

"And how do you plan to see to it?" Blackwood asked with raised brows.

The spark of interest gave Tony hope. "I intend to steal her away from him as he stole her from me. I will take her far, far away, to another country. Westbrook will never find us." He spoke quickly to avoid another interruption. "In the meantime, you can contest the marriage in the courts." He patted the pocket inside his coat. "I have the marriage contracts you and I signed. It will prove beyond doubt that I have a prior claim."

The earl gave an abrupt shout of laughter, then leveled his gaze on Tony. "You fool," he said, his voice laced with contempt. "You think you can take Westbrook's wife and simply hide away somewhere? What do you plan to do once he finds you?"

"He won't."

"Oh, yes, he will. He will track you down and take back what is his. And then, he'll deal with you."

Tony's mouth went dry. "Deal with me?"

The earl nodded. "If you're fortunate, he won't kill you."

A shiver rolled over Tony. Westbrook was certainly capable of it. Tony had seen him display murderous tendencies on more than one occasion, not to mention the threat he'd made that very afternoon. His heart twisted painfully in his chest. Oh, his poor darling Kathleen.

Suddenly, the earl leaned forward and braced his

hands on the rail of the balcony. "Stay away from Westbrook and Kathleen, or you will have to look over your shoulder for more than one threat."

"But . . . Bassett and Channing are out of the country," Tony stammered.

"And don't you think Westbrook has already sent for them?" The earl flicked an ash at Tony's chest. "Now get off my property and don't come back."

Tony brushed the ash away, then turned and stalked toward his carriage, his mind twisting with contempt for the earl. Blackwood was a coward. He was despicable. He would leave his daughter in that nightmare rather than risk Westbrook's wrath to save her.

Well, Tony was no coward. He would do what must be done to rescue his Kathleen.

Yet, in one respect, the earl was right. Simply taking Kathleen and hiding away somewhere would never suffice. He believed Blackwood was correct in saying that they would have to live their entire lives looking over their shoulders. As long as Westbrook lived they would never have any peace.

"Stay away from Kathleen and Westbrook," the earl called after him. "He'll kill you."

Tony's footsteps faltered and bright spots of light exploded in his mind.

Yes! He would kill Westbrook.

# Chapter 37

**T**he candles needed lighting, Kathy thought absently as she sat on the chaise in her bedroom and listened to muffled sounds of activity and the muted voices of Damien and his valet in the adjoining chambers. He was preparing to leave as he had left the last three nights, not returning until long past midnight.

She raised her hands and covered her ears. She didn't want to know when Damien visited his mistress. She did not want to imagine him making love to another woman.

But she could not stop the images from forming in her mind. Images of Damien giving another woman his laughter, his devotion, and perhaps his love.

Love he could not give to Kathy.

She took a shuddering breath and drew her knees up, hugging them to her chest as she stared at the evening shadows reaching across the carpet.

Had it been just three days since Tony had come with information that bled her with every word he uttered? Just three days since Damien had admitted the truth by his refusal to discuss it? A truth that was like a wasting disease, slowly destroying her thought by agonizing thought.

Was that how it had been for her mother? She could understand it now. Love offered few options and even fewer assurances. It could not be fashioned into a shape and size like a suit to be worn on a whim. Just the opposite, it molded every emotion and perception to fit its needs, annihilating self until only the heart spoke and only the soul listened.

And when it was gone, nothing was left.

Kathy feared that most of all. Feared that, like her mother, she would become a hollow shell, feeding off her memories while grief consumed and destroyed her.

A thud from next door echoed through the air.

Lurching to her feet, she glanced around frantically, filled with the urge to run, to escape the noises in the next room that inspired such tormenting thoughts. But where could she run? To the drawing room where she would hear the echo of the front door closing behind him as he left? To the library where silence smothered her with loneliness? To the shops where she could purchase everything but peace?

There was no escape from the knowledge of where Damien was going and who would be waiting for him. No escape from loving him.

She buried her face in her hands, stifling a sob as she groped for strength and reason. Nothing in her life had prepared her for this. The earl had tortured her mind with threats and tormented her body with cruelty, yet she had endured by separating herself from the pain. But how could she endure the pain of losing a part of herself? How could she separate herself from Damien when he had become air and light to her?

She had to separate herself from him. It had been her first instinct when she'd spoken out of anger three days ago, demanding to be released from the marriage. Yet, she hadn't meant it. She couldn't bring herself to end the marriage, just as she hadn't been able to end it at Willow Cottage.

Nothing had changed since then, least of all the terms of their agreement. An agreement she'd made, knowing that she loved Damien beyond all reason. Knowing that he did not love her. She'd been certain she could live with those terms.

She could still do it. She did not have to become like her mother unless she chose to do so. Damien didn't require her to live for him and through him. She could remain with Damien and bear his children and still have a life of her own.

She would keep her word, and in exchange, she would demand that Damien keep his. He'd said that she could have Willow Cottage. She still wanted it. Now more than ever, she needed it. She did not have to stand by and watch as he went to his mistress. She did not have to languish in her room as she waited night after night, for Damien to return.

She would not allow love to destroy her.

She squared her shoulders and crossed the room to knock on Damien's door.

Yates opened it almost immediately, his slight body barring her way.

Her gaze brushed past him to find Damien, then focused on a point beyond his shoulder. She couldn't look at him without remembering the past few months—of how easily he had disarmed her with his presence, forcing her to see the man beneath the hot temper and enigmatic smile, of how stealthily love had stolen her resolve like a thief in the night.

She inhaled slowly, gathering strength, reclaiming that resolve. "May I have a word with you before you go?"

He cocked a brow at her, waiting.

"In private," she said as she slanted a look toward Yates.

The valet left without a word.

"I'm glad to see you have come out of hiding," Damien clipped as he turned away from her to poke his finger through a sandalwood jewel box.

"I've been making plans," she said as she took a hesitant step into the room. "You promised me

Willow Cottage. I should like to begin renovations at once."

"You want the cottage," he said flatly.

"Yes. I haven't changed my mind about it—had you thought I would?" She wandered further into his bedchamber, avoiding the tester bed and the memories that still lay there. "I must have a place I can call my own," she continued, knowing she was perilously close to babbling, "a place where I can retreat and be alone when I feel the need."

"No," Damien said in a monotone edged with anger as he bent his head to attach an emerald stickpin to his cravat.

His reply did not surprise her; she'd expected a battle and welcomed it. An imperious Damien was far easier to oppose than a reasonable one. "Why? It's quite obvious you don't require my presence here all of the time. In fact it should make it easier for you to come and go . . . *as you please.*"

"It is not difficult now," he said mildly. "What would be difficult is wondering if you've taken a lover. I find that I cannot tolerate the idea and I certainly won't provide a trysting place."

She paced the room trying to walk off her sudden outrage at his hypocrisy. "*You* can't tolerate the idea of *my* taking a lover? Do you realize how absurd that sounds?" She stopped, her anger gone as suddenly as it had come. She sank into a chair in an unlit corner of the room, feeling too drained to stand as all her emotions faded into weariness. "Unlike you, I want no one else in my bed," she said softly.

Damien snapped the lid shut on the jewel box. "If that is all, I need to finish dressing."

Numbly, she watched him don his coat. Why was he doing this to her? He was impatient and intolerant, cutting her off at every turn, refusing to speak rationally with her. It was as if the past few months had been a dream and now all was as it had been when animosity and resigned forbearance were all they shared.

She shook her head. It was no use. Love him or not, she could not stay. She could have lived with Damien in friendship, but she could not survive with less.

He strode to a chest topped by a looking glass, picked up twin hair brushes, and ran them through his hair.

She stared at his reflection in the mirror, looking fully upon him for the first time in three days. The light from a candelabra on the chest emphasized the dark crescents that lay beneath his eyes. He looked haggard and weary as if he were as bedeviled and miserable as she. He was suffering too, and his pride would not allow him to admit it.

It had to end or they would both be destroyed, yet the words to convince him eluded her. "Let me go, Damien," she said simply.

He closed his eyes and his head fell back as he braced his hands on the sides of the chest. "I can't," he said in a strangled voice. "I can't let you go, not now, not ever."

Once, she might have felt hope upon hearing those words. But not now, when he spoke them with such unhappiness. Now she felt only grief, for Damien, for herself, for all that they'd shared so briefly and lost so quickly. "And I can't live with you knowing that you go to her night after night."

He sliced his hand through the air, an impatient gesture to silence her, as if he had to speak now or not speak at all. "I have seen her once, Kathy. I gave her funds to see her through a year and severed our liaison. Nothing more passed between us."

"After five years you ended the liaison. Just like that." She snapped her fingers. "And you expect me to believe it." She laced her fingers tightly together and stared down at her lap as she swallowed down the wild laugh rising in her throat.

His loud sigh mingled with the sound of a drawer being opened. His footsteps whispered across the carpet, coming toward her shadowed corner. She glanced up, watched him approach with a branch of candles in his hand, bringing the light with him, an almost perfect circle of gold reaching her, surrounding her, surrounding both of them as he set the candelabra on the table beside her and crouched before her.

He pried her fingers apart and slid something cold and metallic on her finger. "Believe that you are my wife . . . that I want no one but you."

She stared at the heavy gold band on her finger. He was telling the truth. She'd heard it in the sincerity of his voice, saw it now in the plain band that spoke not of wealth nor position, but only of marriage.

"Believe this, Kathy." More gold gleamed as he placed his left hand over hers.

"You're wearing a wedding ring, too," she said, dizzy with the implications of such a gesture. Men did not wear wedding rings. Yet Damien wore one of his own volition. "They match," she added weakly.

He gave her a wry grin. "A fact I hope you appreciate since a goldsmith gave up three days of his life to make them so quickly."

*Three days.* He'd done this for her after Tony had come and it was the most eloquent of gestures. It was the reason he couldn't let her go.

He loved her as surely as his ancestor had loved Fair Alyce.

The realization grew and grew within her, a quiet knowledge that filled her with a sense of peace, of serenity.

Alyce had known all along that her earl loved her. That was why her portrait seemed to glow with serenity. She understood now . . . perfectly. She understood that Alyce had possessed the courage to speak of what was in her heart, to give it to her earl as a gift free of conditions. She understood that she could wait for Damien to speak first or she could fight for him here and now with the same honesty they had always shared whether in dissension or friendship.

"We really are a pair," she said as she traced the line of his ring with her finger. "We have spoken of so many things, shared so much, yet neither of us have dared to give a name to our feelings."

Wariness hooded his eyes and his mouth tightened as he released her hands. "We are married—a pair definitely. We share many things in common including respect and trust and passion for one another. But do not make more of it than that."

"That sounds very much like a warning," she said and heard the quake in her voice.

"It is." He rose and stepped back, his gaze on her harsh, forbidding. "Love me not, Kathy, for you will surely be disappointed." He said nothing more as he turned sharply on his heel and strode from the room.

And Kathy knew then, as she watched him shut the door with a controlled slam, that he didn't want to hear the words.

That he was running from the truth.

She lunged to her feet and ran to the door, determined to catch Damien before he put any more distance between them.

Damien almost ran down the hall, trying to escape what he'd seen in Kathy's eyes and heard in her voice. Trying to escape the lump of anticipation that rose in his throat when he'd realized where her comments about courage and hearts were leading.

*She'd been about to say the words.*

His mind raced as the knowledge chased him toward the staircase. He glared down at the ring on his finger, wanting nothing more than to fling it away from him. What had he been trying to accomplish with his whimsically grand gesture?

Goddammit! He didn't know.

He didn't know anything anymore, other than he

felt guilt for hurting Kathy and he'd felt fear when she'd wanted to leave him.

"Damien wait," Kathy called from behind him.

He glanced back. And now he felt complete panic.

She was racing down the hallway, her hair flying out behind her, her ankles flashing beneath her skirt as she held it up to keep from tripping.

Why wouldn't she leave him in peace? Why wouldn't she leave things as they were?

Why didn't he just let her say the bloody words and be done with it?

Because he couldn't. He was afraid she'd expect him to say them in return.

*He was afraid. . . .*

Sudden comprehension hit him broadside. Emotions he'd refused to acknowledge overwhelmed him as memories threatened to smother him.

He'd been devastated when his mother had died, leaving his father empty, with nothing to give his son and newborn daughter, leaving Damien to assume the responsibility of loving Jillian. He'd buried his feelings, loving his sister too much to risk showing how deeply he'd resented the burden of having to be both brother and father to her. Those years had left him feeling as empty as his father had been.

And now he feared he had nothing left for Kathy when she deserved everything. If Kathy said the words, then she deserved to hear them.

He couldn't give that to her unless he meant it, unless he was sure he could live up to it. Kathy could say the words and he could hear them, but they would be meaningless unless he gave them back to her.

Unless he was certain he meant them, felt them.

He descended the stairs at a dangerous pace, needing to outrun his own treacherous thoughts as well as Kathy.

"Please," she called.

He reached the bottom.

A footman opened the door.

He tried to step outside, to leave her behind, to prove that he could. To prove that he was still free and life continued to proceed on his terms. But at the last minute, he halted and turned toward her, catching her as she barreled into his chest. It would be just like her to follow him outside, unmindful of onlookers passing by.

She glanced at the footman as she panted and tried to catch her breath.

"Leave us," Damien snapped at the hapless servant, then turned his attention to Kathy. "I'm late," he said harshly.

She wrapped her arms around his neck. "Before you go out that door, I want you to know——" She paused and slowly exhaled. "I want you to know that I love you."

He felt crowded—by the walls, by the furniture, by Kathy's body pressing against his. By the words that seemed to absorb the very air around him. Words that would absorb him too if he didn't do something. But do what?

Goddammit! He didn't know.

He reached up to pry loose her hold on him. "No," he gritted. "I don't want to hear it."

"You're lying." She grasped the lapels of his coat. "You've never lied to me before, Damien. Never."

"I'm still not lying," he rasped, feeling strangled. Her arms felt like a vise around his neck as she stood on her tiptoes and pressed closer still, her mouth bare inches away from his.

"We've always talked openly," she said urgently, ignoring his denial. "We should have talked openly three days ago, but we didn't and look where it got us."

It had gotten him in a death grip in the middle of an open doorway, he thought as he again struggled to loosen her hold on his coat. It had gotten him into a trap he didn't know how to escape. He scowled down at her. "I must go——"

She pressed her fingers over his lips as she had done the night she'd come to his bed, silencing him. "You love me, too, Damien, though I know you won't admit it. It's all right. I don't need to hear the words from you. I need only for you to hear them from me."

Ignoring the thundering beat of his heart, he pulled her hand from his mouth. "Let me go, Kathy," he said.

She released her hold on his coat. "You're free to go, Damien. I just wanted you to know that I love you. I want you to understand that it happened and can't be changed. I want you to understand that loving you is both the worst torment I have ever endured and the greatest pleasure I've ever known, and I would not change it if I could." She caressed his cheeks then lowered her hands slightly, holding them palms up. "I love you, Damien, now and always."

She took a single step back, freeing him, giving him the choice to go or stay. And though she no longer touched him, she held him immobile in the threshold with her solemn gaze and outstretched hands, as if she held her love there, giving it into his keeping.

He swallowed as he stared at her, seeing her offering for what it was. Seeing the truth he'd tried so hard to avoid. Love was not a responsibility, but a gift.

Love renewed itself.

He felt it inside him, replenishing him, enriching him. Doubts and confusion disappeared and he wondered why they'd existed in the first place.

Kathy had given him everything he'd wanted. Kindness, gentleness, honesty, courage with beauty as the prize.

Yet, he'd been wrong. Love was the prize.

He had to accept her gift. But more than that, he could return it.

He met her gaze that glistened like a clear blue

pond, hiding nothing. As he would hide nothing. He reached for her, pulled her toward him even as he took a step toward her.

She caught her breath as their bodies met and tilted her head back watching him as her lips curved in a brilliant smile.

"Move away from her, Westbrook," a voice said from the other side of the threshold.

Kathy gasped and paled and swayed as she stared past him.

Damien caught her on her shoulders, holding her upright, holding her close. He knew that voice. A voice that quavered with excitement. He hadn't expected to hear it again.

He slowly turned his head.

Edgewater stood in the open doorway, his hair falling over his forehead, his face shadowed with a day's growth of beard, his clothing wrinkled and dusty. A pistol was tucked into the waistband of his trousers and he held another in a violently shaking hand. "I said, get away from her," he ordered, his eyes skittering as if searching for focus.

He was mad.

Damien ground his teeth, controlling his urge to shove Kathy away from him and launch himself at Edgewater. But any sudden movement might panic him enough to fire and hit Kathy. He had to think carefully, act cautiously, find out what in bloody hell Edgewater was about. "All right."

"No!" Kathy said furiously and wrapped her arms around his neck, pressing closer to him. He could feel the pound of her heart, the shaking of her hands as she dug her fingers into his nape. "Tony," she said with a tremor in her voice, "what are you doing here?"

He blinked and skewed his mouth as if he were confused, then his expression cleared. "Why, I've come to save you, my darling Kathleen," he said brightly. "You must fetch your coat. It is chilly out tonight."

Damien narrowed his eyes as he realized Edgewater had come to abduct Kathy. The man was obsessed with her. He should have seen it before. "Save her from what?" he asked, buying time.

He lifted his chin and glared with hatred at Damien. "From you."

"What leads you to believe she needs to be saved from me?" Damien asked, as he glanced around, searching for Smithy, for a possible weapon . . . searching for anything he might use to disarm Edgewater.

"You dare ask, after the way you stole her from me and forced her into this obscene marriage?" Edgewater said on a shrill note.

"He forced nothing on me, Tony," Kathy said, enunciating each word as if she didn't trust her voice.

Edgewater shook his head and smiled sadly. "Oh, my darling, you don't have to pretend anymore." He lowered his voice to conspiratorial whisper. "I've horses tied to a bush across the street. Wait for me there. When it is over, I'll come to you."

Damien's blood ran cold. Edgewater wasn't here to abduct Kathy, but expected she would accompany him of her own free will. He had come to rid her of her husband, to murder him.

Suddenly, Kathy drew a sharp breath and her arms tightened around Damien. "No," she said in a horrified whisper.

Damien knew then that she was not so afraid she did not comprehend the meaning of Edgewater's instructions. "Do as he says," he hissed, desperate to get her out of the house where she would be safe.

"I won't go," she said.

Edgewater frowned. "You needn't be afraid, my darling. I'll take care of you. We'll be married, as we should have been long ago. Nothing will ever stand in the way of our love again."

Kathy shook her head against Damien's chest. "I

don't love you, Tony," she said. "I don't want to marry you."

The pistol bobbled as Edgewater's face crumpled in distress. "Of course you do. You told me you did, that day in the church, and just the other day you protected me."

Damien held his silence, hoping Kathy's arguments would distract Edgewater long enough for him to attack.

"The earl forced me to say I loved you," she said. "And, the other day, I wanted you to leave so I could speak to my husband in private."

Edgewater paled and steadied his hand. "It makes no difference. In time, you will grow to love me."

"No," she said as if she were speaking to a child. She lifted her gaze and the tremors vibrating through her body became more intense. "I could never love anyone but Damien."

"Kathy, hush," Damien warned, knowing that such words might mean a death sentence for both of them.

Fury clouded Edgewater's gaze and contorted his features. "Bitch," he snarled. "Do you love him so much that you will die for him?"

"Yes," she said.

"Then, you shall die, Kathleen." Edgewater raised the pistol, aimed it between her eyes.

"No!" Damien shouted as he twisted and shoved Kathy behind him, knowing that she would sacrifice herself to save him. Didn't she know that if anything happened to her, he wouldn't want to be saved?

She didn't know. He hadn't told her.

His thoughts scattered as he heard a crack and the breath whooshed out of his lungs. Fire seared through his left shoulder and chest.

"Damien," Kathy sobbed, clinging to him as his legs buckled. He blinked and focused on her face as she fell to her knees in front of him. Her beautiful face, etched with anguish and horror. He glanced down at her hands gripping him, covered with blood.

He'd moved too late. Edgewater had shot her. The pain in his body was nothing compared to the pain of knowing she'd died for him.

The light seemed to dim and he couldn't stay upright, couldn't find enough breath to speak. Pure agony burned through his body as he toppled forward. He tried to twist around to land on his back, to keep from crushing Kathy. He heard another crack, a sound inside him, like bone being struck. Nausea rose in his throat and his head seemed to explode.

"Help me, someone. He's been shot," Kathy cried and she seemed to be floating beneath him, moving slowly as she tried to get out from under him, sobbing with frustration.

He wanted to correct her, to tell her that she'd been shot and he'd merely hit his head on the marble stand by the door.

But then he realized that it was he who had been shot. He who was dying.

He reached for her hair, a flame in the blackness that descended on him. He loved her and he hadn't told her. He should have told her. He had to tell her before it was too late.

He opened his mouth but could not speak. He felt death seep into his bones like a chill and cast its shadow over him.

*Not yet. Goddammit! Not until she knows. . . .*

He opened his mouth again, summoned every bit of strength he could as he felt his life spilling from him, onto Kathy and around her on the floor. Just a few seconds. It was all he needed. All he would ask. A moment to give his heart into her keeping.

But darkness smothered him and the words lay on his tongue like flowers on a grave.

# Chapter 38

"**D**ie! Die! Die!" Tony ranted as Damien's eyes closed and his head fell onto Kathy's shoulder.

"Damien, don't," she cried, acutely aware of Tony raving madly from the doorway, and footsteps running toward her. She ignored it all, caring about nothing but helping Damien. "Please. Open your eyes." She framed his face with her hands, willing him not to lose consciousness, willing him not to die. Praying that it wasn't too late.

Terror lay on top of her as heavy as Damien's weight, crushing her. His body limp and unresponding, his skin cold and paper white as blood poured from a gash near his temple and a wound in his chest. So much blood that she thought he couldn't have any left, that his life had drained out of him, soaking into her gown and spreading a stain across the carpet.

She had to get him off of her, had to get help. Sobbing with frustration, she tried to move him, but he was too heavy.

"Let me help you," Tony said.

She raised her gaze, saw him looming over her, saw him extend his leg, and hook his foot beneath Damien, levering him up and away from her.

Damien moaned as his body rolled away from her and lay still on the floor.

He was still alive. It wasn't too late.

She turned to her side and managed to get up on her hands and knees.

"Watch, Kathleen," Tony said in a voice so shrill she barely recognized it.

She raised her head and focused on him, watched him as he backed away from her, an odd light flickering in his eyes, like a candle flame in a violent wind

"Watch your husband die, my darling," he said as he flung away the pistol in his hand and drew the one tucked in his belt. His hands were steady now and he smiled, a twisted, grotesque expression of madness. "And then it will be your turn."

"Mother of God," a voice said. Smithy's voice. He was here. Everything would be all right now. It had to be all right.

"Stay away," Tony screamed and aimed the pistol at a point behind her.

A sob caught in her throat as she followed the line of Tony's aim and found Smithy at the end of the hall, approaching at a slow, careful walk. "Shoot me, you bastard," he said in a low, deadly voice. "Do it and use up your last shot—" Suddenly Smithy stopped in his tracks and stared at the doorway.

Horror paralyzed Kathy as her gaze jerked back to Tony . . . to the face of a man standing behind him with a pistol in his hand. The earl. He'd come to finish it. To finish all of them. It was over.

A scream froze in her throat as the earl aimed his pistol . . . cocked it . . . fired it.

Tony's eyes widened in surprise. He stared down at the crimson stain spreading quickly across his shirt then up at Kathy. He opened his mouth but only a gurgle escaped his lips. He crumpled to the floor and moved no more.

Without a word, the Earl of Blackwood turned and stalked away.

Kathy didn't care how or why he'd come here. He was gone and she was alive. She could help Damien.

Suddenly the entrance hall exploded in sound and movement. She glanced up at Smithy, heard him shouting orders to the footmen and maids. "Help me," she cried. "Hurry!"

It felt as if forever had come and gone in the time it took Smithy to reach her. Damien didn't have forever. Sobbing, she tore at his coat with one hand and tried to staunch the flow from the wound on his head with the other.

She sobbed again as Smithy reached her side. "His head hit the marble stand. I heard it crack," she babbled as she freed Damien's neckcloth and ripped his shirt open. "He's bleeding so much. We have to stop it—" She gasped at the sight of the hole just below Damien's collarbone, at the blood that just kept spilling and spilling from his head.

Fear shot like lightning through her. There was so much blood.

Jacobs appeared with an armload of linen towels. "I've sent for the physician and the constable."

Kathy grabbed for a towel and pressed it to Damien's head.

Smithy folded another length of linen over his chest.

Damien didn't move, didn't make a sound as Smithy tossed the towel aside and applied a new one. Even his blood seemed to have stopped flowing.

Frantically, she held her hand over his mouth, then beneath his nose.

She could feel no breath.

"He's gone," Smithy said.

She blinked and shook her head. "No. He's merely unconscious."

"He's got no heartbeat."

Smithy's resignation infuriated her. She shoved him aside and leaned over Damien, pressing her ear to his chest.

No breath. No heartbeat.

Nothing.

"No!" she shouted. "He can't be dead. I won't let

him be dead." She clenched her fist and struck Damien's chest. "I'll make his heart beat." It couldn't end this way. Not when they'd just begun their lives together. Not when he'd been about to say what she'd wanted so badly to hear.

She struck him again as fury gathered strength inside her. "Damn you, Damien Forbes. You will not die."

"Lady Kathy, don't," Smithy said in a fractured voice, tears streaming down his face as he gripped her arms and tried to pull her to her feet. "There's nothing else to be done."

She jerked out of his hold and slapped his hands away. "He is not dead," she snarled. "If he were dead, I would be dead, too."

She turned back to Damien. "You're not leaving me," she said fiercely. "You're staying right here. You're going to . . . tell . . . me . . . you . . . love . . . me." She kept pounding his chest, her words keeping time with each blow. "Come back, Damien . . . come back to me." She couldn't see for the tears, couldn't hear for the sobs that shook her body.

But she could feel the sudden rise of Damien's chest, the breeze of a breath that wafted over her arm. She could feel the brush of a hand and the curl of fingers around her wrist. There was no strength in the grip but it stayed her from delivering the next blow.

"Lady Kathy, look," Smithy said in an awe-filled whisper.

Suddenly her sobs ended. Her shoulders heaved as her own heart stalled and she couldn't draw a breath, living on hope alone as she swiped at her eyes with the back of her hand and looked down.

Damien stared up at her, his brows a dark slash above green eyes clouded with pain. His mouth moved, slanting upward at one corner then straightening again as he inhaled and tried to speak. Still holding Kathy's wrist, his hand fell to his chest.

She felt his heart thump beneath her palm, felt his breath as she put her fingers to his lips. She didn't want him to speak. Not now when he was so weak and so pale and she could not bear to see the pain that tightened his features with every effort. Not now when joy filled her so much she had no room for anything else. "You came back," she said softly. "That's all that matters. We can talk later."

He grimaced. "Now," he rasped against her hand. "Must . . . tell . . . you . . . " His voice was barely a whisper.

She shook her head and leaned over him, to silence him with her lips, needing nothing now but to be near him.

But he continued to speak in little more than a strained whisper. "Kathy . . . I . . . love . . . you . . ."

She heard the words and felt them against her lips, a kiss, a promise, a shared breath of life itself.

# Epilogue

*Westbrook Castle*
*November, 1820*

**W**inter robed the landscape in crystal frost and veiled the heavens with luminescent silver. The flowers were gone and the trees were stark silhouettes rising from a colorless earth.

Damien smiled as he approached the arched entrance to the garden, knowing he would find Kathy there, her vivid beauty reaching out like a circle of candle flame in the drabness, the serenity in her eyes and the radiance of her smile a promise of all the bright summers to come.

Still, he lingered on his way to her, knowing she needed a few moments to herself. She would always need some small space in which to cultivate new dreams and gather her thoughts.

Especially today, after the arrival of her—*of their*—family in a furor of trunks and short tempers. They'd come *en masse,* the ship Jillie and Max had taken from America having docked in the Indies to take on Bruce as well as provisions. Max had received Damien's message first since Bruce had been difficult to find while traveling the islands to inspect various properties. Max had immediately chartered a ship and sailed for home.

He'd seen Kathy motion for a servant to bring her a coat as soon as Jillie and LadyLou had taken James to the nursery for his nap. She'd tossed him an apologetic smile and slipped away as Bruce and Max had tersely suggested they retire to the study for brandy and conversation.

The "suggestion" had been an order Damien was anxious to follow. He'd been dreading the moment and wanted only to end it so he could join Kathy.

Her brothers had been in a fine stew over the news that seethed through every conversation in London even now, almost two months after the earl had shot Edgewater.

The Earl of Blackwood was considered a hero for saving the lives of his daughter and her powerful husband. It was the stuff of high drama, Damien supposed. Thwarted suitor goes mad with love and tries to kill his lady and her husband. No one missed Edgewater and the earl finally held the place of honor in society he had always coveted—a small man with a bellyful of self-importance.

No one knew the earl acted only for himself, protecting himself from the retribution Damien had threatened.

Bruce and Max had failed to see the humor in the situation. They had been even less amused to know how closely Damien had come to death.

Damien had refrained from telling them that he'd seen it and felt it. They wouldn't understand. No one would except Kathy.

Kathy who had called him back from that long, narrow corridor that held him trapped and lost in the darkness. All he'd been able to see was the brilliant white light on the other side. It had called to him, luring him so close he'd been able to reach into the light and feel its promise of peace.

Kathy had called to him louder, more insistently as she'd pummeled his chest and ordered him to come back to her. He'd turned toward the sound of her voice and seen her in the distance, a brilliant blaze of color and warmth, offering him anything but peace, promising everything but loneliness.

The white light had lost its appeal.

He saw the fire that was Kathy now, as he paused in the arbor to savor the beauty of her, the only color in a winter landscape. She sat deep in thought, her cheeks rosy with the cold, her hair a flame curling around her face and down her back.

No, only Kathy understood the power she held over him. Only Kathy would dare to beat death into submission to keep what was hers.

Her gaze lifted just then and she tilted her head as she looked at him, smiled at him, drawing him nearer to her as she always did. "Have you put my brothers' fears to rest?" she asked.

He smiled wryly as he strolled over to her and sprawled into the chair opposite hers. "They are resigned to what they cannot change," he said. "But, they still find it difficult to believe that we love one another when only six months ago, we could scarcely bear to be in the same room together. Given the logic of their arguments, I suppose it is difficult to comprehend."

Her expression sobered. "Do you try to comprehend it, Damien? Is that why I see you scowl and stare at nothing, as if something troubles you?"

"No, I'm not troubled, but frustrated and perhaps angry as well," he admitted, unable to keep anything from Kathy. One by one, she had dragged his secrets from him like old clothes packed in the attic. One by one she had shaken them out and held them up, forcing him to see what he'd hidden even from himself for so many years. He'd become accustomed to sharing with her. He needed it as much as he needed her touch.

He sat up abruptly and leaned toward her. "I love you, Kathy. I've said it countless times in the last two months, yet it's not enough. I want to tell you how much. I want to describe it—" He shook his head and raked his hand through his hair. "Goddammit! There are no words to describe—"

She, too, leaned forward and reached out to press

her fingers against his lips, silencing him as she was wont to do when she had a point to make. "I know how much you love me."

He grasped her hand and held it between his. "How can you know when even I can't measure the fullness of it?" he asked.

"I know that you love me enough to die for me." She met his gaze, letting him see the love in her eyes, hear it in the small catch in her voice. "More importantly, I know that you love me enough to live for me."

Damien squeezed his eyes shut as her words swept through him, as he remembered how dull the white light seemed compared to Kathy's vitality, as he realized that life was nothing without the miracle of love.

# Avon Romances—
## the best in exceptional authors and unforgettable novels!

# *Avon Romantic Treasures*

*Unforgettable, enthralling love stories,
sparkling with passion and adventure
from Romance's bestselling authors*

**SUNDANCER'S WOMAN** *by Judith E. French*
77706-1/$5.99 US/$7.99 Can

**JUST ONE KISS** *by Samantha James*
77549-2/$5.99 US/$7.99 Can

**HEARTS RUN WILD** *by Shelly Thacker*
78119-0/$5.99 US/$7.99 Can

**DREAM CATCHER** *by Kathleen Harrington*
77835-1/$5.99 US/$7.99 Can

**THE MACKINNON'S BRIDE** *by Tanya Anne Crosby*
77682-0/$5.99 US/$7.99 Can

**PHANTOM IN TIME** *by Eugenia Riley*
77158-6/$5.99 US/$7.99 Can

**RUNAWAY MAGIC** *by Deborah Gordon*
78452-1/$5.99 US/$7.99 Can

**YOU AND NO OTHER** *by Cathy Maxwell*
78716-4/$5.99 US/$7.99 Can

# Discover Contemporary Romances at Their Sizzling Hot Best from Avon Books

**JONATHAN'S WIFE** *by Dee Holmes*
78368-1/$5.99 US/$7.99 Can

**DANIEL'S GIFT** *by Barbara Freethy*
78189-1/$5.99 US/$7.99 Can

**FAIRYTALE** *by Maggie Shayne*
78300-2/$5.99 US/$7.99 Can

**WISHES COME TRUE** *by Patti Berg*
78338-X/$5.99 US/$7.99 Can

**ONCE MORE WITH FEELING** *by Emilie Richards*
78363-0/$5.99 US/$7.99 Can

**HEAVEN COMES HOME** *by Nikki Holiday*
78456-4/$5.99 US/$7.99 Can

**RYAN'S RETURN** *by Barbara Freethy*
78531-5/$5.99 US/$7.99 Can

# Finally, it was time to return home to a white Christmas...

Paul helped the girls with their luggage and Christmas gifts. Martha saw him peeking at some of the name tags as he placed them in a large trash bag. She'd left a couple unmarked, knowing he'd probably be doing just that.

After loading up the car, Paul and Martha sat in the back while Naomi took the seat up front next to the driver.

"You're so quiet," Paul said at one point. "Nothing to say?"

"I'm just enjoying sitting here next to you. I'm holding it in my memory box."

He laughed and squeezed her hand. "And what else is in that lovely head of yours that you're holding on to?"

"Oh, I've stored all kinds of moments. I remember the day I turned five and my Aenti Lizzy gave me a brand-new box of crayons. Then there was the time I learned to tie a bow, and the time I found my first four-leaf clover."

"Ah, very important memories," he said. "Any about me?"

She looked at him and grinned. "I can't tell you all of them." Then she leaned close and whispered, "But you are definitely one of my favourites..."

**June Bryan Belfie** has written over twenty-five novels. Her Amish books have been bestsellers and have sold around the world. She lives in Pennsylvania and is familiar with the ways of her Amish neighbors. Mother of five and grandmother of eight, Ms. Belfie enjoys writing clean and wholesome stories for people of all ages.

# Love Inspired®

## Discover wholesome and uplifting stories of faith, forgiveness and hope.

Join our social communities to connect with other readers who share your love!

Sign up for the Love Inspired newsletter at **LoveInspired.com** to be the first to find out about upcoming titles, special promotions and exclusive content.

## CONNECT WITH US AT:

Facebook.com/groups/HarlequinConnection

 Facebook.com/LoveInspiredBooks

Twitter.com/LoveInspiredBks

LISOCIAL2019

"At times like this, nobody expects you to be thinking of anything but getting a roof over your *kinder*'s heads."

He didn't reach out to touch her, but she was aware of every inch of him so close to her. His quiet strength had awed her from the beginning. As she'd come to know him better, his fundamental decency had impressed her more. He was a man she believed she could trust.

She shoved that thought aside. Trusting any man would be the worst thing she could do after seeing what Mamm had endured during her marriage and then struggling to help her sister escape her abusive husband.

"I'm glad you understand why I must focus on rebuilding a life for the children." The simple statement left no room for misinterpretation. "The flood will always be a part of us, but I want to help them learn how to live with their memories."

"I can't imagine what it was like."

"I can't forget what it was like."

Normally she would have been bothered by someone having sympathy for her, but if pitying her kept Michael from looking at her with his brown puppy-dog eyes that urged her to trust him, she'd accept it. She couldn't trust any man, because she wouldn't let the children spend their lives witnessing what she had.

*Don't miss*
An Amish Christmas Promise *by Jo Ann Brown,*
*available December 2019 wherever*
Love Inspired® *books and ebooks are sold.*

LoveInspired.com

LIEXP1119

# LEAVING HOME

## *June Bryan Belfie*

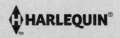

ISBN-13: 978-1-335-49968-4

Leaving Home

First published in 2017 by June Bryan Belfie.
This edition published in 2019.

Copyright © 2017 by June Bryan Belfie

Recycling programs
for this product may
not exist in your area.

This edition published by arrangement with Harlequin Books S.A.

For questions and comments about the quality of this book, please contact us at CustomerService@Harlequin.com.

www.Harlequin.com

**Printed in U.S.A.**

# LEAVING HOME

# Chapter One

How strange to be packing up all her clothing and moving out of the only home she'd ever known. Martha Troyer was on the verge of spreading her youthful wings. Ever since the young man she loved, Paul Yoder, had felt forced to lay a hand on another man, her life had become abruptly changed—perhaps forever.

Amish never allow physical attacks on another human being, and though he had not initiated the confrontation, he was involved. Her loving parents treated her differently now, refusing to meet the young man of her dreams, and the stress she felt in her home caused actual physical pain. She and Paul were prohibited from corresponding, not only by her parents, but the bishop as well.

Hopefully, she would not need to stay away for long. The fear of the unknown, mixed with the excitement of the unfamiliar, created a strange anxiety.

She hadn't set eyes on her future apartment, which she planned to share with her friend Naomi Shoemaker. Martha didn't expect much. She knew she could live simply, as she had done all her life, and needed little to make her content.

She folded her simple frocks carefully and laid them in a carton. Then she added her other clothing and her Bible and notebook, along with a hairbrush and a bar of their homemade soap, which was wrapped in plastic wrap. What else should she pack?

She looked around the room as her mother appeared at the open doorway, unsmiling and appearing depressed, which was her general appearance as of late—a far cry from the jovial, dimpled mother Martha loved so much.

"Don't forget your toothbrush. You can take the rest of the paste. I have another one."

"*Danki.*"

They stood a moment facing each other—so much to say, yet silent they remained.

Then Martha took the three steps to reach her beloved mother and wrapped her arms around her. "I won't be away long, *Mamm*. I promise." She felt her mother's arms tightening around her slim body. Her mother was shaking slightly and a tear landed on Martha's neck. Her heart broke in two as mother and daughter wept together. The realization that nothing would ever be quite the same again was paramount on their minds, though they refrained from uttering their thoughts.

After a few more moments, her mother, Sarah, released her grip and stepped back. "You must promise to keep *Gott*'s laws. Don't ever compromise your morals, *dochder.*"

Martha nodded. "I won't. I just need to get my head together. So much has happened."

"*Jah.* I'm trying to understand. It's hard." She lifted her apron and wiped her eyes.

"If the bishop allows phones, we can talk."

"It won't happen."

"Maybe it will. I know of a community—"

"*Nee*. Not with Bishop Josiah. Nothing will change. But you will come home often, jah?"

"I'll try, Mamm. It will depend on my job."

Sarah shook her head. "It's a dangerous world out there, Martha. You have no idea."

"I'll be careful. I won't go out alone at night and I won't drink or do anything foolish like some of my friends during their *Rumspringa*."

"I know I can trust you, even though…"

"I hope you can forgive the lies."

"I am trying. I can't hold on to anger. That ain't the Amish way."

"I'm praying with all my heart you and *Daed* will agree to meet Paul and give him a chance. He's a wonderful-*gut* man. For a couple of bad moments, he should not be forced to pay for the rest of his life. We love each other, Mamm, and we plan to one day marry. You know that."

"I'm hoping you'll change your mind."

Martha shook her head. "One way or the other, we will marry; but I pray you and Daed will accept him and we will be a happy family, as we once were."

"One day at a time, Martha. Perhaps, eventually… I put a *toot* together with some food for you to take, and Daed left an envelope with a little money in it. Not much, but you'll need to eat gut so you don't get sick."

"You're both so wonderful to me. How can I ever thank you?"

"Just promise you'll be back and you'll live near us when you do marry someone. It would break our hearts if we weren't always part of your life. You know, you're our only child."

"Jah. I know. As much as I'd like, I can't promise I'll live real close-like. There isn't any way I can know the future that well. Please don't ask me to promise something I can't. Even if it's an hour or two away, we will still remain part of your lives."

"But the *boppli*. Your *kinner*. I want them to know us and love us, like you are with *Mammi* and *Dawdi* and all the other relatives. Think of your *Aenti* Lizzy. She thinks of you as her dochder, almost."

"Oh, Mamm. You're not making this any easier." She sat on the edge of her bed and ran her hands over her skirt.

"I guess not. I won't say anything more. You know how we feel about everything. There's nothing more I can do." Sarah turned and walked slowly down the hall to the staircase.

Martha sat and contemplated her choices. It was too late to remain. She had already put down half the rent for November and it was already the first. It wouldn't be fair to Naomi to back out. What *was* fair? Were her parents being fair?

She sighed and folded in the ends of the carton and carried it downstairs, placing it by the front door. When she went into the kitchen, her father was seated at the table drinking coffee. He looked over, grimly. "What time is the driver coming?"

"Naomi's neighbor is doing the driving. They said around noon."

"It's almost that now. There's an envelope for you," he added, pointing to her placemat at the table. "It ain't much, but it should help."

"Danki, Daed."

"Open it."

"Now?"

He shrugged.

She sat at her seat and opened it. There were twenty-dollar bills totaling five hundred dollars. "Oh my goodness! This is way too much."

"It ain't. I wish it could be more."

"Danki. I'm overwhelmed." She felt tears forming. They were always near the surface these days. She swallowed hard to make them stay where they belonged.

"I can pay you back—"

"It's a gift, Martha. I don't want it returned. Just spend it wisely."

"Oh, I will. I definitely will. You know I'm frugal."

"Jah, you have been. Just hope the world don't change you none. I like you the way you are."

She read "love" between the words, but knew her father was too proud to use the word. He'd consider it weak or "girlish" to be so open verbally.

Sarah turned from the counter where she was wrapping a tuna sandwich for her daughter. "You might get hungry on the way. I'll make a couple more for Naomi and her neighbor."

"You are the best parents in the world." It was too late to hold back. She allowed her tears to flow and then reached for tissues and blew her nose. "Sometimes I think it would have been better to just stay and work things out."

"It ain't too late," her father said.

"It is, Daed, but it won't be forever. I'd better go say good-bye to Mammi and Dawdi." She rose and went over to kiss the top of her father's head. He cleared his throat, but didn't look up. Her mother was wiping her eyes.

It was just as difficult to leave her grandparents. It

was as she expected. Her mammi cried buckets and her dawdi remained silent.

After leaving the tearful scene, Martha sat a few minutes on a bench by the house. Spunky, the family mutt, came over to her, his tail wagging. He jumped up on the bench to be closer. "*Hallo*, Spunk. Are you going to be upset when I leave, too?"

His eyes looked sad, but then they always did. She patted him and then wiped tears from her own eyes. She hadn't realized how difficult saying good-bye could be.

As she went back to her house, her aenti Lizzy showed up with several of her sons, along with another buggy full of her grandchildren and the rest of her boys. In a way, it helped, since confusion reigned and everyone was too busy giving advice and tucking bags of goodies into Martha's hands, for her to take in the full impact of this major event in her life.

At exactly noon, a blue Toyota pulled onto the drive and it was time to leave. Naomi got out and gave everyone a hug and then they were off.

After Martha waved to everyone and the house was out of sight, she sat back in her seat behind the driver. Multiple emotions were racing through Martha's brain. Naomi was gabbing away about something, but Martha couldn't concentrate on anything yet. She kept picturing the sad faces of her family she was leaving behind. She decided right then and there to give this new life of hers six months tops, and then return to the bosom of her loving Amish family.

# Chapter Two

The apartment was just as Naomi described it. There was a pull-out mattress in the sofa, which, though a bit lumpy, was clean. Two plump armchairs were squeezed into the small living room with a fifties' style pine end table between them. A scratched-up desk sat under the only window in the room and held a rusty goose-neck desk lamp. A bare bulb served as a ceiling lamp, and though the lighting was poor, to Amish girls who were used to kerosene lighting, it was quite exciting. Martha turned the switch on and off each time she passed by it and grinned at her roommate, who laughed at her friend's childish excitement.

The small bedroom had a double bed and a three-drawer dresser with a matching mirror, which had been painted black. A closet, though small by most standards, was large enough for their few articles of clothing, with a shelf on top for them to store miscellaneous items. The freshly painted walls were off-white, and the bedroom had two connected windows, allowing the afternoon sun to brighten the otherwise drab gray rug and painted woodwork.

There was also a separate kitchen which contained a gas stove with four burners and an apartment-size refrigerator. Counter space was negligible and the single sink had a steady drip coming from the faucet, but they considered themselves fortunate.

The girls danced around, checking out every drawer and nook. There was no tub, but instead a corner shower took up most of the space in the pink-tiled bathroom. At least everything worked and there was even half a roll of toilet paper left on the holder.

The best part of the apartment was the location. They were near a small market and there was a pharmacy and a dollar store within a ten-minute walk. Two restaurants stood side-by-side on the main street, which had a moderate amount of traffic.

Martha's downheartedness was nearly eliminated as she began to explore her new environs. They checked out the neighborhood and when they returned to their apartment, Naomi pulled a cell phone from her apron pocket.

"Look what I treated myself to," she said proudly.

"Oh, wonderful! I'll pay half if you'll let me use it, too."

"Of course! I figured you would since your mamm didn't give your other one back. It's not that expensive. Does Paul know you're moving in today?"

"Jah, I wrote to him a few days ago and gave him all the information. He's pretty excited. We'll be an hour closer by car."

"I wonder how long it would take on a bicycle."

"It's way too far, and dangerous. It's about fifty miles to Lewistown from here, but he makes decent money and he doesn't mind getting a driver. It seems like for-

ever since we saw each other. Hopefully, he can come next weekend."

"You're so lucky to have someone love you that much. I hope I meet someone while we're here. Martha, I'm going to go with my cousin Valerie tomorrow to the thrift store nearby and buy some English clothes. Do you want to come? It would be easier to get a job if we don't look like Amish people."

Martha raised her brows. "I hadn't even thought of that. Jah, I'd love to go. It would feel so weird though, and I don't know how Paul would feel seeing me all fancied up."

"He'd love it. You can wear your hair down now. No one has to know where we come from. We can make up some fantastic stories. Maybe I'll say I was a New York model, but got tired of all the autographs I had to sign."

Martha giggled. "And I was a singer in a night club, but I didn't like working those late nights. This could be fun!" Then she dropped her smile. "We're not really going to do that, are we?"

"*Ach*, probably not, but it's fun to pretend. I'm just so excited, Martha. I'm finally out of the house. Those kids were getting on my nerves, even though I miss my little Patty already."

"Aww. I bet."

After hanging up their dresses and wiping down the counters and the refrigerator, they went out again to go grocery shopping. They felt at home to see a buggy pass as they walked together to the market. It was so much fun to make all the decisions for themselves or do absolutely nothing, if they so desired. They hated to see their first day of freedom come to an end.

The next morning, after a restless night, they went to

Valerie's and met her English friend, Dawn, who was only sixteen. She spent a lot of time with Valerie, who treated her like a younger sister. Dawn had offered to drive, since she had her own car and the thrift shop was about ten miles away. When they arrived, they noted that clothing with blue tags were half price so they sorted through the racks looking for the bargains. After selecting several items, they crowded into one small dressing room and tried everything on. Sometimes, they'd pass the same pair of jeans around until the person who had the best fit would add it to her pile.

By the time two hours had passed, Naomi had seven items, Dawn and Valerie each had two pairs of jeans, and Martha had ten different items! She'd even found a cocktail dress in red, which she figured she'd probably never have occasion to wear, but it only cost three dollars with the discount. She felt extremely extravagant, and slightly guilty.

When they got back to Valerie's house, they had their own fashion show and paraded around the living room in their new-found clothing. Naomi insisted on Martha taking down her hair and removing her sneakers so she could walk in the new heels she'd purchased. Martha decided to skip the heels since her foot was still somewhat tender from her sprain. She certainly didn't want to end up in pain again, especially since she needed to work. Bare feet looked better than her old sneakers.

After they tired of their modeling, the girls went into the kitchen and helped themselves to iced tea and pretzels. Before joining them, Martha twisted her hair into a large bun and pinned it back. She felt exposed with it loose.

Dawn asked them where they intended to work.

"No idea," Naomi answered. "Any suggestions?"

"I think my mom mentioned her friend needing a sitter for her two toddlers. Her old sitter just moved away. It probably doesn't pay much, but it would be something."

"Oh wow! Martha, do you want to apply if there's an opening?"

"It doesn't matter what I do. Actually, I think I'd like to work in a store maybe. A fabric store or even sell clothing."

"I know they're looking for a waitress in the 'Pink Pantry' restaurant. They have a sign in the window and it's just a few doors down," Valerie said.

"That would be wonderful-gut, too. I think I'll go there tomorrow morning and see if they'll hire me. Of course, I have no experience."

"Are you kidding? You're Amish, aren't you? Think of Sunday meals and when we do weddings and stuff. It's practically the same," Naomi reminded her.

"Jah, true."

"You'll have to say 'yes' now and not slip into the *Deutsch*. No more 'danki' and 'gut' for us now," Valerie said emphatically.

"It's gonna be hard. I hope I can remember," Martha said.

"So, I'm curious," Dawn said as she reached for another pretzel. "Why are you guys here? Don't you want to be Amish anymore?"

"I'm not sure what I want to be," Naomi confessed, "but Martha couldn't stand being at home after the fight took place."

"Fight?" Dawn said, leaning forward with a huge grin. "That sure doesn't sound like the Amish I know."

"It wasn't actually a fight," Martha began. "Well, I

guess maybe it was, but I was going with a guy and then decided I didn't really want to marry him since I wasn't in love with him."

"And she went to help someone take care of her kin-ner, and met a gorgeous Amish guy who fell madly in love with her," Naomi added.

"Well, kinda. I mean he's handsome and Amish, but it was his fun personality and his kindness and his love of *Gott*—God—which really attracted me to him."

"And his looks, though I haven't seen him yet," Naomi added.

"Go on. What was the fight about?" Dawn asked.

"One day, Daniel, the guy I no longer liked—"

"But he still loved her," Naomi interrupted.

"Jah, anyway, he came by and wanted to show me his new horse, which I thought would be okay since I love horses and he knew I had to get right back, so I said I'd go and we were headed out of the drive when a car turned in and Paul, my new guy, jumped out. I was so excited to see him that I told Daniel to stop so I could get out. He got real mad and didn't want to, but finally he stopped. I jumped out, like a little kid, landed hard in a ditch-like spot and sprained my ankle. Before I knew it, Paul had me in his arms—"

"Oh, how romantic!" Dawn said, drawing her hands to her heart.

Valerie nodded in agreement. "Go on."

"Well, I guess Daniel was so mad, he came back later and said to Paul that he should leave because I was going to marry him! Daniel! Which wasn't true at all. Any-way, Paul said Daniel should be the one to go, and that I didn't want him around again and before you knew it, Paul had a bloody nose and Daniel was wrestling with

him till my daed came and broke it up. Then he was all mad and told them both to get out and never come back."

"Jah, but Paul did! Tell them about that." All four girls were huddled close together in order not to miss a single word.

"The next day, Sunday, I stayed home because of my ankle and Paul, who had slept in our barn in secret, came in—after seeing my folks leave for church service—and we spent at least an hour together, talking about how we felt about each other."

"I can't stand it! It should be a movie!" Dawn was enthralled. "Did he kiss you?"

"Well, I don't usually talk about stuff like that…"

"He did! I know it!" Dawn, the script-writer, added.

"Jah, I may as well confess."

"Was it a great kiss?" Valerie asked.

"Oh, jah! And we made plans to see each other. He even bought me a phone later on, but my *mudder* found it and that's when things really exploded at home. The bishop came and I couldn't lie when he asked if I still saw Paul. My folks were so disappointed in me. It was awful, but I couldn't promise never to see him again. We do love each other and we want to get married—soon."

"Oh, I can't take it," Dawn said, leaning back in her chair. "That's the most romantic story I've ever heard. I have to come to your wedding."

"I don't know when that will be. He lives in Lewistown and my family is all back in Paradise."

"That's not that far," Valerie said.

"By buggy, it would be impossible."

"Oh, I forgot. But you can get drivers, right?"

"It wouldn't be the same. I'm an only child and my

mudder, mother, and I are very close. It would kill her not to see me every day and play with the little ones."

"And you'd have a bunch, I bet," Valerie said.

"Hopefully. Whatever the Lord gives us. We both want a big family."

"Well, you *have* to get married. You just do," Dawn continued, nodding emphatically.

"So, I'm here to try to clear my head and make the right decision about my life. The best thing would be if Paul agreed to move back to Paradise, but he has a real good job right now and, of course, all his family lives nearby. There's so much to think about."

"He should move. What does he do?" Dawn asked.

"He's a carpenter, and a real gut—oops, *good*—one, too."

"I bet he could open his own shop then and do okay," Dawn said.

"That's something we'll probably end up talking about when we're together."

"Tell me everything, Martha. It's so cool. Could you give up being Amish if you had to?"

"That's nothing I'd want to do. I really love being Amish."

"Except for the lack of electricity," Naomi teased. "She got nutty over lights yesterday."

They all laughed and the subject went back to jobs. Dawn promised to check out the sitting job for Naomi and then they discussed what Martha should wear to check out the waitressing job. They decided on a pair of her new slacks, which were navy blue, and a long-sleeved white sweater. Martha refused to wear her hair down though, but agreed to leave off the prayer *kapp*.

"I won't lie about it though, if the subject of Amish comes up."

"It might actually help, Martha. Everyone knows you guys are good workers," Dawn added. "You might even get away with some of your own dresses, if you wanted."

"Maybe, though I'm kinda curious to wear my new English clothes, just to see how it feels."

"Me, too," Naomi said. "When I stayed with Valerie, I even wore a sweatshirt one time. Remember, Val?"

"How could I forget? You looked better in it than I do."

When they returned to their apartment, Martha spotted a familiar person standing in front of their apartment door. Paul stretched out his arms and she flew into his embrace. Another wonderful-gut surprise. Hopefully, her heart could take it!

# Chapter Three

"You're here! I can't believe it! How long can you stay?" Martha could barely believe her eyes.

"Only a couple hours, I'm afraid. My friend drove me and he has to get back to take his wife to a concert or something. I'm just lucky he was willing to drive me here. I couldn't wait another day, my *liebchen*."

Martha stood back, suddenly remembering her roommate was standing by the doorway waiting for her to unlock it. She looked over and Naomi was grinning at the two of them. Martha took his hand and led him over to introduce them. After a few pleasantries were exchanged, Naomi mentioned she wanted to take another walk. "I meant to pick up some paper napkins at the dollar store. Go show Paul our apartment, but just leave the door unlocked. We need to get another key made," she added.

"It was nice to meet you," Paul said, nodding in appreciation for her quick disappearance.

"Jah. Likewise."

When they got into the apartment, Martha took his hand again and showed him through. It didn't take long,

since it was such a small place. Then they sat together on the sofa and she rested her head against his chest. "I've missed you so much."

"It's been hard. Even though I put in more hours to stay busy, I can't get you out of my mind," he said. "I don't know how long I can stand this arrangement."

"I know. It is difficult, but we're closer now. We can see each other more often, jah?"

"Hopefully. Let me look at you. Where's your kapp? And are those jeans?"

"The kapp is in the dresser. I brought my Amish clothing, but Naomi thinks we should wear English clothes when we look for jobs. I'm just trying them out tonight. Do you like them?"

"I guess. Actually, nee. You look too different. At least you have your hair tucked up. You won't let it down in public, will you?"

"Probably not. I wouldn't feel right."

"Would you understand if I told you I'd be upset? I want you to show your beautiful hair only to me—as your husband."

"If it means that much to you, I'll keep it pinned up. I promise."

"What kind of a job are you looking for?"

"I'm open to most anything, but there's a waitressing job advertised in a small restaurant nearby. Close enough for me to walk. I'll try there first. I hope to go first thing in the morning."

"You'd be gut at that, I know for sure."

"Now, how do you know?" she said with a grin.

"Because my sweet, you'd be gut at anything. I especially like your gut sweet kisses and you haven't given me one yet."

"I'd better correct that right away." She lifted her chin and closed her eyes as she felt his hand rest against her cheek and then his lips touch hers—first gently, and then with passion.

"Just as sweet as I remembered," he whispered. "But we're going to limit it before I forget myself."

"Jah, gut idea. Limit it to how many, sir?"

"Uh, three thousand?"

"Umm. Maybe a little less."

"Like?"

"Like three?"

"Mmm. Not quite what I had in mind, but for now, I guess it will have to do." He added another gentle kiss and then said he'd save the last for later, when he left.

They talked about his family and his job and he mentioned they'd had snow flurries early in the afternoon, but they hadn't amounted to much.

She told him about going shopping with her friends and how much fun they'd had. "And the best thing was, all ten items only came to twenty-four dollars since they were all on sale."

He nodded his approval. "Want to show me?"

"You'll laugh."

"Nee, I promise."

"Well, you'll think I'm weird or something with one thing I bought."

"Okay, let me see that one then and I'll decide whether you're weird or just cute."

She went into the bedroom and came back with the red satin dress on its hanger. His eyes nearly popped out of his head.

"What is that for? Halloween?"

"Oh, you're mean. I know I'll probably never, ever, wear it, but isn't it beautiful?"

His smile dropped. "It looks like a bad woman would wear it. It's definitely not for you." She couldn't tell if he was actually angry, but her heart dropped. It had been a foolish thing to do. "Maybe they'll let me take it back."

"I doubt it."

"Then I'll put it in the Salvation Army as a donation."

"Jah, that would be wise. If you ever wore it, men would try to take advantage of you."

"I never thought of that. In fact, I really didn't think at all." She felt she might cry.

"Martha, you look so upset. I'm sorry. Please don't be. I'm sure you'd be very beautiful in it, but we're Amish and always will be. These things are frivolous and wasteful to spend money on."

"It was only three dollars."

"Three dollars that you could have used for food or a gift."

She plopped the dress over the side of one of the chairs and sat back down beside him. "I've disappointed you, haven't I?"

He put his arm around her once again. "It's not important. What is important is we're going to see more of each other and each day brings us closer to our wedding day. We need to set a date and then you should go back home and prepare for your baptism."

"You've forgotten something. My parents are totally against us marrying. You know that. Until they accept you, we can't plan a wedding."

"I'm going before the congregation next week to confess my sin of displaying anger to Daniel. That should help. I'm actually glad to be going before them. It's both-

ered me terribly to know I lost control like that. What has happened with him?"

"I'm not sure. Last I heard, he was refusing to admit he was wrong. He claimed you struck the first blow and he's showing terrible pride. I can't stand him. I hope they *bann* him."

"He hasn't been by to see you, has he?"

"Nee. My daed would put a stop to that, real quick, but that's one reason I came here. I don't want him to know where I am."

Paul sat back and pulled on his suspenders. "I have forgiven him, but I can't get over my bad feelings for him. I don't trust him. I hope he moves to California or somewhere far away."

"Poor *maedel* in California, if he does."

"Let's not talk about him. Do you want to go for a walk and show me around?"

"I barely know my way around myself; but sure, I'll take you by some cute houses we passed yesterday. I'm so glad you came. Oh, and Naomi has a cell phone, so we can talk every day if you want to. I'm going to pay her half of the cost."

"That's great! So your mamm didn't give you back the one I bought for you."

She shook her head. "She probably threw it out. I'm real sorry, Paul."

"That's all right. I understand her fears. She doesn't want you to leave the Amish and there are temptations. You'll probably get used to electricity now. Maybe you should buy a kero lamp and try to stick with our customs."

"Oh, no. I love it. Watch." She walked quickly over to the wall and began switching the overhead light off and on until she had Paul laughing. He rose and came

over and surrounded her with his arms and kissed the side of her head.

"Uh, oh. That was three," she said, teasingly.

"Doesn't count," he said softly as he pressed his mouth against hers and lingered for several moments. Then they heard Naomi as she knocked loudly before entering. "Gut thing I got that one in, in time. Here comes your roomie."

It was difficult to say good-bye again, but now at least they'd be able to talk on the phone and they made arrangements to get together in two weeks. He suggested just coming for one day so he wouldn't have to pay for a motel room. At first, she was disappointed, but he told her he'd put that much away in saving for their home. That helped and after he left, she sat and told Naomi all about his visit. Well, almost everything.

# Chapter Four

Martha's mother, Sarah, crossed off the day on the calendar and returned to the table and sat across from Melvin, who was stirring sugar into his second cup of coffee.

"It's been two weeks, jah?"

She looked surprised as she took a sip of her coffee and laid the mug down. "You miss her, too."

"Sure. You should know that. It's been awful quiet lately. Maybe we need to pay our dochder a visit."

Sarah's whole face brightened. "That would be ever so nice. You think she'd be ready for company yet?"

"Ask her. You write her every day, jah?"

"Almost."

"I ain't seen but one letter back. Can't be that busy."

"She puts in a lot of hours at that restaurant she works at. You know, I still have that cell phone I took from her room. Maybe it still works. I could try to call her—"

"Sarah, what did I tell you about using phones? Ain't we in enough trouble with the bishop over our dochder's behavior? You want to add more grief?"

"I was just thinking out loud."

"Throw the thing out, if it's tempting you."

"I can't do that. It's not mine to deal with."

"I'll throw it out for you then."

"Just forget I ever said anything about it. I won't use it if you feel that strongly about it, but I ain't about to throw out someone else's object."

Melvin took several gulps of his coffee and then let out a deep breath. "Write to Martha and see when she has time off and I'll ask Hank if he can drive us. At least it's only about an hour away. We'll just stay for the afternoon."

"Maybe we can stay longer. We could get a motel room."

"Who says they even have one, and besides, we don't have that much to talk about. Not till she gets her senses back. Maybe by now she's gotten over her crush on that Paul boy." Melvin added an extra teaspoon of sugar to his coffee mug and stirred it several times.

"It will take longer than two weeks, the way she was going on about him. Are you going to ask her if she ever sees him now?"

"Probably not. Don't want any more lies."

"Maybe we should at least meet with the young man again. She said in her last letter that he's going to confess to his congregation," Sarah said.

"I'll believe it when it's done. Not until."

"If it does happen, could we try to be nice to him?"

"I'm nice to everyone."

"Humph. Says who?" Her lips turned up as she tilted her head.

He let out a laugh. "We'll take it one day at a time, my dear *fraa*. Now get your husband something sweet to go along with this *kaffi*. I know you're hiding something from me."

She giggled as she poked in the cookie jar for a wrapped piece of crumb cake.

\* \* \*

Martha wiped down the small deuce table in the front window after a couple she'd waited on headed for the door. They'd left her two dollars, which wasn't bad since she'd only served them coffee and donuts. She then checked her other two tables, one with four women and the other with an elderly couple, to see if they had enough coffee and water. Things were going smoothly, considering it was only her second full week of waitressing. She'd taken to it quickly and the owners, Joe and Betty Finley, seemed quite pleased with her performance. They were in their mid-thirties, each married for the second time, with no children on either side. Whether it was by choice or God's design, Martha had no way of knowing. They seemed totally absorbed in their business and each other, and were pleasant to work for.

Being used to hard work, waitressing seemed easy and though she was on her feet for hours at a time, she still found the energy and time to use her sketchpad and try her hand at pen and inks. She'd done a few in class when she was younger, but her father discouraged it at home, thinking it was a waste of time. She had occasionally done pencil sketches and then hidden her work in her dresser. The better ones, she'd shown her mother, who told her she had talent, but should not spend too much time developing it, so as not to upset her father.

Now Martha felt free to try her hand once again at an art form, and she truly enjoyed it. Sometimes, during her lunch break she'd sit on a public bench and sketch a tree or building she found attractive. When Naomi saw her notebook one evening, she encouraged her to mat them and try to sell them at an upcoming craft show the town held each spring. "You have all winter to draw, Martha. You might make a lot of money. I'd buy one if I could."

"Goodness! You can have as many as you want. I'll even frame them for you."

"Really?" Naomi's brows rose. "Well, maybe for my birthday in June, you could do one of our apartment building. I'd love to have one to keep."

"As gut—no, *good*—as done. I'll start it next."

Each night, before going to bed, Martha and Paul spent about half an hour chatting on the phone. She looked forward to it and counted the hours till she'd hear his voice. Their love was growing stronger, even though they saw little of each other. He did come by briefly to see her at work one afternoon. He had tagged along with an English friend, who had business in the next town, but since his friend had to return to Lewistown when his work was completed, it didn't leave them much time.

After he left, Betty Finley asked why she was interested in an Amishman and Martha explained for the first time that she herself was Amish and only dressed the way she did to make her job easier—fewer questions and definitely fewer stares. Betty seemed to understand, but often asked her questions about her faith when there was a slow period in the restaurant. According to Betty, she and her husband were Methodists, but had fallen away from their faith during their difficult divorces, years before. They'd met and married five years before they opened the restaurant and found they enjoyed running the business together.

Naomi liked working for the family with the toddlers. She admitted one evening though that she missed her family at home. "I didn't think I would, but I even miss Mamm. They have a phone now, which is sort of a secret, I guess, but I talk to her every few days now."

"I'm so glad, Naomi," Martha said as the two of them

sat with their Bibles. They had begun reading together
when they had the opportunity, and they discussed Bib-
lical questions they each had. It was an interesting time.
Another freedom they had not known—to even question
some of the ideas they'd been taught. Rumspringa was
important to them. When they did settle down and go
through the baptism, they wanted to be ready and sure
of their belief system. This seemed to be strengthening
their faith, which would probably have been a surprise to
some of their friends and family back home. Definitely,
a surprise to the bishop.

"Do you ever talk to little Patty?" Martha asked.

"I did once, but Mamm said she started to cry."

Martha noted her friend looked about to cry herself,
so she quickly changed the subject. She was glad that
they only had a six-month lease though, and then it would
go month-to-month. That way if either of them wanted
to return home, they could, though they'd agreed to wait
until they were both ready to leave, rather than leave one
with the whole rent to pay.

Between their two incomes, they were able to put
money aside and still live comfortably. Having lived
simply all their lives, it was not difficult at all. Martha
knew her father wouldn't want the money returned, but
she hadn't even touched it, since her tips took care of her
expenses. The Finleys gave her free meals whenever she
worked through a mealtime, which helped considerably.

Once when it was slow, Martha made a large batch
of Whoopie Pies, some with peanut butter filling. They
became so popular that Betty paid her extra to keep
them supplied. Martha expanded her selection by making some with pumpkin and cream cheese filling, and
even experimented with lemon raspberry filling.

It was mid-November now and they'd already had six

inches of snow one weekend. Paul had been forgiven by those in his district after confessing his sin publicly. He felt better himself and told Martha he was now praying for Daniel, asking the Lord to bring him to his knees as well.

Martha was encouraged to do the same, but as hard as she tried, the prayers seemed hollow, and she felt hypocritical even attempting to pray for him. Hopefully, the anger would pass. It was painful to realize she still held unforgiveness in her heart, and she asked Paul to pray for her so she could come before God's throne without guilt in her spirit.

Martha was given three days off over the Thanksgiving holiday, even though the restaurant would remain open. It meant that the Finleys would have to hire some of their past employees to fill in. At first Martha refused to leave them at such a busy time, but Betty insisted. She was aware of the importance of Martha being with her family over such an important holiday after talking to her at length about their lives and learning how close the family was—at least until her move.

Once she realized she'd be back home for Thanksgiving, Martha wrote to her parents and begged them to allow Paul to come by on Friday, after the actual holiday. It was time for forgiveness on everyone's part. The fact he'd gone before his congregation seemed to impress her father and they gave her permission to ask him. He'd have to spend the night with her aenti Lizzy, though. That was part of the arrangement.

When she saw Paul the next day, he was practically giddy. "This is our chance, Martha. Danki! Gott is gut!"

"Jah, all the time," Martha chimed in, grinning widely. Patience was paying off.

# Chapter Five

Paul was whistling as he prepared to stain a small end table. His boss, Jeremiah, looked over and grinned at his friend. "Gut to hear you sound a little chipper. You got to see your girlfriend yesterday?"

"Jah. Only for about an hour, but it was wonderful. She's such a sweetheart."

"Have you popped the question yet?" Jeremiah asked as he wiped his hands on a rag.

"We talk about marrying, but I've told you about her parents and how they don't have very nice feelings about me."

"Jah, but now that you've been forgiven by the church…"

"I guess it did make a difference, because they're willing for me to meet with them again over the Thanksgiving weekend. You know Martha is going home for three days."

"Jah, I remember you saying that. So they're going to let you be with their dochder again. That's a gut sign, jah?"

"The best news I've had in a long time. I just hope I don't mess up."

"You won't. You're a decent guy. They should be glad

you're interested in their dochder. Maybe it will help to know you're gonna be making real gut money. I've been holding off telling you till you were more yourself, but I'd like to go into a partnership with you. You know as much, if not more, than I do about this carpentry business. I've really been impressed and I'd like to expand, but I could use a partner I'd trust and who'd be willing to make some investment toward a larger building. It's getting tight here and the work is piling up. I need to expand and even hire a couple new guys."

"Oh, wow! You're serious? A partner?"

"Why not? We get along real fine, don't you think?"

"Jah, we do. I don't have a lot of money saved. How much were you thinking you'd need from me?"

"I haven't gotten that far. First we'd need to find the right building. I'd rather buy than rent. If you're thinking of joining me, we could look together."

"This has taken me by surprise, but I sure like the idea, Jeremiah. I would like to hear all the requirements and possibilities before actually signing my name on anything though."

"Oh, jah, no huge rush, but I'd like to call a couple realtors and get started on looking around. I want to stay in this area though, since I've built up a pretty gut reputation."

"Of course. I understand. Funny you mentioned it today. I actually was thinking of looking for a small place to live in. I want to surprise Martha and present her with a home before I set a date for our wedding. It would be my present to her. I have a few thousand saved, but I guess I could use it for our business instead."

"We've got a lot to think about, but right now, I'm

starving. Let's break for lunch once you're done staining and we can talk some more."

"Danki. Boy, you never know what doors Gott is
going to open next, do you? I don't think I'll mention it
to Martha till things are finalized. Looks like things are
starting to go our way."


Martha couldn't wait for the holiday vacation. Her
parents seemed just as excited as she was, judging by
her mother's letters. She sounded so much happier once
she knew they'd be together for Thanksgiving. Her aenti
Lizzy wrote to say she was pleased to put Paul up at her
house for the night. Martha knew she would also give
him the third degree while he was there. She hoped he
wouldn't mind, but that was the way her aunt was. Very
protective. She always had treated Martha as if she were
her own child, causing occasional jealousy to crop up
with Sarah, her younger sister by eight years. Sometimes, it was amusing, but there were other times, it got
pretty touchy. Since her aunt and uncle had eight adult
sons and lost their only girl at birth, Martha had always
played a special part in their lives.

She loved her aunt almost as much as she loved her
parents. Lizzy had played a major role in her life as she
grew up, so her acceptance of Paul as a future husband
was nearly as important as her parents' approval. Poor
Paul, he had an important time coming up. She wouldn't
tell him too much, since it might make him more nervous than he already was.

The weather had gotten much nippier now that it was
late November. There were some persistent leaves on
the pin oak outside their living room window, but otherwise, the trees were now stark skeletons against the

sky and most days were dreary and gray. Occasionally, a few snowflakes would coat the dry brown grass, but it was still early to anticipate heavy snows. Even though Martha's walk was under a half mile to the restaurant, she'd added a sweater of late under her woolen jacket. She was allowed to wear slacks to work and fortunately had picked up three pairs of dressy pants when the girls had gone shopping together.

Naomi was given some time off over the holiday as well, so she and Martha decided to share the cost of a driver, arranging their trips to coincide. Dawn had offered to drive them, but she was a fast driver and Martha preferred paying someone professional, especially since the weather was unpredictable this time of year.

Wednesday before the holiday, the girls left for Paradise around noon.

Sarah was sitting by the window watching for the car. She'd already baked off three batches of Martha's favorite cookies and she had just tucked four pumpkin pies in the oven to take to her sister's. The aroma was tantalizing. Sarah hadn't yet mentioned that the main meal was going to be at Lizzy's home this year. Maybe it was depression because of Martha leaving home, but Sarah just hadn't felt up to preparing for so many people this time. With her parents and Lizzy's whole family, it would have ended up with over thirty people. Maybe it was just a case of aging, but when Lizzy offered to have it at her house, Sarah had jumped at the opportunity. In the past, she'd take the Thanksgiving meal and Lizzy would do Christmas.

At last, a car turned down the drive and she knew it was Martha.

"Melvin, she's here!" she called out to her husband,

who was changing into fresh clothes for the occasion. He reached the first floor as Martha climbed the steps to the front door.

Sarah opened the storm door and met her daughter at the stoop. "It's so gut to see you again, *lieb*. Come in. Come in. It's windy out here."

"Jah, it is cold." Martha waved back to the driver and brought in her overnight bag, closing the door behind her. Oh, it smelled so wonderful-gut! No one made pies like her mudder. She reached for her father's hands after hugging her mother and he ignored them and wrapped his arms around her, holding her so tightly, she nearly stopped breathing.

"Let's see my employed dochder. Are they working you too hard?" he asked, grinning widely.

"Nee, I really enjoy it and they're wonderful nice people."

"Jah? Gut tips?" her mother asked as they walked toward the kitchen.

"Pretty gut. I save a little every week."

"Jah? Gut for you," her father said, nodding. "Our little *maed* is growing up. Jah, Mamm?"

"She sure is. Goodness, she's a real woman now."

"Oh, I don't feel very different-like. It smells so gut in here. I can't wait till everyone gets here tomorrow,"

"We've had a change, Martha. We're all going to Aenti Lizzy and Onkel Leroy's for dinner. I hope you're not too disappointed," her mother said.

"That's fine, but why? It's always been here."

"Your mamm decided it would be too much for her this year," her father spoke up.

"Now, don't put it that way, Mel." Sarah turned to Martha. "We just needed a change, is all."

"It sure doesn't matter to me, as long as we're all together," Martha said, putting her arm around her mother's waist. "You look gut, Mamm. Are you feeling okay?"

"Pretty gut. Just not as peppy as I'd like."

"Ach, none of us are," Melvin added. "When do we eat dinner?"

"Anytime. I have a roast in the oven. Can you smell it?"

"The pies are all I can smell," he said. "But I love your cooking. Hungry, Martha? Ready for some gut food for a change?"

"Now, Melvin, our Martha is a gut cook. You know that."

"We don't cook a whole lot, Mamm. Working at a restaurant, I eat most of my meals there."

"Do they charge you for them?" her father asked.

"No, they're free and I can even eat their desserts."

"I bet you love that," her mother said as she went over to the stove to check the potatoes, which were gently boiling. Sarah poked them with a fork. "Done."

"Let me put them in the colander for you, Mamm," Martha said as she turned the water spigot on to wash her hands.

"No, you work too hard as it is. I'll take care of it and you and your daed can chat while I mash them up. Just stay in the kitchen so I don't miss anything."

Martha and her father sat down at the table and she told them all about the restaurant and the Finleys, as Sarah mashed the cooked potatoes and listened with happiness filling her heart. It was like a real home now once again. Oh, how she'd missed her darling daughter. Perhaps she was ready to come back home and stay. That would be an answer to prayer, for sure and for certain.

# *Chapter Six*

Thanksgiving was wonderful as always. There was laughter, hugs and kisses, plus cheery children's voices—though somewhat muted since they'd learned the ways of their Plain heritage and were taught to respect their elders and limit their louder voices to the outdoors. Everyone was excited to learn of Martha's new life; however, her cousins assumed it was about to end and she'd be returning home before Christmas.

"Nee, I have a six-month lease, so maybe in April or May, if things work out," she was telling one of her aunt's daughters-in-law. "I have a gut job waitressing, too. I'm trying to save money."

"Jah? You buying a car?" the young woman asked, facetiously.

Martha giggled. "Maybe a new bike. I really want to fill my hope chest."

"Ah, anyone we know?"

Martha shook her head. "Nothing to report officially yet."

Her mother had been cutting pies next to Lizzy at the counter next to the sink while Martha and Judy, the

daughter-in-law, were conversing. She looked over at her daughter and smiled. "You can tell them they may be meeting a possible suitor tomorrow."

Martha was surprised to hear her mother use the word "suitor" and it lifted her spirits. She grinned and nodded. "Jah, I am pretty fond of a man I met when I was helping Cousin Deborah. He's coming in tomorrow for one night to get to know the family better."

"Oh, that's the secret my mamm was trying to hide from us," Judy said, grinning. "She was freshening the guest room at the top of the stairs, but she wouldn't tell us why. Maybe we'll get to meet him, too."

Sarah moved the now empty pie pans to the sink and filled it with water. Then she dried her hands and turned toward Martha and Judy. "Hopefully, if he's the one, they'll find a nice plot of land right nearby."

"Mamm, you're getting way ahead of yourself."

"Just suggesting," she said, with a wink at Judy.

"I know of five acres coming up for sale about half a mile from here," Judy said. "Part of the Bonner track. They're dividing it up into five-acre lots. Builders are snatching some up, but they had over five hundred acres."

"I know that land. It's really gut soil. It won't last long," Sarah said, nodding.

Martha tucked the information away in her mind. Between what she was saving and what Paul had in his account, perhaps it would be enough for a portion of land. What a great location. And he could build a shop next to their home...

"Martha, did you hear me?" Aenti Lizzy was saying. "We need the cookies you brought put on the table. Do you mind? And Judy, your *sohn* just spilled a whole box of pretzels on the living room floor."

"Oh dear. See you later," Judy said as she headed for the broom and dustpan. "He's always into something."

"Your mamm has been so sad with you gone, Martha," Lizzy said. "I hope you'll be home to stay real soon."

"Probably spring, Aenti." Martha reached for some of the larger dinner plates and started arranging cookies on them.

Lizzy sat down at the table to watch. "Jah, she walks around like a corpse sometimes."

"Lots of people leave their homes at my age. Why can't she accept that?" Martha looked over at her aunt, looking for an answer that would make sense.

"I guess since you're her only child, it makes it harder."

"It kinda puts a burden on me though. I don't feel free to live my own life."

"Ain't that what you've been doing?"

"I guess so, but I feel so much pressure and even guilt. You have no idea how strained it was here before I left."

"That's because they were hurt that you lied to them."

"They forced me to lie by not trying to understand my feelings for Paul. They wouldn't give him a chance." She stopped when the plates were filled and sat next to her aunt.

"Well, he did punch a man, jah?"

"Golly, he was pushed to. I told you how it happened. He may be Amish, but he's still a man. Sometimes, even a gut man weakens when he's pushed too far. Daniel is the one at fault, really."

"Just don't jump into something. He might end up being a wife-beater."

Martha rolled her eyes and shook her head. "I know

him, Aenti. He's gentle and loving, and he just got pushed over the edge. I have no fear of him being a gut husband and daed."

"I'm a pretty gut judge of character. I'll let you know how I feel after I spend some time with him."

Martha let out a long sigh. "Please don't give him the third degree. We aren't even engaged. I don't want people to scare him away."

Lizzy let out a guffaw. "I won't get too personal with the lad, but I ain't about to let my sweet niece get tied into a bad marriage. I promise I'll be gentle."

Martha reached across and patted her aunt's left hand. "I'm counting on that and I do listen to my elders, so your opinion counts."

"Danki." She covered Martha's hand with her right hand and squeezed it gently. "Now let's put these on the buffet and see how the table's coming. Should be set up by now."

Martha checked her watch every few minutes, wishing time would go faster. She wondered what Paul was doing at that same time and guessed he was also wishing things would move along so they'd be together sooner.

At last it was time to go back home. Her grandparents had been dropped off at their place earlier by one of Lizzy and Leroy's sons, and those with young children had left to prepare them for bed.

In the meantime, the kitchen had been *redded* up to Lizzy's satisfaction. Martha and her parents were the last to leave. It had been a delicious meal and even Martha was exhausted from all the work entailed. No wonder her mother, who was frailer than her older sister probably due to her earlier battle with cancer, had decided against

taking on the meal at their home. There would probably come a time when Martha would have too many kinner to add to the family meal, and Sarah and Lizzy would have to have their celebrations separately with their immediate families.

Of course, that was a long way off, but on the way home, Martha sat back as her parents discussed the day, and pictured living nearby with her own large family. It would be fun to have eight or ten children, she thought, and tried to picture them. Maybe some would have her coloring while others would be blondies with those wonderful sky-blue eyes Paul had inherited. Once again, she wondered who in her family had given her the genes for her nearly black hair and dark eyes.

"Mamm," she asked, leaning forward from the back seat. "Who did you say I got my dark hair and eyes from?"

Her parents exchanged glances and Sarah cleared her throat. "I'm not sure, Martha. Why do you ask?"

"Just wondering," she answered as she moved back on her seat. Same answer she got last time. She'd have to ask her aunt Lizzy next time. She'd know, since she was older and probably had a better memory about some of the elders who had already passed on.

It was difficult to fall asleep that night; though Martha was physically tired, she was too excited as well as nervous about Paul's visit. Her aunt Lizzy could be a problem if she didn't like someone. She was known as a feisty woman and Martha had seen her put others down from time to time, while her mother was the more placid member of the family. Finally, she fell asleep though her dreams were constant and vivid. She dreamt Paul was married to someone else and she lived at home without

her parents. The worst part was he lived in the same house with another woman and was surrounded by a multitude of wonderful blond, blue-eyed children. Of course, his wife was absolutely gorgeous, while Martha felt old and bedraggled. It was good to wake up and realize it had merely been a dream—or nightmare in this case.

At noon, a car pulled around the drive and Martha, who'd been watching since ten in the morning, grabbed her woolen shawl off the peg in the kitchen and ran out to greet him. They didn't touch, but their eyes exchanged tender love as he paid the driver and walked over to her. By now, her parents had also come to greet him. Her father shook his hand and she could tell he did his very best to look welcoming, though she sensed he was fighting negative feelings.

Her mother was genuinely sweet and her smile radiated on her lovely rounded face. Martha knew she could count on her mother to be a wonderful hostess.

Paul looked wonderful as always. He had a small satchel with him and carried it into the house as Martha's mother led the way into the kitchen. After a somewhat cool greeting, her father excused himself and went back to the barn.

"I bet you're hungry, Paul. We're nearly ready to eat our dinner."

"I admit, I am kinda hungry, ma'am. Sure smells gut in here."

Sarah walked over to the stove and took a wooden spoon and stirred the contents of the large skillet. "Making goulash with ground beef. Just waiting for the noodles to cook. Why don't you two walk around in the sun? It would be gut for you, Martha. You look pale."

"You sure you don't need me, Mamm?"

"Nee. The table's already set. I'm fine."

"Danki." Martha replaced her shoes with boots and Paul followed her out the back door. They walked swiftly to the hen house, which was out of sight of the barn or the kitchen, and Paul immediately put his arms around her and kissed her soundly on the lips.

"I've missed you so much."

"Jah, me, too."

"You look wonderful. I don't think you're pale," he said, tracing his forefinger down her cheek. "When do you have to go back?"

"Tomorrow. Our ride is coming around ten. How about you, Paul?"

"Around the same time. It doesn't give us much time together."

"Better than nothing. When can we see each other again?"

"I'm not sure. We're so busy trying to catch up on our jobs. Seems like everyone wants their furniture before Christmas. We're going to look for more help."

"That's gut," she said, disappointment in her voice in spite of the positive words.

"Maybe you can come one day to visit me, Martha. You could even come to work with me so we'd be near each other. Jeremiah would give me breaks, I'm sure."

"Maybe. I usually get Wednesday off. And now that I'm making money, I can pay for a ride or maybe have one of my new English friends drive me there if I pay for the gas."

"It's not that far away. It was a short ride. Oh, I have a surprise for you." He reached into his pocket and pulled out a new cell phone.

"Oh, you shouldn't have. I don't have the money for two phones, Paul. I share the expense with Naomi, remember?"

He looked so disappointed, she was sorry she'd seemed so ungrateful. "But I guess I can afford to have two."

"I'm paying the whole thing on this one. It's like a family plan, sort of. I'm making gut money right now. In fact, I'm saving..." He stopped. It wasn't time to divulge his possible partnership, which might never materialize, or mention looking for a house. It would take away from the surprise he had planned when he made an official proposal.

"Jah? Saving for what?"

"The future," he answered, avoiding details.

"Me, too. I'm looking to fill my hope chest. I need to work on pillowcases next," she added. "I embroidered the hem of a sheet. It's real cute, but I won't show you. I want to surprise you someday."

"Kiss me again, Martha. I just heard the dinner bell. Who knows when we'll be able to be in private after this. I don't want your folks to distrust us."

"You're right." She put her head back and closed her eyes, waiting for the thrill of his lips on hers once again. His breath was always pepperminty. She liked the fact that his hair was clean and tidy, too. Some of the young men were negligent about their grooming, but not her Paul. He wasn't vain, just careful about his appearance.

After a sweet kiss, they walked back, meeting her father along the walkway.

"How's your cow you were worried about?" Paul asked as they made their way to the back porch.

"She's doing pretty gut now. Still needs to be watched and babied a bit, but she's a gut ole milker."

"I'm glad to hear that," Paul said.

Martha glanced over at her father, who looked pleased at Paul's concern. Score a point for Paul, she thought. It was her aunt Lizzy she was afraid of—not her parents.

# Chapter Seven

There was very little conversation during the meal, but it was not uncommon for the family to concentrate on their food and leave the talking for later. When they were finished eating, Paul complimented Martha's mother on the goulash and she nodded. "I like cooking. Always have."

Melvin wiped his mouth after pushing his plate aside. "When's your *schwester* coming, Sarah?"

"Lizzy said she and Leroy would stop by around seven tonight. They'll take you back with them then, Paul. As you know, you'll be spending the night with them."

"*Jah*, that's very nice of them. I sure appreciate it. I also want to thank you folks for letting me see your *dochder* again. I don't know if she told you, but I went before my church family and confessed my sin about the fight, and I've been forgiven."

"*Jah*, we heard," Melvin said, sitting back and pulling on his long beard. "Glad to hear it. You wouldn't be here if you hadn't."

"I understand," Paul said softly.

"I heard a couple days ago that Daniel Beiler has been officially banned," Melvin said dispassionately.

Martha exchanged looks with her mother. "Daed, why didn't you tell us?"

"Didn't see that it mattered much. You ain't gonna be getting together with him anyway."

"I feel better knowing he's not around, though. That was one reason I went with Naomi and got an apartment."

"Mmm. Thought it was to get away from us for a while," he said, frowning.

"I… I think you know it was for several reasons."

"One reason we thought it would be gut to have you come by in person," Melvin continued, as he turned toward Paul, "was to let you know we won't tolerate lying. Not from Martha—not from you. We want everything to be aboveboard, so if you two want to see each other, we want to know about it."

"Daed, this is so embarrassing," Martha said, close to tears.

"Shouldn't be. We're all adults here, ain't we?"

"Sir, I will be truthful with you. I love your dochder and I hope someday she'll marry me. I never meant to be sneaky. We felt forced to, I'm afraid, and it wasn't right."

Martha thought about the cell phone hidden away in her apron pocket and she was filled with guilt. Then she reached in and removed it, setting it on the table. Paul's brows rose and his mouth flew open, though not a word was uttered.

"So what have we here?" her father said, leaning forward.

"We were going to use this to talk. I hope we still will, but I want you to know about it."

"And if I forbid it?"

"I hope you won't, Daed."

There was silence. Loud silence. Sarah suddenly began coughing and Martha leaped up and brought her mother a glass of water. She took a gulp and placed her hand on her chest. "Danki."

"Your mudder already took one phone away."

"Sir, we just want to talk to each other. We can't see each other, because we live an hour apart by car, but we have to be able to talk. After all—"

"I'm going outside—alone for a while," Melvin said as he pushed his chair back and stood. "I need to think this over. It pains me to hear my dochder speak to me as she does."

"But, Daed—"

He walked past her and went out the back door, forgetting his jacket as he left.

Sarah rose and walked quickly to the pegs and took her husband's jacket as well as her own shawl. "He'll catch a death of a cold. I'll go out and make him put it on."

"Can I take it for you?" Paul asked, as he stood up.

"Nee. Not a gut idea. Stay with Martha."

After she left, Martha put her head in her hands and wept. "I don't know why I did that. Please don't be mad at me."

He came around and knelt by her chair, resting his hand on her arm. "I can't be mad at you, Martha. I understand. We have to do things right. I shouldn't have bought the phone. I guess you'll have to tell them about Naomi having one and the fact that we do talk nearly every night. I want them to trust us."

"Take this one back," she said, as she pushed it toward him.

He put it in his pocket and stood straight. "Do you

think I should get a ride back to Lewistown today, if I can? I don't want to make things worse for you."

"No, please don't leave. I don't think I'll come home again—not for a long time. They're so mean all of a sudden. Don't they want me to be happy? What's the difference if we use phones? Lots of bishops allow them now. Ours is so old-fashioned. Maybe I'll change and become a Mennonite. They even allow electricity and they still believe in Gott."

"You know you don't mean it. We both love being Amish. We'll get through this and someday your folks will understand and accept us."

"I don't know. You haven't even met my aenti yet. She's even tougher. Why can't they just relax and let me run my own life, for Pete's sake?"

The door opened and her mother walked back in alone. "Daed wants the phone gone." She looked at her daughter, whose eyes were swollen from her tears. "I'm sorry, Martha. Really, I am."

"I've already given it back to Paul, but I can't promise not to talk to him on my friend's phone. I just won't agree to that, and if it means he disowns me? Well, so be it."

"Martha Martha. Don't talk like that. We'd never disown you. I'll try to soften his heart so he'll understand."

"It was easy when you two were young and courting," Martha continued. "You lived about three farms apart, right? When you lived in Ohio?"

"Jah, that's true."

"And yet when you married, you came all the way to Pennsylvania. I know your parents and family came, too, but Daed's didn't. Why? Why did you leave and come so far?"

"It's a long story, Martha. Not now."

"You always change the subject. How come it was okay for Daed to leave, but you expect me to promise to live nearby? Maybe I will, but why should I make a promise I may not be able to keep. Maybe Paul doesn't want to leave *his* family."

"Martha." Paul moved next to her and touched her arm. "You're upsetting your mamm. Let's all stop and cool off. I hate that I bring pain to this family. Maybe I'm wrong for you."

*"Paul, how can you say that?"* Martha nearly shouted. The shock of his statement tore into her soul. Was he so ready to call it off? Just because of her family?

"Now let's all calm down," her mother said quickly. "Before your daed comes back in, we should just settle down. If it's Gott's will that you two one day marry, then we have to accept it, no matter where you settle. Jah, we want to be part of your life, Martha, always; but I want you to be happy and living right before the Lord, first and foremost."

Then Sarah turned toward Paul. "I believe you love my dochder and if you do, you shouldn't be so quick to leave. I don't understand. You should pray for peace to settle on this household and acceptance. If you're a man of Gott, then act it and don't be sniveling."

Paul couldn't hold back his grin. "You're right. No more sniveling." He placed his arm around Martha, who was trying with all her might to hold back further tears. "This is the maed I plan to marry. And marry, we will, regardless of what anyone says."

Martha managed to smile ever so slightly.

"That is, if she'll have me," he added.

She nodded and took a deep breath. "I need some air.

Too much strife. I can't take any more. Maybe I should go back to my apartment today."

Her mother shook her head, vehemently. "Please don't, Martha. Not like this. We need to all calm down and enjoy the time we have together. Come help me redd up the kitchen. Paul, you can relax. There's a puzzle started in the sitting room."

"Danki, but I'm not real gut at puzzles. I can help dry dishes if you want."

"Nee, you're our guest. Just sit and keep us company then, jah?"

"If Martha will allow me to stay."

"Oh, Paul. Sometimes I could strangle you, but then I'd have to go confess and I'm too timid to confess something in front of others."

They laughed together and soon the thick atmosphere of dissent turned into a tranquil setting. Even when Melvin returned, there seemed to be God's peace over the home. Martha was certain it was an answer to her prayers. There was a right way to live, and a wrong way. She wanted to follow the Godly way of living with all her heart. Surely, that would include Paul as her husband, and love would win out.

# *Chapter Eight*

Lizzy showed up around seven with her husband, Leroy. "I've never seen so many buggies on the road at one time," she said as she leaned over and pecked at her sister's cheek. "Guess everyone was visiting family today."

Melvin had gone outside to help with the buggy, but Paul and Martha joined the women in the kitchen. Introductions followed and Martha watched as her aunt gave Paul a thorough going over. He kept a pleasant smile on his face, but Martha could tell he was a wee bit nervous by the way he wiped his hands on his trousers.

"So this is Paul," Lizzy finally said. "I hear you make nice furniture."

"I try."

"We could use a new headboard someday, that's for sure. It creaks something fierce when you move around in bed."

Martha swallowed hard. That remark left too many thoughts in her imagination and she silently asked God to forgive her lustful images.

"I'd be happy to show you sketches of some we've

made, whenever you get serious about it. No charge, of course."

"Well, you can't survive if people don't pay you for your time." She took off her jacket and placed it over the back of a kitchen chair. "Any kaffi?"

"Jah, I made a fresh pot a while ago. Help yourself, Lizzy. Lots of cookies to choose from settin' on the counter," Sarah added, pointing across the stove to the counter top. "We'll join you. Come, Paul, take some more kaffi and relax with us."

Lizzy poured herself a mugful and sat down. "Oh, my feet are sore today. I was on my feet seemed like for two days getting ready for Thanksgiving. I'm getting too old for this. My kids will have to take over next year."

"You still plan on doing Christmas?" Sarah asked her sister.

"Not if I can get out of it. You sure you don't want to do it? By then, Martha will be back and you'll have lots of help. Don't forget, you're a lot younger than I am."

"Aenti, I'm not going to be back living here for a while yet. I signed a lease."

"Well, you're sure planning on being here for Christmas, ain't you?"

"I most likely will, but I haven't even thought about Christmas. I have to check with my boss. Hopefully, they close the restaurant, at least for the day. I'm close enough that I could just come for the twenty-fifth, if I have to."

"I'll be strong enough then," Sarah said. "Besides, some of your kinner go to other relatives on Christmas day. Last year, you only had about twenty, didn't you, Liz?"

"I forget. Seems like a long time ago. You have a big family, Paul?"

"Jah, I have three older brothers and two older sisters. All married with kinner. I was the boppli of the family."

"Spoiled, I'll betcha," Lizzy said with a grin.

"Jah, I admit, I was treated pretty gut. Never had to clean much, but I had to help my daed with the farm from a pretty early age."

"So why ain't you farming? More money in carpentry?"

"It depends. I just enjoy working with wood better. I work for a very nice man. In fact, he's the same age as me."

Now was not the time to spring anything about his possible partnership. No, he wouldn't even bring the matter up to Martha, until something was finalized. He suspected her family wouldn't be thrilled to learn that he'd want to remain two hours away from them. Even Martha might be disappointed to learn of his ideas. Of course, once she saw the little house he had in mind to build, he was sure she'd be more than willing to make the move. They weren't that far from her family, and he'd make a concerted effort to visit them frequently. Might get difficult after they reached more than four kinner, but that was a long time off..

Martha's grandparents came over to see Paul, but her grandfather wasn't feeling up to snuff, so they left shortly after they'd spent an hour together with the family. Martha noted her grandfather seemed to be limping more prominently, and walking was somewhat of a struggle. It saddened her to see them aging before her eyes, though it was the way of life and accepting the inevitable was just part of God's plan.

* * *

Paul liked Lizzy's husband right away. Though Leroy
had a quiet nature, he smiled almost continuously and
seemed accepting of his future nephew-in-law. All-in-
all, the visit went well. Before they were ready to leave,
Lizzy suggested he say good-bye to Martha alone in the
small sewing room off the sitting area. There was no
door to shut, but they were able to remain out of sight at
the far end of the room where there was a small loveseat.

He reached for Martha's hand and squeezed it. Then
he lifted it to his lips and kissed it silently. "Do you think
it went okay?" he asked in hushed tones.

"Jah, but the real test comes when Lizzy gets you
alone. Be prepared," she said, giving him a wink.

"Think it's safe to give you a good-bye kiss?" he
asked, now in a whisper.

"If we make it quick-like," she said just as quietly.
Then she leaned over and without releasing her hand,
their lips met and they exchanged a sweet gentle kiss.

"I'll call you when I get back to my apartment," she
said. "I won't make a promise not to talk to you. I'd have
to break it, so I won't lie about it."

"Jah, no more lies." They rose and returned to the sitting room, where the other adults were discussing Christmas gifts for the younger children.

"Ah, there they are. That was short. Ready to leave?"
Lizzy asked Paul.

"Anytime you say. I really appreciate you putting me
up."

Lizzy and Sarah stood at the same time and hugged.
"I'll stop by sometime tomorrow afternoon and we can
go over the gift list," Lizzy said as her husband went for

their jackets. "Did you give your driver directions to our farm?" she asked Paul.

"Jah, Martha told me where it was." Paul picked up his satchel, which was by the doorway, and shook Leroy's hand as he nodded to Sarah. "Danki for a nice day."

"Jah, it was gut to get to know you better, Paul," Sarah said. Her husband merely nodded.

Martha followed them to the door and she patted Paul's arm as she handed him a toot with several cookies. "This is for the ride back," she said, holding in her emotions. Hopefully, they'd get together sometime over Christmas. And maybe before, even if just for a couple hours.

After they left, Martha wiped down one of the counters while her mother rinsed out the coffeepot and laid it on a towel to dry. "What do you think, Mamm? Do you think Daed likes Paul any better now?"

"I think so. I'll learn more later. We haven't had time to talk. He seems like a nice young man. I'm sure it took a lot for him to confess the way he did."

"I'm still glad I'm not around here, not knowing what Daniel is up to. Please find out where he's living before I see you at Christmas. It's just like him to show up and spoil things."

"Ach. He wouldn't dare. Not after he saw your daed's face the day of the fight. He'd be a *dummkopf* to come back here uninvited."

"Jah, you're right about that," Martha said with a grin. "Daed can look pretty tough when he wants to."

"Maybe you should tell Paul about the land for sale. He might have enough money to buy a five-acre plot. That would be large enough for a small house, a building for his carpentry, and a garden, don't you think?"

"I might mention it. I'll see. It seems early to be talking that serious-like, but I can put a bug in his ear."

"I need to sit awhile. Daed went out to check the animals. Maybe we can work on that puzzle together. What do you think? You take over the sky part. It's too hard for me, bein' all the same color."

"I'll give it a try, but I'm not too gut at it either." Mother and daughter went into the sitting room and moved the card table under one of the wall lamps for better lighting. It was something they enjoyed doing together—something she'd miss once married.

# Chapter Nine

"You can put your satchel upstairs, Paul," Lizzy said, pointing to the simple pine staircase leading to the second floor. "Your room is at the end of the hallway on the left. You'll be using the bathroom at the top of the stairs. I put extra quilts at the foot of the bed, since it's supposed to get real cold tonight."

"Under twenty," her husband remarked. "I'd better bring in some more coal."

"I'll help you, sir, as soon as I take my things out of your way," Paul said as he headed for the stairs with his satchel and the toot of cookies.

"Sure could use the help," Leroy said. "I'll be out back."

Once they'd brought several buckets of coal up to the back porch, they came back in, and while Leroy was adding kerosene to some of the lamps, Lizzy motioned Paul to follow her into their sitting room. She pointed to an armchair and sat across from him on the worn brown sofa.

"Thought we could talk a bit while we're alone, Paul.

You know, of course, that Martha is the apple of my eye. I'm sure she's told you how close we are."

"Jah, she has. She loves you very much. And your husband."

"So, I want to know all about the man she plans to marry. Tell me what kind of husband you'll make." She sat back and folded her arms, waiting for the poor young man to sell himself to Martha's very special aunt.

"Well, I hope I'll be a gut husband. I can tell you this. I've never felt this kind of love before. I just want to make Martha happy and I think about her all the time, wondering what she's doing, if she misses me, things like that. We get along so gut when we're together."

"Ever had an argument? Disagreement?"

He thought a moment before answering. "I can't think of a time, but I know we probably will disagree from time to time. That's to be expected, jah?"

"True. It's how you settle things that counts. Martha's been raised to look up to her father, and her mamm knows when to give in to her husband and when to assert herself. Martha ain't a wimp, but she's a Godly woman. I just want to know you'll treat her like Christ treats his bride. You know your Bible, jah?"

He nodded. "I'd always consider her feelings. We may have to learn to compromise sometimes."

"Well, one thing she can't compromise on is where you'll settle down. It would absolutely break my schwester's heart to have her dochder living far away. Ever since she knew she couldn't have kinner, she's considered Martha a gift from Gott. When she first saw her she was only a month old—"

"Why did they keep her away from her mudder?" he asked, confused by Lizzy's comment.

"What do you mean? What did I say? Oh mercy, forget what I just said."

"Please, explain. Was my Martha adopted?"

Lizzy shook her head and rolled her eyes. "What a stupid thing I've done. Jah, Paul, she's adopted, but she doesn't know it. You can't let on."

"Why wasn't she told? I don't understand. Who are her real parents?"

"It's a long story, but I've gotten this far. Just promise, you'll keep this to yourself."

He nodded. "Go on."

"Sarah discovered shortly after she was married that she had cancer in the womb. That's why she hadn't gotten pregnant right away. She was hoping for a boppli the first year. The cancer had advanced somewhat when she finally went to the doctor's. She's lucky to be alive. After they did a hysterectomy on her, she fell into a deep depression. Between the treatments, not knowing if they caught it in time, and the fact that she'd never have her own child, she was in sad shape. We were all worried about her. She wouldn't even leave the house and spent most of her time in bed. Poor Melvin. He was so patient with her, but he, too, was grieving.

"When I heard about my friend's dochder going off during her Rumspringa and getting into trouble, and that the maed couldn't marry the father, I suggested adoption. The girl still had three months to go before the boppli was due. By the time she was ready to deliver, she agreed to the adoption idea, but only if the child would be raised in an Amish home."

"So, she was Amish?"

"Jah, but not the man. He was an exchange student from Italy. Handsome lad. I believe he loved Rosie, the

maed, but he went back home before she realized she was pregnant."

"Did she write to tell him about it?"

"She was too ashamed. I was going to write to him myself, but no one would give me his address. Such pride. *Hochmut.*

"When I went over and approached Sarah about the idea, at first, she was too shocked to make a decision, but in a matter of a couple days, she suggested we all get together and discuss it. I think she feared the girl would change her mind after a few months and the grief would be unbearable if she had to give the child back. She was smart enough to want it done legally."

"So, when she saw Martha?"

"Oh, love at first sight. It was beautiful. Even the boppli, who wasn't even a month old, seemed to know something was special. She came into the house crying her little eyes out. Sarah reached for her immediately and held her against her bosom. The child stopped crying within moments and nuzzled against Sarah's apron.

"We all ended up crying. I felt so bad for the young mother, but she loved the child enough to want what was best for her. The girl's own father was a cold, strict Amishman and he refused to allow his daughter to stay with them if she kept the baby.

"From that day forward, Martha became Sarah's special blessing. She took her everywhere and never allowed a sitter to stay with her, except her immediate family. I helped out the most, not to brag. After all, I wanted to. I adored Martha from the very beginning. Maybe you heard, but I lost the only maed I ever carried.

"When Martha was about a year old, Sarah got the idea of moving away from Ohio so no one would tell

the child she was adopted. We all argued with her, telling her she should tell Martha from the beginning. Why not? Certainly, it wouldn't affect their love for each other, but I think she had actually convinced herself that she was the real mother by then. So, Melvin went out ahead to Lancaster County and purchased the home they're in now and within a year, we had all moved out of Ohio."

"That's where she got her coloring from then. Her father."

"Jah, she looks so much like him. I actually have a photo taken of him while he was staying with the neighbors that year. Martha has never seen it of course, but I can show you, if you're interested."

"Jah, I would be, maybe later. I'm just stunned. I hope I don't let it slip."

"Like I did, right? I'm so upset with myself. All these years…"

"But maybe it's better this way. Do you know anything about the father's health? His family history? Things that might make a difference down the road?"

"No, nothing."

"Did the birth mamm ever come around or stir up trouble?"

"Nee, she kept her end of the agreement. I heard she left the Amish a year or so after giving Martha to Sarah. I don't know where she lives or if she ever married. I suppose I could find out from friends back in Ohio, but I have no reason to poke into the past."

"Martha speaks so lovingly of her parents. That would never change. I'm sorry she doesn't know the truth."

"Jah, I agree with you. She should know, but I'm not the one to tell her."

"Neither am I. It would have to come from her par-

ents. Hasn't she ever wondered where she got the beautiful black hair?"

"Oh, she's asked each of us more than once. We've learned how to change the subject real quick-like. I always get a pit in my stomach. I feel like we're living this huge lie and yet Sarah had a fit when she found the cell phone, accusing her daughter of lying. It sure don't make much sense, when you think about it."

When Leroy came back to the living room, he sat down next to his wife. "So, you two look pretty serious. Anything wrong?"

"You won't believe it, Leroy. I let it slip about Martha being adopted."

"Huh. Seems to me, it's about time the girl knew about it herself. You should press your schwester to tell Martha the truth. Lies are never gut."

Paul nodded. "I know it wouldn't change Martha's feelings one bit. She loves her parents with all her heart. But I'll tell you this much, it won't come from me."

"It should be Sarah's place to tell her," Leroy repeated. "Lizzy, try to talk to her about it."

"Are you kidding? I've talked till I'm blue in the face. Even our mamm has tried to convince her, but she's a stubborn woman, I'll tell you that much."

"Runs in the family," Leroy said with a grin. "Maybe you're lucky Martha ain't related blood-wise, Paul."

After about half an hour passed, Leroy made his way to his bedroom for the night. Then Lizzy went over to her desk and rummaged around till she came upon a small envelope with no writing on it. She opened it and removed the photo of Martha's father.

She took it over to Paul, who held it near the lamp.

"Golly, she sure does have his dark eyes. And his hair. Is hers wavy like his?"

"Oh, you'll have to wait to find out, young man," Lizzy said, smiling. "I'll tell you this much, she's a beauty, through and through."

"Jah, that's for sure and for certain."

The picture went back in its hiding place and they walked upstairs together.

As he lay in bed, Paul found himself praying for the poor young woman who had given up her daughter so selflessly in order to provide a stable home for her with a good Amish family. That was true love. He prayed that she had found some happiness in her own life.

## Chapter Ten

When Paul returned Saturday morning to Lewistown, he went directly to work. Jeremiah had arrived about two hours earlier and was finishing up a dining room trestle table with a dark oak finish.

After changing into a work shirt and overalls, Paul asked about Jeremiah's Thanksgiving.

"It was nice. There were about forty people in and out for dinner. It got kinda crazy. I had a nice talk with your old girlfriend, Hazel Miller, though. First time I ever took the time to really talk to the maed. Nice girl."

"Jah, she is. Just not right for me. Maybe you'll hit it off and get hitched."

"We're going to go to a talk at the library together next week about health."

"That sounds exciting," Paul said, grinning.

Jeremiah laughed. "Jah, real exciting, but then we'll go for kaffi and a donut. How did things go with you?"

"Well, they didn't kick me out this time."

"Real progress, buddy."

"That's what I thought. I didn't get much time alone

with Martha, but it was still wonderful to see her again. I don't know how long I can handle this separation thing."

"Maybe you won't have to wait too long. I read about a building for sale about four miles from here. It's an old car repair place. Lots of room and a large parking lot with half an acre of grass. That means there's room to build a house or two. Like for you and one for me. Interested?"

"I don't know. Things were told to me that make me wonder if I can settle around here, after all. What's the price?"

"They're asking too much, but maybe they'd bargain. It's been on the market awhile now. Since July."

"Right on a main road?"

"No. It's a back road, which would be gut for the home part. Maybe not so gut for the business end."

"You have a reputation. People would find you."

"Think so?"

"I know so. When I tell people I work here, they all seem to know about it. It would be better off the main road, if you plan to live there, too. Better for the future kinner."

"Anyway, I'll call the realtor and we can take a look at it next week, if you're interested."

"I'd like to consider it. I know Martha wants to stay in Paradise, though."

"Well, she might change her mind when she hears about you being a partner. Take a look with me and we can talk about the financial end of things, too. I was working out some figures last night. We could work on commission maybe, and use the rest for expenses. It looks like you could be earning about twice what you're getting now."

"Wow! That's definitely something to consider. One thing I know for sure, I want to marry Martha. The more I see of her, the more I care about her. I think she feels the same about me. We've never talked real serious about where we'd live, though it sounds like she's open-minded. First, I'm going to check with the bishop tomorrow and see when I can get baptized, or there won't be any marriage this year."

"Jah, you should get started with the classes. They take about eighteen weeks, and if you start now, then you could get baptized in the spring."

"And married in the fall! Perfect! I'll tell Martha, she needs to get started, too."

"Can she do it where she's living now?"

"I know she goes to a service every other Sunday with her friend. I suppose she could get started on the classes anyway. You know, I thought now that we were closer, we'd see more of each other, but between her schedule and mine, and all the other obligations we have, it's been hard."

"Marriage is the way to go. So tell me again, why didn't you stay with Hazel?"

"Look, we're two very different people. You might be perfect for each other. I hope you do end up together."

"Think she and Martha would like being neighbors? Martha knows you two were going out, right?"

"Jah and she understands. There's no problem there. They're real gut friends. They got to know each other well when Martha was helping Deborah with the kinner."

"I'm surprised she hasn't been back to visit."

"She wants to, but the waitressing job takes a lot of her time. Especially on weekends. There was also the prob-

lem with her parents not wanting us to see each other, but I guess we can put that behind us."

"Let me show you the benches we need to make for the trestle table I'm working on. They're sort of like the last ones we made, but the people want a heart shape cut out on each end."

"Ugh. That's a pain."

"Make the customer happy, right?"

"Oh jah, that's for sure," Paul said, exaggerating his nod.

On his way home, Paul stopped by to see Deborah and Ebenezer. It was a bit chaotic, with the twins both screaming and the triplets running around the house playing horsey, but they calmed down when they saw Paul, and he got them to lie down and pretend it was night time.

Eb shook his head. "I don't know how you do it, Paul. You always come up with some gut ideas for calming down the kinner. Hope you're as successful with your own someday."

Laughing, Paul agreed. "I'll have you to help me. Your kinner will be near grown-up by then."

"When are you going to marry that maed, anyway? Don't let her get away."

"We're working in that direction. Plant some extra celery in the spring, jah?"

"Sure will," Eb said as he went to take one of the twins from his wife, who had joined them. He sat on the sofa as she handed him a bottle of juice for Miriam.

Then Deborah sat down next to him and gave the other twin, Mary, her juice. She told Paul she'd written to Martha to see when she planned to visit next. "I miss

her so much. Martha was a life-saver. Thank goodness, Hazel still helps a lot. Did you know she and Jeremiah seem to like each other?"

"Just found out today. I'm glad. I think they'd be gut for each other, don't you?"

"Time will tell. There was a time I thought you and Hazel were going to marry and look how wrong I was there."

"It wouldn't have been the right marriage for me. I feel so much more for Martha."

"When do you think you two will marry?" Deb asked.

"I'm thinking next fall. We haven't actually set a date."

"Does she mind moving here away from her family?"

"That hasn't been settled one way or the other yet, but I'm hoping when she hears about me becoming a partner with Jeremiah, and I have a house prepared, she'll want to move here."

"A partner? That would be wonderful-gut," Deborah said.

"Jah, it would be," Eb said. "She doesn't know about that yet?"

"It's not definite."

"Well, you'd be the man of the household. You should make that decision, jah?" Eb asked.

"It's not that easy. I'd want my wife to be happy. She's real close to her parents and she's an only child, as you know."

"Mmm. It's not that far away. It's not like you'd be moving to Alaska," Deborah said.

"I'm gonna pray about it. I need Gott's direction."

"When she does visit, I'll kinda push the idea," Debo-

rah said. "I'd love to have her for a neighbor—and you, Paul."

He laughed. "Jah? I was hoping you'd add that."

"Are you hungry?" she asked. "We haven't had supper yet."

"My mamm will be expecting me, but danki for asking. In fact, I should head home now. Just wanted to check in."

When he got home, his parents were just getting ready to eat. His mother came over to him and patted his head. "Happy? Still feel the same about Martha?"

"Jah, only more so, Mamm. We get along real gut and her family seems okay now about me."

"I guess when they found out you'd confessed your sin?"

"Jah, that was key. The other guy's been banned."

"Oh mercy. What a shame."

"He wasn't a gut Amishman, Mamm. Too prideful."

"Sounds that way. Well, wash your hands. I made corn chowder for tonight."

He handed her the bag with the cookies. "And we can have these for dessert."

She peeked inside. "Yum! With the tapioca pudding from yesterday. Sounds real gut."

How blessed Paul felt to be raised in such a good home and now he had the love of a woman who would bear his children and share her life with him. He thanked the Lord as he reached for the faucet handle and washed his hands in preparation for his favorite soup. He'd even been blessed with a mother who made the best corn chowder ever!

## Chapter Eleven

As the days grew shorter, and colder, Martha relied on her short conversations with Paul each evening to lift her spirits. She missed her family and Paul more each day. It was good to keep busy at the restaurant and at least she was able to save quite a bit of money each week. She rarely thought about Daniel anymore. The fear she'd experienced toward him faded as time went on.

Toward the middle of December, she took off two days mid-week to visit Deborah, and of course Paul, who was able to shorten his work hours so they'd have some time together. Dawn, one of her English friends, drove to save her the money for a professional driver.

It was wonderful to see Deborah and the little ones again. The boys gave her huge hugs before rushing off to wrestle with each other. They were still rowdy, but when their father spoke up, they listened, which impressed Martha. Deborah told her that Eb was much more involved with the children, which gave her the energy and time to get some of the housework done. Martha took over some of the care of the twins while she was there in order to allow Deborah some free time.

Deborah's sisters, Hazel and Wanda, came by to spend time with Martha, but left before Paul arrived in the mid-afternoon.

While Martha was visiting, she and Paul went to the bishop's house the first evening and talked about taking the course for baptism together. Dawn had a close cousin living in Lewistown, and she was more than willing to drive Martha every week so she could attend her class. While Martha took the course, Dawn planned to spend time with her cousin. She wouldn't even take money for gas, so it was a plus-plus for Martha. She'd accomplish two things at once—prepare for baptism and see her darling Paul.

The bishop was very pleasant and encouraged their decision to one day marry. Martha wondered if he'd be so nice about it, if he knew they might be living in Paradise.

Deborah insisted Martha and Paul eat supper both nights with them, but they weren't allowed to help clean up, even though Martha protested vigorously.

"Nee, this is your time to be with Paul. Now, go. Do something fun. Use our buggy if you want to take a ride."

Even though it was bitter cold, they added extra horse-hair buggy robes and took advantage of the opportunity to be alone together. It was so much fun to be able to hold hands and talk without interruption. Their love continued to deepen.

She hated to see the time end, but knowing Christmas was just around the corner helped.

When she and Paul parted the evening before she left, they found themselves alone in the sitting room while the children were being put down for the night. Paul put his arm around her as they sat on the sofa discussing Christ-

mas. "I haven't had much time to tell you how much I love you, but you know I do, jah?" he asked, after kissing her gently on her lips.

"I think I do, jah. And you are my sweetheart, Paul. I can't wait until we can be together always. At least we'll see each other every week now when I come for the classes."

"I'm excited about that. Think we can have an extra hour or two afterward, before you need to leave?"

"I'll ask Dawn, but I can't push it since she's really doing this as a favor for me."

"I understand. It's real nice of her. I'll take whatever time we have and be grateful."

Martha smiled and leaned over for another kiss, which was longer and sweeter than the first. "I'm glad my parents seem to like you now."

"Jah, me, too. It's important to get along with our families."

Eb came into the room, but Paul kept his arm around Martha. They talked a few minutes and then Paul rose to leave. "I know it's everyone's bedtime now. I'd better get home."

Before they parted, Paul mentioned the arrangements he made with Skip Davis to pick him up around nine on Christmas Eve morning and then drive over for Martha and Naomi before making their way to Paradise. Martha had written to her parents the week before to check about Paul spending Christmas with them. She'd been surprised they were receptive to the idea.

Her parents, however, were not thrilled to learn of Martha taking the baptismal classes in Lewistown. They knew Paul's bishop was more lenient than their own bishop, since he allowed cell phones. This displeased

her father in particular. They discussed their opposition to Martha's plan, but Sarah convinced her husband not to bring up the subject over the holiday, as it might be a source of contention. "At least Martha is going to take her vow to remain Amish," she said in conclusion.

Fortunately, the owners of the restaurant had decided to close for those three days so they could spend the holiday with their own family. Martha was relieved, since she would hate to leave them stranded, and would have shortened her visit home if they'd needed her.

Dawn showed up early the next morning to drive Martha back to her apartment. When she got there, Naomi had already left for her sitting job. Since Martha was scheduled to wait tables for the lunch and dinner meals, she needed to prepare to be at work by ten thirty. It was just as well she'd be busy, since she already missed Paul.

In the evenings when Martha wasn't working, she knitted mittens for Deb and Eb's children and some of her young cousins. Her biggest project was a knitted woolen black vest for Paul, which he had once mentioned needing. She had to guess at his size and make it ample enough in case he put on weight.

Naomi had off each day around five from her sitting position, so she, too, was making most of the gifts for her family. The girls took full advantage of the electricity in the evenings, and spoke of the restrictions put upon them by the old-order Amish rules.

"I sure wish Bishop Josiah would bend a little," Naomi said one evening as she knitted a sweater for her mother. "It's so nice to be able to see gut at night."

"Jah, I wish he would, too. I don't see anything evil about letting a wire come into your house."

"It ain't evil, but it does tie you into the government sort of, and that's when you can have trouble," Naomi reminded her.

"I guess. I'm almost done with all my presents. When I finish this pair of mittens, I'll wrap them along with the others. Then I'll just have Paul's vest to finish. Goodness' sakes, it's almost Christmastime."

"You're not sorry you came here, are you?" Naomi asked unexpectedly.

"Nee. It's been gut for me. Do you feel it was the right thing for you?"

"Jah, at the time, but now that I've been away this long, I kinda miss everyone back home. I'll probably leave when you do."

"When the lease is up in April?"

"Jah, though we can go month to month until we want to leave," Naomi said. "What are your plans? Or haven't you decided for sure?"

"I like being closer to Paul and as it turns out, we'll be together once a week now for the classes. Once they're done, I may as well go back home. It's nice to know Daniel isn't around anymore, and my parents have kind of accepted the idea of Paul and me getting married one day, so there's no reason to stay away. I have to admit, I miss my mamm something awful."

"I know you talk about her a lot. Did you finish the hemstitching on her guest towels yet?"

"Jah. And I made my aenti Lizzy a pillow."

"The floral one you were sewing last week?"

"Jah, she loves tulips, especially pink ones."

"Oh, she'll love the pillow then. Before we leave, I have something for you."

Martha grinned at her friend. "And I didn't see you making it?"

"Nope, because I bought something already made. Want it now?"

"Sure, why not? And I'll get yours, but you did see me making it."

"I hope it was that blue knit scarf."

"Jah, you guessed right." Martha went into a drawer in the dresser and took out a wrapped package, as Naomi returned with a present wrapped in colorful candy cane paper. They switched and opened their gifts.

Naomi laughed and swung the long scarf around her neck. "I could use this tomorrow. It's supposed to snow. I love it!"

"I'm so glad." Martha pulled the paper off her gift and opened the box. It was a pair of pajamas with little red hearts and red trim around the collar and the hem. "Oh, they're so cute!"

"I hope you really like them. Maybe I should have gotten a nightie instead," she said, looking over slyly.

Martha winked at her friend. "I like these just fine."

"I'm afraid they're not very romantic," Naomi said.

"But they'll keep me nice and snug. Danki, dear friend." The girls hugged and then went back to finishing their projects.

The next day it did begin to snow. They ended up with about six inches, but the roads were cleared by the time they needed to travel back home.

At last, it was the big day. Skip arrived around ten in the morning and Paul helped the girls with their luggage and Christmas gifts. Martha saw him peeking at

some of the nametags as he placed them in a large trash bag. She'd left a couple unmarked, knowing he'd probably be doing just that.

After loading up, Paul and Martha sat in the back, holding hands, while Naomi took the seat up front next to the driver.

"You're so quiet, Martha," Paul said at one point. "Nothing to say?"

"I'm just enjoying sitting here next to you. I'm holding it in my memory box."

He laughed and squeezed her hand. "And what else is in that lovely head of yours that you're holding on to?"

"Oh, I've stored all kinds of moments. I remember the day I turned five and my aenti Lizzy gave me a brand-new box of crayons. Then there was the time I learned to tie a bow, and the time I found my first four-leaf clover."

"Ah, very important memories," he said. "Any about me?"

She looked at him and grinned. "I can't tell you all of them." She leaned close and whispered, "But your first kiss is one of them."

Her face was so close to his that he took advantage of the moment and kissed her lightly on the lips. "Jah, I remember it pretty gut myself."

"Of course, my memory bank has bad moments, too, though I try to forget them."

"Like what?"

"Like when I was punished for telling a lie. I had to sit in the corner for what seemed like hours. It was probably ten minutes or so, but I felt horrible."

"My memory bank has quite a few moments like that," Paul said. "A couple included a gut swat on my bottom. Not often, but I remember hitting my friend

for not throwing a ball to me. I guess I was about six or seven. My mamm sure set me straight in a hurry."

Martha laughed. "What did she think when she heard about you and Daniel?"

"She had a fit. 'Didn't I teach you anything?' she asked. 'Do I need to send you to your room like a little kinner?' she added. Oh, jah, she wasn't happy about that time."

"But now that you've confessed…"

"Sure, everything is okay. After all, Gott forgives our sins when we confess and repent. Could my mamm do less?"

"Nee. Not when you put it that way. We're clean as the snow out there, right?" she said, pointing to the beautiful pristine rolling hills covered with a blanket of sparkling snow.

"Jah. Gott is gut."

"Jah. All the time."

On the ride over, Martha suggested they could visit the local carpentry shop in Paradise, but they decided there wouldn't be enough time during such a short visit, and the shop would probably be closed anyway for Christmas. She noted he didn't seem that enthusiastic about the idea.

The ride went quickly and after dropping Naomi off, Skip made his way to Martha's home. As Paul paid him, they agreed upon a time for the return ride. Then Paul carried their two pieces of luggage and Martha carried the large bag with the presents.

Her mother hadn't heard the car and was surprised to see them at the back door already. She opened it quickly and called her husband, who was upstairs.

"What a sight for sore eyes," Sarah said as she held her daughter in her arms. Martha kissed her mother's cheek and embraced her for several seconds before releasing her and then turned to hug her father, who had just arrived in the kitchen. Her parents greeted Paul, with a lot more warmth than in the past, and told him where to put his belongings.

"You're staying with us this time," Sarah said. "Lizzy has no room, I'm afraid. Some of our cousins are coming from Philadelphia area and need a place to stay."

"That's fine. I just need a place to put my head. I can sleep anywhere," he said.

"Jah? Even the barn?" Melvin asked with a crooked smile.

Goodness, did her father know about his staying there once? She couldn't tell by his face.

"If I had to," Paul answered, licking his lips, wondering the same thing as Martha.

"I'm glad you're here in time for our dinner," Sarah said.

"I can smell it. Venison?" asked Martha.

"Jah, your daed just went hunting last week. I'm roasting it with potatoes."

"I was only out for an hour. Just as well, it was pretty cold," Melvin said. "I'll be back in a few minutes. I have to put a few tools away."

"It sure does smell gut," Paul said, as he took off his jacket. "I'm pretty hungry."

"Yum. I'm starving, too," Martha said as she placed both her jacket and Paul's on hooks by the door. "I'll wash up and give you a hand."

"I have everything just about ready," Sarah said.

"Come, you two, sit a minute while the beans cook, and Martha, tell me all about your job."

"It's going real gut. I've saved nearly six hundred dollars."

Sarah's brows rose. "Really? That's amazing! You must get gut tips."

"I guess I do. I enjoy waitressing. I often get the same people asking for me. It's fun."

"You get gut tips because you're so pleasant with people," Paul said.

"Sometimes I wish I could work outside the home," Sarah said, softly. "It's a bit lonely here sometimes."

"But you have Mammi and Dawdi next door," Martha said. "Where are they now?"

"They'll be here any minute, but they don't stay around here so much now. Your dawdi feels poorly a lot of the time. He don't get around as much as he did. And especially in the winter, he stays cozied up by the kitchen stove."

"I'm sorry to hear that."

"Well, you'll be back soon, so I won't worry about being lonely much longer."

Martha nodded, but wondered how her mother would react if she and Paul decided to live in Lewistown once they married. They still hadn't discussed it seriously, but he had told her he was now in partnership with Jeremiah, which was a sign he might want to remain. Martha looked over at Paul, but he remained silent.

There was a quick rap on the kitchen door, as Sarah's parents let themselves in.

Martha and her grandmother hugged first and then everyone greeted each other with handshakes and em-

braces. Melvin came back and rubbed his hands together. "Sure ain't gettin' any warmer out there."

"Well, the beans are done," Sarah said as she poked one with a fork. "Everyone take your places and Martha and I will serve it up."

It felt good to be back home with her loving family, made even more wonderful with Paul present. As usual, there wasn't much conversation at the table until the coffee was served at the end. Then they conversed a few minutes until Melvin asked Paul if he'd go out to the barn with him. He intended to build another stall for a new work horse he was contemplating on purchasing and wanted Paul's opinion about the structure, since he was in the carpentry business.

Martha's grandfather picked up his cane and made his way into their sitting room. Not like him to miss an opportunity to talk "man-talk." The women followed him into the sitting room, where Martha visited with her mother and her grandmother, while her grandfather read the Amish newspaper, the *Budget*.

The room smelled luscious from the fresh pine draped on the fireplace mantel and on the window sills. A fire was crackling in the open hearth. There would be no tree, but her mother loved to decorate with greens and candles. Her mother always made it look inviting and added her special touch with colorful bowls of fresh fruit and wooden bowls filled with nuts. Plain, yet festive.

Her grandfather was less talkative than in the past, though he'd never been loquacious, but her mammi seemed just the same. Vivacious and happy. "I'll show you the quilt tomorrow," she said to Martha. "We're coming along real gut on it, ain't we, Sarah?" She turned toward her daughter.

"Oh, jah, thanks to Lizzy. She comes by twice a week to work on it. She thinks you'll need it soon, I guess." Sarah looked over at her daughter, questioning with her eyes.

"Maybe," Martha said with a grin.

"Well, I hope it's soon," her mammi said. "I want to be around for the big event."

"I heard there are only a few plots of land left from the Bonner property, Martha," Sarah said. "Maybe you should go look at them while you're here."

"There's time for that," Martha said, wondering if she should even mention it to Paul. Perhaps, before they went back, she'd broach the subject and see what his reaction would be. Where they'd eventually settle was a subject they avoided.

"Think I'll head back," her grandfather said. "This woman talk ain't for me."

"Join Melvin and Paul," Sarah suggested.

"Nee. I'll go back and get my legs up. They're swollen like a birthing cow."

"When did that start, Dawdi?" Martha asked.

"It's been bad for a while now."

"You should get it checked out, don't you think?" Martha continued.

"Oh, he'll never do anything sensible like that," Mammi said, scowling. "I've been after him for weeks."

"It'll get better on its own," he said as he reached for his cane and jacket. "Take your time, Nancy. I ain't too talkative tonight anyway."

After he left, Martha's mammi wiped tears from her eyes. "I think it's his heart. He gets out of breath easy-like. Barely has to move to feel all wore out."

"I wish you could talk sense into him, Mamm," Sarah

said, as she clucked her tongue. "He's almost eighty and I don't think he's seen a doctor in ten years."

"At least twenty. Hates to go. Says that's when people get sicker."

Martha shook her head. "Why is he like that?"

"Happened to his daed. He went to see a doctor for the first time in his life and died two months later."

"He had a stroke, didn't he?" Sarah asked. "How can you blame the doctor for that?"

Mammi shrugged. "Can't rightly answer that. It's just the way it is. His daed was also ninety-two at the time. Had to die of something, seems to me."

"You two stay here and relax," Martha said to her mother and grandmother. "I'll go finish redding up the kitchen."

"Oh my goodness gracious! I forgot all about the mess we left," her mother said, standing abruptly.

"Stay with Mammi. When Paul gets back, he can dry the dishes. I just want to get them washed."

"A man who dries dishes?" her mammi said, amused. "Bless him. You'd better snatch him up real quick-like."

Martha laughed and nodded. "I intend to." Then Sarah sat back down and kept her mother company while Martha tackled the kitchen. When Paul returned, he automatically picked up a dishtowel and started helping. Martha looked over and grinned.

"I told my mamm and my mammi how you would help out."

"Not manly enough?" he asked grinning.

"It's sure fine with me. Hey, I help sometimes with the milking. It won't kill a guy to lend a hand in the kitchen."

He took two steps over and kissed her cheek. "I just want to be close to you."

She turned off the faucet and wiped her hands on her apron. "Done. I just need to wipe down the counters and put the dry dishes away." They worked together for a few more minutes before joining the women in the sitting room, where they took seats across from them.

"Well, look at the happy couple," Mammi said, as she sat back against the sofa pillows and folded her arms. "They make a right nice-looking couple," she added. "We should get some cute boppli out of their union."

Martha felt herself heat up as a blush rose on her cheeks.

"Now, Mamm, don't go embarrassing the poor young people," Sarah said. "They ain't even engaged to marry yet."

"Well, before that Daniel boy realizes what he's lost and tries to get her back, Paul—you better take the right steps."

"Mammi, Daniel isn't even around anymore. Is he, Mamm? Have you heard anything?"

"Oh, he's still hanging around Lancaster. I heard he's staying with some *Englishers*. Probably getting himself into more trouble. He ain't gonna make his presence here, that's for sure. Melvin would put a quick end to that."

"I'm sorry if I embarrassed you, Martha," Mammi said. "Sometimes I don't know what my head's doing. I forget things now. Like the day they brought you here to meet us…"

"Mamm." Sarah jumped up from her seat on the sofa. "Let's go next door and make sure Daed's okay."

Mammi's mouth dropped. "Did I say something bad?"

"No, no. I'm just worried about Daed, is all. Come on now."

Her mother pulled herself up by holding on to the arm

of the sofa. She looked at Martha and shrugged. "I'm sure he's just fine, but if you'll feel better checking…"

After they left, Martha and Paul moved over to the sofa. "I wonder why Mamm acted like that. Like she was scared out of her mind over something. Strange."

"I guess she's just concerned about her daed."

"I guess, anyway, till Daed comes in, we're alone," Martha said as she rested her head on his shoulder. "I've missed you so much."

"Me, too." He patted her head and then turned so he could kiss her on the lips. When they heard the back-door open, they separated, moving about a foot apart. When her dad came in, he complained about the cold and then stirred up the fire while adding an extra log. That was the last chance they had to be alone for the rest of the evening.

When it was time for bed, her father motioned for everyone to go up at the same time. Well, at least they were bending and seemed to accept the fact that Paul would most likely be a part of their lives from this day forward. Hopefully, they'd have a long lifetime to share.

## Chapter Twelve

Christmas was always special, as loved ones gathered to celebrate the birth of their Savior. It was such a festive time, even in their small family. Martha and her mother baked off five apple pies to take to Lizzy's house for the main meal, but before leaving, the family opened their gifts. Paul was delighted with the vest and modeled it for the family, exaggerating his stance as if posing for *Gentlemen's Weekly*. Martha giggled and shook her head. Even her dad smiled broadly at Paul's antics.

Paul's gift to Martha was a large picture book of Lancaster County's bridges and local scenery. It was passed around the room so everyone could enjoy it. Her dawdi seemed stronger today and he went through the book twice, commenting on the photos he recalled. "Yup, it's one pretty place to live. Bet you can't wait to move here, young fellow," he said, addressing Paul.

Paul and Martha exchanged looks and he merely smiled back at the elderly man.

Sarah took note and made her own interpretation of their visual exchange. She'd just keep praying for her daughter to settle nearby. What more could she do?

After opening up their gifts, they took the large family buggy over to Lizzy and Leroy's home for the main meal. Already most of Lizzy's adult sons had arrived with their wives and children. Some of the daughters-in-law were bustling about setting up three long tables. Partitions had been moved away, which normally separated the double sitting rooms from the long, narrow kitchen, allowing everyone to be seated in a common area. As many of their Amish neighbors did, they built their home to accommodate large groups so when it was their turn to hold the preaching service, they could seat close to a hundred people. Barns were also used by some, as well as open basements. It sure helped when it was a holiday to have so much available seating.

The men hung out in one section of the room while the women busied themselves preparing for the Christmas banquet. No one's oven could handle the number of turkeys needed, so the women planned ahead, appointing some to bring roasted turkeys and others to supply the vegetable casseroles. In spite of the work involved, it was Martha's favorite time of year and she thrived on being a part of this loving family. She glanced over at Paul frequently. He fit right in and she could tell he was thoroughly enjoying his visit. Oh, that he would want to settle here. She lifted her prayers to the Lord as she quietly folded napkins for the tables.

The meal took over two hours. They'd stop between courses and while the women cleaned up from that part of the meal, other platters and serving plates were set around the tables. The youngest children were allowed to play in a closed-in porch, which had a coal stove burning to keep it warm. There were blocks, puzzles, games and miscellaneous toys scattered about. Some of the older

children watched their siblings and kept things from getting out of hand.

Then when their plates were ready, they'd return to eat some more, though the youngest cared little for food with all the excitement of the holiday.

All afternoon, distant relatives arrived, some staying only a few minutes, while others remained longer. Though the Amish don't like to announce their future mates until close to their wedding date when it was posted at the church service, most of the family assumed Martha and Paul were courting. After all, most single men celebrated the holidays in their homes with their families. Of course, most young men courted women in their own districts and could spend a part of the day with their families and then scoot over to visit with their loved ones. Being two hours apart by car made that difficult. In a way, Martha was glad. This way she got to be with Paul for the entire day—and beyond. Hopefully, by this time next year, they'd be in their own home, or living with her parents till they had a home built.

Around seven, her grandparents were ready to go home. Some of the families with the young children had already parted. Paul offered to hitch up their driving horse and bring the buggy around to the front. Melvin seemed pleased at the suggestion, so after saying their good-byes, Martha joined Paul and they went out to ready the buggy. Before hitching up the horse, Paul took her in his arms and gave her a long, passionate kiss.

"Whew!" Martha moved back and blinked several times. "My goodness, Paul. You are some gut kisser. Maybe a wee bit too gut, jah?"

He laughed and put his hands on each side of her

head and gave her a mini peck on the lips. "You like that better?"

"Nee, but my legs got wobbly with the other kind. You'd better hold off on them till we say our 'I dos'— don't you think?"

"You're right, of course. I'm sorry."

"Oh, you needn't be sorry. I like it, that's for sure, but we have a while to wait."

"Jah. You are absolutely right. Let's get Chessy ready for the ride home. Your dawdi looked pretty wore out."

"Did you like the family?" she asked as he prepared the buggy by hitching up the horse. Then he took hold of the reins and they walked the horse around to the front of the house.

"They are wonderful-gut people. All of them. Jah, I'm a lucky man to be marrying into such a nice family."

"I know you probably missed your own family, but if we do end up here…"

"Oh, Martha. We really need to discuss where we'll be living. I keep putting it off."

"That sounds like you've made up your mind."

"Not really. Tomorrow, we can spend some time weighing everything. Okay? Let's not get into it now."

"Okay."


The family seemed unusually quiet on their ride home. Probably just exhausted, Martha thought, but after her grandparents went into the *dawdi-haus*, her mother mentioned he'd been complaining of pain in his chest.

"We'll get him to a doctor this week," Melvin said. "No more excuses."

"Ach. We may have to drag him there," Sarah said, sadly. "He's a stubborn Amishman."

"Jah, but so am I."

Martha never gave much thought to the age of her grandparents. They had always seemed youthful, even though her dawdi used a cane and no longer worked. The realization that she might lose him alarmed her. Later as she was saying good night to Paul, she got teary. He knew without asking why she was upset.

"Tomorrow, we'll skip talking about important things and just enjoy time with your family. It's important."

"Danki. I'm glad you understand."

"Jah. I do, my lieb." He sneaked a tiny kiss in while her mother's back was turned and then they headed for the stairs.

"See you at breakfast, Paul," her mother said as she headed toward her bedroom. Her eyes were reddened and Martha realized she'd been off by herself for the last half hour.

Martha prayed before going to sleep. This time not about herself, but about her family. *Sometimes it's a good thing we don't know what is in our future*, she thought, as she pulled the quilt up around her neck and tried to sleep.

The next day was an extension of the Christmas celebration. The family had more visitors and then in the middle of the afternoon, Aenti Lizzy came by with several of the grandchildren. She stayed only briefly, since she planned several other stops. Food was never a problem. When anyone arrived, they brought cookies or brownies, or sometimes a casserole with vegetables. The constant flow of guests kept the women in the kitchen most of the time, serving or cleaning—whatever was needed.

When things settled down, Martha and Paul bundled

up in their warm jackets in order to take a walk around
the property. Paul made sure he added his vest, which
was about two sizes too big, but a welcome addition since
it was made of wool, and the temperatures had dropped
into the teens.

To get a little warmth, they went into the barn, and
took advantage of the heat the animals generated. Once
they knew they were totally alone, Paul surrounded her
with his arms and they kissed several times, though he
didn't "knock her socks off," as she warned. "There will
be plenty of time for your wonderful-gut kisses after
we're man and wife," she said, smiling coquettishly.

Spunky, the family's mutt, came through the barn
door and nudged against Martha's skirt for attention.
She patted his head.

Then they went over to Milly, the family's oldest cow,
and patted her head while she chewed her cud. "She's
doing better now," Martha said. "For a while we were
afraid she wouldn't make it. She's old, you know."

Paul nodded and placed his hands in his pockets for
warmth.

"Jah, everyone and every animal is given so much
time and then the Lord takes away their breath. I know
you're upset about your dawdi, but you have to be ready."

"Jah, I know. It's hard, is all. My mammi is so close
to him, I don't know how she'll manage."

"She knows he'll be with Jesus, jah?"

"She has said that. Some of her friends scold her, saying no one knows, but Mammi says she reads her Bible
and there are lots of places where she says it's pretty
plain. If you give your heart to Jesus and believe He's
the Sohn of Gott, you will be saved and live in heaven
with Jesus. She believes it."

"I kinda agree with her. I just keep my mouth quiet when I'm with my Amish friends. People believe different things, but your mammi sure knows her Bible. She talked with me this morning while you were redding up the kitchen about some of the verses she loves, and it seems pretty much a sure thing about Jesus making a way for us."

"Jah. Through his death and resurrection, right? She's shown me lots of places in her Bible, too. In fact, our whole family believes the same way. We just don't talk about it much."

"My bishop believes it, too," Paul said. "When we marry, you'll be freer to talk about such things at our church. It's a newer order than yours, for sure."

"It means a lot to you to stay in Lewistown, doesn't it, Paul?"

"It makes sense. I have a gut future with Jeremiah, Martha. He found a new property the day before I left for Christmas that he wants to take me to see when I get back. It even has two small houses on it. He said we could live in one and he'd take the other. I think maybe Gott is opening doors for us."

"Is it different from the one you told me about before? The one that was an auto place?"

"Jah, they wouldn't bend on the price. This one sounds better though."

"My only sadness would be leaving my parents."

"It's not that far, honey. And we could try to visit them often, and they'd always be welcome at our home. Your mamm has survived you being away, right? First when you helped out with Deborah and now, while you're living apart with Naomi. It shows she can handle it. Jah?"

Martha nodded. "And she has Daed and her par-

ents and her schwester, Lizzy, and all of Lizzy's family. You're right, Paul. I'm sure she'd get used to it. My place is with you and as you said, it's not like we're moving far, far away. Goodness, sometimes people move across the country. I will live with you wherever you decide to settle."

He leaned over and kissed her gently. "I can't wait to see the new property. It's three miles closer to your family, too."

Martha laughed and raised her lips for one more kiss. "We'd better go back in. My toes are freezing."

After they all went up to bed, Martha lifted the window shade by her bed. The moon was nearly full, and the scene of all that was familiar to her became more poignant than ever, as she realized she'd agreed to live away from her family. She studied the shadow of the large oak in front of the house as it formed a pattern of twisted limbs on the untouched snow. It was the very tree she used to swing from for hours when she was a child, often wishing she had a sister to join her. Even though she had many friends nearby, as well as an extended family, she had frequently experienced loneliness.

She prayed for a large family when she married Paul. Her parents wouldn't be close enough to enjoy their grandchildren on a daily basis, but with Paul's potential income, they could afford a driver to bring her parents and grandparents frequently for visits. Paul was kind. He'd keep his promise to make every effort to spend time with her family. She felt she'd made the right decision. After all, it was a woman's place to follow her husband. She pulled the shade and returned to her bed. Now that the decision was made, she felt a certain amount of relief and fell asleep almost immediately.

## Chapter Thirteen

Three days after he and Martha parted, Paul and Jeremiah spent over two hours going through the property with Bill Mason, their realtor. It had a total of three acres. The main building had adequate space for their business—more than double the area they used now. It was clean and had several large windows for natural lighting as well as a heat source, which they could connect to a gas generator.

A separate building, which was the size of a double garage, would be used for extra lumber and materials. But what intrigued Paul the most were the two cottages in the back of the property, which looked almost identical.

The houses had two floors and small porches in the front. When the realtor took them through the first house, Paul was amazed to see that it contained three small bedrooms on the second floor, as well as a finished family room in the basement with plenty of room for a wringer washing machine. The kitchen was not as large as he'd like, but there was room to expand, and with help from his friends, he could add an extension at any time. After

all, they wouldn't need a huge kitchen at first. It was a bright home and would need very little work. Since it had been owned by a fellow Amishman, it was devoid of electricity, yet had a generator large enough to supply their needs. He wished he had one of those fancy cell phones with a camera built in, so he could send pictures to Martha, but he took out the small notebook he carried with him for notes, and sketched out the floor plan.

"The other home is a little larger," Bill said as he locked up the doors and they trudged through fresh snow to view the other house, which was about a hundred yards away. "There are two brothers who own this property, but they're moving to Ohio, so they're anxious to sell."

"What did they do for a living?" Paul asked. "There's not enough land to make a living, farming."

"No, they used the large building for storing merchandise, which they sold online. They had a Mennonite partner who did the business end of it. I think they told me they sold vitamins and health items. Had quite a good business going apparently, but they missed their families. They can do the same thing in Ohio, I guess."

"When did they move out?"

"About two weeks ago, but I got the property only a few days ago. Haven't put it on the multiple listing yet, because when I saw it, I figured it was just perfect for you guys—even with the two houses. And the price is right."

They reached the front porch of the second house and Bill unlocked the door and motioned for them to enter. "Pretty much the same, except the kitchen is larger and there's a fourth bedroom upstairs. They used it for a nursery."

It was a nice home, but would need painting through-

out, which did not present a problem. It would work better for Paul, with the large kitchen and extra bedroom, but he would leave it up to Jeremiah to choose first.

After they'd inspected every inch of the buildings, the three men walked back to Bill's car.

"We'd need to take out a mortgage," Jeremiah said.

"Shouldn't be a problem," Bill said, confidently. "I have connections at the bank in town and with a healthy down payment, it should go through quickly."

When he told them how much they'd need to put down, Jeremiah shook his head like it would be easy. Paul swallowed hard. He had only a quarter of what he'd need to pay for his half. Where would he get the rest? Then he remembered his father telling him a couple years back that since he was the youngest, he'd be entitled to the family's estate someday. Maybe he'd be willing to put some money forward at this point. At least it was a possibility.

The men shook hands and the realtor mentioned it wouldn't be on the market long. Jeremiah nodded. "We'll talk it over and get back to you as soon as we can."

After they returned to their workshop, Jeremiah talked non-stop about the potential of the property. He was excited about the prospects for their business to thrive, and talked of nothing else all afternoon. "What do you think?" he finally asked Paul. "You can have either house, if you'll come on board."

"I'd love it. I might have a problem coming up with half the down payment, though. I'll talk to my daed about it tonight. Maybe I can have an answer for you tomorrow."

"Sounds gut. We can't sit on it. It's such a reasonable price."

* * *

After supper, Paul sat with his parents in their sitting room, and his father asked him to read the scriptures. When they were finished, Paul brought up the subject of the property. His father sat and pulled on his beard, thoughtfully. He nodded. "How much do you need?"

Paul told him.

"I'll have it for you tomorrow. Need to go to the safe deposit box."

"I'm so grateful, Daed. And there's room for you and Mamm to have a dawdi-haus there someday."

"We won't need that, sohn. Your *bruders* have plenty of extra space. Maybe your future in-laws will need a place, though."

"Jah, of course they'd be welcome as well. I can't believe how things are falling in place. It's got to be Gott."

His mother, who hadn't said a word, nodded. "Of course it is. He wants what's best for his kinner. You're a gut faithful believer, sohn, and you will be blessed."

"It sure don't mean you'll go through life without problems, and sometimes even tragedies," his father said. "But you stay faithful to Gott and he'll never leave nor forsake you, sohn. It's a promise in the Bible. That's for sure."

"And for certain," his mother added, nodding her head in agreement.

"Danki. I'm so glad you're my parents." Paul got up from his chair and went over first to his mother, whom he kissed on the cheek, and then to his father, who stood up for an embrace. Paul felt tears form and though he was embarrassed, he noted his father seemed choked up as well.

Later, Paul called Martha and told her about the house

and property. Then he mentioned the exchange he had with his parents.

"They're so generous to you, Paul. What wonderful-gut people I'm getting for in-laws."

"Do you think you can get an extra hour next week when you come for the instructions, so I can show you the place? You could bring your friend, Dawn, if she wants to see it."

"I'll ask her. Actually, I'd like to go alone with you, Paul. It's such a special time for us."

"I understand. I can't wait to show you. Jeremiah said we can have the larger home. The kitchen's much bigger, but if you like the other one better when you see them, I'll leave it up to you. Anyway, we'll probably make an offer in the next day or so."

"Even before I see it?"

"Golly, I'd hoped…"

"It's okay. If you like it, I know I will, too. You go ahead and do as you think best, my darling. I trust your judgment."

"Have I told you how much I love you yet tonight?"

"Nee. I'm waiting." She grinned into the phone.

"Well, I love you tonight even more than I did last night, though it doesn't seem possible."

"And I love you more each day, as well," she said.

"I'd better get some sleep. I have to be in early tomorrow," he said. "We're putting a kitchen in and it's huge. Oh, Jeremiah hired a new carpenter to help out. Nice guy. He's a Mennonite. Not married yet, but working on it. He should be easy to work with."

"I hope he doesn't want our house," Martha said, joking.

"He's *our* employee, Martha. Catch that? *Our?*"

"Wow! Sounds pretty gut. How come you weren't in on the hiring then?"

"I read his application and he sounded so qualified, I told Jeremiah it was his decision."

"That's gut. Sounds like things are really going to work out."

"Before you left, did you mention anything to your parents about where we'll be living?" he asked.

"Nee. I knew they were too concerned about Dawdi, and I didn't want to add to their worries."

"Did they convince him to see a doctor?"

"Mammi told me the next morning before I left that he finally agreed to see someone."

"Let me know how things turn out. They'll probably have to do tests."

"He'll love that," she said facetiously.

"I'll pray for you all. Maybe it was just indigestion."

"I hope that's all it was. I'll tell you all about it when Mamm writes. She said she'd send a letter as soon as there was any news. I'll let you go now. Sleep well, my lieb."

"Jah, and you, too."

Goodness, everything seemed to be falling right into place. Imagine, a home of their own right away! And one had four bedrooms and could be theirs! They should fill them up real quick-like. She sure hoped so, anyway.

## Chapter Fourteen

It was frustrating not to be able to talk to her mother. Martha was anxious to hear about her dawdi. Hopefully, they'd gotten him to a doctor by now.

Because of the holidays, the bishop had skipped a week of the baptismal lessons, but tonight after work, Dawn was picking Martha up to take her to the class. Dawn seemed more than willing to spend extra time with her cousin in order to give Martha time to examine the property. Jeremiah and Paul were supposed to hear sometime today whether their offer had been accepted.

Finally, the work day ended and Martha, bundled up in her warmest jacket and scarf, waited outside for her ride. Her teeth chattered as twenty-mile winds swirled around her. It was the coldest day of the winter so far. January was not Martha's favorite month, but knowing she would be seeing Paul helped with the winter blues.

Dawn pulled over and Martha, shaking from the cold, climbed in the cozy Subaru. The girls chatted the whole way and Martha told her all about the property.

"He put in an offer and you haven't even seen it yet?"

"Jah. But I trust his judgment."

"Wow. I'm afraid I'd be upset if it were me. What if it's horrible?"

Martha laughed. "If it were horrible, Paul wouldn't want me to live there."

"You're very trusting."

"Well, Amish women…"

"Yeah, I know. Whatever the husband wants…"

"On most things, but we do use our voice when we need to."

"My parents argue about everything. Maybe it's better the way you do things, though believe me, I could never give up my English things or ways. It's probably what you're born into."

"Jah, true. I'd like to have electricity, though. It would be ever so nice to have air conditioning."

"I can't imagine life without it."

"We really do manage, Dawn. During the heat of the day, we keep the shades drawn to keep out the sun and we often hook up fans to our generator. Also, Daed planted trees around the house when they bought it and so we get a lot of shade. It's not really that horrible, though there are some days…"

"What I'd like is your food. I've eaten at Naomi's and, boy, can her mother cook."

"Jah, we like our food. I'm trying to learn to cook like my mudder, but I need more practice. Poor Paul, he'll have to put up with my experiments."

"He seems to like anything you do. He's real nice, and he sure is a looker."

Once they got to Deborah's farmhouse, Dawn dropped her off and they made plans to meet three hours later for their trip home.

Deb was in her rocking chair, one twin tucked in

each arm, singing a soft lullaby when Martha let herself in. She kissed her friend's cheek and whispered so she wouldn't disturb the babies. They spoke softly for a few minutes and then Paul arrived. Eb was bathing the boys upstairs, but when they were dressed for bed, he came down to greet his friends.

"I hear you're going to go see your new home."

"Oh, was the offer accepted?" Martha asked, turning to Paul.

"Jah, last night after we talked, but I wanted to surprise you. Danki, Eb. You have a big mouth."

Eb laughed. "So my wife tells me. Sorry, I didn't know you hadn't told Martha yet."

"It's okay." Paul took hold of Martha's hands and nodded. "It's ours. Or will be in about fifteen years when the mortgage is paid off. We'd better get over to the deacon's house. Classes will start real soon."

After the instructions, Paul climbed into the buggy next to Martha.

"Okay. Ready to go see the property?"

"Oh, jah! It's freezing out though. We won't be there ~~ long, I'm afraid."

Eb's, ~~ought about that already and on my way over to you'll ~~ted a fire in the fireplace of the home I think house." ~~d brought some extra blankets from the

"You're s

you use the fi

"Nee. I aske~~l, but won't the owner be mad if

fine with it."    ~~ly?"

"Let's go then, ~~e's a great guy. He was

blanket tightly around ~~

As they approached ~~    ~~pped the horse

~~nted out

the other roads which led to it. "It's a great spot. I can't believe we got it for the price."

Then he pulled over to the wide parking area, which was still covered with a thick layer of packed snow and some ice. When they got out, he laid a horse blanket over his driving horse before he took Martha's hand and led her to the building, which would be the future shop.

"It's wonderful," she said, looking around with the aid of a battery-operated lantern for light.

"It's hard to see everything," Paul said, "But it has all the space we'll need, at least in the beginning."

She checked out the lavatory and the area for the offices, nodding her approval as they went. Then they left and walked toward the farthest house. Smoke rose gently from the chimney and soft lighting glowed through two of the downstairs windows.

"It's so cute, Paul. Would that be ours?"

"Jah, if it's the one you like best. I sure hope you like it. Remember it looks better in the daytime."

When they got to the front door, he unlocked it and took her hand, leading her with the lantern to the back of the house to show her the kitchen and dining rooms first. Then they moved up the stairs and che____ ___ out the bedrooms.

"Four. That's gut," she said, nodd__ _____ _____ them."

"I hope so," he said, lean__ _____ _____ ours," he said as

"Here's the big room____ ___ "Goodness, I don't have they walked int_ ___ 's nice anyway."

"Oh my ___ __t his arms. She went over to him hand _____ Paul placed the lantern on the

and they embraced. He kissed her—a lovely lingering kiss on her lips. Then he pulled back and spoke softly. "This can be our room. Our house."

"I love it, Paul. And I love you with all my heart."

"My sweet love. But it's freezing up here. Let's go down before you catch a cold. You haven't seen the sitting room yet."

When they arrived back on the first floor, he opened the door to his right and the room was at least twenty degrees warmer. The fire glowed and formed shadows against the white walls. The dried applewood crackled and sputtered, inviting the two young lovers to gather warmth from its dancing flames.

They sat on three folded quilts right in front of the fire and Paul placed a fourth quilt around their shoulders. Neither of them spoke for a couple of minutes, taking in the pleasant scene.

"Will this be in your memory bank?" he asked.

She turned and kissed him lightly. "It's there already. I can't remember being this happy. It's really going to happen, ain't? We're going to be a family one day."

"Jah, I believe so with all my heart. I can't imagine life without you." He squeezed her arm fondly and nuzzled his face against her wrapped hair. Her kapp was now on her lap.

"I guess you don't want to take your hair down," he said.

"Nee. Let's wait. We don't have that much longer. November, right?"

"Jah, but that's ten months away. It seems like an eternity."

"I'm afraid to let my hair down."

"Why, honey?"

"Because it might make you want more."

"Maybe it would. I still love to picture you in my arms with your gorgeous black hair surrounding your shoulders."

"See? That's almost lustful—naughty *bu!*"

"Oh, I wish we could marry right away. We should have gone through the baptism last year."

"We didn't know we'd be so in love then, or we would have."

"The English get married any old time."

"I know, but we sure ain't English," she said, grinning. "Nor do I want to be. I love the way we live for Gott and our families."

"It works for me, too, Martha." He glanced at his watch. "We should probably let the fire die down now. I need to get you back soon."

"I wish I could stay longer."

"I know. It seems you just arrived. I'll come back here after you leave with Dawn, just to check and make sure the fire is out." He reached into the fireplace with a poker and spread the embers to cool them. "You still haven't heard about your dawdi?"

"Nee, but I should get a letter in the next day or two."

"I'm praying for him every night," Paul said.

"Danki. Of course, so am I. I worry about my mammi. They're so close. It's upsetting, she's getting real forgetful lately. She's always misplacing her glasses and sometimes they're up on her kapp and she doesn't even know it."

Paul smiled. "Old people do forget more, but she seems pretty gut to me."

"She said something strange the day I left. I was twisting my hair to tuck under my kapp and she made a com-

ment about my handsome daed, saying I look just like him. I don't look anything like him, Paul. He's so fair and blond. What a funny thing to say. Do you think she's going blind?"

Paul wiped his lips. How to answer. "Nee. Maybe you have some of his expressions."

"Maybe. I don't even look like my mudder. I don't know who I took after. Funny, how the genes can go back a bunch of generations."

"Mmm. Funny." Paul stood up and reached for her hands. "We'd better leave now, honey. I don't want to make Dawn wait. She's been so gut about driving you. I hope she's a gut driver."

"Jah, she's real careful when there's snow on the roads. She drives much slower now. I'm real glad."

As he locked up the front door, Martha slipped her hand over his. "I couldn't be happier, Paul. You did a great job finding us a home. I don't even have to see the other one."

"I'm relieved to hear that. It has only three bedrooms and a smaller kitchen. I was afraid you'd think even this kitchen was too small."

"But we can always add on, if we need to, and it will be a few years before we need more space, that's for sure."

"Unless you have triplets and twins like Deborah," he added, grinning.

"Oh, I hope I have them one at a time. I don't think we have many twins in the family."

Before they left the car for Deborah's home, they kissed one more time. "You'd better not kiss me so much next time, Paul. We do have almost a year left to wait. It might make it harder."

"I'll try, honey, but when I see you, I just want to be close."

"I know. But let's try to keep it to one or two kisses each visit. Please."

"Jah, you're right. You're a wise young maed, Martha. Another reason to love you."

When they came in, Eb was having coffee at the kitchen table alone. "Deborah's upstairs with the twins, Martha, if you want to say good-bye."

"Oh, jah. I'll be right down."

Paul poured himself some coffee and joined his friend while Martha went upstairs.

Martha found Deborah sitting with Mary, nursing her before putting her down for the night.

"So you like the house?" Deb asked.

"I love it! I can't wait. It has four bedrooms."

"That's gut. You know we're expecting again, right?"

"I wasn't sure, but I suspected. Are you okay with that?"

"I don't have a choice, but I'm getting used to the idea. I'm not as sick as I was in the beginning, and Eb really has changed. He does a lot around here now. Of course, he has more time in the winter, but he promised he'd help when the new one arrives. And of course Hazel will give me a hand. She's got a beau now, though, so I don't know how long I can count on her help."

"Jah, he's Paul's partner, Jeremiah, right?"

"Oh, of course you knew about it."

"I'm relieved she has a new boyfriend. I always felt a little guilty talking about Paul around her. I know she cared deeply for him at one point."

"Jah, Jeremiah seems much better for her. I can't explain why, but she seems happier around him."

"We might end up being close neighbors."

"I know. How strange is that? I don't think Jeremiah has mentioned marriage yet, so I won't say anything about the house to her."

"Gut idea. We might be jumping ahead of ourselves. Now I have to tell my parents we won't be living in Paradise. I dread it."

"It may be easier than you think. After all, you've been away quite a bit. Maybe they enjoy having an empty nest."

"I never thought of that. I'd be delighted if that ends up being the case. I hate to hurt them in any way. They're such gut parents. I've been blessed."

"It ain't that far away, Martha. Certainly, you could get back for holidays and birthdays and things."

"That's true."

"Martha," Paul called up the stairs. "Your friend just pulled in."

"I must go." Martha leaned over and kissed her friend's cheek. "I'll see you soon. Maybe we can come a little earlier next week when I come for the class."

"Oh, try. I miss you, dear friend."

"And I, you."

She turned and went down as Dawn started to get out of the car.

"Wait in the car where it's warm. I'll be right there," Martha called out.

Paul had her jacket and held it for her while she put her arms through the sleeves. Then he twirled the scarf around her head and then her neck. "I'll call you tomorrow night, Martha. Have a safe trip."

"Okay." She nodded over at Eb, as Paul held the door open for her.

As she slipped by, he stopped her briefly and whispered, "I love you," and then kissed her cheek. He stood and watched as she climbed in next to Dawn.

Ten months. Seemed like a long time, but at least he had the new business to think about. He would be busy, that was for sure.

# Chapter Fifteen

Naomi was waiting for Dawn and Martha to arrive. She paced around the apartment, humming a song as she went. At last, she heard them approach the outer door and nearly ran to open it.

After they greeted each other, Martha studied Naomi's expression. Something was different. She was positively glowing. "What's going on? You look different from when I saw you earlier."

"My whole life is different. I haven't said a word, because I was afraid it would never come of anything, but that's all changed."

"So tell us!" Dawn said as she slipped off her jacket and sat on a chair.

Martha hung her things on a hook and returned to the sofa, where she and Naomi sat next to each other.

"I'm in love!"

"Well, I'll be!" Martha said. "I didn't even know you knew a guy here."

"I met him the first day I babysat. He lives next door with his parents. He came over all the time pretending he just wanted to play with the kids. Of course, I suspected

it was more. But today, he asked me to go steady! I can't believe it! He's the coolest guy I ever met."

"Wow! But is he Amish?"

"Nope. As English as they come. Actually, his ancestors came from England! I'm so excited."

"You'll have to leave the Amish, won't you?" Dawn asked.

"I've been considering it for a while now anyway. Right, Martha? You know how I've been."

"It's a huge decision, Naomi. You'd better not jump too quickly," Martha said, shocked by her friend's sudden news.

"Well, he hasn't asked me to marry him yet. He goes to community college at night, but he wants to become a social worker, so he'll try to go to college away from here next year. I hope we get married first so I can go with him. I don't mind working full time for a few years."

"You haven't known him very long," Dawn mentioned.

"Long enough to know I'm madly in love. He's everything I've ever wanted in a husband. He's even cute."

Martha pulled on her kapp strap as she stared at her friend. "You won't see him much when we leave in April. Your feelings may change."

"Oh. I'm going to stay on, even if you leave. I can try to get another roommate to help pay the rent, but I'll wait for you to decide if you want to stay on a few more months first. Don't forget, you're closer to Paul this way."

"Jah, true. I'm just totally shocked. You never even mentioned a guy. What's his name?"

"Tyler Monroe. Such a cool name. Like a president or something."

Dawn giggled. "You've caught the love-bug. I can't wait to meet him. You girls lead such exciting lives!"

"Wait till you see. He gave me a picture." She took a photo out of her pocket and showed her friends, who were impressed.

"Nice," Dawn said.

"Jah, pretty 'cool' just like you said. Nice curly hair."

"He's dreamy, and he loves me! I'll never sleep to-night."

"Well, I need to get to bed," Dawn said, reaching for her jacket and heading for the door. "I have early class and I haven't even done my homework."

"Danki for the ride, Dawn," Martha said. "I really, really appreciate it."

"No prob. My cousin and I love to get together. She's a bit gossipy, but has a good heart. I'll come by the restaurant in a couple days and see how things are going. I hope your grandfather is okay."

"Jah, me, too."

"Oh, I picked up the mail," Naomi said, coming down to earth. "You did get a letter. It's on the kitchen table."

"Oh, I totally forgot to check the mailbox before I left this evening."

Dawn waited while Martha opened it. When she was finished reading, she looked over at her friends. "He's having tests done. The doctor is checking out his heart first."

"I'm glad he's finally getting care," Naomi said. "Why are some men so stubborn?"

"I don't know," Martha said. "Maybe your Tyler will be better."

"He'd better be, or he'll hear it from me."

"Oh, she sure doesn't sound Amish anymore," Dawn said, laughing.

"Aren't you worried about telling your family?" Martha asked.

"They probably won't be too shocked. They know I've been unhappy for a while now. I haven't been baptized, so I can't be shunned. It's not like I'll never see them again."

"Still…"

Dawn shook her head. "I'm glad I'm free to marry anyone I want. You're really restricted, aren't you?" she said, turning to Martha.

"I wouldn't even consider leaving the Amish," Martha stated. "Even though there are some rules I would change if I could, I love being part of the Amish community. We really take care of our people. The generations enjoy living together—"

"Not everyone, Martha," Naomi said, interrupting. "My mother can't stand her mother-in-law."

"Well, I'm sure there are exceptions," Martha admitted. "But on the whole families are pretty close."

"I have to get going," Dawn said as she reached for the doorknob. "I'm happy for both of you. Now I wish I could meet someone. There's absolutely no one in my future."

"You're still young," Naomi said. "English marry later, usually."

"True. I have a lot to accomplish before tying myself down. See you later."

After she left, Naomi got up and danced around the room, amusing Martha. "Goodness, you act like you're ten years old."

"I feel like a kid. Oh, it's so much fun to know I'll be free someday."

"If it doesn't work out with Tyler, would you still want to jump the fence?"

Naomi stopped and put her hands on her hips as she contemplated her answer. "I don't know, actually. I haven't thought about that much. Maybe not."

"Then don't go upsetting your family just yet. Keep it to yourself, Naomi. No sense in causing a problem if it ends up not being one."

"I guess you're right. I'm definitely going to stay on here though. I love making my own money and now with Tyler in the picture..."

"I'll think about staying beyond April then. It's month-to-month, right?"

"Jah."

"You'd better learn to drop the Amish expressions or your new friends will make fun of you."

"Oh, Tyler loves to hear me talk the Deutsch. I'm teaching him."

"Really? How sweet of him."

"Everything's sweet about him. He's just about perfect."

"I feel that way about Paul, but I know no one is perfect except Jesus, so I'm prepared to accept him with any faults he may have, as long as they're not terrible bad."

"That's a gut—good way to think, Martha. You're smart for your age."

Martha laughed. "Just common sense, I guess. I'm going to turn in early. I'm doing breakfast and lunch tomorrow."

"And I have to write to a friend back home. Maybe I

won't mention anything about Tyler. It would get around like a brush fire if I told Becky."

"Wise move."

As Martha said her prayers, she gave thanks for her family and for her new home. Then she prayed for her grandfather and asked that God give everyone strength to get through whatever lay ahead. She felt peace after laying her problems in His hands. What a blessing to know Jesus as her friend, as well as Savior. She fell asleep quickly, knowing her prayers were heard.

Sarah sat at the kitchen table, stirring cream into her coffee, when Melvin came in with the morning mail. He handed her a letter from Martha and poured himself a mugful of the dark delicious brew. "Looks like our dochder finally had time to write."

"It's only been a few days," Sarah said in her daughter's defense. "She works hard, you know."

"Jah, that's true. I guess I'm too critical. It's just I see how hard it's been on you with her gone. I'll be glad when she's back in April."

"So will I. I miss my sweetie. Lizzy's excited, too, and Mamm talks about it all the time now. I think with my daed being so tired all the time, it's draining on my mamm. He used to help around the house, but now I have to go do the sweeping and all."

"Two houses are too much for you. Lizzy should help more."

"She has her own family to care for. Her one daughter-in-law is expecting any day now. Lizzy goes over to help her nearly every day with her other kinner."

"I suppose she is pretty busy. Then I'll help with the cleaning more."

She patted his hand. "You're a gut Amishman. Danki. I hope Paul is as gut as you. Our Martha deserves the best."

He shook his head. "So open the letter."

"I'll read it out loud.

*Dear Mamm and Daed,*

*I'm sorry I haven't written in a while. I've been working a lot of hours at the restaurant and then taking my instructions every week. It keeps me busy and I go to bed early when I can. Everything is okay here and I was glad to get your letter about dawdi seeing a doctor. Please write as soon as you know what's going on with him. I hope his heart is okay. Maybe he is tired just because he's old.*

*How are you both doing? Don't work too hard, Mamm. You, too, Daed. It will soon be time to start the crops, so you should get your rest in while you can.*

*I'm reading my Bible more when I have a chance. I like the gospels the best. I try to remember everything you've taught me about being a good person and I try to treat all my customers with kindness.*

*Love and hugs to each of you. Give Aenti Lizzy and Onkel Leroy my love as well as Mammi and Dawdi.*

*Martha."*

Sarah smiled as she folded up the two-page letter and tucked it back in its envelope. "She sounds real gut."

"Jah. Likes making money, I think."

"Well, that's okay, as long as she doesn't make it into something too important."

"She didn't mention visiting. You have a birthday in February. I hope she remembers."

"Oh, jah," Sarah said. "When she left last time she said she'd do her best to come home for a couple days when I have it."

"It's a Monday, right?"

"Jah, it's gut it's not a weekend. She works just about every weekend, I know."

"You should remind her when you write back."

Sarah nodded. "I will. I'm gonna wait till tomorrow after taking Daed to the doctor. I'll have more to tell her."

"Any more of that breakfast crumb cake left?"

"Jah, but dinner will be ready soon. Don't you think you should wait?"

"Oh, I guess so. Smells gut. What are you cooking?"

"Meatballs and sauce. We're going to have spaghetti."

"Thought so. You're right, I want to leave room for that. You make the best. You must have Italian blood in you."

Laughing, she added, "Nee, but our dochder does. Though she doesn't know it, she may turn out to be a better spaghetti maker than me."

"Don't you think it's time you told the maed?"

Sarah's mouth drew down and she shook her head. "I don't know if I'll ever tell her at this point."

"But we're living a lie, Sarah. You know lying is a sin."

"I think Gott understands it. He knows my heart. Martha and I are real close. I don't want that to ever change."

"For Pete's sake, girl, why would it change? We've been her parents her whole life."

"I know. But I get scared thinking about it. Please try to understand."

"I try, but I can't say I do. It's not such a terrible thing to be adopted."

"I've heard some people leave and go to find their blood parents and forget all about their adoptive family. I couldn't take that, Mel. It would kill me, for real."

"It wouldn't happen, I'm absolutely sure of that, but I'll leave it up to you. Just pray she don't hear from someone else. Then you'd be in a bad way for sure."

"Very few people know."

"Your parents and Lizzy and Leroy know. How 'bout their kinner? Do they know?"

"Nee. Lizzy made an oath not to tell anyone. Her older boys were too young to remember when we moved here with Martha. Besides, we'd already adopted her."

"Where do you keep the papers hid?"

"In our bedroom, deep in my hope chest. She'll never go in there—not while I'm alive."

"You'd better hope not."

"Don't talk about it anymore. I'll put the pot on for the spaghetti."

"Gut, I'm just about starving."

He sat and finished his coffee while Sarah set up their table for four and went next door to tell her parents dinner would soon be ready.

# Chapter Sixteen

Sarah and Melvin sat in the waiting room while her parents were in the doctor's examination room. Her father had insisted on having only his wife in with him. Sarah flipped through several old copies of *Better Homes and Gardens* and then replaced them on the end table and folded her hands in her lap. There were several other people waiting, all of them in English garb. The Amish didn't attract much attention in Lancaster County—by the locals anyway. They were used to their Plain neighbors.

"They've been in there quite a while," she whispered to Melvin.

"Takes time. He has no records, probably."

"Jah. True."

"Think they'll know what's wrong just by examining him?"

Melvin shrugged. "We'll have to wait and see." He picked up a magazine about farming and became engrossed in an article about corn. Finally, her parents came out and joined them. They looked none too happy.

"Come on. We can go home now," her father said abruptly.

When they were seated in the buggy, her parents in the back and Melvin as the driver, Sarah turned and addressed her parents. "We're not moving until you tell us what they found."

"Your daed's heart is kinda weak. They want to run some blood tests tomorrow morning and do some kind of a stress test. Then he may have to have another test. What did they call it, Rubin?"

"I wasn't listening all that much. I think it was cath or something like that."

"I remember Josiah Helmuth's daed had that done last year," Melvin said. "They put something in the heart. Think it was called a 'stint' or a 'stent' and he's been just perfect ever since."

"Jah," Sarah said, nodding. "I remember. They can do all kinds of things to make the heart work better. I'm sure you'll be gut as new, Daed. Just have to listen to the doctor."

"Jah, I'm listening. I'm listening. First, I have the three of you gabbing about my heart, then I have to put up with the doctor and—"

"Well, maybe you wish we didn't care so much," his wife said, annoyed at his attitude.

"Gut grief. Don't take it the wrong way, Nancy. I'm just tired of hearing about it, is all."

"Well, you'll continue hearing about it until you listen and do what you're supposed to."

"I made it here, ain't?"

"Start the buggy, Melvin. I want to get home. I left dishes in the sink."

It was quiet all the way back. Sarah wasn't sure she should be worried or not. At least they didn't put him in the hospital. That was a good sign for sure.

After they all shared vegetable soup and cheese sandwiches for an early supper, her parents went back to their dawdi-haus and Sarah cleaned up the kitchen.

Melvin went out to take care of the stock and then returned and sat in the sitting room next to his wife, who was searching through her sewing box for a needle with a larger eye. "My eyes ain't doing so gut anymore. I may need glasses."

"Get some at the pharmacy. Mine work gut. Wanna try them?"

"I did already and they don't work for me. Maybe I should check with a doctor."

"If you'd feel better doing that, jah, call and make an appointment."

She nodded and finally found a large enough needle to thread. "I should be writing to Martha instead of sewing, but I just want to wait a little while and calm down."

"Honey, I didn't know you were all upset still." He put his newspaper down and wrapped an arm around his wife. "It's gonna be fine. They have all kinds of medicine now to help people with messed-up hearts. We know quite a few people who take medicine for blood pressure and even diabetes. We've just been fortunate to be as healthy as we've been. Bet it's your gut cooking."

Sarah smiled for the first time all evening. "I can't take credit for our health. Only the gut Lord gets credit for that, but danki for the compliment. You're right, I'm sure everything will turn out just fine. I wish Daed wasn't so difficult though. Poor Mamm."

"She has her hands full, that's for sure."

They returned to the clinic the next day and in spite of Rubin's objections, they took several vials of blood

and then sent him into a special room with a treadmill, monitors and cots. No one else was allowed in. About an hour later, he came out, rather pale, and plunked down on a chair next to his wife.

"Well? Did they find anything?"

"They want me back in two days for that cath thing. I have to get stuff to make me sleep, or close to it. I hate being out of it. I like to know what's going on."

"I'm sure they know what they're doing. Who's doing the test?"

"A different doctor. He's a heart doctor. Forgot his name."

"Mr. Detwiler," the receptionist called over. "We have your paperwork here."

He rose and walked over to her desk, where she explained the procedure and then gave him several sheets of instructions and forms, which he signed.

"We'll see you Friday then at nine," she said as he turned to leave.

"If I make it," he muttered. The family followed him out and again they rode back in silence. Sarah noticed her mother's eyes were glassy. It was difficult enough, without her father acting this way. She wondered if he was just plain scared and this was his way to cover up.

Later she talked to Melvin about it.

"I guess he is nervous, honey. I would be, too, wouldn't you?" Melvin said. "The heart's pretty important."

"Jah, you're right and he's never been sick, as far as I can remember. Of course, he had that bad accident years ago, but other than that, Daed's been in really gut health."

"He should be thankful."

"Jah. He probably is," Sarah said.

"Jah. Just doesn't show it, I guess."

"I guess."

"Now why don't we play checkers and try to get our minds off things," Melvin suggested.

"Should I write to Martha yet? Or should I wait till after the testing?"

"Better write tomorrow and let her know what's going on. That way she can be praying for your daed. Tell her to pray for all of us. He ain't making it easier on anyone."

Sarah smiled. "You can say that again. Okay, I want the red checkers."

"Like always," he said, leaning over and kissing her on the tip of her nose. "That's why you usually win."


Martha was disappointed not to receive a letter of information about her grandfather, but she figured no news was good news in this case.

Finally, on Friday, she got word that he'd been to the doctor and had blood work done and had a heart catheterization scheduled for that very day. How frustrating not to have a phone. It seemed ridiculous in this day and age that she'd have to wait to hear. She should have given them Naomi's phone number and had them use the common phone at the Schultzes' barn. Next time. If her mother sent a letter off this afternoon, she could get it Monday and definitely by Tuesday. She'd just stay in prayer every time she thought about home.

That evening, when Paul called, she told him about the procedure. He reassured her by telling her about a couple of people he knew who had gone through it safely, and it ended up being the only procedure they required.

"I'm going home for my mudder's birthday the middle of February," she told him. "I may not be able to get to the baptism class. I hope it's okay."

"Sure. I'll explain it. It's important for you to get home, honey. I know it means a lot to your parents."

"And to me. Jah, but I'll miss you, Paul."

"We're making settlement on the property sometime around the middle of February. We're just waiting to hear from the bank. I'm getting excited. Then we'll move all our supplies and equipment over. Maybe it will be the same week you go home, which means we probably wouldn't see each other anyway that week."

"Will you move into our house?"

"Not without you, but I can start painting it and getting it ready. Still want all white walls?"

"Jah, but like slightly off-white."

"Maybe I should wait for you to choose."

"I can send a sample or get a name or something. I'll stop tomorrow at the hardware store and pick one. Oh, my golly, it's actually happening! I'm sorry now I told my folks I'd come home in April. It means we'd be further apart again."

"Can't you change your mind and explain it to them?"

"I don't think Mamm would understand. I'll see what I can do. I won't have a phone while I'm home for her birthday, but I'll only be gone two nights. I don't like to miss work."

"You're a gut employee."

"How's your new worker coming along? Do you like his work?"

"Jah, but he's still learning about the finer points. He's quick to learn though. I think it will work out fine. Mamm's calling me. I promised I'd fix her oven tonight. I'd better go. I love you."

"And I love you. *Gut nacht*, Paul."

"Gut nacht."

She hated hanging up, but it wouldn't be forever. Tomorrow was the last day of January and she counted the days till they could marry. Paul planned to talk to his bishop about getting married on the first Thursday in November. It seemed like a long time to wait. She hadn't talked to her parents about getting married in Paul's district. That was not going to go over well. She'd just have to remain strong. It was difficult when she knew how it would affect her parents. At least she wasn't jumping the fence like Naomi planned to do. That would have crossed the line, for sure.

# Chapter Seventeen

The catheterization went well, though the doctor found it necessary to insert a stent. When he was coming out of the mild anesthesia, the surgeon told him he'd be on medication for his heart. He grumbled, but seemed relieved to have the procedure completed.

His wife, Nancy, stood beside the bed, as Sarah and Melvin remained in the background.

"When will they let me go home?" he asked her.

"Not yet. You're too groggy. Rest."

"I'm resting. The animals need feeding soon."

"I'll take care of them," Melvin said softly. "Don't worry about a thing."

"Humph. Hope these people know what they're doing," Sarah's father said, within earshot of a nurse.

She didn't say a word as she continued writing on a chart.

"Do you want to nap?" Sarah asked.

"Nope."

"Thirsty?" his wife asked.

"Nope. Just want to get home."

The nurse turned her attention to the patient and came over to check his blood pressure. "Good, your pressure

is almost normal. It won't be long, Mr. Detwiler. We'd like to watch you for another hour or so before we discharge you. You did very well."

"He's a strong person," Sarah said.

"He must be."

"Well, them cows are gonna be burstin' by the time we get back."

"They'll be fine, Daed," Sarah said. "It's not that late. Besides, Melvin does all the milking now—usually by himself."

He scowled and closed his eyes.

Sarah looked over at her mother, who puckered her lips and shook her head.

Finally, he was given the prescription scripts he needed as well as the necessary follow-up papers. The nurse insisted on taking him to the buggy in a wheelchair when he was discharged. He didn't say a word, but his expression told it all. He was not a happy man.

There was little conversation on the way home. Once he was settled on his couch, Sarah and her mother, Nancy, tended to his needs while Melvin went out to milk the cows. Had his father-in-law forgotten it was Melvin's responsibility now? Perhaps he was trying to impress the nurse and make her think he was farming by himself.

Once back at her house, Sarah took out a piece of paper and wrote to Martha, explaining what they'd done. She was quite relieved that there was no mention of the need for further surgery. Apparently, he was in better shape than they'd all imagined. It was fortunate they treated the problem before it became worse.

She also reminded her about the upcoming birthday, which until now had remained in the background of her mind.

She signed off and set the envelope by the door. She'd

already missed the mail carrier, so it could wait until the next morning.

When Melvin returned from the barn, he asked about the prescriptions. "Should I try to get them filled to-night?" he asked.

"The nurse told me it could start tomorrow. It's getting dark out, dear. Wait until it's light tomorrow. I'll be glad when this winter is over. It seems twice as long as usual."

"Jah, especially without our Martha."

She nodded. "You miss her, too, don't you?"

"Jah. Sure. She's my baby, too."

"Come sit next to me, Melvin. Sometimes I forget about your pain, I'm so busy thinking of myself. Forgive me for being selfish."

"Honey, you're the most unselfish person I've ever known. Don't you worry about it. I know it's harder on you. Mamms have it worse when their young ones grow up and leave. Do you think they'll settle here near us?"

"I'd like to think so, but his business, you know. A man has to think about making a living. I will accept whatever they decide to do. As long as I have you, I'll be fine."

He squeezed her hand. "Jah, I know what you mean. I feel the same. Hopefully, we have many years ahead to be together."

"Jah, I pray so. Now, I'll put some of yesterday's soup on for supper. I want to take some over to the folks. Daed won't be up to coming over here tonight. It's way too cold out and he was shaky when we brought him in. Did you notice?"

"Jah. Gut thing he used his cane getting in the house. I had his other arm, just in case."

"I know. You're a gut sohn-in-law, Melvin. Even Mamm says she's glad I married you."

"That makes two of us."

"No, all four of us, oh, make that five. Martha thinks you're the best daed in the world. She told me that herself."

He grinned. "Can't argue with that. Now, I'll take the soup over when it's ready. Put it in an extra large pot in case they want more later."

Sarah nodded as she stood. Then she leaned over and kissed the top of his head before taking the soup out of the refrigerator. She was a very fortunate woman. *Danki, Gott.*

The next morning, Sarah flipped the January page to the back of the calendar and replaced it on the wall next to the refrigerator. Fourteen days until her Martha would be coming for her birthday. Now that she felt some relief about her father's condition, she could concentrate on planning the meals while Martha visited. She planned to stay two nights before returning to her job at the restaurant. Good thing she had such nice people to work for. They tried to oblige her requests for her visits home. Of course, soon she'd be home for good—or so Sarah hoped.

Melvin came in from the barn after removing his boots and sat at the table for his morning break. "Any kaffi left from earlier?" he asked.

"I just made a fresh pot. Mamm stopped over with fresh wheat bread. She's been baking up a storm now that she's happy again."

Melvin chuckled. "That's gut for us. Is she planning to make that fudge she's so gut at?"

"I think she'll bring some for my birthday. That's

been a tradition since I was little. A dozen pieces of the dark chocolate and a dozen of the white chocolate. That's probably why I've always had a hard time losing weight."

"You look just fine to me, Sarah. Don't change a thing."

She laughed and dimples appeared in her cheeks. Melvin loved her laugh. She was just about perfect in his eyes.

"The bishop just stopped by," he mentioned as she set the pot on the table.

"I thought I heard a buggy, but I was upstairs changing sheets and didn't take the time to look out. Didn't he want to stay for kaffi?"

"I asked him, but he was on his way to his bruder's. Anyway, he wanted to mention that Daniel Beiler is back and living down the road from us. He's renting a room with the Kitchens. Bob Kitchen and his wife are taking in roomers now."

"I'm not happy to hear that. Martha will not be pleased."

"He won't come around here, if he knows what's gut for him. Don't you worry none."

"I'm not concerned, but Martha seems afraid of him. Ever since that time…"

"I know. But she ain't here to worry."

"If she learns about it, she'll be afraid to come back in April. I just know it."

"I guess we need to tell her, though."

"Maybe we don't have to mention it."

"Now, Sarah, that ain't right. You tell Martha she should never tell a lie and then you say that?"

"I guess."

"And not to tell her she's adopted. I think it's a big mistake."

"Now, you promised, Melvin. That's one secret I intend to keep to myself. Please don't betray me."

"Now, you know better than that."

"Well, I know it wouldn't be on purpose, but you sometimes forget."

"What came in the mail yesterday that you grabbed so fast and kept quiet about? That ain't like you, Sarah. Who was it from? I saw it was postmarked from Ohio."

"It's nothing to worry about. Just a letter from an old friend."

"Mmm. A man friend or a woman friend?"

"Oh mercy! A woman, of course." She clucked her tongue.

"Okay, don't make me drag it out of you. What friend?"

"Oh, I may as well tell you. It was from Elizabeth, my friend who I went to grade school with. You met her a few times."

"Jah, I remember Elizabeth. Nice girl with freckles and big teeth."

"Now, you always said that. They weren't too big. Just came out front a little. Anyway, she heard from Alice Zook who heard from Rebecca Schultz that Rose Esh was in town."

"Martha's mudder?" His mouth dropped open. "After all these years? What did she have to say?"

"That's why I didn't want you to know. She wanted to know where we were living now. She asked all kinds of questions about Martha. Melvin, I was scared to death when I read the letter, but Elizabeth said no one told her a thing. Actually, Rebecca doesn't even know where we moved to. The only one I told was Elizabeth and she swore she'd never tell a soul. Apparently, Rose had heard

we'd moved to Lancaster County from one of the merchants, but Elizabeth shrugged when she mentioned it."

"Then we have nothing to fear. Lancaster's a big county. You should throw that letter out and forget you ever read it."

"I might do just that. I don't know yet. I'll read it over at least once more. Elizabeth has moved over to her dochder's dawdi-haus so I want to write down her new address first. That's why I didn't sleep gut last night."

"I heard you walking around. Thought you just had indigestion from that fried bologna we had for supper."

"Well, it didn't help any, but it was the letter that really kept me up."

"Come here and sit with me." She sat across from him and wiped her eyes with her apron. "Now, Sarah, just put it out of your mind. Everything is just fine."

"I know I shouldn't be worried and I tell myself that over and over, but sometimes I don't believe it."

"She knows the maed is all grown up. What purpose would she have in wanting to know more now? I heard she'd married. Ain't that what you heard a few years ago?"

"Jah. Maybe she still is. I don't know and I don't want to know. Even hearing her name…"

"Well, we owe that young woman a lot, Sarah. We were mighty fortunate she was willing to let us adopt Martha. And she's stayed away all this time."

"Jah. You're right. I'll pray for a softer heart. I don't have ill feelings for her, but I don't want to have her in Martha's life."

"I understand."

"I hope you do. Sometimes I think you don't really understand me. Sometimes I don't understand myself.

Maybe it's fear… I don't know. I'd rather not talk about it now. I have dishes to wash. Let me redd up the kitchen and then maybe we can go over the budget tonight. I'd like to make a new *frack* for Martha before she gets here. I thought maybe a pretty blue dress. I just want to be sure there's enough money in the till."

"I'm sure there is, Sarah. You go buy the fabric. I have cash in my dresser drawer. Take as much as you need."

"Danki. You're a gut and generous husband."

"Jah well, you're a very special fraa. The best."

She stood up and before starting the clean-up, she went over and kissed the bald spot on his head. He grinned his approval and took a sip of the fresh brewed coffee. He was one fortunate Amishman, that was for sure and for certain.

# *Chapter Eighteen*

Martha had to call for a driver to take her back to Paradise for her mother's party, since it was mid-week and Dawn was busy during the day with her studies. Martha had saved more money and was glad she could afford the expense of a driver. She had purchased a colorful banquet-size table cloth for her mother's birthday. It had a white background decorated with bright sunny yellow tulips with fresh long green leaves. Best part was, it didn't need ironing, just a good steady breeze to flush away any creases.

After wrapping it and packing a few clothes, she waited by the window for the driver. It had warmed up considerably for February and was in the low forties. A storm was expected, but not until the day after she'd be back home. She had packed her high boots just in case it arrived earlier.

Paul had considered meeting her in Paradise, but with the settlement and the amount of work they had at the shop, he decided to wait until things were calmer.

Though disappointed he couldn't make it, Martha was excited to see her family. She missed her mother

the most, but she was also anxious to see her father and grandparents, as well as her aunt and uncle and all the cousins. At last her driver arrived and she made her way to the car, carrying everything in her arms.

He put her things in the trunk and invited her to sit up front. She'd met him once before and he was old enough to be her father, so she felt comfortable doing so. They had a nice chat and then he had to concentrate on the road as flurries descended unexpectedly and increased in intensity, making it slightly difficult to see clearly. It gave her time to think. She'd have to wait until she got back to her apartment to talk to Paul again. The next day they were having the settlement. He sounded excited when he talked about it. Things were actually happening now, which made it all the more realistic to marry soon.

Even though it was her mother's birthday, she felt it was now time to tell her family she'd be living in Lewistown after the marriage took place. Since everyone was used to her being away, she figured it wouldn't come as too much of a shock at this point. It would be a hurdle jumped. The next hurdle would be telling them she'd be joining a less conservative church after her marriage. Though still Amish, it would be too liberal in her parents' eyes. The cell phone was permitted by Paul's bishop, and her father saw that as heresy.

When she arrived, she noted her aunt's buggy was already parked by the barn. Her uncle still hadn't repaired the side door handle. No one had come to open the front door, which meant they hadn't heard the car pull up. She could surprise them if she tiptoed through the front. What fun! She used to do that as a child.

After paying the driver, she waited until he was on the road before checking the front door. It was unlocked, as

she'd expected. Her heart beat quickly, reminding her of her childhood surprises. She could hear her parents talking in low voices to her aunt and uncle in the kitchen. Oh gut—more family members to surprise. She stood where they wouldn't see her and quietly removed her jacket.

"I think you should tell her before someone else does," her father was saying.

"Especially since her real mother is searching for her now," her aunt Lizzy said.

"Nee. I've kept it from Martha all these years, I'm not about to—"

"To what?" Martha stepped into the kitchen, fear transcending every pore in her body. What had she just been witness to? *Real mother?*

Sarah gasped as she saw her daughter. "Why did you sneak in here?"

"No, why are you talking about a *real* mother? What does that mean? You're my mother! What's happened?" Martha burst into tears as Sarah rose and went to surround her daughter with her arms. Everyone else was stunned into silence as they watched the scene unfold.

"Stop!" Martha drew away. "Tell me the truth," she sputtered through her tears. "Have you been lying to me my whole life? I was adopted? Why would you lie about it?"

"Honey, I feel like I gave birth to you. You have always been like my own child."

"Why wouldn't you tell me? Did you think it would really matter? Did you have so little faith in me? In my love for you?"

Melvin rose and came over and put his arm around his wife. "She was afraid you'd feel different about her."

"Nee! Not if I'd known from the beginning! But now! Now, after all these years of being lied to!"

"Oh, Martha. Martha. Please try to understand," her mother started saying as she, too, began to weep.

"I can't." Martha shook her head over and over. "I have to go to my room. Please leave me alone. I need to… I don't know what. Come to grips, I guess." She turned and went up the stairs, leaving her belongings by the front door.

When she got to her old bedroom, she crawled under the familiar hand-made quilt and wept. The pain of being lied to all these years… The hypocrisy of her parents being so shocked and upset over her using a phone… Who else knew? Obviously, her aunt and uncle were in on it. Maybe all their children and their children's children. Was she the only one in the dark?

She turned to her side and reached for the box of tissues on the nightstand. Who was this woman who had given birth to her? And the father? No wonder she didn't look like anyone in her family. It wasn't *her family*. She was an outsider. Had never really belonged. Had she suspected down deep? The black hair—the dark eyes—her height. Maybe her parents were English, searching for her. Hadn't she heard that? What were the circumstances that made her blood mother give her away? Was she too young? Or too selfish? Or sick?

She wanted to know everything. What did she feel toward her parents now? They'd been so good to her all these years, but why lie? She felt betrayed. They had so little faith in her. And they seemed so ready for her to move away after the episode with Paul and Daniel. Were they regretting their decision to adopt her? Had she disappointed them that much?

She rolled over to her back and stared at the blank ceiling. If she could only make her mind as blank. If only she'd made her presence known. But wasn't it better to know the truth?

There was a faint rap on her door as her aunt's voice came through. "Martha, can I come in?"

"I'm not ready to talk. Please just go away."

"Your mother is so upset—"

"Jah? Well, so am I! Please leave me alone."

There was a moment's hesitation and then she heard her aunt's footsteps recede as she headed for the staircase. Aenti Lizzy. One of the special people in her life. She'd known all along and never said a word. Probably everyone knew but Martha. What a joke.

What would Paul think? Would it matter to him? If she was born to a single mom, which was most likely the case, would she be considered… Her mind flew from one thought to another. It was as if her very life had been a lie—a joke.

How foolish to see it that way. She'd had a wonderful childhood. She loved her parents dearly—that wouldn't change, but right now, the shock and disappointment in their lack of faith in her love overshadowed everything else.

Should she return to her apartment now? Or go to Lewistown? She so wished she could talk to Paul, be held by Paul. He'd know how to handle it. But it was her mother's birthday. She couldn't hurt her that much. No, she'd stay and try to pretend things were okay. It would be a strain on everyone. They were waiting for her to accept the whole situation, but could she so soon after learning the truth?

Her tears had dried and she sat at the edge of the bed.

Soon, she'd go downstairs. Soon, she'd embrace her parents. Her adoptive parents. But not quite yet. She knelt by the bed and prayed. She prayed for everyone involved, including herself—for strength and wisdom. And then she prayed for her blood mother…and father. And most importantly, she prayed He'd remove any anger she still felt. That was the hardest.

She'd give herself a few more minutes before joining the family.

The settlement took place and the realtor handed Paul and Jeremiah two sets of keys and shook their hands. When they got outside the two men slapped each other on the back and high-fived.

"I'm treating you to lunch, my friend," Jeremiah said, grinning.

"I'll take you up on it," Paul said, smiling back. "But I'll pick up the tip."

They made their way over to a local luncheonette and ordered soup and grilled cheese sandwiches. Then Jeremiah asked if Paul would be moving into the house right away.

"I think I'll wait till I'm married. It will make it more special that way. Besides, I want to do some work. It needs painting throughout."

"Jah, I'm glad you wanted the larger house. The other one doesn't need a thing. I'm going to move in in a couple days."

"Do you want help moving?"

"Sure, why not? Though I'll have plenty of help."

"How are things going with Hazel?" Paul asked as he waited for his chicken noodle soup to cool down.

"Gut. Real gut. She may be the one."

"Think it's mutual?"

"Oh jah. No regrets on your part, friend?"

"Nee. None, whatsoever. My Martha is everything I've ever wanted in a mate. I miss her so much when we're apart. She wanted me to come to Paradise for her mudder's birthday."

"So, why don't you go? We're pretty caught up at the moment."

"Think I should?"

"Hey, you should celebrate with Martha. Look at what's happened. You're a young man to be part of a business and own your own house."

Paul nodded. "She'd like me to be with her. Maybe I will. I'll call Skip and see if he could take me this evening. It would be fun to surprise her."

"Jah, women like stuff like that. It shows you care, know what I mean?"

Paul nodded and took a spoonful of soup as the waitress returned with their sandwiches. He wanted more than anything to see his Martha and share the exhilaration he felt. Nice being part owner, and he and Jeremiah were not only partners, but close friends as well.

# Chapter Nineteen

Martha checked the small wall mirror in her room. Her tears had dried up and she had readied herself for uniting with the family. An hour had passed. When she joined them, they were still sitting in the kitchen. Her mother's eyes were puffy and red, though there were no tears to be seen at this point.

When Martha appeared, all conversation stopped and her mother looked at her daughter, questioning her with her eyes.

"I'm sorry I reacted the way I did," Martha began. "It was just such a shock." She went over to her mother and knelt on the floor beside her chair. Sarah reached over and surrounded her with her arms.

"I guess it was wrong to keep it from you, Martha. I'm real sorry."

"I know you did it for your own reasons. I'm sorry, too, but it doesn't change my feelings for you and Daed."

Melvin got up from his chair as Martha rose and he hugged her tightly in his strong arms.

Then her aunt and uncle stood up and waited for her to reach out to them.

"My sweet maed," Aunt Lizzy said. "No one ever wanted to hurt you."

"It may take me a while to get over the shock," Martha said, turning back to her mother, who nodded.

"I understand."

"What I'm going to say next was something I decided before today, so don't take it as anything but what it is—a decision I've made after giving it much thought. You all know I plan to marry Paul." Everyone nodded and each of her family returned to their chairs and sat down, as they listened attentively.

"It's okay with us," her father stated. "Now that he's right with Gott."

"You know he's just become a partner in the carpentry business and they just purchased a building—along with two houses."

"We didn't know all that," Melvin said, a frown setting in.

"Jah, it's a wonderful opportunity for his future. And we will live in one of the houses."

"Oh, mercy," Sarah let out.

"Mamm, we decided it a while ago."

"You never said a word."

"I wanted to tell you all in person. Paul has said over and over that we'll visit with you often. It's not that far."

Lizzy clucked her tongue. "Too far to take the buggy."

Martha looked over at her aunt. "Jah, but we can use drivers. It's only a two-hour ride."

Lizzy shook her head and looked down at her hands. "It's your life."

"We'll never see you," Sarah said as she lifted her apron to her eyes once again.

"Of course you will," Martha reassured her. "And

everyone can come and stay as often and as long as you want. Our house will always be open to you."

Melvin stroked his beard and looked at the floor. "Not the same."

"I've been away a lot lately. You should be used to it by now. Somehow, everyone has survived."

Lizzy spoke up again. "It ain't been easy on your folks. None of us."

"I'm sorry," Martha said. "You all came here from Ohio and away from Daed's family."

"We did that for you, Martha," Sarah said. "We didn't want people asking questions."

"I guess it was foolish in the end, Mamm. Don't you think people wondered when a maed with black hair and dark eyes was supposed to be your blood dochder? I hope you can tell me more someday about where I came from. I think I have a right to know."

"Not now, Martha," her father said, sternly. "Your mamm's been through enough today. Let's not be cruel."

"I didn't say that to be mean, Daed."

Lizzy stood up. "I'm gonna frost your cake, Sarah, before the layers dry up."

"Aren't we celebrating tomorrow?" Martha asked.

"Jah, but I wanted to bake it today."

"Lizzy used my oven."

"And your cake flour, schwester. Guess that was a funny thing to do."

"Ach. We're family. We share everything."

The tension seemed to recede and Martha went to the door where her belongings were still sitting and took them upstairs to get the place in order and to be alone for a while. It had been awkward, but at least there were no secrets now between them. She'd probably wait to tell

them about Paul's church and that their *Ordnung* was not as strict as the old order her family followed. No point in upsetting them any further. She also figured she'd hold off on questioning them about her roots. Her aunt would be the one to talk to, that was for sure.

Paul checked his watch as he sat with the driver, Skip Davis. He was relieved Skip could come right over after he returned from his lunch with Jeremiah. He should arrive in Paradise about an hour before supper, which would be good since it would give him a chance to be with his sweetheart alone first. She sure would be surprised. She had told him once she loved surprises. He was not usually this spontaneous, so he knew she'd not be looking for him.

Skip congratulated him on his new business facility and asked for business cards once they were printed out. "I know lots of people who would use your services," he added.

"Jah? I'll be sure to get some over to you. Jeremiah mentioned cards today. There are so many things to think about."

"So are you going to pop the question to your girl-friend?"

"We already know we're marrying, but I want to talk to her family while I'm visiting. I just hope they don't get upset with me for arriving unexpectedly. Of course, Martha asked me before, but I didn't think it would work out. It's her mom's birthday tomorrow."

"Oh, I bet they make great cakes."

Paul laughed. "Jah, they do. Nothing fancy of course, but gut homemade ones. Lots of butter and sugar and—"

"Stop, you're making me jealous. My wife buys all our desserts. Not the same."

They talked about other issues and even got on the topic of politics, though Paul's knowledge of current events was somewhat limited.

Finally, they pulled onto the back road leading to the Troyers' place. Paul could feel his excitement growing the closer they got. He pictured Martha's face and how surprised and pleased she'd be to see him. It was more fun this way. He was glad it had worked out, and hopefully, her family would be as pleased.

Martha was glad her aunt and uncle were planning to stay until evening. Two of their sons came by and left off some baked goods for the next day since they'd be unable to attend the party. She wondered if they knew she'd been adopted. Probably, since it seemed everyone else knew. No one spoke about the revelation and she tried to forget the feelings it had harbored. She would always love her family, that wasn't the problem. No, it was the feeling that somehow, she'd been betrayed—that they felt her feelings of love were perhaps too shallow to accept the truth. She tried to put herself in her mother's shoes. If she decided to adopt someday, would she want to keep it a secret from the children? She doubted it very much, but it was twenty years ago. Maybe in those days people thought it was a good idea to let the adopted children go through life without knowing the truth.

Martha was washing coffee mugs when she heard a rap on the kitchen door. Probably another of Lizzy's sons, she thought, as she dried her hands and went to answer it.

My goodness! It was Paul! Oh, what an answer to prayer.

She swung the door wide open and reached for his hands. "You came!"

"Jah, I'm here all right." He walked in and before anyone arrived in the kitchen, he kissed her lightly and quickly on the lips.

"I can't believe it! I was missing you so much," she said.

"Are you okay?"

"Jah, now I am. Come into the sitting room. My aenti Lizzy is here with her husband, Onkel Leroy. You're in time for supper."

"Well planned, jah?" he said grinning.

He followed her into the front room. Everyone was surprised by his appearance, so unexpected. Martha noted her mother's cool greeting and felt a pit in her stomach. Too much emotional trauma. It was so important to have good relationships with family. It would crush her to cause grief to her parents. Paul was such a good man, surely, they'd treat him well. The thought of future division in the family was unacceptable.

He went over to the men to shake their hands and nodded to the women.

"Didn't expect to see you," her mother finally said. "But of course you're welcome," she added weakly.

"Mamm, I have the platters of meat and cheese ready. Maybe Paul and I will take a walk before we eat."

"Jah. Okay. I guess I can set the table."

"It's already done. I just need to add one more place for Paul, but I'll do it when we return. It will only be a few minutes."

"Don't go far. We'll ring the bell when we're ready to eat."

Once out of the house and out of sight, Paul reached

for her hand and they made their way to the far field where they embraced. "Your mamm didn't seem too happy about me coming. I probably should have stayed home, but I wanted to see you in the worst way."

"I'm glad you came. I needed to see you. I had a shock today."

He pulled away so he could see her face. "Honey, what happened? You didn't look like yourself when I came in."

"You'll never believe it. I just found out I'm adopted. I wasn't supposed to hear about it, but I was just outside the kitchen door when I overheard them. I was going to call out, 'Surprise,' but in the end, I was the one surprised."

Paul stood staring at her. She looked quizzically at him. "What's wrong? Does it make a difference to you?"

"Of course not."

"You act funny. Aren't you surprised?"

"Martha, I already knew."

"You *what?* How could you have known?" She moved apart from him and stared in disbelief.

"Your aenti accidentally let it out."

"Why didn't you tell me? Was I the last one in the world to find out?" Her voice cracked and she put her hands over her eyes and shook her head.

"She made me promise not to tell you."

"You shouldn't have promised." She put her hands down to her sides and allowed tears to flow once again. "I can't even trust you to tell me the truth."

They both heard the dinner bell, but they made no effort to return to the house yet.

"Honey, it would—"

"Don't call me that! I can't trust anyone." She turned and walked quickly back to the house, but instead of

washing up for supper and helping, she walked briskly past the family and went back to her room.

When Paul got to the house a few moments later, he noted her absence. Everyone waited for an explanation. It was strange. Everyone just stood motionless staring at him. Finally, he looked at Sarah and spoke. "I had to tell her I knew about the adoption."

"Oh, my," Lizzy said as she plunked down on one of the kitchen chairs.

Sarah gaped. "How did you know?"

"I told him by mistake, Sarah," came Lizzy's timid response.

"And I promised not to tell Martha, but she was angry with me for keeping it a secret. I had no choice though. I'd promised."

Melvin folded his arms and solemnly nodded. "She'll get over it. Right now, she feels we all lied to her."

"And we did, I guess," Lizzy remarked.

"Should I try to talk to her?" Paul asked.

"Nee, leave her be," Melvin said. "She needs to think it through. She'll come around."

"We may as well eat," Leroy said.

"That's all you think about," Lizzy said. "Your stomach."

"Well, we can't do much else," he said, chagrined.

"I guess I shouldn't have come," Paul said. "Maybe I should call my driver. He couldn't have gotten too far."

Sarah nodded. "Might be a gut idea."

"Well, he came all this way," Lizzy said. "I think you should stay, Paul. Martha may realize she needs you. She just has to spend some time by herself…sort through everything. It's been quite a shock to the poor maed."

He looked over at Sarah. "Is it okay?"

"You can stay with us," Leroy offered. "Then by tomorrow, everything will be just fine, I'm sure of that."

"Jah, go home with Lizzy and Leroy," Sarah said. "She'd probably be more upset if you left town. And she'd most likely blame it on me."

"Now, Sarah, don't say such things," her husband said. "She's a *schmaert* young woman. She'll realize everyone was just doing what they thought best. Give her time." He turned to Paul. "I agree with Lizzy. You should stay with them tonight and come back tomorrow. We'll try to have a nice birthday party."

Paul nodded. "Poor Martha. She thinks we've all betrayed her."

"Foolishness," Lizzy said. "She'd better get over it."

"Now, Liz," Sarah said. "It's been a shock for her. It ain't foolishness."

Lizzy scowled over at her sister. "Let's eat now. I'm starving and you make the best potato salad around."

The meal was eaten in silence. Not a peep was heard from upstairs. Paul ate only enough to stay alive. If only he'd stayed home or kept his mouth closed. His poor Martha was hurting and he couldn't even think of a way to help.

After they ate, he followed Melvin and Leroy out to the barn where they took care of the livestock. Women were too complicated, the men decided. But until Gott came up with a better plan, they were stuck with them. Their billy goat came over and nuzzled his owner—as if he understood and agreed.

## Chapter Twenty

Daniel Beiler had allowed his mustache to grow while he lived with his English buddies in Lancaster, but now he was back in his district and he'd done enough damage to his reputation without balking about the shaving restrictions in their Ordnung. He put shaving cream on his upper lip and slowly and methodically removed his blond lip whiskers. He had removed his beard already. His hair lay over his collar. With a towel over his shoulders he trimmed it to just below the ear lobe.

Then he stood back and smiled into the mirror over the sink. Pleased with his reflection, he went back to his room and changed into a clean Amish blue shirt and attached his *galluses,* or suspenders, to his trousers.

Hopefully, by now, word had gotten around about his accepting responsibility for that fight he'd had with Paul Yoder, the puny carpenter from Lewistown. Surely, it was Martha he'd seen in the car the day before as it made its way to her home. Perhaps she was home to stay. Certainly by now, her father had gotten over his animosity toward him and would allow him to visit his daughter from time to time.

The weeks he'd been away had been quite an experience. The girls he'd met had been quite fascinated with him, probably because he'd been Amish and it was a challenge, but for whatever reason, they'd been agreeable to his attention and he'd had his ego built up. Surely after all this time, Martha would be willing to take a second look. If not, well, he'd check out the other girls at the next sing. He could always go back to Molly Zook. She was pretty cute—not as good looking as Martha, but she was an agreeable girl and he knew she was probably still carrying a candle for him.

His father gave him permission to use the family buggy and since the roads were pretty clear, he harnessed up their newest driving horse and headed over to the Troyer farm.

That morning, the Troyer house was being set up for Sarah's fiftieth birthday party. Some of her great-nieces were already blowing up balloons for the occasion, and Lizzy had just pulled in with her husband and Paul. It was nearly noon.

Martha had come down for breakfast earlier. She'd barely spoken after wishing her mother a happy birthday. She'd set the wrapped tablecloth in the sitting room in a corner after making sure the card was included. Sarah had tried to make light conversation with her daughter, but it was obvious the girl was still harboring ill feelings. When Paul came in, Martha was wiping down the sink with cleanser. She barely looked up. Her eyes were swollen and her expression looked grim. He came over and asked if he could help. She merely shook her head and went on scouring.

Sarah looked over and suggested he help bring chairs

in from the barn and line them up in the sitting room. He went over to Melvin and offered to assist him with the job.

As he was returning with three stacked folding chairs, Daniel pulled into the drive. Not expecting him to be the driver, Paul merely waved, assuming he was waving to a family member coming for the party. Then he set the chairs around in the large room and headed back through the kitchen. There standing at the open door was Daniel, immaculately dressed and groomed. The men stared at each other and then Martha's father came over. "You ain't welcome here, Daniel. I'd like you to leave without a fuss."

"How come you allow this guy?" he asked, pointing over at Paul. "He was in the fight, too."

"He confessed to his congregation. He's been forgiven and Martha invited him."

"I've repented as well. Don't you give me the same credit?"

Paul had heard enough. "Look, Dan, it's over between you and Martha. We're going to be married soon. Just accept it and leave her alone."

"I want to hear it from her."

"She's upstairs."

"I'll wait."

"Nee, you have to leave now." Melvin glared at the young man.

"I don't want to cause trouble. Tell Martha if it's true she's marrying this guy, she needs to tell me in person. I'll stop by next week."

"She won't be here," Paul said, his voice firm and steady.

"Where's she living now? With you?"

"Go." Melvin took a step closer and the young man turned and left the house.

"He never gives up," Melvin said under his breath. "What's going to happen in April when Martha comes home?"

Martha's voice came from the hall. "I'm not coming back as long as he's still around. He scares me."

"Martha, I thought you were upstairs," Paul said.

"I was, but I saw him get out of his buggy from my bedroom window and I wanted to see what he was up to."

"I'm glad you didn't talk to him." Paul went over and stood next to her, without touching her hand.

"I never want to talk to him again. I think you should speak to the bishop, Daed. His confession was probably fake."

"I don't doubt that, but we can't judge a man's heart."

"I doubt he has one," she added. Then she turned her attention back to Paul. "Can we talk alone in the sewing room?"

"Sure." Paul turned toward her father to get his approval. Melvin nodded.

They walked together to the small room and sat on the loveseat, barely touching.

"I'm sorry I acted the way I did, Paul."

"It's okay. I understand."

"That's gut, because I don't. I have so many feelings going through me right now, I hardly know who I am. It's as if my identity is gone. Like I have amnesia or something and I don't even know my name. I don't understand what's happened to me."

"Oh honey, I'm sorry you're going through this."

"What do you know about my background? Did my aenti tell you anything else? Please be honest now. I won't accept anything else."

He told her about the events surrounding her adoption as they'd been related to him. Then he told her about her Italian father and that the young man had never been made aware of her existence.

She listened intently without comment. He also told her about the first time Sarah had met her and the immediate bonding that took place. His words brought a smile to Martha's lips as she pictured it.

"I heard my blood mother was looking for me. I want to find out more, but I don't want to hurt Mamm. She's upset as it is. Can you find out more from my aenti?"

"I'll try, if there's an opportunity. Maybe after we go back to their place. I'll try to come back in the morning to say good-bye, Martha."

"I'm leaving early. I'm scheduled for the lunch shift."

"Honey, we've barely spoken. When can I see you again?"

"I don't know. Dawn plans to take me to Lewistown for the instructional class next week. I'll try to get some extra time. I know we need to talk more. I'll be afraid to come back here, now that Daniel is back. At least it didn't end up like last time. I guess he's learned his lesson."

"I sure hope so. I'm glad you'll stay where you are until we can marry."

"It won't go over too gut with my folks."

"I think they understand now. I hope your daed speaks to the bishop about that guy. I was hoping he'd be banned for good."

"Jah, me, too. I don't trust his so-called remorse."

"Do you think I could kiss you once before we go back?"

She nodded and leaned over, closing her eyes.

"Wow! Look at Martha kissing!" one of her young cousins yelled out from the open doorway.

Martha pulled back and turned to the grinning child.

"Stop, Lucas! Shame on you," she said, feeling shame herself.

He giggled and took off.

Paul shook his head. "I guess we'll wait."

"I hope the grown-ups didn't hear. My daed would not be happy."

"I'm sorry, Martha. I just want so much to be close to you. I hope you're not still mad at me."

"Nee, not really. Just confused about everything. Let's go back in and I can give my aenti a hand with the food. We expect over forty people in and out today to help celebrate. I don't know how much time we'll gct together. I want to hear about your settlement and the house and a million other things, but everything's so messed up."

"I know, honey. At least I get to be in the same room with you. It was worth coming."

"I think Gott wanted you here to be a support. I'm glad you came. Just knowing you were near was a comfort— after I got over my anger. I felt so guilty having so many mixed feelings about the very people I love the most. I hope I'm forgiven. I've been praying a lot about it."

He ran his hand down her cheek. "You're very special. You know I love you."

"I know." She smiled her first radiant smile since she arrived home. "And I, you."

The rest of the afternoon was so busy, no one had time to talk about what was on everyone's mind. After Paul left, Martha's mother went up to bed. In a few short hours, Martha would return to the safety of her small apartment, her job and her friend. She looked forward to the morning and her normal routine.

# Chapter Twenty-One

As Martha prepared to leave the next morning, her parents seemed reluctant to part with her. Sarah held her closely as she said her good-byes, and her father watched with sorrowful eyes as he waited his turn. Martha feared the tears would begin and she'd never be able to leave.

"Try to come next month," her father said when it was his turn to embrace her.

"I'll see how it works out, Daed."

"Your mamm needs to know things are okay between you, jah?"

Martha nodded. "We'll all be fine. Just may take a little more time for me to get over the shock."

Sarah wiped her eyes. "Write to us soon, Martha."

"I will." She went back to her mother and took her hands. "You know I'll never stop loving you both, don't you?"

Sarah was unable to verbally respond at first. She could barely swallow, but she nodded and smiled tenderly.

"Now, my driver is waiting. I must get back in time for the lunch crowd. I'll try to write tomorrow."

Melvin stood beside his wife and watched as the driver placed Martha's belongings in the trunk. As the car pulled away, Melvin placed his arm around Sarah's waist and waved with his other hand.

Martha waved back to them and then settled into her seat next to the driver. She was thankful that he was quiet on the drive home. She needed to think about all the events of the last two days. She was more anxious than ever to learn about her birth parents and the circumstances that led to the adoption. Paul had told her the mother had been Amish. It would have been a terrible disgrace to find herself pregnant and unwed. And her father, an Italian exchange student at the time, had no idea of Martha's existence. Without his full name and some idea as to where he lived in Italy, it would be impossible to trace him.

That didn't prevent her from dreaming about the possibility. When Paul had told her he'd seen a photograph of him, she'd felt almost resentful her aunt had never shared it with her. Didn't she have a right, after all, to know her roots? In their short visit together, there had been no opportunity for her to even question her aunt about the photo. Surely, she'd part with it now since Martha knew about him. She planned to write to her first thing and request it be sent to her. It was the least her aunt could do.

Martha arrived to find Naomi still at the apartment. The children Naomi sat for were both sick from a virus, so she wasn't going to be working for a day or two. The children's mother took time off from her job to stay home with them.

Since Martha had an hour before she had to be at

work, she changed into her waitressing clothes and sat at the kitchen table with Naomi, who was mending the torn sleeve of a blouse. When Martha told her about being adopted, Naomi placed her mending aside and listened attentively. After Martha finished telling her what she knew, Naomi sat in silence for several seconds. Finally, she spoke softly to Martha. "Oh wow. I don't know what to say. You must be totally in shock."

"I was, but it's finally sinking in. It explains a lot of things in my past. Mainly, my appearance. I never could understand why I didn't have blond hair and blue eyes like my whole family. When I'd bring it up, there was never a real explanation. It made me curious about my forefathers. There were other things, too. So often when my aenti was over, she and my mudder would be talking and the minute I came into the room, they'd hush. I figured they were discussing something about me and I could never imagine what I'd done."

"Are you going to try to meet your real mudder?"

"I would like to. Apparently, she wants to meet with me. I couldn't get much information this time. My folks were real upset that I knew. It was hard on everyone."

"They shouldn't have lied all those years. Why did they keep it a secret?"

"Mamm was afraid I wouldn't love her as much, I guess."

"I think that's silly."

"Of course. It wouldn't have mattered at all. But now, I'm pretty determined to find my birth mom. Her name is Rose. That's a pretty name, don't you think?"

"Jah, real pretty. I hope you can find her, Martha. And maybe someday you and your daed can meet."

"That would be so wonderful-gut. Well, I'd better head over. I have a few things to do first."

"And you said Paul showed up."

"Jah, but we'll talk tonight. There's so much to tell you. By the way, I will probably stay here until I marry."

"Really? Because of your folks?"

"Nee. Because of Daniel Beiler."

"Goodness, you sure have a lot to tell me, Martha. I can't wait until tonight."

Martha rolled her eyes as she nodded. "Jah, quite a drama, don't you think?" She grinned over as she made her way to the bathroom to fix her hair.

It was difficult for Sarah to talk about what had transpired. She put all her energy into scrubbing the kitchen floor. The heavy traffic from the day before had left its toll on the first floor, but especially on the kitchen linoleum. The physical effort helped calm her nerves. Maybe Lizzy would come by to chat. If not, her mother was always available. Melvin kept to himself most of the morning, mucking the stables and adding hay for bedding.

Once she completed her task, she rose and stretched her arms above her head to take the kinks from her sore back. Then she placed the coffee pot on the stove and sat at the table waiting for it to brew. Reaching into her apron pocket, she found the letter her friend had sent from Ohio.

Sarah reread the letter from Elizabeth and then tucked it back in her pocket. She should write back and thank her friend for keeping her informed. It might have been better not to know Rose was interested in finding Martha, though. Goodness, why, after all these years? At

least she'd stayed out of their lives while Martha was growing up. She was very thankful for that.

The sound of a buggy arriving interrupted her thoughts and she went to the window pleased to see it was Lizzy. Melvin took the reins from her sister and they spoke a few moments before Lizzy made her way to the back door. Sarah opened it for her sister, and after she was standing next to her in the kitchen, they embraced. Normally, they didn't bother since they saw each other so frequently, but today was special.

"Did you sleep okay last night?" Lizzy asked.

"Pretty gut. I was wore out from the party."

"Jah, you sure had a lot of people come through. Has Martha left yet?"

"Sure. She left early. She has to work lunch."

After hanging her woolen shawl over a peg, Lizzy went over to the stove and helped herself to a mug of coffee. "Any cake left from yesterday?"

"Oh jah. Back in the cupboard. Help yourself."

Lizzy picked out a sweet bun and laid it on a plate. "Want anything?" she asked before sitting at the table.

"I'll just stick to kaffi right now."

Lizzy sat and stirred in a teaspoon of sugar and then looked over at her sister with a solemn expression. "Think Martha's forgiven us all?"

"I ain't sure. She says everything is fine, but it just felt different. Did you notice?"

"To tell you the truth, after she took time to think about it all, she seemed like the same Martha we all love."

"I hope so. It was not an easy time for anyone. Don't think it helped to have Paul show up."

"He's a gut fellow for Martha. Just wish he didn't want

to stay in Lewistown. It sure doesn't seem right for him to keep her apart from her family."

"Don't forget he has a business now and a home. We have to look at the bright side."

"Schwester, I'm real proud of you. You're taking it better than I am."

"There just ain't much any of us can do about it, so I'm trying to make the best of it."

"This bun is gut. Who brought it?" Lizzy asked, changing the subject.

"I don't even know. There were so many people dropping food off the last couple days."

"You sure have a bunch of people who care about you."

Sarah laughed. "Jah, you'd think I turned a hundred with all that attention."

"Well, you're halfway there, schwester."

Sarah's smile faded as she stirred cream into her mug. "You think I should tell Martha about the letter I got from Elizabeth?"

"I don't know. Maybe, if she asks you for more information."

"I don't think she will. She knows it would hurt me more if she tries to meet with Rose."

"She's going to be curious, Sarah. You know that and you can't have any more lies between you."

"I guess. I'm not going to tell her though. If she asks me straight out, I won't lie, but I'm hoping she won't."

"If she asks me, I'm going to have to tell her what I know. I'm sick of keeping things inside."

"I'm sorry I asked you to. It wasn't right of me. I know that now."

"You were just afraid, is all." Lizzy reached across the table and patted her sister's hand. "I ain't upset with you."

"I hope that's true. I have to talk about something else." She cleared her throat and looked over at Lizzy.

"Sounds serious. What is it?"

"I found a lump. In my breast."

Lizzy's hand went to her mouth as she gasped. "Dear Gott. When?"

"A couple days ago. I'm going to call the doctor when I can get to the community phone."

"Another reason for allowing phones," Lizzy said, her brows lined with concern. "Does Melvin know?"

"Nee. What's the point in upsetting him? It may be nothing."

"You'll have to tell him. He knows you never bother to go to the doctor. No more secrets, Sarah. Tell him, or I will."

Sarah let out a long sigh. Then she put her hands up to her eyes. "I'm scared, Lizzy," she said faintly.

Lizzy moved over to Sarah's side of the table and put her arm around her sister. "I know. But you're right, it may be nothing to worry about. I'll go with you to the doctor, if you want."

"Jah, I would like that unless I end up telling Melvin," Sarah said, resting her head on her sister's shoulder. "I don't know what I'd do without you. And now with Martha…"

"I'll always be by your side, as long as the gut Lord allows me. Don't forget Gott, Sarah. Go to him in prayer. He'll provide you comfort."

"I've been praying a lot lately. He's making me stronger, Lizzy. I feel it."

Lizzy patted her sister's arm. "I'll take you in my buggy this morning to make that call. Don't wait."

Sarah moved away and used her apron to wipe away a tear. "Jah, that would be gut. And I'm not going to lie to Melvin, but we just don't have to mention anything quite yet, okay?"

"All right. For now, but he should go to the doctor with you."

Sarah nodded. "Jah, I guess I'll tell him after I make the appointment. Poor man, he don't take news like this too easy."

"No one does, but he has a right to know. Come on now. We can come back and heat our kaffi up after you make that call. I won't rest until you do."

"You sound more like Mamm than my schwester," Sarah said, attempting humor. The women went out to the buggy, leaving their coffee time behind. Sometimes it seemed like problems came in bunches. This was sure one of those times.

## Chapter Twenty-Two

Paul and Ben Johnson, the new carpenter, worked together at the new building, painting the walls of the area they expected to use as a showroom. Jeremiah continued to work on the cabinet samples they planned to add, now that they had the space for display. With three men working, he and Paul wanted to expand their inventory.

It helped to stay busy. When Paul was finished with the business end of the decorating, he had plans to work on their new home.

Martha was able to convince Dawn to spend an extra hour with her cousin on the evening of the baptismal instructions. This would allow time for her and Paul to catch up on everything. They spoke every night for at least half an hour—and usually longer, but it was still better to talk face-to-face about important things.

When she arrived at Deborah's a few minutes early, Martha ran upstairs to say good night to the boys first, and then she came down and sat with Deborah and held little Mary while she told her friend about the adoption.

"You may not believe this, but I always wondered how

you got that wonderful head of hair of yours. I'd have a hard time keeping mine covered if it looked like yours."

"Well, now I know why I'm darker, too. It's cool to realize I have Italian blood in me. I've always had a passion for pizza, so now I understand why."

"Goodness, I love it, too, but I'm totally German and Dutch." Deborah smiled over as she finished nursing the first twin, Miriam, while Mary continued sleeping in Martha's arms.

"Did you tell Paul yet?" Deborah asked.

"Jah, but he already knew." Martha then explained the whole situation and told Deborah she wanted to meet her birth mother eventually.

"I'd feel the same way, and it doesn't change how you feel about your adoptive mamm, right?"

"That's right. I'll never stop loving her and Daed. They've been truly wonderful-gut parents. I couldn't have asked for better, but there's something inside of me that needs to know about my blood family. Maybe I have half-bruders and schwesters, as well. I doubt I'll ever meet my daed though. I wouldn't know how to even begin looking for him."

"I wonder if he stayed in Italy. You should at least try. Maybe your blood mamm will know where he is."

"I doubt it. She didn't even tell him she was carrying a boppli."

"And you're going back home in April?"

Martha explained the circumstances with Daniel returning and the preference to stay away from Paradise for a while longer. As they talked about the arrangements, Paul came through the door. He looked so wonderful. She felt her heart swell at his sight. They held hands in

front of their friends, but they saved anything more intimate for their moments in private.

Ebenezer came down after reading a bedtime story to the boys and greeted Paul. "You must be nearly done with your instructions by now," he said. He reached for Mary and held her against his chest, patting her gently.

"We won't finish till April," Paul said.

"Well, next week is the beginning of March," Ebenezer said. "Time goes fast."

"Not fast enough," Paul said. He looked over at Martha, who smiled back.

"Jah, way too slow for me, too," she noted.

"We'd better head over, Martha. We don't want to be late. Is Dawn giving us any extra time?"

"She is. We'll have more than an hour after we're finished."

"I'm glad."

"We'll leave you alone when you come back," Deborah remarked. "I know it's hard to always have people around."

"That sounds gut, Deborah. Danki," Paul said.


Their instructions went well and when they returned to Deb and Eb's house they sat in private and discussed everything they hadn't had time to talk about when he visited Martha's home for the party.

"I hope Daniel won't be a problem," he added after discussing his return to the community.

"That's one reason why I've decided to stay on at the apartment and continue working. That way I won't run into him, and I'll be putting money aside for our expenses."

"I feel better knowing you won't see him. Were your folks okay about you staying put?"

"Not thrilled, but they've pretty much accepted that I'm independent now. Maybe they're even a little relieved. It's hard to tell."

"And I'm glad they know about our plans."

She nodded. "I think we're more open with each other now, since the adoption thing. No more secrets. At least, I hope it's better now."

"We must never keep things from each other, Martha. Even if it's hard to talk about some things, we need to be open."

"I agree, Paul. So far, you know everything there is to know about me."

He leaned over and kissed her for the first time that evening. "And I love everything about you."

"You aren't upset about me being adopted?"

"Not at all. Just don't get an Italian temper."

"I'm sure that's way exaggerated. One of the other waitresses I work with has Italian blood and she's the sweetest, calmest maed I've ever met."

"I'm teasing. I'm the one who has to watch his temper. Though without Daniel around, I don't have much of a problem."

"Jah, he brings out the worst in people, that's for sure."

"I just heard a car on the drive. I'm afraid it's your ride."

Martha nodded. "Jah, it's time to leave. I can't wait until we never have to say good-bye again."

"Soon, sweetheart. Soon." He walked her out to the car and watched as they drove away. Then he went back to the house to see his friends. Good thing for friends.


Sarah and Melvin sat in the doctor's waiting room together. Melvin reached for an outdated *Time* magazine

and flipped through the pages, barely absorbing a single word. Sarah just sat and looked at the television hanging on the wall across from them. It was a news station and a panel was discussing the situation in the Middle East. Always war, she thought. Would it ever be otherwise? If everyone thought the way she and her Amish friends thought, there'd be no such thing as war. Why didn't they just wake up?

"Mrs. Troyer?" a nurse asked the waiting group scattered about the room.

"Jah, that's me," Sarah said, her heart quickening as she and Melvin stood at the same moment. They followed the young red-headed woman down a hallway where there was a scale set up along with some other equipment.

"I'll get your weight and your blood pressure first." After the preliminary work was done, they were taken to a small cubicle with an examining table and a small desk set up with a computer. She was given a hospital gown and told to take her clothing off above the waist and then hang her clothes on a hook for that purpose. "Dr. Butler will be with you shortly," the nurse said, smiling sweetly.

"Danki. Thank you," Sarah said softly as her husband nodded. He took a seat and began pulling on his blondish-gray beard. Sarah did as she was told and then sat down next to her husband.

"Now don't be so nervous," she said to Melvin. "We've been through this before."

"Jah. Jah. I know. I ain't nervous."

She clucked as she shook her head. With this, there was a soft knock on the door and a tall thin man in his fifties came in and greeted them. He was somber look-

ing, but neatly attired in a white coat. "And what brings you in, Mrs. Troyer?" He took the revolving chair by the desk and swiveled the chair to face them.

"I found a lump. Here." She pointed to her right breast.

"Sarah had cancer when she was young," Melvin added.

"I see. Let me get some of your history then before I examine you." It took a few minutes for him to get the information he needed. Then he asked her to sit up on the examining table. He took his time checking her breasts. When he was done, he told her to dress and he'd return shortly. He then took her chart and left the room.

"He didn't say much," Melvin noted.

"Not yet." Her hands trembled as she pulled her dress over her head and adjusted the pins.

"You need help?"

"I got it." She sat down and reached for his hand. "I'm a little scared."

"I know, honey. Me, too."

"I wish Martha was here."

"She'll be home next month, maybe."

"I miss her, that's for sure."

He nodded. They sat silently, but he cupped her hand between his and raised it to his lips. An unusual display of affection and much appreciated.

The doctor returned and took a seat. His expression never changed. "We'll do a mammogram when I'm done here. We have the equipment on site. When's the last time you had one?"

"I never had one. I don't even know what it is."

"I see. It's like an x-ray, but more specific. You do have a tumor, but this will give us more precise infor-

mation. Fortunately, you discovered it while it was still fairly small."

"Jah. I was washing with soap and I felt—"

"Yes, you mentioned it before. I'll have the results by tomorrow afternoon. I don't suppose you have a phone."

"Nee. I want one, but my husband—"

"I know. It not part of the rules. Can you call us then from a public phone?"

"Jah, we'll call you," Melvin said gruffly. "What time?"

"Around four tomorrow. The radiologist will need time to read it. There are others ahead of you."

He rose and mentioned the nurse would come in and take her for the mammogram.

After he left, Melvin grunted. "Not real friendly."

"As long as he's gut."

"It would help if he wasn't so quick talking."

"Jah, but everyone says he's the best doctor around. Even Lizzy knew about him."

"Jah, and your schwester knows everything," he said sarcastically.

She rolled her eyes and folded her arms. There was no love lost between her husband and her older sister. There were times they barely spoke to each other.

Finally, she had the mammogram and they headed back home. Melvin barely spoke. She knew he was worried, just as she was. It had been years since her hysterectomy, and they'd ceased to be concerned about the cancer reoccurring.

"We should stop off and tell Lizzy and Leroy what we know," Sarah suggested.

"We don't know much of anything."

"Well, Lizzy will worry if she doesn't hear what happened."

"All right. We'll stop, but it will be time for milking soon, so we can't stay long."

A few minutes later, he pulled the buggy into their drive and secured the horse to a hitching post. "Remember what I said."

"Oh, jah. How could I forget," she said under her breath, irritated by his mood.

Lizzy seemed pleased that she'd had the tests done and tried to reassure her that it was probably nothing. After a few minutes, they left and arrived home just in time for their normal milking hour. Often Sarah helped Melvin in the barn, but not today. She headed over to her parents' home and let herself in the door. They had not yet been informed of the potential problem, and Sarah had no intention of mentioning it quite yet. No sense in getting everyone all worked up, when it might be nothing.

Her father was lying down and she told her mother not to bother him since she would be leaving shortly to start supper.

"I don't think we'll come over for supper tonight, dear," her mother said.

"Because of Daed? He's too weak?"

"I guess you could say that. He don't want to go out when it's cold. I have eggs so I'll scramble them up with some potatoes."

"I can bring rice pudding over later."

"Jah, he'd like that. How come you weren't over earlier? I thought we'd work on Martha's quilt."

"I had to run errands with Melvin. We can work on it tomorrow maybe."

"Gut. It's slow going. My eyes just ain't what they used to be."

A few minutes later, Sarah saw Melvin heading for the house. "I best be going now, Mamm. Say hi to Daed for me." She stood up and put her jacket on.

After supper, with conversation at a minimum, they sat in the sitting room and Melvin read from the Bible. Then he prayed out loud, which was unusual. After going through a litany of family and friends, he began asking God to help Sarah. His voice cracked and he stopped speaking altogether for several moments. Sarah peeked over and realized he was fighting back tears. She reached for his hand and he stopped praying and looked over. "Honey, I'm so afraid I'll lose you. You have to promise to fight hard if it's bad news. I don't know how I'd manage without you."

"Oh, Melvin. I know you're afraid. That's why you acted so grouchy before, jah?"

"Did I now? I didn't realize. I'm sorry, peaches."

"You haven't called me that in years. Not since that time we worked in old man Joe's orchard picking peaches."

"I guess I haven't. I hope Gott forgives me for cutting Him off like I did."

"I'm sure he understands. We can finish silent-like if you want."

"Maybe."

He continued to hold her hand as he bent his head down and remained still. When he looked up, Sarah was still praying. He looked at her sweet face. Such peace. She'd already come to grips about the possibilities that lay ahead. She was a wonderful-gut woman and he hoped he'd have many years left with her. *Let it be Gott's will.*

# Chapter Twenty-Three

Sarah busied herself the next day in the dawdi-haus. First, she cleaned the white tile bathroom for her parents and then scrubbed their kitchen from top to bottom. Her mother, Nancy, watched in wonderment as her daughter accomplished in two hours what would take her two weeks. What a blessing!

After dumping the dirty water outside, Sarah put everything back in its rightful place and then sat on one of the straight chairs in the sitting room waiting for the floor to dry in the kitchen. Her father seemed more cheerful than usual. Sarah pulled one of their small accent pillows over from the sofa next to her, plumping it up before placing it behind her back. "Do you need anything done, Daed?"

"Nope, you've worked enough for one day."

"Mamm and I are going to quilt this afternoon till Melvin and I go out."

"Where you going?"

"Oh, just an errand or two."

"Can you get me some cough drops when you're out, Sarah?"

He called over to his wife, who was pulling out the quilting frame hidden behind the sofa. "Give Sarah some money, Nancy."

"It's okay, Daed," Sarah said. "I can certainly afford to buy you a box of cough drops."

"Know the kind I want?"

"Jah, the ones you always get."

"That's right, and make sure it's the same flavor. Eucalyptus."

"Are you getting a fresh cold, Daed?" she asked.

"Don't think so. I just like to suck on them. They feel gut on my throat."

Nancy looked over and frowned. "You wouldn't need anything if you hadn't smoked all those years. You're lucky you don't have lung cancer."

Sarah shook her head in agreement.

"Well, I stopped ten years ago. Give me credit for that."

"I'm glad we stopped growing tobacco when we did. It ain't healthy for anyone."

"We didn't know much back then. People lied to us. Makes you wonder what's true even today." He turned to his daughter. "You're mighty lucky that cancer never came back to you, Sarah."

She looked down at the floor and nodded, but didn't look over at her father. Hopefully, the results would be favorable when they called the doctor's office later.

"Jah," her mother added. "After six, seven years, or something, they say you're cured. It's been that long for you, Sarah. Gott is gut."

"Mamm, Gott is gut whether he lets me be healthy or lets me get sick. I don't blame Gott when things go wrong. We live in a sinful world."

"That's for sure."

"We'd better sew now because I'm leaving around three thirty to run my errands."

"Don't you forget them cough drops," her dad reminded her as she walked over to her mother and helped her steady the frame.

They weren't even halfway through their project yet. She was surprised her sister Lizzy hadn't arrived to help. If it was a serious condition, Sarah wanted to make sure the quilt was finished before... Nee, no sense dwelling on the sad things in life. "I'll push it by the window with you, Mamm. We need good lighting if I'm going to keep my stitches the way Lizzy likes them."

Her mother laughed and nodded. "Jah, you'll hear about it if they ain't just right, for sure."

Later that afternoon Melvin and Sarah headed out to make that crucial phone call. Melvin directed their horse to the neighbor's barn where the community phone was available. "You want me to make the call?" he asked.

"Maybe. Jah."

He checked the business card they'd given him and plugged in the numbers. He was surprised to hear the doctor's voice as he answered. "It's me, Melvin Troyer," he responded. Sarah watched her husband's expression, which never changed during the entire conversation. She hoped it would offer her a clue. It didn't.

When he hung up, he turned his eyes to hers. "He wants us to come in tomorrow morning. It ain't gut news." Then he turned away as he cleared his throat.

Sarah knew he was trying to be strong for her. She kept calm as she took his arm and led him back to the

waiting buggy. "It's okay, Melvin. I feared it was not gut. We'll get through it, and I'll be just fine again."

He nodded, but his gait told her all she had to know. His normally quick steps had changed to those of a defeated old man, and he wasn't even old.

"We have to stay strong, Melvin. For each other."

"It's sure hard, Sarah. I hate to think of you going through all that again."

"I know. I know. I ain't looking forward to it, but I'm a strong Amish woman. You'll see. I beat those old cancer cells once, I can do it again."

"I think sometimes, you're stronger than I am," he added as he took her hand to help her into the buggy. He sure hadn't done that for years.

Sarah smiled at him and quickly wiped her forming tears as he walked around the back of the buggy to get the driver's seat. He was such a good man. And he was hurting. Her sweet husband was suffering—perhaps more than she was.

When they got back to the house, she spotted Lizzy's buggy. Maybe she should tell everyone at the same time. Dreading it, she and Melvin went into the dawdi-haus together. Lizzy looked up from the quilting frame, questioning with her eyes.

Their mother was concentrating on her stitches, but looked over her reading glasses at her daughter. "What an honor, you brought your husband with you. I bet you're looking for a goodie," she said directly to Melvin.

Sarah's father came in from the bedroom. "Hope you remembered my cough drops," he said. After seeing the serious expression on her face, he stopped walking and

looked from his daughter to her husband. "What's going on? Somebody die?"

"We have to tell you all something," Sarah started. "I didn't mean to look so upset. Can I have a cup of kaffi?"

"Well, sure now. Of course." Her mother removed her glasses and they all walked back into the kitchen. No one said a word, but Nancy pulled out some mugs and poured the hot liquid into each container as the others took seats at the table.

Sarah sat and looked over at her husband as she stirred her coffee.

"You want me to tell them?" he asked.

"Jah, I think so."

One could have heard the proverbial pin drop.

"We ain't real happy to have to tell you, but Sarah may have the old cancer back."

Nancy's hand went to her mouth as she shuddered. "Merciful day."

"In my breast," Sarah said, looking over at her mother.

"They have a lot of good results today," Lizzy stated after a few silent moments, futilely attempting to believe what she was saying. She looked over at Sarah, who was bravely holding back her emotions.

"That's true," Sarah said, nodding. "Tomorrow we'll get more information."

Her parents, who were sitting next to each other, held hands. Nancy's eyes became glassy. "Do you want me to go with you to your appointment?"

"Nee, that's okay. Melvin will be there. He can take notes, right, honey?"

"If you want."

"You'd better. I forget sometimes what they tell me."

He nodded, but became silent.

Lizzy cleared her throat. "Jah, Annie Jones had breast cancer, remember? She did real gut getting better. They didn't even have to do chemo."

"And that was at least ten years ago, right?" her mother asked.

"Jah. And I'm sure they know a lot more now."

"I hope so," Sarah said. She took a sip of coffee as the others sat quietly, each contemplating the news and the effects it had on the family and them personally.

"I just want everyone to know," Sarah started, "that however it ends up, I'm real sure I'm going to be okay. I have faith in Gott and I trust Him here in my heart." She touched her chest with her hand. "I know His will, will be done. I hope it's His will that I'll get through this and be well again, but if not..." She turned her eyes to Melvin. "Just take care of my dear Melvin if he is alone someday."

Melvin put his hands up to his eyes and shook his head.

"This is too much," Nancy said, her voice trembling. "I ain't going to let you say any more, dochder. We are going to look at the bright side, for certain. Now, let me look in the cupboard for the rest of those molasses cookies I baked a couple days ago and we'll stop with this sad talk right here and now. Gott will make you better and that's that."

No one argued with Nancy when she got her dander up. Slowly, the group settled onto more pleasant conversation and Nancy passed her delicious soft molasses cookies around the table as she put a second pot on to perk.

The hard part for Sarah was writing to Martha. Finally, after several false starts that evening, she told Mel-

vin she'd wait to talk to her daughter in person. She needed to know how serious her condition was as well. Perhaps it wasn't even cancerous. Why get her daughter worked up for nothing?

The next day, Melvin and she went once more to the doctor's office. They were barely seated when the nice nurse came over to tell them the doctor was ready to see them. Again, they made their way to his office. He was already sitting at his desk, working on the computer. He looked up as they entered and waved his arm toward two chairs and then finished typing something into the computer.

Melvin turned his dark felt hat around in his hands as he stared at the floor. Sarah felt a hot flash come on and waved an old magazine to cool her sweating forehead.

Finally, Dr. Butler rolled his chair around to face them. "I told your husband that the mammogram showed a tumor. Before we can plan your treatment, we need to know exactly what we're dealing with. I'm sending you over to Dr. Harriman, who is the head of oncology. I've discussed it with him, and he wants to start the testing immediately. With your history of cancer, we need to work swiftly."

"Will they do testing today?" Melvin asked.

"I imagine so." He rose, took the folder with her charts and led them down a long hallway, through double doors and into a separate area with a waiting room filled with patients, some of whom wore scarves over their bald heads. The doctor introduced them to a pleasant, round-faced woman in her forties and then wished them well, as he turned to leave.

"Danki," Melvin said, frowning. He hoped Dr. Harriman would have a better manner.

"Now, it will be a few minutes before the doctor can see you," the nurse informed them. "Would you like to wait where you can watch the television?"

"Nee. Don't like what I see on that thing," Melvin said firmly. "We'll wait by the fish tank."

"That's fine. I'll let you know when a room is available. My name is Milly if I can do anything for you. Coffee?"

Melvin shook his head and looked over at his wife.

"No, thank you," she said. "We'll watch the fish."

Waiting was always difficult and this was no exception. After what seemed like an hour, but was only about twenty minutes, a pleasant looking man of average build and curly white hair came out to greet them. They liked him immediately. "Well, folks, you can follow me. I have the last office on the left. Take seats and I'll be right behind you."

After they were all seated, the doctor sat back in his chair and looked directly over at them. "It's difficult to tell you how we'll proceed until we do some studies to determine how far the cancer has spread—if at all. Hopefully, we've caught it early. We'll do some blood work and take a chest x-ray today. Then we'll set you up for a CAT scan. Once we decide whether it's confined or has made its way into your lymph nodes, we can do the staging."

"Staging?" Sarah asked.

"Yes. We want to know the exact size, the form it's taken, whether it's lobular or ductal—"

"Those are big words," Melvin said, raising his hand. "We just need to know if it's real bad or not, and will you be able to cure her."

"These are ways of determining her prognosis. If it

has spread, we call it metastasis, and that will be important to know in order to determine whether she'll need surgery at this time, or perhaps we'll need to start with radiation or chemo. I know you're anxious for answers, but I don't want to make predictions until we know exactly what we're dealing with.

"Our goal will be to cure you with the least amount of trauma for you to deal with. We're a team here, Sarah. We will be working together. It may be a fairly simple procedure, but we have to evaluate the treatment after the testing is done." He cleared his throat and folded his hands on the desk. "Do you have any questions for me?"

"Nee, do you, Melvin?"

He shrugged. "I guess we just have to wait and see."

"I know it's difficult, but it is for the best. Now, I'll write up the tests we need and have someone take you down to the lab and get things started." He rose and extended his hand to Melvin, who also stood up.

"Danki," Melvin said, shaking his hand.

A few minutes later, a new nurse came in and took them to yet another area of the building where they drew a number and sat and waited to be called. It was reassuring to Sarah to be in the clinic where the people surrounding her seemed to know what they were doing, and showed concern for her and Melvin. She was confident she was going to beat this thing—the big "C."

Melvin smiled over at her. He, too, looked more confident now that there was a plan. Besides, God was in charge.

# Chapter Twenty-Four

It had been nearly a month since Martha had learned of her adoption. She figured enough time had passed, and she could write to her aunt and request more information about the whereabouts of her birth mother. She was also anxious to have the photo of her father. Now that it was no longer a secret, there was no need to keep the picture in hiding.

One evening after a slow day at the restaurant, she sat down to write her request, when she heard the doorbell ring. Naomi was out with her new boyfriend, so she went to answer. When she opened the door, she nearly fainted. It was Daniel Beiler!

"How…how did you know where I live?" she asked, standing rigid with her hand on the door knob.

"Now, that's not very friendly. I thought you'd be pleased to see an old friend."

"Daniel, you know you're not welcome here."

He removed his hat and softened his tone. "I just wanted to see you again, and tell you I'm sorry for what I've done in the past. Please give me a few minutes. I'll leave whenever you ask."

Releasing a long breath, she stood back from the door and waved him in. "You can sit on the chair over there," she said, pointing to a chair opposite the sofa.

He nodded and quietly took his appointed seat. She moved over to the sofa and sat on the edge of the cushion, waiting for him to start the conversation.

"I overheard one of your relatives talk about you last Sunday at church service. I got in on the conversation and they told me about the town where you were living and about the restaurant you worked at. I went there and talked to one of the other waitresses about you and said I was an old friend from school. She told me where you lived. I know things were bad last time we saw each other. I just didn't want to leave it that way, Martha. We once loved each other, so at least we can be friendly to each other, jah?"

It made sense at the moment. "Okay. We can talk to each other when we are together at functions, but that's all."

He nodded. "I'm seeing Molly Zook now."

"I'm glad, Daniel. She's a nice maed, and I think she's always had a crush on you."

"I'm not saying it's serious, but I'm trying to get over you. I just wanted you to know. I'm sorry for the way I acted before, especially with Paul. Are you still seeing him?"

"I am, and it is serious. It wouldn't have worked out between you and me, Daniel. We thought too differently from each other. I can't live so somber-like."

"I understand. I'm trying to be lighter with people. It's hard. Well, you know my family. I don't think I've ever heard my parents laugh."

"That's sad."

"Jah, I realize that now. Too late, I'm afraid."

"Maybe Molly can make you laugh more."

He actually grinned over. "She tickled me once. That was funny."

Martha giggled. "Guess I never thought to do that."

"I'm gonna leave now, Martha, but I just wanted to let you know, I'm not the weird guy you thought I was."

They rose at the same time. As they reached the door, he replaced his hat and then stopped and turned toward her. "Sorry to hear about your mamm."

"What are you talking about?"

"Her cancer. It's a shame."

"She got over that years ago."

His brows raised. "Nee, haven't you heard?"

"Stop! Tell me! What's going on?"

"I guess I shouldn't have said anything, but I just heard Sunday that she's got cancer."

"Oh, dear Gott, can it be true?"

"Maybe I heard wrong, Martha. Check with your daed. I hope I didn't say something I shouldn't. I can't seem to stay out of trouble with my mouth."

Martha began to shake. She grabbed on to the door trim, fearing she was about to faint.

"Are you okay?" She felt Daniel's hand on her arm.

"I… I don't know."

"Sit down," he said, leading her back to the sofa.

"Why would they not tell me?" she muttered as she put her head on the back cushion. "I thought we weren't going to have lies between us."

"I think she just found out herself. Maybe she wanted to tell you in person."

"I must get home. Can you drive me back with you?

I can get a driver to bring me back here when I'm ready. I have to see my mamm."

"Sure. Of course. But you'd better wait till you're feeling better. I'll get you some water."

"Jah. Water. I'll call in tomorrow to the restaurant. I wasn't scheduled anyway till the following day. Oh, this is horrible! I can't believe it! Poor Mamm." Martha burst into tears as Daniel returned with a glass of water.

He set it down on the coffee table and patted her arm. "They cure a lot of people now, Martha. Think positive."

"She had cancer before. Oh, this is terrible."

Daniel held on to her arm and then encouraged her to drink some water.

She took a sip and pushed the glass away. "I need to pack some things. Do you mind waiting?"

"Of course I don't mind. Anything I can do for you?"

"Nee. My head is clearer now. I'll be quick."

"Take your time, Martha. I'm in no rush."

"How did you get here?"

"A friend brought me. He's waiting in his car."

"Oh mercy, maybe you should go tell him what's going on."

"I will. I'll leave the door unlocked and be right back. Don't try to carry your things yourself. You're too shocked. You might fall."

As she reached for her few pieces of clothing, she realized her hair was in a long braid and uncovered. She flushed as she realized Daniel had seen her that way. He hadn't mentioned a thing about it, which was good. Maybe he hadn't noticed. She quickly wrapped her braid around her head and placed a kapp on top. Then she threw several days' worth of underwear in a small suitcase, added her bible, her toothbrush and her hair brush

and snapped it shut. She looked around the room. She'd have to leave a note for her roommate, which she wrote hurriedly in pencil and placed on the kitchen table.

Daniel returned and took her suitcase in one hand, leaving his other hand free in case she needed support. She managed without his help and suggested he sit up front with his friend while taking her place in the back seat. His English friend seemed polite and she closed her eyes and prayed once they got on the road for Paradise. They stopped once on the way where they used the facilities and Daniel purchased hamburgers for all three of them, which they ate in the car before taking off again.

It was eight thirty when the friend pulled up at Martha's home. There were still lamps on downstairs, though the dawdi-haus was dark.

Daniel walked up to the kitchen door as Martha turned the knob. It was unlocked. She opened it and called out. Within a minute, her father was in the kitchen, lantern in hand, to see if he'd been hearing things. "My goodness, Martha, you gave me the fright of my life! Daniel, what on earth are you doing here?"

"I heard Mamm is sick! Tell me it isn't true, Daed!"

"Oh, honey. I'm sorry. It is true. She has breast cancer."

"Oh, dear Lord in heaven." Martha began crying uncontrollably. Melvin put his arms around her and added his own tears. Steps were heard from the hall, as Sarah came into the room with her own lamp. She already had her night clothes on and she held her bathrobe in place. She nearly dropped the lamp when she saw her daughter and Daniel standing in the kitchen with her Melvin weeping aloud.

"Martha! My word, why are you here, practically in

the middle of the night?" She looked over at Daniel, questioning with her eyes.

"I'm afraid it's because of me. I went by to tell Martha I was sorry for the way I'd acted, and then I said I was sorry about you being sick, and then… Well, here we are. She insisted on coming."

"Mamm," Martha said, "Why didn't you tell me? I thought we weren't going to keep secrets anymore. I'm so upset."

Sarah reached for her daughter and they embraced. "I was waiting to get more information, honey. I didn't want to worry you for nothing."

"But you're sure it's cancer?"

"Jah. We just don't know how serious it is, or what they will do. I hope they can cure me without the radiation. I don't want my hair to fall out again."

"Oh, Mamm, who cares about hair? I just want you to be all better. You have to be." The tears continued to flow.

Daniel had stood watching quietly from the doorway. "I'll get your suitcase, Martha. Then I'd better go."

She turned to Daniel. "Danki for bringing me home. I'll never forget it."

He nodded. "Perhaps my friend can take you back when you're ready. I'll stop by to see how you're all doing tomorrow and maybe you'll have a better idea about when you'll need a ride."

Melvin thanked him and went out with him so he could bring the suitcase in and save Daniel a trip.

"I'm sorry you got so upset, Martha," her mother said, reaching for a tissue in her robe. She handed an extra one to her daughter, who wiped her eyes.

"You got through the other time, Mamm. You can

do it again. They know a lot more today about treating cancer, that's for sure."

"Jah, you're absolutely right and I need to be at your wedding."

"And my children's weddings," Martha added.

"Come sit beside me on the sofa. Tell me about your job. And Paul. How's he doing?"

The two of them went and sat together, Martha's arm around her mother's shoulder. It was good to be home. Now that Daniel was not a threat—in fact he was actually kind to her—she could move back sooner. If she needed money, she could work part time somewhere, though her place would now be with her mother. She would offer her support. They would fight this malignancy together, and with God's strength in them, they'd defeat those horrible cancer cells and have many wonderful-gut years together as a family.

# Chapter Twenty-Five

Eventually, Martha and her parents made their way to bed, though it was at least an additional hour before Martha closed her eyes. She left the kero lamp burning with the wick lowered, which flickered, causing shadows against the white walls of her familiar bedroom. She'd always felt safe within these walls, with the knowledge of her parents' protection and love. Her childhood had been lonely at times when she'd feel the absence of siblings, but with so many relatives in her life, the happy times far out-numbered the moments of sadness.

Her mother was so brave. She didn't look for pity or show anger toward God. No, she accepted it as God's will and remained strong in her faith. Melvin, too, assured Martha the family would get through this and the pain and suffering would indeed pass. "Look how Jesus suffered on the cross," he said once during their discussion, "and it was for us. Suffering makes us stronger. Builds our character." Sarah had smiled as he spoke, nodding in agreement. "Jah, I'm going to have a nice character, that's for sure," she said with a wink at her husband.

Light from the half-moon came through the window.

Martha had forgotten to pull the shade. She allowed her childhood memories to once again drift through her mind. How many nights she had fallen asleep thinking about the amazing world her creator had made, and his unwavering love he had for his people.

"Danki, Gott. Just be with my mamm and daed…and me, as we struggle to remain strong through these next months. And help me make the right decisions about my future. Whatever I decide, help Paul understand and support me."

She stopped and sighed, then finally continued, "Help me forgive Daniel for the past and not hold anger in my heart. And bless my other mother, whom I've never met. Somehow let her know she did the right thing by letting me grow up here in this wonderful family. Amen."

She opened her eyes briefly, aware that the need to sleep was taking over. After lowering the wick till the light went off, she rested her head on her pillow and went into a deep and peaceful sleep. She was where she needed to be.

The next afternoon, Aunt Lizzy came by and was surprised to see her niece visiting. Martha told her what had happened and how she'd found out about her mother's illness. "Do you plan to move back, Martha?" her aunt asked.

"Jah, real soon, but I need to return and explain to my employers, as well as Naomi, about my change of plan. There's a girl Naomi knows, who might move right in with her. I hope so, since she'd have trouble paying the rent on her income alone. If it is a problem, I'll help out for a couple months till she finds someone. I'll miss my job, but my place is here."

"Does Paul know your plans?"

She shook her head. "I need to get in touch with him. I wish we had phones."

"If you need a buggy ride to the community phone, you can use my buggy."

"Danki. I probably should let him know at once. I also plan to go back tomorrow and work the dinner shift, since I'm scheduled. Then I can talk to everyone about my change of plan. I know they'll understand. They're wonderful-gut people. I'll try to be home here by the weekend."

"Martha, I'm so glad you're coming back. Your mamm would never ask you to, but I know she wanted you here with her during this time. She loves you very much."

"I know, Aenti Lizzy. And you know I feel the same. That will never change."

Results from all the tests were back now and an hour-long appointment was scheduled for the following Monday. Martha planned to come back Sunday, if all went well. Now, more than ever, she knew she was needed at home. The three of them would go together to get the prognosis and hear the plan for treatment.

When Martha called Paul, he sounded rushed, so she spoke quickly about all that had transpired. When she told him about the cancer, she heard him take in a quick breath. "Oh, Martha, I'm so sorry. How did you learn about it?"

Martha told him about the surprise visit from Daniel and his accidentally mentioning it. Paul was silent for several moments.

"Daniel Beiler? He came to your apartment?"

"He wanted to apologize for his behavior."

"I bet. And play the consoling friend, no doubt."

"Paul, it wasn't like that. He was very sincere. He's changed."

"Don't believe it, Martha. A zebra doesn't lose its stripes. Remember that. After he told you about your mother, did he try to comfort you?"

"I don't like your attitude, Paul. It's like you're accusing me of something."

"Martha, not you, but I don't think Daniel would lose a chance to touch you or embrace you."

"He patted my arm. That was absolutely all."

"And you allowed it?"

"For heaven's sake, Paul, you're jealous! He merely acted as any friend would act."

"Okay. So then what?"

"Well, I wanted to get right over to my parents, so he let me go back with him."

"You couldn't wait to get a regular ride?"

"Paul, did you hear me? My mother has cancer! She needed me to be with her. I didn't care how I'd get here, I just wanted to get home. Surely, you understand."

"I'm trying. I really am, but it blows my mind to think of his being with you like that."

"And I'm shocked at your reaction. Don't you trust me?"

"It has nothing to do with trust." Paul's voice had an edge to it.

"Oh, I think it does. You act like I'm going to fall all over him, just because my mother is ill. We can be friends, you know."

"I'm sorry, I guess I did overreact. Forgive me?"

"Of course. But please don't act so jealous again. I don't like it."

"It was childish of me. When can we see each other next? I think we need to get past this."

"I don't know. I have to go back, work the rest of the week and be home by Sunday, since Mamm's appointment is Monday. It's an important session, since we should know better about her treatment then."

"You'll miss the baptism class."

"Jah, I expect I will."

"Well, I guess it can't be helped. I'll call the bishop and explain."

"Danki. Now I need to go help Mamm."

"Tell her I'll be praying for her, and for your whole family. I love you, sweetheart."

"Danki. Love you, too, and I'll tell them. We can talk tomorrow evening. I'll be back at the apartment."

"You call me when you have time. I'll probably be at our house painting the kitchen."

"Okay. Gut nacht, Paul."

After she hung up, she stood a moment thinking about their conversation. It was really the first time they'd been angry with each other. Certainly, a poor time to act like a jealous husband. My goodness, how childish!

She made her way back to the waiting buggy and headed home. She wanted to bake a cherry pie—her mother's favorite—before leaving for her apartment the next day. She pictured her mother's face when she'd see it bubbling up in the oven.

"Hey, Paul, what's wrong? I haven't seen a smile all day," Ben Johnson, their new carpenter, asked.

"Sorry, I've just had stuff on my mind."

"It's okay, but if you need to talk, I'm always here."

They painted in silence for several minutes, and then

Paul laid his paintbrush aside temporarily. "I know it shouldn't bother me, but I can't help it. My girl's mother just found out she has cancer, so Martha's going back to live at her home for a while."

"I'd think that was the right thing to do, don't you?" Ben asked as he bent down to paint along the floor molding.

"Sure. That wasn't the problem. She found out about her mamm when an old boyfriend stopped by to tell her."

"Still don't see a problem."

"He lives more than an hour away and he's Amish. Not like he can just up and drive himself."

"Yeah, now I'm following you, I think. There's more?"

"I think he planned the whole thing so she'd break down and he'd be there to offer comfort, if you know what I mean."

"I thought you were going to marry this girl."

"I still am."

"Then I wouldn't worry about it. Maybe they're just friends now."

"You think I'm just overreacting?"

He smiled over. "Sounds that way to me, Paul. What did she say about it?"

"That they're just friends." He smiled a crooked smile. Paul picked up his brush again, dipped it into the paint and picked up where he'd left off.

"There you are. Not a big deal in my book. She probably wouldn't have mentioned him if he meant more than friendship."

"You'd have to know the guy to understand my feelings. He and I got in a major fight over her once."

"A real fight? Literally?"

"Almost."

Ben whistled through his teeth. "Sounds English to me."

"I'm not proud of it, but boy, did that guy push it. He's one guy I don't like."

"Well, it sounds as if you're letting those thoughts color your feelings. Unless your girl acts differently around you the next time you're together, I don't think there's anything to worry about. I'm sorry about her mother. Hopefully, she'll make it through okay."

"Jah, I sure hope so. She's a nice woman and she's not very old." He told Ben about her earlier bout with cancer and then he mentioned the adoption.

"I met your girl once, didn't I? She came in the shop to see you?"

"That was her."

"She seems like a really nice girl. You're lucky. I'm dating a new girl now. She's a Methodist, but she's agreed to attend the Mennonite service next week with me. I think she'd consider changing churches, if we got more serious."

"That would be a big step," Paul said.

"We agree on a lot of things."

"And also disagree on some according to your beliefs, jah?"

"Yes, but we agree on the most important things. Like Jesus is the son of God. Salvation is by grace. Important things like that."

Jeremiah came into the room and put his hands on his hips as he turned completely around to check on their painting job. "Looks real gut," he said. "You guys have done a lot today. I'm going to go pick up a couple pizzas. Want anything on them?"

"Plain is fine," Paul said.

"Yup, plain like us," Ben said with a chuckle.

# Chapter Twenty-Six

Martha was relieved to know Naomi's friend was excited to move in to the apartment when she left, and Joe and Betty, her employers, were understanding about her sudden departure. They planned to hire someone to replace her, but in the meantime, one of their past employees arranged to come in on a temporary basis.

Everything seemed to be falling into place.

"I'll sure miss you," Naomi said as she sat on the edge of the bed and watched Martha packing up her few belongings. "You never even got to meet my boyfriend. I wanted your opinion."

"Bring him by later tonight. I don't have to work."

"Jah, but he does. He's putting in hours stocking shelves at a hardware store in the next town just so we can be ready to marry sooner. Oh, I'm so excited."

"Have you told your folks about leaving the Amish yet?"

"Not yet. I haven't had the courage, but when I go home in two weeks, I'm going to tell them."

"I owe you some money on the phone this month," Martha mentioned.

"It's okay. You haven't even been on the phone that

much this week. How come? Paul putting in too much work?"

"We just don't seem to have much to say right now."

"Still upset about his jealousy thing?"

"I'm trying not to be, but even after telling him how I felt, he still asks if I've heard from Daniel. It's annoying."

"Have you?"

"What? Heard from him? No, and I probably won't."

"What if he knows you're back and comes by to see you?"

"I can handle it now. It's easier since we're just friends."

"Right. From what you've told me, he probably still has hopes."

"I've told him outright that Paul and I are going to marry."

"That wouldn't stop some guys. Not till you're actually married."

"If he becomes a problem, I'll let him know that he can't come around anymore. I really don't think he'll bother. He's seeing Molly Zook again."

"They'd probably make a gut couple. Both on the boring side."

Martha laughed. "That sounds so mean, Naomi. Shame on you."

"I guess it wasn't nice to say, but you have to admit, it's true. Molly talks about her two dogs constantly. Goodness, what's to say about dogs?"

"I've seen them. They're both German shepherds. Really nice animals."

"But they're still animals."

"Jah, true. I think it's a gut match though. She's really a sweet person."

"When is your ride coming?"

"Tomorrow around noon."

"I'll be at work. We'll have to say good-bye tonight. I'll miss you a ton."

"Me, too. Come by to see me when you visit your family."

"I will. I'll try to anyway. You'll have to come visit me, too. You have to meet Tyler. I know you'll love him."

"Not love, Naomi. You don't really mean that."

She giggled. "That's for sure, but you can like him a lot."

"I'm sure I will."

The next day, Martha finished her breakfast and then cleaned up before making a last-minute check. She'd packed everything she'd brought with her, plus a few more things she'd added since being there. She left the beautiful red dress in the closet for Naomi. If she left the Amish, maybe she'd have occasion to wear it. Hopefully.

It was the first day of spring and it couldn't be any nicer. The sky was a rich blue with a few skimpy clouds along the horizon. The temperature was in the mid-sixties and clusters of daffodils attracted her eyes as she waited for her ride. At last, she saw Hank Hudson pull in. He gave her a hearty greeting and placed her carton and suitcase in the trunk.

Another chapter in her life was coming to a close. Maybe she'd keep a journal, she thought, as she buckled her seat belt and made her way back to Paradise.

Her parents were delighted to have her home again and her mother had baked some of her favorite cookies and bars. Goodness, if she ate them all, Martha would

expand her waistband by several inches. She'd limit herself to four cookies a day and encourage her father to pick up the slack.

On Monday, they sat quietly in the buggy as they made their way to the doctor's office, leaving a few minutes before schedule. Martha could tell her mother was nervous by the way she kept licking her lips and pulling on her kapp ribbon. No wonder. Her father, too, was displaying his telltale signs. He kept clearing his throat as he yanked one of his suspenders with his free hand.

After tethering the horse, the three of them went to the waiting room where they sat for nearly half an hour before being led back to the doctor's office. Then Dr. Harriman came in and introduced himself to Martha. He sat at the computer and brought up Sarah's information. After taking a few moments to review her chart, he turned to the silent family.

"We believe from the tests that the cancer's at a fairly early stage, which is a good thing. However, we'll know more after we extract the tumor surgically, and at that time we'll also remove the sentinel lymph node and test it for cancer cells. If it's clean, we won't need to worry about any other nodes being infected. If it has spread though, we'll have to go further, and depending upon the extent of the cancer, it might be necessary to start chemotherapy afterward. It's too soon to know."

"Oh, I hope not. It made me so sick before," Sarah said, tearing up.

"I hope it won't be necessary," the doctor said, nodding over. "The CAT scan showed the tumor to be five centimeters, so it needs to be removed."

"Will you have to take off the whole breast?" Sarah asked.

"Not at this point. I'm planning on breast conserving surgery, but it will mean radiation afterward to make sure the cancer hasn't spread."

"That ain't as bad," Sarah added, twisting her hands in her lap.

"When do you think you'll have time to do the surgery?" Melvin asked.

"I'd like to schedule it for late this week. My nurse will come in to discuss it with you. I'm sorry I couldn't be more encouraging."

"It's okay," Sarah said, her lips trembling. "I'm not worried—too much."

Martha hadn't said a word. There was so much to grasp. "Will my mother have to stay in the hospital for long?"

He turned his attention to Martha. "Hopefully not. If all goes well, it will only be a few days. Any other questions?" he asked, addressing all three of them.

"Nee. I guess not," Melvin said.

"Then if you'll remain in here, I'll get my nurse to come in and discuss the date for the surgery." He typed a few notes into the computer and then nodded as he left the room.

"He seems nice, Mamm," Martha said after he left.

"He's supposed to be gut," her father said. "I asked around and a couple of my friends had heard about him."

"Jah, I have gut feelings about him," Sarah stated. "I ain't scared."

"Oh, Mamm," Martha said as she reached for her mother's hand.

The nurse knocked and then entered. "Maybe you re-

member me. My name's Milly," she said as she smiled at them. "We'll try to get you in right away and start making you well again," she said pleasantly to Sarah.

The date and time were established. It was set up for Friday of that same week at seven in the morning. Then Milly made an appointment for the pre-surgical testing and handed several papers over to Sarah, who handed them to Melvin, who handed them over to Martha.

A few more things were discussed and then they made their way back to the waiting horse and buggy and they began their journey home. Again, it was a silent trip, but the clip-clopping of the horse's hooves on the pavement added a touch of normalcy. Martha loved hearing it even from the time she was a child. It was steady and reassuring. Things would turn out just fine, of that she was sure and certain.

## Chapter Twenty-Seven

That evening, Paul and Martha spoke for over an hour on the community phone. She wished he was there with her as she relayed the conversation with the surgeon. "Mamm tries to be so brave, but I can tell she's scared. I feel so bad."

"It's got to be hard on everyone. No one wants to see a loved one suffer. I'm sorry you have to go through this, Martha."

"I made the right decision about coming home. Even Daed mentioned it yesterday. He said it helped him, too, to have me here."

"I guess you haven't talked about our wedding."

"Nee, this isn't the time for wedding talk."

"You don't think we'll have to delay it, do you?"

Martha bit her lower lip. "I hope not, but things are too mixed up right now. I can't even think about the future."

"I'm glad they're going to operate right away. The sooner the better."

"Jah, that's for sure. I'll try to call you when it's over."

"You should call me when she goes into the operating room, too. We can pray together."

"Danki. Jah, I'll call, if it's possible."

"Is your aenti going to be there, too?"

"Jah. We stopped on our way home earlier and she and my onkel will be there. Probably my mammi and dawdi, too."

"That's gut. Families need to be there for each other."

"I wish you could be here, Paul, but I know you can't. I do understand. Well, I'm so exhausted and we've been talking a long time. I'm headed right for bed when we say good-bye."

"I imagine you are exhausted. Call me tomorrow night, if you're up to it. I'm going to go talk to the bishop tomorrow to tell him what's happened. I'm sure he'll understand why you can't make it."

"You should finish the classes and get baptized, even if I can't."

"Would your bishop finish up the classes there, so you could get baptized?"

"I have no idea. Probably not, since he's not as lenient as your bishop. He'd probably have a fit if he knew some of the things your bishop allows—or about me using the cell phone."

"It could delay the marriage."

"Paul, it can't be helped! Please try to understand. I want to marry every bit as much as you do, but I have to put my mudder ahead of my own feelings."

"Don't get so testy, Martha. I merely said what was on my mind."

"I'm sorry, it's just that this is a hard time for me. Don't make it harder."

"We won't talk about it again. At least, not until your mamm is on the way to recovery. Okay?"

"Danki."

They were silent a few moments and then Paul said good night and Martha, calmer now, told him she loved him."

"I know, honey. And you know I love you. Everything will be fine, I'm sure."

"Jah, if it's Gott's will."

"Jah. And may it be His will."


Aunt Lizzy knocked on the kitchen door the next morning around nine o'clock and then let herself in. Martha and her mother were already preparing a pork roast for the noon meal when she arrived. After placing the roast in the oven, Martha poured out the remaining coffee from breakfast and started brewing a fresh pot.

"I hope you have some of your sticky buns left. I didn't eat breakfast this morning," Lizzy said as she removed a shawl from her shoulders and placed it over a peg by the door.

"They might be a bit stale," Sarah said as she unwrapped a plate with several remaining buns and set it beside her sister.

"It doesn't matter. I like them anyway. How did you sleep?" Lizzy asked her sister as they sat together at the table waiting for the coffee to brew.

"Pretty gut, considering."

"How did Mamm and Daed take the news?"

"Quietly," Sarah said as she ran her fingers over the woven placemat.

"Jah, I can just imagine. Are they going to the hospital Friday?"

"I don't think they should. Daed's been feeling poorly lately. I worry about him."

"Well, let others do the worrying, schwester. You have enough on your mind."

Martha brought out a few small plates and set them next to the buns. She nodded at her aunt's comment. "That's what I told her, too. Dawdi is strong. He'll be fine."

"I still don't want them sitting over at the hospital all day. They'll probably keep me in recovery after the operation. That's the way they do things."

"Jah, I agree," Lizzy said. "I'll have a talk with them later."

"Mamm keeps talking about the quilt, Lizzy. She's driving me crazy about it. Please tell her not to worry so much about it," Sarah said.

"You know Mamm. She has to worry about something."

"She has her dochder to worry about now," Martha said. "If the quilt isn't finished by the time of the wedding, I'll take the one off my bed."

There was another knock on the door and Martha looked up to see Daniel Beiler peeking through the window in the door. "Oh no," she murmured as she rose to answer it.

"Hi, Martha. I just wanted to see how your mamm's doing." He stepped over the threshold and nodded over at Sarah. "Hi, Mrs. Troyer. How are you feeling?"

"Fine. Let the young man sit, Martha, and get him some kaffi. It's sure done by now."

"Jah." Martha stood back and pointed to an empty chair and then went to find another mug, which she set in front of him. She placed the coffee pot on a trivet and instead of sitting, she began peeling potatoes for their dinner.

"You're starting them too soon, Martha," her mother said. "Come sit."

With reluctance, Martha wiped her hands on a dishtowel and sat across from her guest.

"Martha's mamm is going to have surgery on Friday," Lizzy said.

"Oh, it's gut they're not waiting. I'm glad," Daniel said, as he reached for the pot and began pouring coffee into his mug.

"Jah, me, too, though I can't say I'm looking forward to it," Sarah said as she passed the plate of buns over to Daniel. He nodded as he took one and reached for a clean plate to set it on.

"Will they do the surgery in the morning?" Daniel asked Sarah.

"Jah, I have to be there by seven," she answered.

He nodded. "I'll try to stop by to see how you're doing."

"That's not necessary," Martha said quickly. "She'll be too out of it to have company. We want just family there."

"Oh, sure. Of course." He looked embarrassed as he took a large bite of the sticky bun. "These sure are gut," he said. "Did you make them, Martha?"

"Nee, Mamm did."

"But she makes them just as gut," Sarah said. Martha looked over at her mother. Goodness, was she still hoping for a reconciliation after all that had happened? Certainly, she didn't think it was over between Paul and her. She'd have to have a talk with her mother once they were alone. No point in giving the man false hope.

Melvin and Lizzy's husband, Leroy, came in and joined them. Melvin nodded at Daniel, but didn't say a word to him. At least, he knew it was over.

Martha was afraid her mother would invite Daniel to stay for dinner, but before she even had a chance to ask, Daniel stood up and headed for the door. "I'll be praying," he said with a holier-than-thou expression on his face. Martha wasn't impressed, but her mother thanked him vociferously. Then the door closed behind him.

Lizzy looked over at her niece. "Well, that was a surprise. Last I heard, he wasn't allowed to step foot in this house. What's changed?"

"I guess you could say Daniel's changed, but my feelings are the same," Martha said. "We're just casual friends now. That's all I want, really."

"Does Paul know you see him now—as a casual friend?" Lizzy asked.

"He understands."

"Well, I don't," her father said, his mouth turned down. "I don't think people change that much. That guy is still hoping to get your attention. Don't be too friendly, Martha."

"I'm not."

"She's not," Sarah repeated. "We have to forgive, Melvin. You know that. What kind of Amish person would you be if you held a grudge? We have to give him a chance now, don't we?"

"I suppose. I can forgive the boy without wanting him to come around our dochder."

"I'm an adult now, Daed. I can handle things. Please don't get involved. I love Paul and that's not going to change. I've told Daniel and he said he's interested in a friend of mine now, so it's going to be okay."

"Just keep your wits about you, Martha. Don't let him sweet-talk you." Her father continued. "Paul's a better man, if you ask me."

After an awkward pause, the family discussed the upcoming surgery and the recent warmer weather. After a while, the conversation turned back to food.

"That roast smells gut," Lizzy said.

"Oh, I'd better get those potatoes started," Martha said as she rose from the table and headed for the counter.

"And I'll cut the beans," Sarah said.

"I'll set the table," Lizzy said, rising.

"And we'll get out of your way," Melvin said as he nodded to his brother-in-law to head for the door. "Ring the bell when you're ready," he reminded his wife as they took off.

"Men!" Sarah said with a half grin. "Sure can make a fast exit when they want to."

"Jah, you can say that again," her sister agreed. "Now, I'll work on the gravy. This kitchen sure smells gut."

## Chapter Twenty-Eight

To appease Mammi and keep their minds off the upcoming surgery, the three women joined Martha's grandmother Wednesday and Thursday afternoons to work on Martha's quilt. Martha decided not to discuss her mother's behavior toward Daniel. Her poor mother had enough on her mind without getting into a discussion about that relationship.

Thursday night when Martha called Paul on the public phone, they prayed aloud about her mother and the upcoming surgery. Martha wasn't able to hold back her tears. Paul reiterated how he wished they were together so he could comfort her.

"I know she'll be fine in the end," Martha said, "but I hate to have her go through all this, especially since she's already had to deal with cancer years ago."

"I know. It's rough. They know a lot more about treating cancer now, I'm sure of that," he said trying to reassure her.

"Still."

"I know."

"Can we talk a little longer, Paul? I know you've got a busy day ahead of you—"

"We can talk all night, if that will help," he said, tenderly.

"What would I do without you?"

"Hopefully, you'll never have to find out," he said.

They stayed on for another hour and then feeling the tug for sleep, Martha told him she felt better and could finally get some rest. She went right up to her room when she got back from making her phone call.

Once in bed, she laid on her back and thought about some of her early memories. They always included her mother. She was her best friend growing up. When she was a young child, she taught Martha all about Jesus and how He was also her friend. Martha didn't hear that part in church. God always seemed remote and a little scary, but when her mother talked about Him, she would see Him differently. She'd picture Jesus calling the children to His side. He had a beautiful smile and kind eyes. This was who she prayed to, and she felt He was present—holding her.

The next morning, Martha dressed hurriedly and then went downstairs. Her mother was already cleaning up from Melvin's early breakfast. She smiled over at Martha. "Daed is hitching up Chessy. My folks decided to stay home. It would be a long day for them. Can you be ready in half an hour?"

"Jah, I'm nearly ready now. I just want a little oatmeal first."

"I left some in the pot. Finish it up."

Martha went over to her mother first and took hold of her hands. "How did you sleep?"

"Just fine. I'll be happy to get it over with. I'm hungry though."

"Jah, I bet. I'm sorry you can't eat." Martha placed her arms around her mother and rested her cheek against hers. "You're very brave, Mamm."

"Nee. Not brave, dear. I just put my trust in Gott. He knows what's best for each of us. Whatever happens, I'm ready."

"I love you, you know."

"Jah, I know. I can't tell you how much it means to me to have you here alongside of us. I was so fearful when you found out about…you know. The adoption. I was afraid you'd feel different."

"That couldn't happen, Mamm. You'll always be my mudder. Always."

Sarah cleared her throat as she pulled back slightly. "Remember when you were little and you'd ask me how much I loved you?"

"Jah, and you'd say, more than there are stars in the sky and sand on the beach."

"That hasn't changed, my *liebschdi.*"

Just then, Melvin came through the back door. "Ready?"

"Jah, we're almost ready. Martha has to eat some cereal and I have to use the bathroom again. Take a snack with you, Melvin. There's a banana left." Sarah went upstairs as Martha added a little milk to her cereal. Though it was difficult to swallow, she knew it might be a while before she'd eat again. She needed to remain strong for her mother—and her father.

When they arrived at the hospital, they pulled the buggy next to two other Amish buggies. One was

Lizzy's. "She beat us to it," Sarah said with a crooked smile.

"Poor Aenti Lizzy. She's pretty worried for you," Martha said as her father secured the reins and then took out a small overnight bag with a few items for Sarah. He helped his wife out of the buggy and then reached for Martha's hand.

"She ain't the only one," he said under his breath.

"Now, I don't want anyone upset. I'm gonna be just fine. I know it."

"Mmm." Melvin took hold of her arm and they made their way inside to the special waiting area for surgical patients and their families.

Lizzy looked up with a pained expression, though she turned it into a smile for her sister.

"We got here only ten minutes ago. Did you sleep at all last night?" she asked her sister as they exchanged hugs.

"Not too bad. Better than Melvin. I heard him stirring every few minutes."

Then Lizzy reached for Martha's arm and they embraced. "How 'bout you, Martha?" she asked.

"Okay, I guess. In a way, I was relieved that the surgery was scheduled for today. The sooner they get that awful tumor out, the better. Jah?"

Everyone nodded in agreement. "I'll go to the desk with you, Sarah," Melvin said. They went over to the nurse in charge and then Sarah was led out of the waiting room to a hallway. The nurse leading her turned to the family first. "We need to get some vitals and have her change. We'll get her settled down and then one or two of you can go in with her while she's prepped for surgery."

Melvin let out a long sigh and sat down, folding his

hands together. The rest of the family took seats once again and made small talk for the next half hour. When Sarah was ready for company, only Martha and her father were allowed in. Lizzy and Leroy didn't look happy to be left behind, but no one objected aloud. Everyone was aware of hospital protocol.

Sarah was lying on a hospital bed with an IV inserted in her hand. She was calm and chatting with one of the nurses when they arrived. "And this is my husband and my daughter," she said to the nurse. They exchanged greetings and then the nurse proceeded to ask Sarah more medical questions. An anesthesiologist came in and went over his plan. Then the surgeon came by, and nodded to everyone before telling them what he planned to do, once again.

About a half hour later, two attendants came in to wheel her to surgery. Melvin patted her legs as she passed him, and Martha went as far as the swinging doors leading to the surgical rooms. They stopped momentarily to allow her to lean over and kiss her mother's forehead.

"I've traded my prayer kapp for this funny green shower cap," her mother joked before disappearing behind the doors. Martha was amazed at her mother's calmness. It had to be God. She truly wasn't afraid. Martha said a silent prayer as she returned to her father, who had his eyes closed and his head bent down slightly. What did people do who didn't trust in a higher being? It would certainly be harder to face moments like these.

They made their way back to the waiting room, and the vigil began.

# Chapter Twenty-Nine

After a few minutes, Martha found a public phone and called Paul to give him a full report about her mother. They prayed together for several minutes and then she went back to the waiting room where two of Lizzy's sons, along with their wives and a couple of their older children, had joined the group. They had brought brownies and buns along with bottles of water for the others.

It seemed as if the clock hands on the large round wall clock never moved, or at such a slow pace that it seemed time was standing still.

Martha turned pages of an old cooking magazine, but nothing caught her interest. Around noon they still hadn't heard anything. Some of the family had left, but two cousins came to take their place. Everyone who came brought food of some kind with them, but Martha had no appetite and politely refused anything they offered. Any time she felt fear well up, she'd turn to God for comfort. He never failed to provide it.

Then around half past twelve, they were told that Sarah was now in recovery and had gotten through the

surgery well. It would be a while before she'd be awake enough for family members to visit.

Out of the corner of her eyes, Martha noted a young Amishman coming through the doors. It was Daniel. He went right over to her and asked about her mother's condition. After she relayed what the nurse had told them, he sat down and folded his arms. Martha passed the plate with brownies over to him and he helped himself to one. "I can't stay long, I'm afraid," he said. "I have to get back to work."

"Well, danki for coming by, Daniel. It was real nice of you."

"No problem. I'll come by tomorrow, too, to check on things. I'm glad you're okay with me stopping by."

"Jah, it's nice you care."

"I do, more than you know."

Martha looked at his expression. Uh oh. That had more meaning than she wanted to admit. Goodness, why was she pushing it? She thought she'd been clear about her feelings. Her father was probably right in not trusting him to keep it at the friendship level. It was nice of him to come by to check though. Maybe she'd misread his last comment.

Finally, they were allowed to visit Sarah, though she'd been moved to a private room on a different floor. When they went over to the elevator, Daniel decided to take the stairs. He walked away at the same time the elevator arrived. Martha said good-bye, but her father barely nodded as he departed.

Martha was relieved Daniel hadn't attempted to touch her. Of course, in public, it was rare any Amish person showed signs of affection. It simply didn't happen.

Sarah was asleep when the four of them entered the

room. Lizzy and Leroy stayed in the background, allowing Martha and her father time to talk to Sarah. She opened her eyes and let out a slight smile. She whispered something and Martha leaned over and asked her to repeat her comment.

"I'm glad it's over, but I hurt pretty bad."

"Jah, Mamm. They gave you something before they brought you to your room. The nurse said you'll get more in about an hour. Try to rest."

"Jah." She closed her eyes and barely moved. Martha stood back as Melvin patted her mother's free hand.

"We'll be right here, Sarah. Lizzy and Leroy are here, too."

She smiled again. "Danki. Love you all."

"Jah." He coughed and wiped his eyes with the back of his free hand. "Now don't try to talk. Just rest."

"Mmm." She did as he suggested.

"I think I'll go sit in the waiting room we passed down the hall," Martha said. "Maybe she'll sleep better."

"We'll go with you," Lizzy said. "Melvin, are you staying?"

"Jah. I'll come out later." His eyes never left his dear Sarah. Martha squeezed his shoulder as she headed for the door. "We'll be waiting."

"Why don't you get something to eat? You must be hungry by now."

"Maybe. She'll be fine, Daed. She got through the worst."

"Jah," he said with a nod. "She's strong."

"And strong in the Lord."

"Jah, that's for sure."

When Martha got to the waiting room with her aunt and uncle, she was shocked to see Paul standing by the

large window. She almost thought she was imagining it, but he came right over to her. "Surprised?"

"Oh jah! Shocked!"

"I wish I could hold you in my arms," he whispered.

"Oh jah!"

He turned and addressed her aunt and uncle, who looked equally surprised.

"Gut you're here," Lizzy said. "Our Martha could use your support."

He nodded. "I'm glad she's in a regular room already. They told me to come here when I got to the information desk. Can I get anyone something to eat from downstairs?" he asked.

"We're fine," Leroy said. "People have been bringing stuff, but you should get Martha to eat something. She ain't even snacked."

"Come on then, Martha. You have to keep up your strength. Then you can tell me all about your mudder. The nurse wouldn't tell me anything, except she was done with the surgery."

"I guess I could eat something now. Okay." As they approached the entrance to the cafeteria, they spotted Daniel clearing a tray into the trash. His back was toward them and Paul stopped and put up his hand. "I don't want to have to talk to that guy. Let's go to the far end where he won't see us."

She felt her heart pounding as they walked quickly to the opposite side of the cafeteria. When she looked back, Daniel was gone.

Without speaking a word, she followed Paul over to the long line of people working their way along the large display of available food, some stopping for an employee to hand them a plateful. Martha asked for the meatloaf

platter and Paul decided to have the same. After they received their food, they stopped to pay, and then seated themselves next to a window.

Only then did Paul mention Daniel's presence. "So, was he waiting with you?"

"Nee."

"But you saw him."

"Jah, he came by earlier, just to see how Mamm was doing." She cut the meatloaf with her fork, but didn't attempt to eat.

"How nice."

"Well, it was nice, Paul. He's known my mamm for years."

"Oh, I'm sure that's why he stopped by. It had nothing to do with you." He reached for his knife and spread a butter pat on his roll. His mouth was firm.

"I don't want to talk about him, Paul. Let's just try to have a nice lunch. I'm really glad you came. I've missed you so much."

"As it turns out, you had company without me."

"Please don't. You know I hate it when you act all jealous. There is nothing—and I'll repeat it—there is nothing between me and Daniel. I've made it very clear to him. So, I wish you'd stop acting childish."

"Childish? Would you like it if I continued to see Hazel every chance I could get? I could, you know. We live close by and I wouldn't be surprised if she still cares a little about me, but I wouldn't do that. I definitely wouldn't encourage her."

"Well, I don't encourage Daniel to stop by. Not at all!"

"How do I know that?"

"Paul, please. It's been such a hard day."

He was silent for a few moments. Then he laid his

knife aside and leaned over. "I'm sorry, Martha. Really. I don't know what got into me."

"A little green devil, if you ask me," she said, trying to lighten the mood.

"Maybe that was it. I won't mention it again. Not today anyway. Come, let's say grace and eat now."

"If I can."

"Everything's fine, Martha. You know how much I love you."

"Jah, okay. I'll try to forget everything and enjoy this meal. I don't know when I'll eat again."

They managed to keep the conversation light and fairly impersonal.

When they were done, they walked back to the family. Her aunt was visiting the bedside alone while Martha's father and uncle stood talking to Dr. Harriman.

Martha and Paul joined them in time to hear what the doctor had to say. He nodded over to them as he continued speaking of her surgery. "We had to go deeper and remove more lymph nodes since the sentinel node was infected. We'll know more after we get the results. I won't schedule her for radiation immediately. I'd like her to recover from this surgery first. Probably next week."

Martha felt herself tremble as she digested his words. They had hoped that the cancer had not spread. This was not the news she had anticipated. She felt Paul take hold of her arm. "You okay?" he whispered.

"Not really," she whispered back.

"Let's go sit down. Then I'll get you some water. You're so pale."

The doctor told them he'd be checking on Sarah before he left for the day and then he excused himself. Melvin

and Leroy returned to the waiting area and sat silently, frowns spread across their faces. It was not good news.

After finishing a cup of water, Martha looked over at her father. She sure wasn't much of a help. Her poor daed looked devastated and here she was almost passing out. "I need to be with Daed," she said softly to Paul.

"Get a little stronger first. I'll get you more water." He took the cup and returned a minute later with it refilled. After drinking it, Martha moved next to her father.

"She'll be okay, Daed."

"I sure hope so."

"Remember, she's strong."

"Jah. I should go back in. She'll need me there with her."

They looked up to see Lizzy returning. Melvin stood and walked over to her. They spoke a moment and then he went into his wife's room as Lizzy joined the others.

Leroy moved over to allow his wife to sit next to Martha, who proceeded to repeat what the doctor had told them about his findings.

"Oh, that's not gut," Lizzy said, lifting her apron to her eyes. "My poor schwester. Mamm will be heartbroken."

"Maybe we don't need to give her all the details," Leroy said.

"Nee. No more lies in this family. She'd want to know, Leroy. Sarah's a fighter. I thought we might lose her when she had her last cancer bout, but she fought like a trouper to get well."

"And she did," Martha stated, nodding vehemently. "She can do it again."

"Jah, absolutely," Lizzy said, patting her niece on her hand.

"Martha," Paul started, "my ride is coming in half an hour. Do you think I can go in and see your mamm?"

"Sure. I'll go in with you. Was she trying to sleep when you left, Aenti?"

"No. She just got another shot for pain. She's prob ably still awake."

Martha led Paul into the room. He seemed uncomfortable as he looked about at all the hospital equipment. There were monitors everywhere. Then he went over to Sarah, who opened her eyes. "Hallo, Daniel," she said in her semi-conscious state.

"Mamm, it's Paul," Martha said, feeling the pit return to her stomach. Goodness.

"Oh, jah. Sure it is. How are you, Paul? It was nice of you to come by."

"Jah, well, I'm glad for your sake that it's over. Sorry you have to go through all this."

"I'm sorry, too. Be sure you take gut care of my Martha now."

"I will, Mrs. Troyer. Don't worry about that." He smiled faintly over at Martha, who had all her attention on her mother.

"Paul has to leave soon, Mamm, but he wanted to say hallo first."

"Well, ain't that nice? Say hello to your mamm, Rebecca. Maybe she'll be able to come by."

Paul looked over at Martha, questioning with his eyes. "My mother's name is Helen," he said, confused.

"Oh my. I was thinking of Mrs. Beiler, wasn't I? I'm so confused."

"It's okay, Mamm," Martha said. "It's probably from the anesthesia. Not to worry. Come, Paul, Mamm needs her sleep." She kissed her mother's cheek and headed toward the door as Paul followed her out.

He didn't say anything about the faux pas. They were

the only ones in the elevator when it headed toward the floor to the entranceway. Paul leaned over and swiftly kissed her cheek. "I'm sorry I can't stay longer, but my driver has to get back for some reason. He did me a favor to drive me here today."

"Danki for coming, Paul. We didn't even have time to talk about your visit with the bishop."

The door opened and they walked together to the entrance. His ride was already waiting.

"Not much to report, but call when you can. I sure wish you'd break down and get a cell phone."

"I've thought about it, but I don't want my parents upset with me again. Not now."

"It's real frustrating."

"I know. For me, too, Paul."

She watched as he got in the front with the driver. He waved to her and within seconds they were out of sight.

She turned and headed back to her mother. It had been a long day. And she knew others would follow.

# Chapter Thirty

A few days later Sarah was released from the hospital. Melvin called their driver, Hank, for the trip home since he wanted a smoother ride for his wife than was possible with the buggy. Martha sat up front with Hank, and Melvin sat next to his wife.

The doctor had stopped in before discharging Sarah, and told them because of the spread of the cancer cells, he planned to start radiation within a week. The news cast a pall over the family and conversation on the way home was sparse.

Once home, Sarah changed into night clothes for comfort's sake, and Martha made up a bed for her on the sofa so she could avoid the stairs until she felt stronger. Fortunately, they had a lavatory on the first floor. Martha planned to help her sponge bathe until she was ready to climb the stairs and have a regular shower.

Even though Sarah might have preferred a few days without visitors, neighbors and family members stopped by briefly to pay their respects and drop off casseroles and desserts for the family. It was much appreciated, though Sarah was exhausted by the end of each day

from having company. Martha also wished she could find more time to relax. The stress had only added to her fatigue. Melvin, though busier than ever due to the demands of early spring on farmers, spent as much time as possible keeping Sarah company. Through it all, Sarah kept a cheerful demeanor, and her positive attitude was a leading factor in giving the whole family courage to face the future—whatever it would bring.

When the radiation was started, she convinced Melvin she wanted to be taken back and forth in the familiar buggy. It wasn't just the expense involved, since they could have well afforded it, but she enjoyed the ride with their beautiful chestnut-colored horse leading the way.

One evening, Daniel came by the house but didn't stay long. He was very polite and did not cause any concern on Martha's part. He truly seemed concerned for her mother.

When Martha found the time and energy to call Paul, which was now about every three days, they did not discuss Daniel at all. Martha was relieved, but there were moments when Paul hesitated in the conversation and she wondered if he wasn't debating whether to ask questions about him.

Paul told her he was making plans to come visit, but since his free time was limited now with their business in full swing, they didn't finalize a date.

Sometimes, if Martha had some time to herself, which wasn't often, she asked herself about her feelings toward Paul. She knew she still loved him, but with so much on her mind, she found she thought of him less and less. It scared her somewhat, but she figured once her mother was done with radiation, things would settle down and

she'd have time once again to concentrate some of her thoughts on her own future.

Naomi stopped by one afternoon when she was home visiting her family. She had her new boyfriend, Tyler, with her. He seemed perfect for Naomi, and Martha liked him immediately. Naomi showed her a ring on her finger, a small diamond solitaire set in a simple gold setting. "It's beautiful," Martha said. "So, your parents know about your plans?"

"Jah, they weren't terrible surprised."

"And they seemed to like your fiancé," Tyler said, grinning.

"Jah, for sure. And they're probably glad their daughter is finally going to be married and not running around like the English girls."

"I can't believe they weren't upset about you leaving the Amish."

"They were at first, but we don't have to cut off ties since I wasn't baptized. That helped, I think."

"I'm sure it did."

Sarah was glad to see Naomi again. Once they were gone, she added her approval of the young man she was to marry. "He reminded me of Daniel," she added.

"Only nicer. Much nicer," Martha added.

"Well now, Daniel is a nice bu. I wasn't crazy about his parents, but he seems like a nice enough young man."

"Please don't hold out any false hopes, Mamm. That's been over for a long time."

"Maybe for you, Martha, but I think the young man still has eyes for you."

"I'm marrying Paul, Mamm. Nothing can change that."

"Well, one never knows, Martha. Sometimes life leads

you in strange ways. I guess time will tell. I'm thinking maybe tomorrow I'll try to go up the stairs and take a real shower. That would feel wonderful-gut."

"Sure, Mamm, if you're up to it."

That night Martha took the buggy to the community phone to call Paul. She hadn't talked to him in two days. The phone rang several times before a girl's voice answered. Martha wondered if she'd called the wrong number. It was after seven. Surely, he'd be home by now.

"Is Paul there?" she was finally able to ask.

"Jah. Wait a minute."

Martha strained to hear the conversation between this girl and Paul, but all she heard was mumbling.

A few moments later, Paul's voice came across. "Hallo."

"It's me, Paul."

"Oh, I was hoping you'd call tonight."

"Who was the girl?"

"Hazel. She didn't recognize your voice either, I guess," he said haltingly.

"Why is she at our house, with you?" Her voice began to tremble.

"Actually, I'm at work. We have to finish cabinets for a kitchen being used in a builder's sample home. The deadline is next week."

"I've tried to call you and you haven't answered."

"I wondered. You didn't leave messages. I figured you were just too busy with your mudder to call."

"I always called when I thought you'd be home from your job."

"I appreciate that, Martha, but the truth is, I've been working evenings till after nine all week. I'm beat."

"So why is Hazel there? Does she work for you now?"

"She brings dinner for us. We'd work straight through our meals if she didn't cook for us."

"That's nice of her," she said disingenuously.

"Jah, it sure is. She's a gut cook, too."

"Oh."

"You sound funny. You aren't jealous, are you? You know she's seeing Jeremiah, right?"

"I also know she's never quite gotten over you."

"That's silly."

"When are they getting married?"

"I don't think that's been settled yet."

"Maybe I am a little jealous. She's with you and I'm only able to talk on the phone once in a while."

"Well, now you know how I feel about Daniel. Has he been by lately?"

"He stops in once in a while—to see my mamm, of course."

"You know better than that. He's there to see you. Watch out for that guy. I don't trust him at all."

"He's changed."

"Really? The leopard's lost his spots?"

"I don't want to talk about him."

"Well, I don't want to talk about Hazel. She only comes by to help out."

"You haven't asked about my mamm. Don't you care?"

"Martha, why would you say something stupid like that? Of course I care."

"Stupid!"

"Well, not stupid, maybe foolish."

"I have to go now. I don't know when I'll call again."

"Don't hang up feeling like that. Call me tomorrow

night. Hopefully, I'll hear the ring. I'm using noisy tools right now."

"Well, sweet Hazel can always answer."

"Martha."

"What?"

"This isn't like you."

"Maybe you don't really know me."

She heard him take a deep breath, but he didn't respond. Then he told her softly that he loved her—in the Pennsylvania Dutch.

"Okay. Me, too. I'll try to call tomorrow night. No promises. Gut nacht."

"Gut nacht," he responded, his voice still lowered.

Martha hung up and leaned against the wooden frame of the door. Goodness, was their love fading? With a sad spirit, Martha climbed into the buggy and headed back home. Her future looked very uncertain and she was too exhausted and melancholy to even care. *Dear Gott, give me strength to accept whatever my future holds.*

The next day, her mother seemed peppier after making it up the stairs for a shower. After she was dressed, she lay on her bed and motioned Martha to come sit by her side. "That felt real gut, Martha. Almost like I'm normal."

"Someday, Gott willing, you will be normal again, Mamm."

"Jah, Gott willing. I'm going to fight as hard as I can to make it through this, Martha. For Daed and for you."

Martha took her mother's hand and stroked it with her other hand. "You're a brave woman. Tomorrow, you get your radiation treatment. Does it make you scared?"

"Nee, not scared. I don't like losing all my hair again, but that's vain-talk, jah?"

"Oh, I think every woman likes having her own hair. Yours goes below your waist, ain't? You hardly ever have it down when I see you."

"Your daed likes it down. He even brushes it sometimes for me."

Martha grinned. "I can't picture him doing that."

"Oh, your daed was very romantic when we married. He still can be."

"That's sweet. I hope Paul is just like him."

"I hope so, too. It's been a gut marriage—your daed and me. We've only argued three times in all these years and he was right two times out of the three."

Martha looked over sadly. "Goodness, that's amazing. Already, Paul and I have had disagreements. Even now, things aren't quite right."

"Then take your time planning your marriage, Martha. As my daed used to say, 'You're a long time married. Make sure you pick the right one.' He was right, you know."

"I know Paul is the right one for me," Martha said, feigning confidence.

"Then Gott will make it happen. If I don't make it… to see you marry…"

"Mamm, please don't talk like that. Of course you'll make it. You have to!"

Sarah squeezed her daughter's hand. "Honey, no one knows when the gut Lord is calling them home. It can be years or hours, but as long as we trust in our Jesus and keep Him in our hearts," she added softly as she took her hands away and crossed her heart with her arms, "it will be okay. One day we'll all meet again in Gott's

glorious kingdom, so I don't want people grieving if I don't make it."

Tears streamed down Martha's face as she nodded. "I understand, but I can't promise not to grieve."

"Then for one day, you're allowed, okay?" Sarah said, smiling gently at her daughter. "Daed will need you. I know you will want to live in the home Paul's fixing up if you do marry him, but maybe you can visit Daed often. And of course there's Lizzy. You're like a dochder to my schwester."

"I'll try to come home often, Mamm. You mustn't worry about Daed. He could live with us when he gives up farming. Our home will always be open to him—or Aenti Lizzy. You know that."

Sarah wiped away a stray tear and then smiled. "Jah, you'll always do the right thing, Martha. That's just the way you are. Even as a little maed, you tried to do things right. You used to say Jesus was watching you, and you wanted to please Him."

"I guess I still feel that way. I don't even like hurting Daniel's feelings. I hope he'll be happy with Molly."

"I doubt it. He comes by so often and I don't think it's really because of me. I see the way he looks at you. If things don't work out gut with you and Paul, give the young man a chance, Martha. I think he's changed."

Martha shook her head. "It's Paul I love, Mamm. I think it will always be Paul."

"Now, how did we end up talking about the men in your life, dochder? I think I'll take a little rest before coming downstairs. I'm pretty tired today, and this way, if anyone else shows up, I can escape seeing them. Is that a terrible thing to say?"

Martha smiled. "I know what you mean, Mamm, and

no, it's not terrible at all. You need to rest before tomorrow. And Mamm, if you lose your hair, I have enough on my head to cut half away and still have a mop."

"A beautiful 'mop' of almost black hair. Now, wouldn't that be fun—for me to have a wig made of your lovely dark tresses? I might just let you do that."

Sarah lay back and pulled a quilt up to her chin as she closed her eyes. Martha leaned over and kissed her cheek and tip-toed out the door and down the stairs. Her father would be looking for his meal soon. Her responsibility was to care for her parents now, as they had cared for her for the last twenty years. Yes, it was her turn and marriage would have to wait and Paul would have to accept her decision.

A good man would understand, and Paul was a good man. That was for sure and for certain.

* * * * *

*Christmastime brings a single mom and her baby back home, but reconnecting with her high school sweetheart, now a wounded veteran, puts her darkest secret at risk.*

*Read on for a sneak preview of*
The Secret Christmas Child *by Lee Tobin McClain, the first book in her new Rescue Haven miniseries.*

He reached out a hand, meaning to shake hers, but she grasped his and held it. Looked into his eyes. "Reese, I'm sorry about what happened before."

He narrowed his eyes and frowned at her. "You mean…after I went into the service?"

She nodded and swallowed hard. "Something happened, and I couldn't…I couldn't keep the promise I made."

That something being another guy, Izzy's father. He drew in a breath. Was he going to hold on to his grudge, or his hurt feelings, about what had happened?

Looking into her eyes, he breathed out the last of his anger. Like Corbin had said, everyone was a sinner. "It's understood."

"Thank you," she said simply. She held his gaze for another moment and then looked down and away.

She was still holding on to his hand, and slowly, he twisted and opened his hand until their palms were flat together. Pressed between them as close as he'd like to be pressed to Gabby.

The only light in the room came from the kitchen and

the dying fire. Outside the windows, snow had started to fall, blanketing the little house in solitude.

This night with her family had been one of the best he'd had in a long time. Made him realize how much he missed having a family.

Gabby's hand against his felt small and delicate, but he knew better. He slipped his own hand to the side and captured hers, tracing his thumb along the calluses.

He heard her breath hitch and looked quickly at her face.

Her eyes were wide, her lips parted and moist.

Without looking away, acting on impulse, he slowly lifted her hand to his lips and kissed each fingertip.

Her breath hitched and came faster, and his sense of himself as a man, a man who could have an effect on a woman, swelled, almost making him giddy.

This was Gabby, and the truth burst inside him: he'd never gotten over her, never stopped wishing they could be together, that they could make that family they'd dreamed of as kids. That was why he'd gotten so angry when she'd strayed: because the dream she'd shattered had been so big, so bright and shining.

In the back of his mind, a voice of caution scolded and warned. She'd gone out with his cousin. She'd had a child with another man. What had been so major in his emotional life hadn't been so big in hers.

He shouldn't trust her. And he definitely shouldn't kiss her.

But when had he ever done what he should?

*Don't miss*
The Secret Christmas Child *by Lee Tobin McClain,*
*available December 2019 wherever*
*Love Inspired® books and ebooks are sold.*

www.LoveInspired.com

Looking for inspiration in tales
of hope, faith and heartfelt romance?

Check out **Love Inspired**® and
**Love Inspired**® **Suspense** books!

**New books available every month!**

---

"Are the *kinder* okay?"

"Yes, they'll be fine." Uncomfortable with his small intrusion into her family, she said, "Kevin had a bad dream and woke us up."

"Because of the rain?"

She wanted to say that was silly but, glad she could be honest with Michael, she said, "It's possible."

"Rebuilding a structure is easy. Rebuilding one's sense of security isn't."

"That sounds like the voice of experience."

"My parents died when I was young, and both my twin brother and I had to learn not to expect something horrible was going to happen without warning."

"I'm sorry. I should have asked more about you and the other volunteers. I've been wrapped up in my own tragedy."